THE GRANTCHESTER MYSTERIES

SIDNEY CHAMBERS
AND
THE PERILS OF
THE NIGHT

JAMES RUNCIE

ISIS
LARGE PRINT
Oxford

First published in Great Britain 2013
by
Bloomsbury Publishing

Published in Large Print 2014 by ISIS Publishing Ltd.,
7 Centremead, Osney Mead, Oxford OX2 0ES
by arrangement with
Bloomsbury Publishing

CIP data is available for this title from the British Library

ISBN 978–0–7531–9248–1 (hb)
ISBN 978–0–7531–9249–8 (pb)

Printed and bound in Great Britain by
T. J. International Ltd., Padstow, Cornwall

For Marilyn

Contents

The Perils of the Night 1

Love and Arson 67

Unholy Week. 140

The Hat Trick 221

The Uncertainty Principle 284

Appointment in Berlin 335

The Perils of the Night

As the afternoon light faded over the village of Grantchester, the parishioners lit fires, drew curtains and bolted their doors against the dangers of darkness. The external blackness was a *memento mori*, a nocturnal harbinger of that sombre country from which no traveller returns. Canon Sidney Chambers, however, felt no fear. He liked a winter's night.

It was the 8th of January 1955. The distant town of Cambridge looked almost two-dimensional under the moon's wily enchantment, and the silhouettes of college buildings were etched against the darkening sky like illustrations for a children's fairytale. Sidney imagined princesses locked in towers, knights leaving on dangerous quests through forests, and woodcutters bringing supplies to stoke the fires of great medieval halls. The River Cam was stilled in time, its waters frozen and embedded with fallen branches, scattered twigs and dead leaves. The snow that settled on Clare Bridge made the decoration of its parapet rails look like fourteen snowballs that had been left by a giant standing astride a model of an English university. Set back and to the south, across whitened grass, the magnesian limestone that comprised the fabric of King's College Chapel was given extra luminance by the snow that gathered on the roof and pinnacled standards of its turrets. Wind gusted round the edges of the building, throwing white flurries against the mouldings and mullions of the windows. The stained glass was darkened, as if waiting for something to happen — a new Reformation perhaps, an air raid, or even the end of the world. The stillness of the night was broken by only a few sporadic sounds: a passing car, a drunken shout, the footsteps of university proctors making their rounds. In Sidney's college of Corpus Christi, stalactites clung to the guttering while uncertain weights of snow slithered off the eaves-cornices of Old Court and fell in heavy slabs from the keystone of the main gate. Bicycles lay against spiked railings, the spokes of their wheels frosted white. It was an evening for drawn curtains, hot toddies and warm fires; for sitting in a favourite armchair with a good book and a companionable dog.

Sidney had enjoyed a couple of pints at the Eagle with his good friend Inspector Geordie Keating and was beginning his journey home. It was after ten, and most of the undergraduates were locked in their colleges. Admittance after that time was through the Porter's Lodge and on payment of a "late-fee" of one shilling. This latitude extended until midnight, after which there was no legal admission. The only option open to those wishing to return to their rooms in the small hours was to behave like a cat burglar and break in. Sidney had done this when he was a student, some ten years before he had become vicar of Grantchester, approaching the college in Free School Lane, mounting the railings by St Bene't's Church, shinning up a drainpipe, and making his way across the roofs and over the conservatory before climbing in through an open window of the Master's Lodge. Soon after this escapade, Sidney had discovered that this was a rather better known route than he had thought, and that the Master's daughter, Sophie, often left her bedroom window open deliberately in the hope of a little late night entertainment. The practice of night climbing had become something of a Cambridge sport, as students pursued a hobby of illegal mountaineering in the name of "high jinks". Onions had been rolled off the appropriately shaped dome of the Divinity School, umbrellas had been left on the Tottering Tower of the Old Library, and a Canadian student at King's had become obsessed by a fanatical desire to put a herd of goats on his college roof.

The possibility of discovery, and the potential penalty of being sent down as a result, had deterred Sidney from taking a full part in such proceedings, but rumours of daring feats of architectural mountaineering still fed the gossip in college common rooms. The university authorities had increased the number of torchlight patrols in an attempt to stamp out the practice, but undergraduates still risked their future university careers in the name of freedom and adventure, conspiring in low voices about the challenge of photographing each other while climbing the Great

Gate of Trinity, the New Tower of St John's, or the north face of Pembroke.

The ultimate challenge for those driven by "pinnaclomania" was an ascent of one of the four octagonal turrets of King's College Chapel. Valentine Lyall, a research fellow of Corpus, was leading an expedition that very night. The consequences were to prove fatal.

Sidney was alerted to the situation by a commotion on King's Parade. Such was its volume that he made an immediate detour, turning right out of Bene't Street rather than his customary left.

Lyall was a seasoned night climber who was well known throughout the university. He was accompanied by Kit Bartlett, his postgraduate student, a blond-haired athletics blue; and Rory Montague, an altogether stockier third-year undergraduate who had been called upon to photograph the expedition for posterity.

The three men were dressed in polo-neck sweaters and gym shoes and the climb took place in two stages, from ground to roof and from roof to north-east turret. Lyall had taken the lead by placing his hands between the clamps of the lightning conductor and pushing himself up twenty feet with his arms. He carried two coils of hundred-foot rope over his shoulder. He used his feet to lever his body outwards and upwards against the wall, while a hand-over-hand movement worked in a semi-contrary motion, keeping him tight against the stone while sustaining his ascent.

The accompanying students followed with torches, and, after a brief rest on a broad sloping ledge, they began to "chimney" up the fissure between two walls, their backs against one wall and their feet against the other, thrusting themselves upwards with their legs. The stone flange against which they pressed their feet was four inches wide and the ascent was performed at an oblique angle. Sidney could see one of the men stop and look down to the iron railings below. He was fifty feet from the ground, with forty still to go.

The university proctors were already at the scene. "Can anyone go after them?" Sidney asked.

"They'll kill themselves if they do," one of the men replied. "We'll get their names when they come down. We don't think they're from this college. They must have been hiding when the porters did the rounds. This has got to stop, Canon Chambers. They may think it's a sport, but we'll end up taking the responsibility if it goes wrong."

The climbers gathered at the base of an octagonal turret that rose from the roof in six stages. Some sections were easy to climb, with pierced stone latticework offering opportunity for handholds, but the height of the parapet was forbidding. Valentine Lyall began his traverse round the base of the pinnacle and found a series of air holes in the clover-leaf stonework above the first overhang. They were fifteen inches deep and across, and he could use them as a short ladder. He was now over a hundred feet from the ground.

He climbed up on to the parapet and approached the chessboard stonework near the top of the pinnacle before calling down. "Careful, men, the stone gets crumbly here. Make sure you have three grips at once; two hands and one foot, or one hand and both feet."

Rory Montague was losing his nerve. As he approached the second overhang he noticed that there was no handhold for a distance of five feet. "I can't do this," he said.

"Don't give up," Bartlett urged. "Use your knees. Keep close to the stone. Don't lean out."

"I'm not going to."

"There's only twelve feet to go."

Lyall was already on the second overhang. "We need a photograph."

"Not now," hissed Bartlett.

"Help me," Montague cried. "I'm stuck."

"Don't look down."

"It's as dark as hell."

Lyall shone his torch. "Get round to your right. There's a drainpipe."

"What if it gives way?"

"It won't."

"It stops before the parapet."

"That's only a few feet."

Montague called up, "I need the rope."

"Give me a minute." Lyall reached the last parapet. He leant outwards at full stretch, grasping it with both hands, and pulled himself up by using the gaps in the stonework until his feet reached the topmost hole.

Bartlett followed and the two men threw down the rope. Montague caught it and used it as leverage to make the final ascent.

Sidney had moved further along the exterior of the north side of the nave to get a better view. Snow fell in his eyes, while the high and distant figures appeared as silhouettes against moon and torchlight. "There's nothing to protect them if they fall," he said.

"They never fall," one of the proctors replied.

"I imagine the descent is much harder."

"Once they've got back down on to the roof they return through the interior; if they've got a copy of the key, that is."

"And have they?"

"I wouldn't put it past them."

"So you'll wait for them at the bottom?"

"Once they're in the roof space they can hide amongst the main timbers until they think we've gone home. Last year a couple of men were in there for hours. We just barred the staircase from the outside and waited until they were hungry enough to give themselves up."

"You mean there's no escape?"

"No one's managed it so far."

The wind dropped. Lyall gave instructions to Rory Montague. "Hold on to the rope and lower yourself down. Use the clover-leafs as footholds, and then make a traverse to your left. We won't be able to see you but we can feel you."

Montague began the descent. All seemed well until the clover-leaf stopped. He then missed a foothold. "Bugger." He pushed himself away from the wall and let the rope take his weight.

"What the hell are you doing?" Lyall called.

"I can't get a foothold."

"Use a hand. I can't take all this weight."

"I need both hands on the rope. I'm not strong enough just to use one."

"Push your feet into the wall. Get the strain off the rope."

"I'm too far away from the building."

Montague's left foot hovered against the side of the parapet, trying to find a hold.

He began to sway above the abyss.

A porter shouted up: "COME DOWN AT ONCE."

Montague let his hands slide down the rope. He felt his palms burn. His right elbow hit a gargoyle. "Slacken off," he ordered.

"What's going on?" Lyall asked.

Montague began a short abseil down the side of the building and found a foothold. There he rested before pulling at the rope again.

"What are you doing?" Lyall called down. "You have to tell us when you've finished with the rope so I can untie and make my descent. I don't need it."

"I do," Montague replied. He wondered where the hell his friend Kit Bartlett had gone.

"I'll lean out and give you some more," said Lyall. "We've got enough. Are you safe?"

"I think so."

"Good. I'll just . . . hell . . . wait . . . oh . . ."

He fell away from the building, backwards through the night air and the snow, past the contorted faces of the silent gargoyles, the body gathering an inevitable momentum until its hard arrival on ground that would never be soft enough to stop death.

There was no scream, just silence, the fall, and the dull sound of a landing without echo: a gap in time, filled only with the incomprehensible disbelief of its witnesses.

"My God," a proctor said quietly.

"Was that Mr Lyall?" Montague asked. "The rope's loose. I can't see Bartlett. I'm on my own. I don't know how to get down."

One of the porters called up, "Take it slowly, sir."

"DID MR LYALL FALL?"

"Get back down to the roof, sir, and someone will come and get you. Do you know the interior staircase?"

"Where's that?"

"There's a trapdoor in the roof. Wait there and we'll come and get you."

"I don't know anything about a trapdoor. Where's Kit? What's happened to Mr Lyall?"

The porter did not answer. "We need to get you down."

"I don't want to die," Montague shouted back.

"Who is with you?"

"I've told you. Kit Bartlett. But I don't know where he is. DID MR LYALL FALL?"

"Where are you from?"

"Corpus."

Montague clambered down and jumped the last few feet on to the roof. He searched the length of the chapel for the trap-door that led down to the interior staircase. Had his friend Kit already found this or was he hiding somewhere else? How had he managed to disappear so quickly?

An ambulance made its way down King's Parade.

Sir Giles Tremlett, the Master of Corpus, was deeply distressed by the death of one of his fellows and asked Sidney to come and see him the following evening. "I am assuming that you will be prepared to take the funeral?"

It would be Sidney's third that year already. He saw so much natural death in winter and it saddened him that this was so needless. "I didn't know Lyall well."

"Nevertheless, it would be appropriate for a fellow of the college to be buried at Grantchester."

"I take it he was not a churchgoer?"

"These days, scientists seldom are." The Master poured out a stiff sherry and then stopped. "I am sorry. I always forget you don't like this stuff. A little whisky?"

"With water. It's rather early."

The Master was distracted. Normally he would have a servant present to pour out the drinks but it was clear that he wanted an uninterrupted conversation. A tall man with long clean hands and elegant fingers, Sir Giles had a precision about his manners and exactitude in his dress that diverted any suspicion of the fey. His speech was as crisply ironed as his shirt, and he wore a three-piece suit in dark navy from Savile Row, together with the regimental tie of the Grenadier Guards. He had fought in the Great War alongside Harold Macmillan, and he was a good friend of Selwyn Lloyd, the Foreign Secretary. His wife, Lady Celia, always dressed in Chanel, and their two daughters had married into minor aristocracy. Decorated with a KBE in his early fifties, Sir Giles was considered to be a key figure in the British establishment; so much so that Sidney wondered if he thought a Cambridge college was something of a backwater.

As a former diplomat Sir Giles was used to the ambiguities of political discourse and the technicalities of the law, but, since taking up his post only a few years previously, he had been surprised how personally academics took to their disputes and how difficult it was to find lasting and satisfactory resolutions to their problems. It was bad enough discussing matters at meetings of the governing body, but now that one of their own had died in mysterious circumstances, he was going to have to rely on all his tact and discretion to smooth things over. "I was hoping that this could all be kept within the confines of the university, but that wish has proved forlorn. I believe you know Inspector Keating of the Cambridge police force?" he asked.

"I saw him only last night, and I am sure that he will take an interest in the case."

"He already has. He plans to interview Rory Montague this afternoon."

"And Bartlett?"

"It is a tricky situation. It was irresponsible of Lyall to take students out on such a night. I know that some of us have done a bit of night climbing in the past but that was when we were students. You would have thought he might have got it out of his system by now.

11

Rory Montague has been unhelpfully evasive. I was hoping that you might talk to him, Sidney."

"A pastoral visit? Surely the college chaplain could see to that?"

"No, I'd like you to go. You were there, after all. Of course it hardly helps that Kit Bartlett has disappeared."

"There is still no sign of him?"

"None. His parents have already telephoned. They seem to know that something is amiss (God knows how) and will start making their own enquiries. They might even go to the press, which is, of course, the last thing we need . . ."

"Indeed."

"Montague says Bartlett vanished before he started the descent. And there's another curious thing: his rooms are empty."

"As if he had planned to disappear all along?"

"Exactly so."

"And therefore Lyall's death may not have been accidental?"

"I don't think it will take the police too long to reach that conclusion, do you? Keating's not stupid and he's bound to interfere. I can only suppose that Bartlett's in hiding. We'll have to talk to all his friends, of course."

"Did Montague see what happened?"

"He can remember the rope being thrown down to him. After that, he claims his mind is blank."

"Anything else?"

"He suffers from vertigo so he feels guilty. He says that they wouldn't have used the rope if he hadn't been with them."

"It makes you wonder why he went up in the first place."

"He was their photographer," the Master explained. "And I imagine he was keen to impress. Kit Bartlett is a charismatic figure and Lyall was his tutor."

"Pacifists used to do foolhardy things in the war to prove they weren't cowards." Sidney remembered two cheerful friends who had worked as stretcher-bearers, refusing to kill enemy soldiers, acting with daring courage on a Normandy beach before they were blown up in front of him.

"I don't know if that will be Montague's story or not. I am also not sure whether it is helpful if he confesses to any responsibility. It could lead to a manslaughter charge and we don't want that."

Sidney finished his whisky. "We do, however, want the truth."

The Master was irritated. "The last thing this college needs is a scandal. We have already had a generous response to the appeal on our six-hundredth anniversary and I do not want to put that into jeopardy."

"We have to ascertain what happened."

"That, I recognise. We will behave with authority and fairness. It will be my official position."

"Then I must assume you have an unofficial position?"

"It is a delicate matter, Sidney."

"Then perhaps you could explain?"

"I am sure Inspector Keating will keep himself busy. Investigating. Asking questions."

"He certainly will. What of it?"

The Master gave Sidney what he hoped was a confidential look. "I'd like you to tell me what he thinks. I would like some warning if his enquiries become too detailed, particularly regarding the personal lives of those involved. I wouldn't like him to delve too closely, either into their relationships or their political interests."

"I thought Lyall was married?"

"He *was* married, yes. But I think that was very much for show. I am sure you don't need me to spell things out."

"You want me to keep watch over the police investigation?"

"I wouldn't put it like that. But I want you to be our college liaison. Inspector Keating knows and trusts you."

"He won't trust me if he finds out that I am telling you everything he's up to; and he certainly won't take kindly to the idea of me spying on police procedures."

"I don't think we need to put it as strongly as that. One needs to be very careful in Cambridge, as you know perfectly well, about the use of the word 'spy'. It leads to unsavoury speculation and we have quite enough of that already."

Sidney was aware that the university had still not recovered from the ignominy of "the affair of the missing diplomats", the former graduates Burgess and Maclean who, it was assumed, had defected to Moscow four years previously. Keating had been consulted about their disappearance and had protested that he hadn't been given full-enough access to the investigation. Since then, things had certainly developed. There had also been rumours that another Cambridge Apostle, Kim Philby, was "a third man" after his resignation from MI6 in 1951, and Keating had made it clear that he thought the newly formed KGB, led by Ivan "The Terrible" Serov, regarded the university as a fertile recruiting ground.

"I didn't know that Lyall was working for the security services."

"I didn't say that he was."

Sidney waited for the Master to explain but he did not. "You can't expect me to talk in any detail about all of this. Some things are best left in the dark. I am sure there is a discreet way in which we can conduct the matter."

"I am not sure there is, Master. After a death . . ."

Sidney knew there was a murky side to the relationship between the university and both MI5 and MI6 but he had always steered clear of asking too many questions about it. He recognised the appeal of recruiting intelligent agents but wished that it could be kept until after the students had graduated. It was too easy to exploit people who could not anticipate the consequences of their enthusiasm for intrigue; and, once they acquired a taste for secrecy and deceit, they could not always be relied upon to stay on the same side.

"I thought you priests dealt in grey areas all the time. Very few moral dilemmas come in black and white. It's a question of trust. Loyalty too."

15

Sidney was not at all sure that he liked where the conversation was heading. "I am perfectly aware of my loyalties, Master."

"To God, and your country; your college and your friends."

Sidney put his empty glass of whisky back on the drinks tray. "May they never come into conflict. Good evening, Master."

The snow returned once more, covering the ice on the roads and pavements, so that any movement across its surface was hazardous. Few people dared look up and ahead for long, offering only muted greetings to those they knew, preferring to concentrate on securing each footstep against a fall, eager to escape mishap and get home. Such careful responsibility was a far cry from Sidney's childhood enthusiasm for tobogganing with his brother and sister on Primrose Hill before the war. Then danger was a thrill, but now that he was older and into his thirties, he would have preferred to use the wintry conditions as an excuse to stay at home and concentrate on his next sermon.

The last thing he wanted was another tortuous inquiry. He had only just returned from a short holiday in Berlin with his friend Hildegard Staunton. She had been excellent company and it had been a relief to get away, both from his clerical duties and his criminal investigations. Indeed, he was still living in something of a post-holiday afterglow, and so he was as keen as the Master to ascertain that the events on the roof of

King's College Chapel had been unfortunate rather than sinister.

Rory Montague had his rooms in New Court, on a staircase close to the Porter's Lodge. Sidney was not looking forward to the meeting because he found it difficult to provide consolation and extract information at the same time.

There was also the dilemma at the heart of the event. He could understand the idea of some amateur climbing for high jinks. He had done it himself. But for a fellow of the college to encourage his students to attempt such a risky ascent on a dark and snowy night in the middle of winter seemed the height of madness.

Why on earth did they want to do it? he wondered. Could it simply be the excitement: the idea that action is life and here was jeopardy at its most distilled? Was it, as he imagined mountaineering to be, the hypnotism of an immense terror drawing them on, the narrowness of the gap between life and death, the fact that one slip or a lapse in concentration could result in a fatality?

Montague was a nervous, barrel-chested boy with curly brown hair, tortoiseshell spectacles and a small mole on his left cheek. He wore a tweed jacket, a mustard-coloured sleeveless jumper and a dark green tie over a Viyella shirt. There could hardly have been someone who looked less like a climber, let alone a man who might wilfully plan the death of another.

Sidney introduced himself and began with an apology. "I am sorry," he said. "I know you must have had a difficult time."

"Why have you come?" Montague answered. "Am I in trouble? Do people think it was my fault?"

"I was asked if I could talk to you."

"Who by?"

"The college. And I assure you that anything you tell me will be in confidence."

"I've already made one statement. I should have known it would not be enough. I can't think why it happened."

Sidney knew he would have to choose his words carefully. "If you do not want to add anything to what you have said already then, of course, I understand. I know it is a distressing time. I merely wanted to say that I am at your disposal, should you wish to discuss anything more."

"Why would I want to do that?"

"I have some experience with the police. I think it was hoped that I might be able to help smooth things over."

"There is nothing to smooth over, Canon Chambers. It was an accident. Mr Lyall fell. It was a stupid thing to do and I suffer from vertigo. We shouldn't have been up there in the first place."

"And why were you?"

"Kit thought it would be a laugh. He knew his tutor did that kind of thing. They were close."

"And you and Bartlett were friends?"

"Everyone loves Kit."

"And do you know where he is now?"

"I thought he'd gone home."

"It seems he has not. That is a cause of considerable anxiety; both for his parents and, I imagine, for you."

"He probably thinks I can look after myself."

"And can you?"

"I don't know."

"How did you get involved in all this, may I ask?"

"Mr Lyall knew I came from a family of mountaineers. My father was one of the youngest ever men to climb the north face of Ben Nevis in winter and on the ice. Now my brothers have all done it. I'm not so keen myself."

Sidney looked across the room to a neatly stacked boot-rack. "I see that you own a pair of climbing boots."

"In my family, everyone has to have them."

"Have you always had a fear of heights?"

"I don't mind up on the dales or on the fells in the Lake District. It's a sheer physical drop that I can't stand. Anything steeper than a 1 in 5."

"And on the roof of King's?"

"I panicked."

"Even if you could not see all the way down?"

"That made it worse."

"I wonder why you went up in the first place?"

"To prove myself. To try and get rid of the fear . . ."

Sidney stopped for a moment, thinking that the answer had come too easily. He needed to press on. "Can you remember what happened?"

"I had the rope and I couldn't find a foothold. I asked Mr Lyall to slacken off and give me some more rope and I heard a cry. Then I thought I heard Kit scramble down. I'm not sure. It was dark."

"Despite the moon and the snow?"

"I could only see things that were close."

"And you were there to take photographs?"

"Yes, although I never got my camera out."

"You didn't take a single exposure?"

"No. I was going to do so but then everything went wrong." There was a silence before Rory Montague added a further thought which, perhaps, he did not mean to say aloud. "I hate this place."

Sidney was surprised by this sudden turn of emotion. "Have you always felt that? 'Hate' is a strong word."

"Kit's been kind to me. Mr Lyall too. He told me that it doesn't matter where you're from if you have strong beliefs."

"And what are they?" Sidney asked.

"I'm not one for joining the Chapel Choir, if that's what you're after."

"I meant *political* beliefs."

"I believe in equality. We can't live in a country where there is one law for the rich and another for the poor."

"I understand," said Sidney, familiar with the appeal of radical politics to the young.

"You say you 'understand'," Rory replied. "But the Church is part of the establishment. There comes a time when a man has to decide which side he is on."

"I don't think it should be a question of sides." Sidney answered more defensively than he had

20

intended. He did not like to be considered something he was not. "I think it's a question of fairness and justice."

"Then we should agree with each other." Rory Montague almost smiled. "Although I am a member of the Communist Party."

"Some people would keep quiet about that. I admire your frankness."

"I am not ashamed. The revolution will come to this country one day, Canon Chambers. That, I can promise you."

Sidney was not sure if this was a threat or if Montague was speaking for effect. It was odd to volunteer this information so readily. If there was any connection with the KGB, however implausible that might seem, then the boy was hardly likely to draw attention to his membership of the Communist Party; and, by the same token, if he had been recruited on "our side", such a move was an equally obvious act of attempted infiltration. Surely Montague's only fault, if fault there was, was one of political naivety?

Sidney dined in college on braised lamb, hoping the weather might ease, and was late back to the vicarage. Although the nuts, fruit and alcohol of the traditional "combinations" after dinner had waylaid him, he was confident that he would be home in time to take Dickens out for his nocturnal constitutional. As he bicycled carefully through the gritted streets, he remembered that his dog had not shown much keenness to be out in the snow. In fact he had been a little lacklustre of late and Sidney worried there might be something wrong with him. It had been a while since his regular check-up with the vet.

Apart from one light in the kitchen the house was in darkness and it seemed colder than it was outside. Dickens greeted him with his usual mixture of affection and expectation and carried one of Sidney's slippers in his mouth as he followed him into the kitchen, circling his bowl in the hope of a second dinner.

A pan of milk was warming under a low gas flame. Sidney's curate was making his night-time cocoa. "We've had a bit of an adventure," Leonard began.

"Both of you?"

"I'm afraid so. I went out to see Isabel Robinson. You are aware that she has been ill?"

"I am, but I thought that, being a doctor's wife, she would be well looked after."

"I'm not so sure. Doctors sometimes neglect those closest to them. We can all be guilty of that from time to time."

Sidney wondered whether this remark was meant for him, but let his curate continue. "When I returned, the window of your study was wide open and there was a breeze blowing. I thought that perhaps Mrs Maguire had been giving it an airing, but she doesn't come after dark. Then I noticed that some of your papers had fallen on to the floor. It could have been the wind, of course, but Dickens had a copy of *The Cloud of Unknowing* shoved in his mouth. It must have been a ploy to shut him up. Not that he is much of a barker."

"You mean we've had burglars?"

"Yes, but nothing appears to be missing. Perhaps they were disturbed by my return. It is a bit of a mystery."

"Have you called the police, Leonard?"

"I presumed you had just been with them. And I couldn't be sure it means a break-in. As I said, I don't think that anything has been taken. Perhaps you should check?"

Sidney left the kitchen and walked into his study. Nothing seemed to have been removed. The silver cufflinks that he thought he had lost remained on a corner of his desk; the jazz records that he so loved were stacked by the gramophone (the burglar was clearly no fan of Acker Bilk); and the porcelain figurine of a girl feeding chickens, *Mädchen füttert Hühner*, that Hildegard had given him stood in its usual position on the mantelpiece.

"Extraordinary," Sidney remarked as he returned to the kitchen with Dickens padding behind him.

"I can't think why anyone would want to burgle a vicarage," Leonard answered, "especially in such dreadful weather. Besides, people must know we can't have anything worth stealing. It's rather an affront, don't you think?"

"You've lost nothing yourself?"

"As far as I can tell."

"Perhaps your collection of Dostoevsky put them off?" Sidney asked, trying to cheer himself up.

Leonard pretended that he had not heard the remark, raised his lips to his cocoa and blew on it. "Still too hot," he observed. "Maybe they were looking for something specific or someone was trying to frighten us. It might even be a warning of some kind. Is there anything I should know about?"

Sidney had to decide how much to confide in his curate. "I don't think so," he began, but then set off on a different track. "Why do you think people betray their country, Leonard?"

"That's an odd question at a time like this . . ."

"I was thinking."

"Are you referring to the communists?"

Sidney sat down at the kitchen table. "I could understand it before the war, perhaps. It was all part of the fight against fascism; too many members of the British establishment were keen on Hitler. Many of them were anti-Semitic. To fight against them from within must have been considered as working for the greater good. But it's hard to understand why people might do it now."

"I don't think the British establishment has changed all that much," said Leonard. "Communism will always have its attractions. People are fired up by ideas of equality. They want to change the world. Sometimes I suppose they want to take revenge."

"I also wonder if some people pretend to be communists when they are not?"

"That would be very perverse, wouldn't it?" Leonard asked. "Why would anyone want to do that?"

"That's what I may well need to find out."

Sidney took Dickens out and tried to let events settle in his mind. He felt uneasy and he could not quite work out why. It wasn't just the death of Lyall, or the possible burglary, but the sense that this was the beginning of something more sinister; something he could not predict or plan for.

He walked out of the vicarage, down the wide high street with its thatched cottages, its village school, pubs and garage, and took the narrow snowy path behind the Green Man, down to the meadows and frozen river. There were few remains of that day's activity: a completed snowman with coal buttons, eyes, mouth and carrot nose; the tracks of a toboggan; a circled cluster of footsteps from what might have been a snowball fight. Looking back to the easterly edge of the village, Sidney could just make out the silhouette of a group of bombed-out buildings that had still not been rebuilt since the war. The snow covering looked like giant sheeting left by removal men who had forgotten all about them.

Sidney tried to concentrate on something altogether more enjoyable, but found his thoughts about Hildegard and his recent German visit were equally unsettling. He wondered if it was snowing there too, what Hildegard might be doing, and when on earth he was going to see her again. He missed her far more than he had anticipated, and wished she were with him.

After the death of her husband, Hildegard had been the catalyst for Sidney's adventures in crime. He had felt an almost inexpressible sorrow on meeting her and they had begun to share an intimacy that was yet to be defined. She understood what he was thinking better than anyone he knew. She was also able to get away with asking questions that would have been too direct if posed by anyone else.

"Do you think you might, in your heart, be embarrassed about being a clergyman?" she had said.

Sidney wondered if she was right, and if he might feel less anxious (and less distracted by crime) if he had more status; if, eventually, perhaps, he was a bishop.

"A clergyman cannot be proud," he answered.

"Of course not. But he must have the confidence to do his job well. Like a doctor."

"That is not to say that there aren't ambitious priests, of course."

"How ambitious are you, Sidney?"

"I think I aspire to a clear conscience."

"That sounds almost too good to be true."

"It is the truth as I see it; an honest answer, I hope. Perhaps because I gave it to you quickly, it is what I most mean."

Hildegard took his arm. It was another cold night and they walked on through the Tiergarten, past street stalls selling *bockwurst*, toasted almonds, chestnuts and *glühwein*.

"I like being with you," Hildegard said. "You can be so serious and then sometimes I think you are in a world of your own. I wish I could go there."

"Well," Sidney replied. "I can always take you. But what about you? What will you do?"

"The future seems so far away," Hildegard answered. "For now, the present moment, here, now and with you, is enough."

Back in Grantchester, Sidney knew that he had to be careful not to romanticise the memory of what had happened. He reminded himself that Berlin had also been unsettling. He was forever showing his papers. Armed guards at sector checkpoints were continually asking him to prove that he was who he said he was.

Recalling it all now, as he walked Dickens home across the snow-filled meadows, Sidney began to think about loyalty and how hard it was to lead two very different lives at the same time, one in England and the other in Germany. But then, he continued, the idea of duality was also at the heart of Christianity. You had to be both a man and a Christian, and if there was ever a conflict between the two then it was his duty as a priest to put his acquired identity, as a man of faith, above his own essential nature.

Sidney was not sure how successful he had been at doing this. There were times when it would have been far easier to act on his own instincts, and in accordance with his innate personality, but the idea, surely, was that these had to be sacrificed in order to fulfil a more important calling.

He wondered if people working in the field of espionage thought in the same way, perverting the religious impulse, perhaps, putting their conscience above their country, believing in a higher purpose or a different destiny for which they were prepared to betray everything they pretended to hold dear.

Valentine Lyall's funeral took place ten days after his death. Although Sidney had not known him well he was

27

able to talk to a sufficient number of his colleagues to draw up an informal portrait of the man. A keen mountaineer, Lyall had been born in Windermere in 1903, and had been too young to fight in the First World War. Since then, however, his work in radiology at Strangeways Research Laboratory in Worts Causeway had brought him international recognition. His research into the deleterious effects of radioactive isotopes, and the biological impact of atomic explosions, had been of inestimable benefit to the Ministry of Defence; but Lyall had also been determined to uncover the benefits of that same technology in peacetime, putting the similarities between war armament and protection to good use. Consequently, he had written extensively on the application of radiation action in biological and medical investigations.

This gave Sidney the substance for his funeral address; that good could yet come from evil, that darkness could be turned into light.

He was tempted to take his text from the Book of Isaiah. *They will beat their swords into plowshares and their spears into pruning hooks. Nation will not take up sword against nation, nor will they train for war any more.* However, Sidney knew that his academic, and therefore judgemental, congregation would find this too obvious and so, in recognition of Valentine Lyall's love of mountains, he settled for something braver, especially given the context of the man's death. He chose to speak on the subject of Matthew, chapter 17, verse 20: *If ye have faith as a grain of mustard seed, ye shall say unto this mountain, Remove hence to yonder place: and it shall remove; and nothing shall be impossible unto you.*

It was worth the risk. Every time Sidney spoke to the more doubtful, humanist or cynical members of the university he found himself becoming more aggressive about his faith.

Not that he knew everyone who had come to the service. Despite the aspersions cast about his private life, Lyall had once had a wife; and although she had left him shortly after the war and lived in London, she returned for her former husband's funeral and sat with his sister in the front row. The two women were joined by the Master of Corpus, several senior fellows, and staff from the Strangeways Research Laboratory.

Sidney's sermon went well. He had learned that the best way of unsettling the non-believer was to attack with certainty, acknowledging doubt before hitting home with the necessity of faith.

The wake was held in Cherry Hinton Road. Lyall's sister, Hetty, offered guests some rather tired-looking cheese sandwiches, followed by tea and cake, whisky or sherry, while Sidney took the opportunity to have a quiet word with a woman he had never met before.

Alice Lyall, now Bannerman, was a surprisingly tall, elegant woman with magnificent Titianesque hair that had been swept back and curled. Although she could clearly dominate a room she took pains not to, either embarrassed or tired by the effect she could have on a man. She was going to stay for as long as it was polite to do so, and Sidney knew that he would have to choose his words carefully if he was going to acquire information.

"When we first moved in, I thought that we would live here for ever," she explained. "I imagined the children going to the Leys or the Perse and that I would become a don's wife, one of those grass widows you see on their bicycles all over town trying to look as if they belong in a world of men. Now, of course, it turns out that I am merely a widow; of sorts."

"You didn't have children?"

"Not with Val, no, although that is hardly a surprise. I have had two boys since."

"Your husband didn't mind you coming today?"

"I didn't particularly want to come. But when you've been married to a man you have to find a way of coming to terms with what has happened. You have to forgive him in the end."

"Did Mr Lyall require much forgiveness?"

"I don't think this is the time or the place to discuss the failure of my first marriage, do you, Canon Chambers?"

"I am sorry. Please 'forgive' my indiscretion."

Alice Bannerman took no notice. "It's not easy to be married to a liar. I am glad you did not mention it in your address."

"That would not have been appropriate. I presume you are referring . . ."

"There's no need to spell it out. Everyone knows he preferred men."

"Everyone suspects. That is different."

"God forbid anyone at the university ever telling it like it is."

Sidney did not like to press matters. "I am sorry to have troubled you."

"You are not troubling me. In fact, I am grateful. I am also sorry to have been short with you. It's not been an easy day and I do hate Cambridge. Thank you for taking the service."

Sidney was surprised that so many women tended to think in this way. "Do you think your former husband did too?"

"Hate Cambridge? I am sure he loved it."

"Many people find it difficult: the lack of privacy, the two different worlds of town and gown."

"Oh surely, Canon Chambers, there is a hierarchy of etiquette and a constellation of social codes."

"Yes, I can see that," Sidney tried to be conciliatory. "No one quite knows what the rules are."

"There are worlds within worlds when you think about it. Although I never expected to understand my husband on the subatomic level, I must say."

"You are a scientist?"

"I started off as Val's research student."

"I didn't know that."

"When you look as I do, Canon Chambers, very few people credit you with intelligence. Even at this esteemed university, people tend to go by appearances."

"As a priest, I try not to."

"Well, even as a priest, I think you probably have rather a long way to go, if you don't mind my saying so."

Sidney was shocked by this directness. He suddenly felt rather sick. In fact, he worried that he was going to *be* sick. Perhaps it had been one of the cheese sandwiches. "If you'll excuse me . . ."

Alice Bannerman appeared to guess his intentions. "The bathroom is at the top of the stairs on the right."

The walls on the way up were tacked with Ordnance Survey maps and black and white photographs of mountains. Once in the bathroom, Sidney washed his face to quell his nausea. The small hand-towel was damp on a ring beside him. He looked to see if there was another and then noticed a small bathroom cabinet. He wondered if Lyall had kept any Alka-Seltzer or cod-liver oil to settle his stomach. When he opened the cupboard he found that it was half-filled with prescription medicines: mechlorethamine, triethylenemelamine and busulfan. He would have to telephone his father to check what they meant but he was almost sure that they were medicines for cancer.

He opened the window to get some air and then drank a glass of water. He took a few deep breaths and decided to go home as soon as possible.

"So soon?" Alice Bannerman asked.

Sidney could not leave quickly enough. It was early afternoon, but already it was almost dark, the only light coming from the street lamps and the snow. When he got back to the vicarage, he decided, he would make himself a cup of tea and sit by a warm fire in the half-light and pray quietly. Then he would talk to Leonard.

members of the university believed they were a law unto themselves. "Academic ability isn't everything, Sidney," he pronounced, "especially when it comes to crime. You have to know what makes people tick. You have to understand the human character. You can't just get all the answers out of books. That's why you and I get on with each other."

"I agree, although you do need intelligence as well as intuition."

"Then there are different kinds of 'intelligence', aren't there? The public and the private . . ."

"The stated and the concealed."

Such was Inspector Keating's impatience that he was not going to wait to hear Sidney's ideas but pressed on with his own. "We need to establish the truth about Valentine Lyall. Who was he and what were they all doing on the roof in the first place? Was this a relatively innocent escapade or did one or more of them have sinister motives? Did Lyall fall or did Bartlett push him? If he was pushed, was he deliberately lured on to the roof in order to meet his doom? If so, then for what purpose? And why this method?"

"To make it look like an accident."

"There are simpler ways of killing a man. Second, we need to know if Rory Montague saw as little as he says he did and whether he is as innocent as he sounds. Can he remember anything more, and what was his relationship with the two other men? Why is he still here when Bartlett has disappeared? And lastly, why is the Master of your college so keen that I should only talk to you?"

"He is worried that you will think it might have something to do with espionage."

"I wouldn't be surprised. I do have a few contacts in the Foreign Office and they've been warning me about this place for years. Although I don't always get the information I'm after. They can be quite evasive when they want to be."

"I imagine that's their job. But it's always hard to know what's going on and how much people know," Sidney continued. "I'm not a great believer in conspiracy theories myself. People at this university are generally too consumed by their own ideas. You cannot underestimate the limited preoccupations of the intellectual. But whether this is, or is not, an accident, it's certainly unusual for three men to be on a roof together and for one to die and another to disappear from the face of the earth. I also share your doubts about Rory Montague. I think he's hiding something."

"We need to go through their movements as accurately as we can; and that, unfortunately, means getting on to the roof ourselves."

"I imagined you might say that," Sidney replied warily. "I presume we can forgo the use of climbing ropes. There is a perfectly good interior staircase."

"And I assume you know how to get to it."

"My friend, the precentor, will supply us with a key."

"You have friends in high places."

"And some low ones too," Sidney replied, finishing his pint. He told himself firmly that he should not have another.

"You had better not tell me about them. Have you got time to do all this, Sidney? In the past you have always been very quick to remind me about your duties. I assume you have other things to do?"

Sidney looked down at his depressingly empty pint glass and hesitated. It was a busy time for visiting the sick (Mrs Maguire's mother could not have much longer to live) and Leonard had requested guidance before taking the first of his Lenten confirmation classes. There was also the "annual inspection of the fabric" to worry about. This was always testing in wintertime when the church roof was prone to leak and the current weight of snow had already made the situation precarious. Furthermore, Sidney's friend Amanda Kendall had telephoned only that morning and threatened to pay an imminent visit to Grantchester in order to "hear all about the German escapade", and this would take up at least half a day of his time. There was too much going on already.

"Well, Sidney?" Keating asked.

"I think most things can wait," his friend replied uncertainly.

The two men arranged to meet at St Andrew's Street police station the following morning. Before going to King's, Keating asked if they could make a small detour through the college. He wanted to have a look at Kit Bartlett's rooms.

For a moment, as they walked down Petty Cury, Sidney had the feeling that they were being followed. A man in a dark raincoat and trilby, whom he thought he had seen on the way to the Eagle the night before, appeared twice behind them and was in no hurry either to overtake or head off in a different direction. It was unsettling, but Sidney did not want to point this out to his friend for fear of seeming over-anxious.

Kit Bartlett's set of rooms was on the second floor of a staircase in Old Court itself. The outer room consisted of the furniture the college had provided: a couple of armchairs, a desk, chair and card-table. The single bed had been made up, the curtains were drawn and there was nothing personal that could suggest his presence.

"What was he studying?" Inspector Keating asked.

"Medicine. Although I think he was specialising in radiology. Lyall was one of the great experts in the subject. Bartlett won't be short of job opportunities either here or abroad."

"Why do you say abroad?"

"I was just thinking where he might have got to . . ." Sidney wondered if it was too far-fetched to think of Moscow.

"We have no evidence that he has left the country."

"And none that he is still here. Why would a man disappear so suddenly if innocent of any crime? What could his motivation be for killing Valentine Lyall, if kill him he did?"

"Before you start worrying about any negligence on my part, Sidney, I would like to say that I have already alerted Inspector Williams at Scotland Yard. He is watching all the major departure points. London airport has his details."

"He will almost certainly be travelling with false papers. I assume your men have done a full search?"

"They have. The reason I wanted to come is that they have already told me the room was clean: too clean in fact."

"What do you mean?"

"With a student you would normally expect to find something. There should be a little bit of evidence somewhere: an unwanted book, a scrap of paper behind a chair, an old newspaper or something. But here there was nothing. It was a professional job."

"Which means?"

"He did not clear his room himself. It was done for him."

"And who would do that?"

"Someone wishing to leave no trace."

"I thought there was always a trace?" Sidney asked.

"Well, the fact that there is nothing is a clue in itself." Inspector Keating opened the outer door to Bartlett's rooms. "Dark forces, you understand: government secrecy, the national interest."

"I see."

"It was so much simpler in the war, wasn't it, Sidney? You never woke up to find that one of your colleagues in the Northumberland Fusiliers was a Nazi. Peace is more complicated. It's easier to disguise your behaviour and pretend to be what you're not."

The two men walked back across Old Court and crossed King's Parade. Sidney regarded the fan vaulting of King's as the greatest architectural achievement in Cambridge; it was far better than the cloister walk in

Gloucester Cathedral or Henry VII's Lady Chapel in Westminster Abbey. It was like the inside of a beautiful boat or a perfect violin.

Soon the two men were standing at the west end looking up at the interior roof of Weldon stone, eighty feet above them.

"People assume," Sidney began, "that Bartlett must have crawled into the hollows and supports of the vault and waited in the timbers until the coast was clear. But I believe there are other exits."

"Apart from the internal staircase used by Montague?"

"There may be more than one. My friend Robin will no doubt alert us to the possibilities."

A fresh-faced man in a red cassock approached and handed Sidney the key. "Of course we are going to have to change the lock," he explained. "I think one of our visitors must have made an impression into some soap or wax and then had a copy made. It means that now any subsequent tours of the roof will have to be accompanied."

The precentor was in a hurry; one explained by the arrival of choirboys for a rehearsal before evensong. "If you can be down before we start that would be helpful. And please lock the door behind you. We don't want anyone following you up there."

"Indeed," Keating replied.

"I don't think we'll be long," Sidney smiled. "I am not sure about the inspector's head for heights."

"I think I'll be all right," his companion assured them. "It'll be the closest I'll ever get to Heaven. I hope there's a ruddy light."

Sidney turned the key in the rusted lock. "Try not to swear, inspector. The switch is here. Would you like me to go first?"

"If you wouldn't mind. Have you ever climbed this building yourself?"

"I am afraid not," Sidney replied. "I gave up on the nursery slopes: the south face of Caius and the Senate House leap. That was excitement enough. And I have only been to the top of the chapel twice before, and both times by this route. The view is spectacular."

"Which makes one wonder why anyone would have wanted to go up at night?"

The two men climbed the spiral staircase, pausing for a rest halfway. "I always like the mason's marks," said Sidney. "They are the one element of pride in an otherwise anonymous building."

"They remind me of prisoners trying to escape," said Keating. "I can't imagine Bartlett wanting to stay too long up here. What on earth do you think he was doing? He must have known they'd discover him in the end."

"Unless he waited for a few hours or knew of a different exit? Despite what the porters say, I don't think anyone is going to keep watch on the staircase for that long. I imagine he let himself out at around three or four in the morning and caught the first train to London."

"The 4.24? Then he could get down to Dover and be on one of the first ferries. If he did that we've little chance of finding him."

The two men emerged on to the roof. New snowfall had erased all the footprints from the night climb and the frosted stone appeared far less solid when seen at close quarters. Sidney wondered what it must have been like for the first masons, how much they would have had to work in similar conditions and in the limited light of winter. He walked across to the north-east pinnacle. "I imagine Rory Montague began his descent with the rope from the first parapet; although it's hardly straightforward."

Keating glanced down. "It's madness. To think supposedly intelligent people could do this."

Sidney did not like to look for long. "I would definitely hesitate," he said.

"That is interesting. Do you think that if I knew you well . . ."

"You do know me well, inspector."

"That I would *expect you* to hesitate? I could *predict* it?"

"Quite possibly."

"Then I might even be able to take advantage of your hesitation."

"What do you mean?"

Keating paced his way towards the south-west corner of the chapel. "Montague's story suggests that Bartlett disappeared by running the length of the roof and disappearing through a concealed doorway in the south-west pinnacle. Montague's hesitation, his panic, bought his friend time. It was, perhaps, all part of a plan."

Sidney was struggling to come to terms with the direction of Keating's thinking. "What kind of plan? You're not implying that they were all in on it — that the murder, or even perhaps suicide, of Valentine Lyall, the disappearance of Kit Bartlett and the framing of Rory Montague are all part of some greater plot? That the event was deliberately *staged*"?

"I'm not sure. I just cannot believe the whole thing was a simple escapade, Sidney. It's too dangerous."

"But if you want to kill someone surely there are easier ways of doing it? Why go to the trouble of something so melodramatic?"

"Because you want it to be known. You want it to be made as public as possible."

"I'm not sure if I can quite believe that."

"I think you may have to make another visit to the Master's Lodge," Keating replied.

"You think that he hasn't been telling me as much as he should?"

"I think it might be an idea to get things straight. You need to try and find out if all three of these men were really on our side or not; and, if that is the case, whether they were playing a different game, in public, to throw someone else off the scent."

"And you think I can trust the Master?"

"Probably not, but I'd like to know what he has to say for himself. I'll try to make some discreet enquiries with my contacts at the Foreign Office, but I think you're going to have to do your bit, Sidney. Those bloody colleges never tell us what's going on and only call us in when it's too late. It's never the best way to run things."

The two men began their descent from the chapel roof and Keating stopped. "Are you happy to talk to him? It won't compromise your position with the college?"

"Conscience before compromise, Geordie."

The inspector smiled at the off-duty use of his Christian name. "You will tell me everything he says, won't you?"

"You have my word."

"It might be difficult. They'll try and keep you in the dark for as long as possible but you know where your loyalties lie?"

Sidney resumed his walk down the narrow confines of the stairway. It was unnecessary to be asked such a question again. "I have no doubt about that, I can assure you."

Although it had begun to thaw, the sharp wind still cut through the warmest of overcoats and the thickest of scarves. Every foray into the outdoors became a challenge. A man needed to have something to look forward to, Sidney decided, and although he knew that the company would be challenging, he was enjoying the possibility of a warming lunch with his friend Amanda Kendall before his next encounter with the Master.

It was becoming something of a monthly routine. Amanda would take the 11.24 train from Liverpool Street and Sidney would bicycle over from Grantchester to meet her at 12.39. They would then walk over to Mill Road and have lunch at their favourite restaurant Le Bleu Blanc Rouge.

Sidney was not particularly adept at cycling, using the time to concentrate either on his forthcoming sermon or on recent events, and his attentiveness to traffic was not as sharp as it might have been. Nevertheless, he was shocked into alertness by a butcher's van turning left across him into Bateman Street and then mounting the snowy kerb before accelerating away into the distance. Had it been a few seconds later, Sidney would have been knocked down.

This sudden awareness pulled him up short. It would take only one lapse of concentration and he could have died. He really did have to try to pay more attention: unless the driver *had meant to hit him*. Was someone monitoring his investigation into the death of Valentine Lyall? He wondered, once again, if he was being followed and if he should alert Inspector Keating to his suspicions. Or perhaps, he consoled himself, all of this anxiety was merely nervousness at the prospect of seeing Amanda?

His friend was known for her directness and Sidney had not thought too carefully about how open he was going to be with her; either about recent events or, indeed, his last German visit. Amanda liked clear answers to her questions. She was not that interested in either ambiguity or uncertainty despite the fact that their friendship still had its areas of unease. Sidney had been immensely attracted to her when he was younger but, since his ordination, Amanda had stated that any romantic potential had evaporated with his decision "to put God first", and he, in turn, had concentrated on her Roman nose and a snaggle tooth on the top right-hand side of her mouth in order to avoid infatuation.

There remained, however, an immense, and often exclusive, affection between the two friends. They had met shortly after the war, when Sidney had become an interim replacement for Amanda's favourite cousin, Charles, who had been killed at El Alamein. They had a shared sense of the ridiculous, loved "pastime with good company", and hated any abbreviation of their Christian names (she was no more of a "Mandy" than he was a "Sid"). Although she hated jazz, could not understand the rules of cricket, and thought that the clergy should work much harder to make their sermons entertaining, she was irresistibly attracted to Sidney's charm and loyalty. She was also, particularly, grateful for his petty vanities and how he tolerated being teased because of them. He had, she thought, an openly vulnerable humanity and, unlike other clergy, whom she cruelly referred to as "theatrical cast-offs", Sidney could preach a decent sermon. His mixture of decency and optimism reminded her of the actor Kenneth More in *Genevieve*. She also recognised that Sidney was, perhaps, the only man she knew who properly appreciated her intelligence (St Hilda's Oxford, the Courtauld Institute, research into Holbein and the history of British portraiture), her love of music (she played the oboe and sang in the Bach Choir), and the complexity of her social situation (a large inheritance and the resulting hazard of fortune-seeking suitors).

Despite the horrors of a "freezing train and a frightful journey", Amanda was on feisty form on her arrival, regaling Sidney with news of his sister Jennifer and a New Year house party that was full of "handsome men who had never bothered to learn how to be interesting". It was a relief to get back to her work at the National Gallery, she said, and she was glad to be helping her old tutor Anthony Blunt with some research into the later paintings of Nicolas Poussin.

Sidney unfolded his napkin. "It is strange you should mention Blunt. He dined at the college a few nights ago."

"He's not a Corpus man, is he?"

"I think he was a guest of the Master."

"You didn't talk to him? You know he's the son of a vicar?"

"I was a little distracted, Amanda."

"By anything in particular?"

"Nothing too alarming."

Amanda paused while the waitress finished pouring out her glass of wine. "I'm afraid I don't believe you, Sidney. I have seen that look of yours before and it troubles me."

"One of our junior fellows has died. It's been a sad business."

"By 'junior' do you mean that he was young?"

"It was an accident," Sidney answered.

"I assume, by your tone, that it was nothing of the kind."

"It's quite complicated," Sidney replied as their food arrived.

Amanda raised a glass of wine to her lips and made steady eye contact. "Are you getting into trouble again?"

"I can't seem to help it."

"Anything I can do?"

"Yes," said Sidney, poking at a rather unsatisfactory poached egg soufflé. "You can take my mind off it. Tell me about London. What have you been up to?"

"Nothing too exciting. I've told you about all the parties. Your sister is still seeing Johnny Johnson . . ."

"And what about you?"

"There's one chap who's being particularly attentive, but it's too early to tell if he's decent or not. I'm far more careful after the Guy debacle."

It was only a year since Amanda's future fiancé had disgraced himself with a hot-tempered display at a London dinner party and it had taken her months to recover from the embarrassment. "I think I've given up on men for the time being. There's far too much work to do at the gallery. In any case," she continued, "it's not my admirers we need to be discussing; it's yours. I am talking about the famous widow, lest we are in any doubt."

Sidney put his starter to one side. "I was afraid we'd come on to that."

"So you admit that Hildegard is an admirer?" Amanda smiled. "I think I'll have a little more wine."

"We are very good friends. That is all."

Amanda remained silent, forcing Sidney to continue. "I had a marvellous time."

"Is that it?"

Sidney remembered strolling through the Tiergarten to the Badewanne jazz club where they had listened to the Johannes Rediske Quintet play with cool control. It was a relief that Hildegard "got" jazz and understood why he liked its spontaneity and freedom. Afterwards, they had walked back on the Kurfürstendamm, past the bombed-out Kaiser-Wilhelm-Gedächtnis-Kirche. It began to rain, and Hildegard had their only umbrella. When she put her arm through his, so that they could share it, and she squeezed up against him, it had felt the most natural thing in the world.

"Well?" Amanda asked. "Are you going to tell me anything?"

"There's nothing much to tell."

"I don't believe that for a moment. It's simply that you don't want to talk about it. I seem to remember that she is musical."

"She teaches the piano. She plays Bach every day."

"She must be very serious."

"Not all the time. She is also a great fan of Jimmy Cagney."

"You have been to the cinema together?"

"She has taken me. We went to see *13 Rue Madeleine*."

"Intriguing."

"It was rather fun."

"And is she beautiful?"

Sidney was not going to be drawn into any comparisons. "I think so."

"Not classically then, I imagine." Amanda looked at Sidney but it was clear that he was not going to say anything more and she had sufficient tact not to press the matter. "Will I ever meet her?" she asked.

"In due course."

"You mean that she is coming back to Cambridge?"

"I have invited her."

"When?"

"Later this year, I hope."

"That seems rather vague."

"I don't want to rush things."

"Are you in love with her?"

"That's a very direct question."

"Are you prepared to answer it? Or shall I take your silence as assent?" The waitress cleared away their plates. "You can think about your answer over your coq au vin. I'm sorry you found the starter so disappointing. You should have had the onion soup."

"Really, Amanda, it's very hard to know what I think; and yet, at the same time, I quite like not knowing. It's a pleasant confusion."

"That means you are, I would have thought."

"In love? I don't know, Amanda. But I think I feel most like myself when I am with her."

"I thought you got that with me."

"You are, if I may say so, more of a challenge."

"That's what most of my admirers say. Do you think it puts them off?"

"I do think that many men find intelligent women difficult; particularly if they are cleverer than them."

"None of them are as intelligent as you, of course."

"I'm sorry to hear that."

Amanda smiled. "You're not sorry at all. You are extremely pleased."

"Well I do like to be top in some regard. Would you like another glass of wine?"

"That would be kind; although I myself seem to have been displaced from the top spot."

"Not at all. You are very different women."

The waitress arrived with two plates in her hand. "Who's having the daube?" she asked.

"I am. I'm still cold," Amanda replied, before asking, "Do you think you'll marry her?"

Sidney hesitated.

Ever since his ordination to the priesthood, he had resigned himself to the idea of celibacy. He could no more imagine a life shared with a German widow than he could with his dazzling friend opposite. Even if he were to marry he was sure that he would make an unsatisfactory husband. He was incapable of concentrating on the traditionally masculine areas of everyday life. He may have been able to translate Herodotus from the Greek but he was not able to drive a car. He could listen to the darkest fears of his parishioners and comfort them in their hours of anxiety, but he was not sure that he could change a fuse. He was hopeless with money, finding that he always had more pressing things to do than go to the bank or pay his bills. No, Sidney had always said to himself in the past; marriage was not for him. He would take as many wedding services as his parishioners required, and marry hundreds of couples in the course of his ministry, but he was destined to remain a bachelor.

"Hildegard is a widow, you will remember. I don't think she's ready for marriage."

"Does that mean that you are?"

Sidney imagined himself sitting in his study with Hildegard playing the piano in a room across the corridor. He could even picture a small child, a daughter perhaps, standing in the doorway, asking him if he'd help mend her kite.

"Are you going to answer my question?" Amanda asked.

Snow lay heavy on the tiled roofs, turrets and parapets of Corpus; outlining the cinquefoil lights and gabled dormers of Old Court, that most ancient of all the enclosed areas of Cambridge, as Sidney returned from seeing Amanda on to her train.

He remembered how the astronomer and mathematician Johannes Kepler had been intrigued by snow crystals, writing a small treatise entitled *On the Six-Cornered Snowflake*. In 1611 he asked the fundamental question: "There must be some definite cause why, whenever snow begins to fall, its initial formation invariably displays the shape of a six-cornered starlet. For if it happens by chance, why do they not fall just as well with five corners or seven?"

In his treatise, Kepler compared their symmetry with that of honeycombs and Sidney had once heard a sermon that used the miracle of the snowflake as an example of both the simplicity and the complexity of God's creation. It might be worth reviving that idea, he thought, particularly in this weather. Instead of seeing the mass of snow, the congregation could be persuaded to look into the smallest details of it in order to find God.

"STOP!"

Sidney did so.

"STAY THERE!"

A large weight of stone fell from the roof of New Court and landed in front of him.

"Good God, sir," cried the porter. "You could have been killed."

Sidney felt the fear run through him.

"That was close. We've had such trouble with the snow, sir. The college is falling apart. Some of the older buildings can't stand it. It's the water, you see. It gets into the stone and then freezes and thaws, expands and contracts . . ."

"Yes," Sidney cut him off. "I understand the process."

"I'll get one of the men to clear up. You must have someone watching out for you."

"I suppose I do."

"Of course, as a priest, you probably have extra protection. I imagine the angels don't want to lose one of their own. That was a near miss."

"I wouldn't call myself an angel, Bill."

"Better than being a devil, though, isn't it?" the porter winked.

Sidney was irritated. He didn't like people winking, he had to talk to the Master, and he worried that someone was trying to kill him. In a moment of madness he wondered if it was Kit Bartlett. What the hell was going on?

Sidney was determined to have it out with the Master, but when he finally got to see him he found the man was incapable of concentrating on their conversation. He appeared to have lost something and kept rearranging the papers on his desk, looking under the stacks of books that lay on the tables, chairs and piled on the floor. Even the library ladder was so filled with academic paraphernalia that it could no longer fulfil its function in enabling the reader to reach the higher shelves in the study.

"Have you mislaid something, Master?"

"It's a curious thing. It's only notes."

Sidney was bemused. "I'm sure they will turn up."

"I am a little worried because I have been rather acerbic and I would prefer it if they didn't get into the wrong hands. I have looked everywhere."

"Perhaps your secretary has taken them away?"

"Miss Madge knows that she must touch nothing in this room," the Master replied. "I have her well trained."

Sidney wondered how he had achieved this. His own housekeeper, Mrs Maguire, moved everything willy-nilly and her vacuum cleaner took precedence to everything. The result was that after one of her "proper cleans" Sidney could never find anything at all.

"It's very troubling," the Master continued. "It is not just that Lyall is so tragically dead and Bartlett has disappeared. It's the air of uncertainty I can't stand."

"I suppose we all like a semblance of order."

"A semblance? There's no illusion in order. It is what we are supposed to offer in this college. History. Continuity. Academic excellence."

"And you think that the event on the roof of the chapel will adversely affect our reputation?"

"It will if we don't explain the nature of the accident clearly. Lyall was one of our better-known fellows and, even in his lifetime, he attracted a few stories. Now, of course, there are more."

"Insinuations, accusations of a sexual nature?"

"You know the kind of thing. It doesn't take much. I wish I could find these notes."

"Perhaps they have been stolen?"

"I doubt that. Although it *is* irritating."

"Theft is a crime, Master. You could always call in the police."

The Master stopped tidying his papers and asked, "How do you think your man is getting on?"

"Inspector Keating?"

"You've nothing to report yourself? Nothing out of the ordinary has occurred to you recently?"

Sidney was alarmed. Why would the Master ask such a question if he didn't suspect that something had happened or that Sidney had become suspicious? He must *know* that Sidney was being followed. He *knew* that there had been attempts to scare him off the case.

"I don't think so," Sidney replied.

"Are you sure?"

Sidney hesitated. "I am quite sure." He wasn't going to give the Master the advantage in a situation where he wasn't sure whom he could trust.

"You are aware that Rory Montague has returned home?"

"In the middle of term?" Sidney thought that this, too, was unusual. "Why?"

Sir Giles tried to sound nonchalant. "I thought a break might be good for him."

"It was your idea?"

"Just for a few days. While things calm down."

"Do you think he will lead us to Bartlett?"

"I suppose he might. Bartlett's parents certainly hope so; although I have hinted that this is a question of government secrecy and that they shouldn't be unduly alarmed."

"You said that? Even though we cannot be sure? I would have thought that would only make them worry more. Have you told the police about Montague?"

"I imagine they will find out soon enough."

"He is a witness; and, of course, a suspect, Master. I must tell them."

"Yes," the Master answered drily, "I had imagined that you would."

Sidney felt distinctly uneasy as he made his way to his regular Thursday-night drinks session with Inspector Keating. He was now convinced that he was deliberately being kept in the dark. He was also being tailed by the dark green butcher's van that had first cut across him before his lunch with Amanda. What could they possibly want with him? He turned off Silver Street into Queens' Lane. The car followed as he walked past his college and entered the consoling confines of the Eagle.

Once they had greeted each other, sat down in their favourite chairs, ordered their pints, and begun their game of backgammon, Sidney tried to get to the point as soon as he could.

"This is what I think," he began. "Valentine Lyall was recruiting for the security services."

"I'm sure that is the case," Keating replied. "But which? Not that we should be talking about it in here."

"No one is listening."

"The room may be bugged."

"The Eagle? If it was, then you would know."

"Probably. Although you would be surprised by how often I don't."

"There is no one else here," Sidney continued. "It might as well be a private room."

"Well keep your voice down; and don't name any names if you are going to start making suggestions."

"I am not going to say anything indiscreet."

"I wouldn't bet on it. Which side do you think our man was on?"

"That is, of course, the crucial matter. Let us suppose that the victim, and since we are in such an ornithological location, let's refer to him as the Falcon, was with our own intelligence services. The other two, let us call them the Buzzard and the Merlin . . ."

"You think they were working together?"

"I think so. It is clear that the Merlin is in love with the Buzzard."

"Is it?"

"I think so. The Merlin is the keenest to impress, to belong, and therefore pretends to suffer from vertigo.

The Falcon leans out from the pinnacle to give him more rope and, at the moment when he is most off balance, the Buzzard pushes him from the roof. He then heads off down the spiral staircase using a key he has obtained by making an impression on a previous visit."

"While the Merlin is left hanging to make it look like an accident?"

"Not only that. He must then be interviewed and made the centre of all enquiries while his companion makes his escape. It is he who stole the Master's papers and who, probably even now, is with the Buzzard. I don't think they're at home as the Master says. I think they're in either Berlin or Moscow."

"So you think, as I do, that they might be KGB?"

"Not entirely."

"What do you mean?"

"Why was I being followed? Who was trying to put me off? It wasn't one of your men, was it?"

"No."

"And why, of course, did they not succeed in killing me? A professional would have made short work of it. I am sure that it would be a simple matter to dispose of me."

"I'm afraid you are probably right about that."

"And so I think it was for show, Geordie. I had to be seen to be under threat. The people responsible wanted to make our investigation seem dangerous."

"And who would want to do that?"

"Our own side, of course." Sidney hesitated. "I may be wrong but let us imagine that all this was meant to happen. Think of it as a deliberate plot in which the Falcon was meant to be sacrificed. He knew that he was dying. He might as well die for his country. It was his final mission."

"Go on."

"It is a trap, laid by the man at the heart of my college. The Master is playing a double game."

"So our men are double agents?"

"The Russians think that the boys have killed one of the most successful recruitment officers the secret service has ever known, and now have the files on every possible MI6 member from Cambridge . . ."

"The Master's lost papers . . ."

"Although, of course, those papers will be false."

"They might work that out. Don't you think it might have been made a bit too easy for them? The Falcon was known to put his recruits through the odd test or two. That's why everyone turned a blind eye to his night-climbing escapades and, I presume, why no one wanted the police involved. But if it was all a trap to deceive the KGB then there must still be a member of the KGB working in Cambridge; a man who has recruited both of the students who were up on the roof that night?"

"I am afraid so."

"And we don't know who that is?"

"So far we do not."

Inspector Keating took a thoughtful sip from his pint and pulled his chair in and away from the fire. "I've never been told directly about these spying matters but

59

even this complexity seems too straightforward. You don't think the birds of prey could be triple agents?"

"Recruited by the KGB, defecting to the SIS, but only pretending to work for them while retaining their Russian allegiance?"

"Playing us at our own game?"

"But what would they get out of the mission?"

"A safe passage to Moscow, paid for by the British taxpayer."

"That is a possibility."

Keating looked at his notebook. "My official responsibility is quite simple. I have to decide whether the Falcon fell or if he was killed. There is still the perfectly straightforward explanation: a reckless and foolhardy man, who knows he is going to die anyway, takes a couple of students up to the top of King's College Chapel on a snowy, and let's also add 'windy', night and falls off. That's it."

"I am sure that is what the university would like you to think."

"It doesn't seem right, Sidney."

"But what is the alternative? A full-scale investigation into the workings of the British secret service?"

"You are suggesting I turn a blind eye?" Keating asked.

"It is what often happens in the establishment. Inconvenient truths are best left buried. If you don't ask too many questions of a gentleman then you won't be disappointed."

"And this is what makes us British?"

"It is our face to the world," Sidney replied. "Many of us are civilised, charming and perfectly genuine people. Others have developed their reserve into a form of refined deceit. It's why people find the British so intriguing, Geordie. The line between the gentleman and the assassin can be so very thin."

Keating finished his pint. "It's so much easier dealing with downright villains. At least there's an honesty about them."

The following day Sidney decided that he would try to clear up a few things with the Master before evensong. It was another bitter night and he was hardly cheered by the fact that Sir Giles Tremlett had company. Sitting on the sofa, with one arm draped carelessly across it, was the ample figure of the British Foreign Secretary. Sidney apologised for the timing of his visit.

"Not at all, Canon Chambers, you are welcome as always. I think that you two have met before?"

"Only by reputation," the Foreign Secretary answered. "I think you fought with my father in the war. He was in command of your regiment."

"Ah, yes," Sidney replied. "In Normandy."

"And now, of course, we have our own battles to fight. It's a much subtler game, this question of international diplomacy. I just was talking to the Master about our problems with the Russians."

Sidney was not as politically informed as he thought he should be, but he was still perfectly aware that the Soviets had rejected proposals to unify Germany and were attempting to block the Federal Government's attempts to join NATO. "I am sure that the Prime Minister is concerned," he said.

"He is always suspicious of foreign powers, but even Churchill can't go on for ever."

"I imagine you have plans."

"Eden will take over. He's the heir apparent. And we want continuity. Otherwise we'll have to have yet another conference in Berlin. The Master tells me you know the city well."

"I was there after the war."

"Indeed. Giles tells me that you have a friend there."

Sidney hesitated. "I wasn't aware that the Master knew such a thing."

"He likes to keep his cards close to his chest."

"Clearly you both know more about me than I think is necessary," Sidney replied archly and then, emboldened by the confidence of his tone, he pushed on. "Is that why I am being followed?"

"You've noticed?" the Foreign Secretary asked.

"I could hardly not."

"You haven't been in any danger, I can assure you. The police knew all about it."

"Even Inspector Keating?"

"Not him exactly. That would have given the game away."

"It's not a game. I was alarmed."

"Yes, I suppose you were," the Foreign Secretary conceded. "But then we wanted you to behave anxiously."

"Whatever for?"

"To show that you were not working for us."

Sidney was exasperated. "But I was working for you."

"We also needed to offer you a little protection."

"From whom?"

"I think you can imagine."

"You mean that I could have been being followed by two different sets of people?"

The Master gave the Foreign Secretary a look that prevented him going any further. "Perhaps you'd like a drink, Sidney? It will be Lent soon enough."

"The season when we pay particular attention to the forgiveness of our sins," Sidney replied, as pointedly as he could.

The Master poured out a small whisky. "I can't imagine that you have many sins to forgive."

"We pray for the sins of the world."

"And they are manifold," the Foreign Secretary concurred before rising from the sofa. "I am afraid that I must be going back to London."

The Master hesitated. "You will not stay for dinner?"

"My car is waiting. I am very grateful to you, Giles. It's been a complicated business but at least it's over."

Sidney could not comprehend why they had begun a conversation that had by no means finished. "Wait a bit. I need to understand all this. You mean that Bartlett and Montague are our men while pretending to be KGB?"

The Foreign Secretary was surprised that this needed confirmation. "You may *perhaps* assume that."

Sidney asked for clarification. "That's why Bartlett's parents didn't make more of a fuss about his so-called disappearance."

"I did have a word with them . . ."

"And Lyall was MI6?"

"We have let other people believe that to be so."

"It was so. Did he volunteer to be killed?"

"It is probably best that you don't ask too many questions, Canon Chambers."

"I know that Lyall was dying."

"He fell. It was an accident."

"I understand that is the official position."

"It is what happened," the Foreign Secretary insisted. "I must say that both you and Keating have been very diligent."

"That was our job."

"Not entirely. We asked you to report on Keating's observations rather than develop any ideas of your own."

"I could hardly help that."

"No, I suppose you couldn't. But there are sometimes levels of necessary ignorance; when ignorance can even be bliss."

"I don't like to think that I have been kept in the dark."

"You have known as much as you have needed to know, Canon Chambers, as I think we explained from the start. Keating has agreed to accept that Lyall's death was accidental and the case is closed. You are free to resume your clerical duties which, I am sure, are many."

"Is that all?"

"Yes," the Master replied firmly. "That will definitely be all."

Sidney gathered up his cloak and walked back across New Court. It was starting to snow again.

He was angry about being used as some kind of cover for activities he still could not unravel, and he was far from knowing a sure truth. It was like doubt without the faith. He took a seat in King's College Chapel as an ordinary member of the congregation, and knelt down to pray. The candles guttered with the breeze that whispered through narrow gaps in stone.

The precentor began the service with a sentence of the Scriptures: "When the wicked man turneth away from his wickedness that he hath committed, and doeth that which is lawful and right, he shall save his soul alive."

Sidney prayed in the darkness. He thought of the unknown author of *The Cloud of Unknowing* trying to define God through what he was not: how the believer has to "unknow" all human qualities in order to comprehend the divine, just as, he supposed, a spy had to "unknow" all his allegiances. Through this negative theology, the *via negativa*, came the wisdom of ignorance.

He remembered the definition of God that the same author had written at the end of his mystical theology of St Denis: "He is neither darkness nor light, neither error nor truth; nor, all told, can he be affirmed or denied ... his incomprehensible transcendence is incomprehensibly above all affirmation and denial."

Perhaps, Sidney wondered, he had to divest himself of all his worldly concerns if he was to become a better priest. He should give up all pretence at being a

65

detective. He should leave behind all perceptions of the senses, and reasonings of the intellect, and enter that cloud of unknowing, that darkness which would, eventually, be illuminated by flashes of light. This was the paradox of faith, the embracing of darkness in order to find light.

He joined in with the prayers of the congregation. "Lighten our darkness, we beseech thee, O Lord," he continued. "And by thy great mercy defend us from all perils and dangers of this night."

Outside, the snow began to fall on the chapel once more, across its architraves and buttresses, its grand towers and its gracefully balanced roof, and then further, down on to the hats, coats, scarves and shawls of the saints and sinners of the town as they made their way back to their streets, villages and homes. Still it fell, as if there could be no stopping it, with all its unhurried quiet, covering everything with its fragile white flakes until it found its way, at last, on to the grave of Valentine Lyall, where it softly made its rest.

Love and Arson

It was a warm summer evening in the middle of August and Sidney was in an exceptionally good mood. There had been little to distract him of late, many of his parishioners were enjoying their holidays, and he had time to himself. This was what life would have been like for a Victorian clergyman, he thought, as he walked Dickens across the meadows, along the river and out towards the nearby woodland. He had a manageable list of duties, he could concentrate on one thing at a time and he was untroubled by crime. At that moment, all he had to do was appreciate the gifts that God had given him and the amiable companionship of his Labrador.

A group of schoolboys were playing an impromptu game of cricket on a stretch of newly mown grass. Sidney stayed to watch an over. He even felt like joining in. After all, his school-days weren't so very far away in the grand scheme of things, and there were times when he still felt that he hadn't quite decided on the kind of man he wanted to become.

He remembered a traditional medieval round with its cuckooing chorus that he had learned at school and he sang quietly to himself:

Summer is icumen in,
Loudly sing cuckoo!
The seed grows and the meadow blooms
And the wood springs anew,
Sing, cuckoo!

He couldn't remember the rest. Amanda would know, he was sure. She was in Scotland for the glorious twelfth and would doubtless return with stories about rich hosts with names like Angus, Hector and Hamish. Each would have a Highland hunting lodge filled with dancing and house parties. It was a world he could never imagine joining, and so it was just as well that he was getting on so well with Hildegard. She was, he had decided, so much more like him.

Hildegard had not been back to Grantchester since the death of her husband, Stephen Staunton, over four years ago. Despite their affection for each other, Sidney had not pressed the idea of a return visit, preferring to take short holidays in Germany. He had first been to see her in the New Year of 1955, and had made two further trips since then. Hildegard had taken him to Hamburg, to see St Michael's Church and the Trostbrücke, and then, only last year, they had spent a few days in Koblenz where they had taken a boat to Boppard and cruised through the Rhine gorge to Rüdesheim.

Despite intrusive questioning by his friends and colleagues, Sidney had decided not to pin down the nature of their relationship. He had, however, begun to take lessons in German conversation from Marcus

Gruner, an elderly parishioner, and on his last visit he had even surprised Hildegard with the deftness of his first tongue-twister in a foreign language: *Fischers Fritze fischt frische Fische; Frische Fische fischt Fischers Fritze.*

The situation, however, was far from straightforward. Unlike Amanda, who seemed to tell him everything, Hildegard was more circumspect. He had no idea, for example, if she had other suitors in Germany, or if she had decided to renounce the possibility of love and a second marriage altogether. She kept an air of mystery about her even though, Sidney thought, at the age of thirty-one she was surely too young to resign herself to a single life. Could they drift on as they were, or would things have to develop one way or another? His relationship with Amanda was more feisty, he recognised, and he was perhaps more confident of his abilities within it. Perhaps she didn't expect so much of him, or the stakes were lower, or he felt that his failings didn't matter so much because she had made it perfectly clear that she couldn't possibly marry a vicar. Amanda was mercurial, openly flawed, vulnerable and quickly forgiving, whereas Hildegard was quieter, more thoughtful and harder to read. She made him think more deeply about his actions and his responsibilities. In short, she expected more of him, and, as a result, Sidney had an uneasy fear of letting her down.

As he approached the woodland, Sidney was distracted from his thoughts by one of his non-churchgoing parishioners, Jerome Benson, standing under a canopy of chestnut trees. He wore a matching flat cap and tweed hacking jacket, cord breeches and a well-worn pair of shooting boots. He had an untrimmed beard that was more ginger than his hair, and features so roseate that he looked like a man on the verge of losing his temper. He had an uncocked twelve-gauge shotgun by the barrel in his right hand, resting the magazine against his shoulder with the stock behind his back. A couple of partridges were peeping out of the tweed cartridge bag on his opposite shoulder. Sidney bid him a good evening and noticed that Benson's corduroy trousers were tied up with string.

A few yards further on, Sidney passed a parked car, a Triumph TR3 Roadster, in which a young couple were amorously involved. The briefest of glances assured him that the girl was Abigail Redmond, the comely seventeen-year-old daughter of his Labrador breeder, and he guessed that the stylish vehicle belonged to her boyfriend, Gary Bell, the son of the local garage owner.

Suddenly, he heard a shot ring out. Dickens ran off and rapidly returned with a tawny owl in his mouth. He dropped it at Sidney's feet.

"Good heavens!" his master exclaimed. "I am sure that's illegal."

Dickens looked up, expecting gratitude and reward, but before Sidney could decide what to do, Jerome Benson stepped into the light, with his lurcher beside him. "What has your dog got?"

"Did you shoot this owl?" Sidney asked.

"A woodcock. Your dog must be confused."

"I would be surprised."

"I can assure you that I shot a woodcock. Let me see the owl." Benson leant forward, picked up the creature, and began to examine it. "No sign of any shot. A natural death, I should say. I can look after it. I'd best go and look for my woodcock. Your dog seems very eager."

"He is an enthusiast," Sidney replied, uncertain quite how to respond. In the momentary silence he heard a car rev up, speed, and then slow down abruptly as it neared. Gary Bell leant out of the window and shouted, "Perverts," before screeching off.

Sidney wondered what they thought he had been doing. He would have to get over to the Eagle and see Keating. His mellow midsummer mood had melted away.

Cambridge was quieter in August. There were few students around town and people who lived there all year round were more relaxed. This was as close as the city ever came to being just another small market town in the east of England. Although the great university buildings gave Cambridge its historic permanence, as if it could return to its medieval roots at any moment, the town was in repose before the next generation of students arrived in the autumn. It was summer hibernation, Sidney thought: not so much a long vacation as a long siesta.

He had been looking forward to his regular backgammon session with Keating but his spirits descended further when he discovered that his friend was in a teasing mood. A few hours earlier Sidney would have relished it, but the disconcerting encounter with Benson, and the brief moment of abuse from Gary Bell, had made him lose his mirth.

The previous evening Keating had been to see a Doris Day film at the pictures, and he was keen not only to tell Sidney all about it but also to enquire about his friend's interest in the subject of romance, noting, yet again, his twin loyalties to Hildegard and Amanda. "Cambridge is probably a damned sight quieter because we haven't seen so much of Miss Kendall recently," Geordie joshed. "Have you given her the heave-ho?"

"Not in the slightest. She's on holiday in cooler climes: the Highlands."

"Aren't there rather a lot of midges in Scotland?"

"I don't think she'll trouble herself about them."

"I suppose they are more likely to be scared of *her*."

"She's shooting with friends."

"I only hope they don't shoot each other. At least it's out of our jurisdiction."

"Talking of shooting . . ." Sidney began.

Keating stopped. "Oh for heaven's sake, man . . ."

"Don't worry. I don't think it's of any significance, a minor misdemeanour, I am sure, but something happened earlier this evening that troubled me. I am not sure how much you know about the legal protection of wild animals."

"There was a law passed in 1947."

"I imagine the shooting of an owl is an illegal act?"

"It certainly is."

Sidney explained what had happened with Benson. The inspector promised to send a colleague round to have a word. He explained that although it was an offence to kill, injure or take any wild bird, including the tawny owl (*Strix aluco*: Sidney was impressed by Keating's use of the Latin name), it was legal to pick up most animal and bird species that had died naturally.

"That, I would have thought, was a moot point."

"I agree, Sidney, but unless you saw the incident or we can examine the owl and discover shot within it, then there is little we can do. We have to be sure. Just because a man behaves suspiciously, does not mean that he is up to no good. If we arrested every person who acted in an unusual way the cells would be full and you would be one of the first to be admitted."

"I would assume that, were such a situation to arise, you would help me out?"

"But I might be in there too. My superiors have already had a word about our friendship. They don't take too kindly to undue influence."

"But any conversation with a priest is surely above suspicion?"

"Not these days. Priests can be as capable of corruption as any other man."

Sidney stood up to order a second pint of bitter. "I am not so sure about that, Geordie. We do have our standards."

"What about the vicar of Stiffkey?" the inspector called out, enjoying the fact that he had to raise his voice to make his point heard. "The Prostitute's Padre? He had a very 'hands on' way of dealing with fallen women."

"I think he was much misunderstood."

"Didn't he end up applying to manage Blackpool football club and working as a lion tamer?"

"None of that is illegal, Geordie."

"I heard that his daughter became a trapeze artist and went on a date with Joseph Goebbels."

"You are making this up."

"I am not." Inspector Keating was now in full flow. "I will swear on any Bible. It just goes to show how much the clergy think they can get away with. I've learned that you have to watch them as much as anyone else."

Sidney returned with the beers. "I think, in my case, you can make a general presumption of innocence."

"You have always told me to be careful of presumption, Sidney. I am only following procedures that you yourself have influenced. One can't be too careful."

The hot dry weather continued. Away from the meadows, and in front of the Grantchester cottages, the small front gardens and proud English lawns became parched and brown, the blowzy roses shed their petals, and the airless afternoons left many of the villagers too languorous either to weed or water.

It was at the end of one such day, when the sun had beaten fiercely through all the south-facing windows of the village, that two Cambridge fire engines were called to an old summerhouse at the bottom of a field behind the garage. The building had been rented to Daniel Morden, a photographer who was away taking pictures at a wedding in London, and the alarm was raised at such a late stage that the fire had already taken hold by the time anything could be done. Flames leapt up the side of the building and into the roof space exposing its beams and rafters; windows cracked open, glass shattered and the front door fell forwards on to the ground.

By the time the fire brigade arrived, the first floor was on the point of collapse. The heat travelled so far in advance of the flames that it was impossible to get close to the centre of the blaze. A changeable breeze meant that the conflagration was spreading in three different directions at the same time. A small group of people filled buckets from an outdoor tap and both Gary Bell and his parents were terrified that the flames would jump to the garage with its plentiful supply of petrol. Thomas Bell was swearing that they should never have rented out the building in the first place, that he had always thought the photographer was a liability. It was typical of Daniel Morden to have evaded any responsibility by being in London. "I bet it was one of his bloody cigarillos," he shouted to his son, who answered that it was too late to worry about that now.

Suddenly there was flashover. The summerhouse sucked in the surrounding air and burst out of itself in a mighty eruption that filled the entire structure, the violent flames circling in an uncontainable whirl of fire that swept across each surface. This was the full venom of a blaze at its highest temperature. The timber-framed building could offer no resistance. The roof collapsed under its force. The air was filled with the crack of wood, the fall of brick, and the force of a wind that contained pure heat.

Within half an hour the dwelling had been reduced to its skeletal structure. A few supporting vertical poles smoked and steamed against the midnight-blue sky.

Sparks, ash flakes and fire-drops crackled and drifted through a smoke that carried with it the stench of charred wood, burnt fabric and photographic chemicals.

It took over two hours to bring the flames under control and by dawn there were piles of brick, rubble and timber all over the ground, glowing hard, occasionally flaring up with the residue. Only a few items were recognisable amidst the remains: the tangled metal of a photographic enlarger, a melted metronome, a cracked glass ashtray, part of an antler from what had once been a stag's head.

Sidney visited the site before morning communion and found one of his parishioners, Mark Bowen, already at work, wearing heavy boots and thick rubber gloves. He was a fire investigator.

"Is it still going?" Sidney asked.

"In some places it's hot enough to bake a potato. I think the point of origin is near the main windows, but I can't tell yet."

Sidney could see no sign of main windows and any casual passer-by would have had considerable difficulty working out either the structure or the orientation of the building.

"The destruction is much greater than you would expect from a straightforward house fire and there may have been multiple points of origin. I suppose it must have been the photographic chemicals: toner, developer, acetic acid. There are all kinds of nastiness in there. I also found a petrol can near the scene. I suppose that's normal . . ."

"The Bells having a garage?"

"But you wouldn't expect them to be so careless with it. I can't imagine any of the family leaving petrol lying around."

"Which suggests?"

Mark Bowen stood up and started to take off his gloves. "Either that someone started the fire by using a can of petrol and then ran away or . . ."

"Someone put the petrol can there deliberately . . ."

"Exactly, Canon Chambers, although what is strange is that this doesn't feel like a petrol-based fire to me."

"What does it feel like?"

"Something more intense."

Sidney knew that he should head off back to church and check through the readings for the tenth Sunday after Trinity. "You don't think it was an accident then?" he asked.

"The photographer was away at the time. He still doesn't know anything about it. I imagine it might be a bit of a shock when he comes home."

"It could have been an electrical appliance, I suppose. Did the place have power?"

"It doesn't look like it."

Sidney realised that he was out of his depth and should move on but he couldn't help wondering. "Why do people commit arson, Mark?"

"I'm not saying it's arson, Canon Chambers."

"I can see that would be jumping to conclusions. But *in theory*?"

"It's mostly young men. You don't find many female arsonists. Sometimes it is straightforward pyromania. The most common cause, in my experience, is revenge.

But I am sure you know all that, Canon Chambers. You don't need me to tell you that most of the trouble in the world is caused by love and money."

"I suppose sometimes people even set fire to their own homes."

"Not when they are sixty miles away. I haven't found any evidence of a timing mechanism."

"You can't rule anything out, you mean?"

"Whoever did it could even have hired a professional arsonist. They're often around when a business has money worries. The owner claims on the insurance; although I can't think that this place would have been worth very much."

"One would have to check Daniel Morden's policies?"

"That's not really your line of work, though, is it, Canon Chambers? You deal in the more dramatic stuff."

"I don't seek it out."

Mark Bowen had one last thought. "You also have to remember that people sometimes burn places down to get rid of evidence."

"What kind of evidence?" Sidney asked.

"I am sure you can imagine."

"You mean incriminating paperwork, vital clues, that kind of thing?"

"Actually I meant something more than that, Canon Chambers. I meant dead bodies."

A few days later, Keating was able to give Sidney an update on the situation. Daniel Morden had, indeed, been away in London at the time of the blaze, taking photographs at the second marriage of one of his best friends. He had been renting the summerhouse from the Bells for around three years, using it as his studio while he lived in what had once been his mother's flat off Hills Road. He was divorced (his wife had since died, although not in any suspicious circumstances as far as the inspector was aware) and he had a son who lived abroad.

"One wonders why Morden came here in the first place?" Sidney asked.

"He said something about avoiding the temptations of London. He's led what's known in the trade as 'a colourful life'. You know what photographers are like around women. They're like vicars only with sex appeal."

Sidney was about to protest when he realised he was being teased. "He could keep himself to himself here," Geordie continued. "None of the distractions of Soho that you're all too keen on."

Sidney let this reference to his love of jazz and seediness pass. "I imagine he lived in his mother's old flat for free. Do you think he had money worries?"

"Divorce is always more expensive than people anticipate," Keating replied with an air of disinterest that surprised Sidney. "But there's no sign of a lady friend. Perhaps she scarpered too."

"You mean his first wife left *him*?"

"Women do leave as well as men, Sidney. Sometimes they can't stand it any more; as my wife keeps warning me."

"We can't really suspect Daniel Morden of burning down his own studio?"

"Except it isn't his. It belongs to the Bells."

"And you've spoken to them?"

"They're angry, although they could be acting up. They're bound to have needed the money and, besides, the fire's a way of getting Morden out of there."

"So they could have been the arsonists?"

"I don't see why not."

"And they had the insurance, you say?"

"The Bells had the building insurance. Morden was covered for contents. Although there's not likely to be any pay-out until we tell them what happened."

"It can't be a lot of money, surely?"

"No, but it's probably worth burning the place down if you can get away with it. Unless there's something else going on . . ."

Sidney hesitated. "I think that's what Mark Bowen was implying."

"There's no evidence of any dead bodies, if that's what you're thinking."

"Perhaps someone thought that Morden was inside?"

"Attempted murder, you mean? No, Sidney, I'm pretty sure this is some kind of insurance trickery. Go and see the man yourself, if you like."

"I'd have to think of an excuse."

"That hasn't stopped you in the past. It's your job, isn't it, caring for the afflicted? It would be interesting to see what you could get out of him."

"Would you like me to go then?"

"I'm always grateful for any help you can give, Sidney. You know that."

"Then I have your blessing?"

"I'd be glad to be the one giving the blessing. It certainly makes a change."

Sidney thought things through as he made his way home from the pub. He had brought Dickens with him so that the dog could have a good walk on the way there and back. Canine companionship had become one of the great and unexpected treats of his life. Although there were times when his Labrador took the law into his own hands (he could still get excited by sheep, for example, and the lambing season was something of a challenge), Sidney admired his exemplary combination of patience and affection. While other people's dogs yapped and leapt up and slobbered and barked, Dickens kept his curiosity closer to home, straying far less than he had done in the past, contented with his lot in life. He seldom took against people and was slow to anger, and there was a time when Sidney realised that he could learn much simply by observing his dog's good nature.

However, this made it all the more troubling when Dickens became agitated. He had run on ahead but stopped at the stile that led on to the meadows and began barking loudly. It was almost dark and, as Sidney approached, the figure of Jerome Benson ran past them with his lurcher in close pursuit. A girl in a powder-blue cotton sundress was walking quickly away in the opposite direction with her head down. Her left hand scooped back the fall of her blonde hair over the side of her head, and her right hand was shaking. Surely that was Abigail Redmond? Sidney thought. And if it was, what had Jerome Benson done that had distressed her?

A handsome olive-skinned man in his late fifties, Daniel Morden wore a cream linen suit that had seen better days. His brown brogues were well worn and his panama hat had been thrown on to a beaten armchair. He sat at his desk with a weak tumbler of whisky by his side, tapping his cigarillo into a full ashtray. He did not offer Sidney a drink. He merely expressed bemusement at the fact that a clergyman should want to pay him a visit. Although his were hardly the lodgings of a successful man, Sidney recognised, after a few minutes' conversation, that his host had known some level of glamour in the past. In fact, in his heyday, he must have benefited from natural good looks and an easy charm.

"Everything requires so much energy these days," Morden began. "I was ambitious when I was young, but now I have to work hard just to stand still; and that can be rather boring, as I'm sure you know."

"It depends on what you are looking at, I suppose."

"Well, a pretty young girl always helps."

"And you photograph pretty girls, Mr Morden?"

"When I am given the opportunity. These days it's mostly weddings."

Morden had been in the film business in the 1920s, starting off as an assistant to the great English cinematographer Charles Rosher. He had even directed a couple of silent movies, but then had what he described as "a spot of bother" with the financiers and his career had slid back down the ladder through stills and fashion photography to advertising features, weddings and low-level private commissions. Sidney noticed an empty bottle of whisky in the wastepaper basket and wondered how much alcohol had been to blame for this fall from grace.

It was clear that Daniel still had some enthusiasm for life when he talked about things that interested him but his ageing looks and the decline of his career meant that his face, in repose, was one of resignation. His long cheeks appeared to sink, his mouth remained in neutral and his eyes had a faraway look. This was a man who appeared to be able to switch himself on and off.

He explained that he had been in London taking photographs at a society "do" as a favour (although Sidney suspected that the groom was probably doing his friend a service by providing employment). "One has to grit one's teeth and wish them well, of course, when half the time you can tell that the couple are doomed. I imagine it must happen to you as well, Canon Chambers. You must see a bride walking up the aisle and think 'here comes another poor lamb off to the slaughter . . .'"

"Actually, I hope to prevent that. I try to prepare couples thoroughly for matrimony . . ."

Daniel interrupted. "But you're not married yourself. You must have seen enough to put you off."

"Not exactly."

"It always amazes me how people doll up their daughters. All those debutantes. 'Love for Sale.' I used to make such a lot of money taking their photographs and putting them in *Country Life*. Nowadays, of

83

course, there aren't so many of them about; although I once photographed your friend. Miss Kendall."

"How do you know I know her?"

"Oh, Canon Chambers, everyone knows that. She's one of those socialites with a soft spot for vicars."

"You mean there's more than one?"

"A lot of women like to have a clergyman to get them out of a scrape. It's a good insurance policy."

"Talking of insurance . . ." Sidney began.

"It's just as well I paid my premiums, isn't it?" Morden replied quickly. "There should be a tidy sum. I shall have to be careful not to celebrate too lavishly."

"Isn't the money meant to replace the equipment you have lost?"

Morden nodded. "It is. But I am having second thoughts about the rest of my life."

"You won't start again?"

"I was about to give it all up, not that you have much choice in this business. You only know you've retired when the telephone stops ringing. Hollywood is a lifetime away."

Sidney tried again. "There's one thing I'm not sure about, and it's why you rented the summerhouse in the first place."

"It wasn't the most exotic location, I'll grant you. In fact it was falling down, but it had perfect natural light; south-facing, with windows down one side that you could soften with gauze."

"I thought photographers needed a darkroom?"

"I did all the developing here in the flat. There's a bathroom and a spare room at the back."

"I was also going to ask about your family." Sidney thought he knew the situation but wanted to hear Daniel Morden explain it.

"You're taking an unusual amount of interest in my life. Are you like this with all your parishioners?"

"I try to be of service to everyone. I think that's part of my job."

"I imagine some people might find you a bit of a nosy parker."

"That's something of an occupational hazard."

"I suppose that depends on which of your occupations you might be referring to."

"I am a priest."

"And a part-time detective, I hear. Word does get around."

"I hope that one does not compromise the other."

"I'm not so sure, but I'm happy enough to tell you about my family. Not that there's much of it. I have a son. He's in France. We don't speak to each other."

"I'm sorry to hear that."

"We had a disagreement."

"And his mother?"

"She died, although not before divorcing me. It was a bad time."

"I'm sorry."

"Nothing to be done."

Sidney knew he should leave. "You said you were thinking of stopping. I wonder what you might do instead of photography?"

"I'm going to try and paint. I've always wanted to do that. Photography, however, is more lucrative."

"Painting is a slower process, I imagine."

"And time passes all too quickly, don't you think?" Morden asked. "You can't ever really comprehend its momentum. All you *can* do is to take hold of individual moments and analyse them closely: the way light falls through a window, for example. That's why the summerhouse was perfect. You could spend a whole day watching the light."

"Is that what you want to paint?"

"I try to capture beauty," Daniel Morden answered. "I want to find stillness in the middle of movement."

"And youth too, I imagine?"

"Yes, of course, the rose before it flowers. Once it comes into full bloom you can already anticipate its decline. I like to photograph promise, and the moment before full beauty. Then you have expectation; drama. But I am sure I am boring you, Canon Chambers."

"Not at all. You speak with such enthusiasm I wonder why you are planning on giving it up?"

"I'm not sure people appreciate what I am trying to do; and, of course, as with all artists, there is the problem of confidence. Not to mention the balance between doing what you want to do and earning a living."

"Are they very different?"

"Sometimes you have to prostitute yourself in order to earn money, Canon Chambers. It is easier for a doctor, or even a priest, to retain his integrity. People will always be ill, and they will always die, and so you will always be in work. No one really *needs* a photographer."

"And have you lost everything?" Sidney asked.

"I still have the Leica I took to the wedding. And I also carry round an everyday camera. It's a little Minox. I've been experimenting, as a matter of fact."

"I don't think I've heard of a Minox."

"It's the camera spies use for photographing documents, although I've been using it for people. I don't even look through the lens. You have to guess the framing, fire the shutter and hope for the best. It's shooting from the hip but you often discover unexpected angles, surprising accidents, hidden everyday moments; sometimes, if you are very fortunate, the revelation of unexpected beauty."

"Do people know they are being photographed?"

"No, that's the point. You catch them unawares. They have no idea the camera is on them and so they are more like themselves. It means you can be a bit of a voyeur, but I don't mind that."

"It sounds quite hit and miss."

"Life is hit and miss, Canon Chambers; this kind of photography mirrors the elusive unpredictability of our existence."

"As elusive as knowing who would have wanted to burn down your studio?"

"I have no idea about that."

"You have no enemies?"

"I probably do, but they have been very careful not to tell me who they are."

"You have no clues?"

"I don't believe in looking for clues where the results may be distressing, Canon Chambers. I don't like to seek out more trouble than I've already got."

On his way home, Sidney decided to stop at the garage and have a look at the scene of the fire. He also hoped that he might be able to have a word with Gary Bell. Why had a petrol can been left lying around? Did the Bells keep a disorganised garage or were they tidy and efficient? How well did they know Daniel Morden and why had they rented out the summerhouse in the first place?

Sidney approached with trepidation, as he was still sure that it was Gary Bell who had called him a pervert when he had been walking Dickens two weeks previously. The memory rankled.

Gary was working on a motorbike in his blue boiler suit and it was not going according to plan. Abigail Redmond stood beside him, dressed in a gathered white blouse and skin-tight jeans, ready for a ride.

"I don't know what you're doing here," Gary began after Sidney had made his introduction. "The last thing we need is a priest."

"People often say that to me," Sidney began, "and, of course, in many cases it's the last thing people get: a priest at the moment of death." He was not going to put up with any nonsense.

"Well no one has died here."

"It could have been close."

"I don't think so. Morden was hardly ever around. He was always off with his friend Benson, looking at women. I thought you were one of them. What were you doing gawping at us the other day?"

"Yes, I wanted to have a word with you about that. I was merely walking past with my dog. I did not 'gawp', as you say."

"I saw you looking at us."

"I glimpsed as I passed. It seemed you had other things on your mind," Sidney replied firmly.

"Well, I did, as a matter of fact." Gary smirked at Abigail.

His girlfriend spoke for the first time. "That man with the beard and the shotgun. Benson. He's always prowling around. I think he's following me." She lit a cigarette.

Sidney decided not to let on that he had recently as good as witnessed a confrontation between them. He didn't want the couple developing their notion that he was something of a voyeur. "Have you told the police?"

Gary took over the conversation once more. "What's the point of that? They'd probably start following her too."

"They could call Benson in: issue a warning."

Abigail Redmond took a drag on her cigarette. "My dad says we can sort it out ourselves. He's going to go round. He says we don't need the police."

Sidney was concerned. "I wouldn't advise taking the law into your own hands."

Gary Bell looked him up and down. "No, I don't suppose you would. What do you want from us?"

"I just wanted to clear up the matter of the other evening. I was not, I repeat not, spying on you in any way. I was accosting Benson because I believe he had shot an owl, which is illegal. I also came here because I wanted to ask when you last saw Daniel Morden?"

"What's that got to do with you? Has something happened to him?"

"I mean before the fire."

"I saw him that morning. He had called a taxi and he was carrying all his equipment and a couple of round silver cans. I asked if he was going to make a film . . ."

"He was all sweaty," Abigail added.

Gary explained. "That's the drink. If he'd been in there at the time of the fire he'd probably have been too drunk to get out."

"And have you any idea how the blaze began?"

Gary Bell stopped work on his bike. "The police told me they found one of our petrol cans outside. They asked me questions like they thought I'd done it. If I had I wouldn't have been so thick as to leave the evidence next to the scene of the crime, would I?" He turned to Abigail for approval. She nodded, dropped the stub of her cigarette and ground it underneath the sole of her red high heels.

"Yes, I am sure you would not," Sidney replied. "I was also wondering how well you both knew Mr Morden?"

"Enough to say hello. That's all it was."

"And did he never ask to take your photograph, Miss Redmond?"

Gary Bell interrupted. "Why would he want to do that?"

Abigail was defiant. "I don't pose for no one."

As he bicycled round Cambridge, Sidney worried what all this meant. Why would anyone want to burn down a summerhouse of such little value? Could it simply be an insurance fraud or was it something more? Could

Gary Bell, or even Abigail Redmond, have started the fire to get Daniel Morden out of the building? Surely it would have been simpler not to renew his lease? Might there be some romantic history between Morden and Abigail, even though she was still so young? And Benson the taxidermist seemed, from what Abigail had said, to be a bit of a stalker; perhaps he was more than that? How well did Morden know him?

He would have to go back to the photographer. If nothing else, he was sure that Morden had a few good stories in him, and that should be entertaining in itself. Perhaps, since he had worked in Hollywood, he had met some of Sidney's jazz heroes like Eubie Blake and Noble Sissle. He thought of Benny Goodman in *Hollywood Hotel*, Bessie Smith in *St Louis Blues*, Fats Waller in *Stormy Weather* and even Dooley Wilson in *Casablanca*.

It was a Monday afternoon in early September. Morden was glad of the opportunity to reminisce, but he had never enjoyed privileged access to the lives of any of the legendary jazz figures about whom his guest was hoping to hear. "Most of them were after my time, I am afraid, Canon Chambers. I was more of a silent-movie man. The talkies did for me as they accounted for so many others."

"Surely you saw it coming?"

"Of course, but we didn't go in for too many words. If you take the most famous film I worked on, we were determined to tell the story visually. We tried to use cards as little as possible: in fact on one of Murnau's other films, *The Last Laugh*, he only used one card in the whole picture, and that was to explain the ending. He believed the picture alone should tell the story. 'Satis verborum' was our motto. 'Enough of words!' We wanted the audience to look at film and at life as if it were a dream or a memory. It should appeal to a part of the brain that had only just been discovered. We were very pure about it."

Sidney was intrigued. "What was the film?"

"*Sunrise*. It's about a man who plans to murder his wife. Only he doesn't. Most of the drama happens on a lake. It's about forgiveness, I suppose, and it's beautiful. We used all the qualities of dream; flash backwards and forwards, superimposition, composites, fantasy, multiple exposures."

"I'd like to see it."

"The existing print's not very good because they had to make a new negative so it's not as sharp as it was when people first saw it. The blacks have gone grey and the soundtrack's too noisy."

"A pity."

"It's still worth seeing. You can tell it's a masterpiece."

"And what did you do after that?"

"I began to direct myself, even though I wasn't as good as Murnau. Then I had my trouble."

"I'm sorry. You don't need to tell me if you don't want to."

"It's a common enough story. The work didn't go the way I had planned, the demon drink became as much a part of my life as the younger starlets, and I found myself on a plane home."

"And do you keep your old films?"

"Not here. Watching them made me depressed. They're stored at the labs where they were processed."

"I think you took some cans to London on the day of the fire?"

"How do you know about that?"

"Gary Bell told me."

"Him? They were only tests for something I never made."

"What was that?"

"I was going to make a new version of Stravinsky's *The Rite of Spring*. People thought I was mad. The piece is only half an hour long so it was never going to be very commercial unless I put stuff in between. I had a wonderful dancer. Natasha. She was half-Russian. She was a very pale, amazingly thin young girl, with high cheekbones, and dark, dramatic eyes. The camera adored her but the money ran out. I had to come back to England. We got a house near the Oliviers and pretended everything was all right and I was still a player, but it was a fantasy. Then Emma made her move and I took to my medicine." He poured himself a drink.

"Made her move?"

"I came home unexpectedly and there was a man in the house. They didn't even bother covering it up. I thought they could have made an effort, but Emma never had much imagination. Tim was her first boyfriend. He hadn't been glamorous enough the first time round. She had wanted more of a 'catch', which is why she chose me; only I didn't prove to be a

93

big-enough fish, and Tim had worked steadily as a kindly, principled and eventually quite successful stockbroker."

"And your departure from Los Angeles wasn't anything to do with young girls: people like Natasha?"

"People assume it's always about women. There was a girl, as a matter of fact, and although people gossiped I had done nothing wrong. I was more of a mentor to her, a father figure, but everyone jumped to the wrong conclusions and she needed to ditch me in order to save her career."

"And there was no one afterwards?"

"I suppose, until now, there's always been *someone* on the go. I am not a total disaster, Canon Chambers, but there was no one serious after Emma. After she died . . . it was an accident, in a swimming pool at a friend's house . . . I went to stay with my parents. I'm still with them really. Look at me now, in my dead mother's flat with hardly a penny to my name."

"So you'll be grateful for the insurance money?"

"Yes, but that doesn't mean I started the fire, if that's what you're getting at."

"I'm not."

"I think I know you by now. You will remember that I was in London."

"I do," Sidney replied. "The police have talked to Gary Bell about the petrol can but I can't think what he might have got against you?"

"You're right. It's more likely to be someone like Jerome Benson."

"Why him?"

Morden lit another cigarillo. "He wanted to watch me photograph girls."

"And did you let him?"

"Of course not. I have to be discreet. I can't have people *watching*."

"I imagine you can't. Some of the girls you photograph are quite young, I suppose?"

Morden was irritated. "They have to be sixteen. I can't tell with some of them, they're so precocious, but you generally know."

"And are any of them local girls?"

"I don't think it would be wise to tell you my clients, Canon Chambers, but some have been local, yes."

"Abigail Redmond, for example?"

"The name is not familiar; but then, so many of them make up new names. It's all cash so it doesn't matter. They pay and send the photographs on to the modelling agencies. They always ask me for advice, or introductions, and I help out when I can but I only have a very limited influence."

"Do they pay you any extra for that?"

"No, Canon Chambers, I do it out of the goodness of my heart."

"And you don't have favourites?"

"Like children, I love them all equally."

"And you don't get into any scrapes?" Sidney persisted.

"Scrapes? I am amused by your euphemism. Are you asking if I get involved with any of the girls in a way of which their parents might disapprove?"

"Yes, although I recognise that this is none of my business."

"It certainly isn't. But the answer is 'no'. I'm past that stage."

"You mean that you have been at 'that stage' in the past?"

"I like women, Canon Chambers. Don't tell me you don't?"

"That can't have been easy for your wife."

"You deduce correctly. She even thought I was having an affair with Jane Winton, the girl who played the manicurist in *Sunrise*. I did point out that she had only just got married."

"But, as you say, those days are over." Sidney knew he could not sustain Morden's tolerable humour for much longer. "Why did you keep going, I wonder?"

"Money, Canon Chambers. That and the fact that I am incapable of doing anything else."

"It seems quite a step down, if I may say so, from silent films and fashion photography to girls in skimpy dresses?"

"They're not always that skimpy. Sometimes they don't wear anything at all. But it doesn't make much difference. It pays well and, as I say, I need the money. I always need money."

Sidney was bemused by his conversation with the photographer but intrigued by the fact that he appeared to know Amanda. He telephoned to check if what he said was true.

"I think he was the one who took my photograph when I was a deb. If that's the man he was a rather glamorous, but ageing, roué. Has he been up to something?"

"I'm not sure."

"That man had trouble written all over him, I seem to remember."

"Did you find him attractive?"

"That's a very leading question. Men don't normally ask that kind of thing. They can't bear to think of the competition. He's a *photographer*, Sidney. I think I can do a bit better than that."

"I keep forgetting that your prospective marriage has necessary social implications."

"It's my parents as well as the money, you will remember. I don't want to be fleeced."

Sidney imagined that Morden was a man who could probably run through someone else's capital at quite a lick. "You're very wise, Amanda."

"I don't know why you're asking me all this. Most of the time I wish the subject was best avoided. I don't like people defining me by who I might, or might not, love. It's such a distraction and it gets in the way of work. It's all very well for you. At least you've got someone in mind."

"I wouldn't put it as strongly as that."

"For goodness' sake, Sidney. I don't know why you don't just bow to the inevitable and get on with it. Hildegard sounds perfectly nice and I can tell you can't stop thinking about her."

"It's quite a complicated situation."

Sidney returned, momentarily, to the anxiety of his courtship. He worried if it was as right for his potential beloved as it was for him? What if Hildegard's return to Grantchester would end, in any way, as it had done the first time, in unhappiness? What if he could not give her the redemption he felt she deserved?

"Everything's complicated if you worry too much about it," Amanda replied with certainty. "There's never a right and a wrong time. Look at my brother. He ran off with a divorcee and he's perfectly happy."

"I think there's a difference between a divorcee and a widow."

"Of course. But there are advantages. They have seen it all before. They have probably learned all the danger signals in a marriage and can head things off before everything falls apart. You can benefit from their experience and learn from them."

"I suppose that's true."

"Sometimes, Sidney, you just have to act hopefully and get on with it."

Jerome Benson's home was a veritable cabinet of curiosities. The walls of the front room were decorated with traditional examples of the taxidermist's art and concentrated entirely on fish: a pair of perch, three or four pikes, a thick-lipped mullet, a brown trout, a carp, a roach and a flounder. The inner room was stranger, featuring picturesque narrative attempts (a fox with pheasant prey, two sword-fighting stoats) and what could only be described as the macabre: a two-headed lamb, a mummified cat, an armadillo holding a soap dish and a model of the human eye.

Dickens began to panic at the sight of a sheepdog's head mounted on a wooden shield and a terrier contained in an oval glass dome. He cowered when Benson moved closer. It was the first time that Sidney had seen his dog so frightened by another human being.

"I imagine that you have come about the owl," Benson began, "although I thought I cleared the matter up at the time. I can assure you the police are overcome with pressing matters in town and can't be bothered to drive out two miles to Grantchester to check on a bird of prey."

"I don't think that's the case."

"I really don't see why I have to justify my actions, least of all to you. I have a detailed logbook for every specimen and a licence for my taxidermy. I only pick up animals that are already deceased. Of course, friends collect from abroad, and I do deal in Victoriana. I worked for a short while at Cooper and Sons. You may have heard of them?"

Sidney dimly remembered a childhood visit to Walter Potter's museum in Cornwall with its bizarre anthropomorphised images of squirrels playing cards, a kittens' wedding party and rats rescuing each other from a trap.

"I am not familiar with the practice of taxidermy. Do you specialise in certain types of animal?" Sidney asked.

"Birds," Benson answered. "Since you ask."

"Any particular reason?"

"They die so well . . ."

"I was not aware."

"They lie on their backs with their heads to one side, making a heart shape. I try to make their beauty last for ever."

Sidney thought of the photographer Daniel Morden and his desire to create an eternal moment.

"Some of these animals will become extinct, Canon Chambers. That's the purpose of my craft. The crested sheldrake was last seen in 1916; the Layson honeyeater in 1923; the Cuban red macaw in 1864. Thanks to taxidermy we know what they were like."

"And the tawny owl?"

"I did not kill that owl, Canon Chambers. It was dying and I was waiting."

"Then why were you carrying a gun?"

"The law does permit licensed gun owners to shoot any predators or vermin. I also carry it for my own protection. People distrust my wanderings. I have been threatened."

"On what basis?"

"People seem to think I am not looking at wildlife but at them."

"You mean, courting couples?"

"As I say, I have been threatened. Now I often have to leave my binoculars at home. It arouses less suspicion."

"But you still wander out at dusk?"

"It is the best time to find many of the things I am looking for and I do have work to do. I also like my liberty.

100

Sidney noticed that beside a taxidermy brochure and a price list lying on the table was a copy of the graphically illustrated *Sultry* magazine. No dead birds in that, he thought ruefully.

"How well did you know Daniel Morden?" he asked.

"He took the photographs for my brochure. Made it look very professional, I'll say that for him."

"Is he a friend?"

"I wouldn't call him that — but we share similar interests."

"Such as?"

"I can't see that it's any of your business."

"Would it, for example, include the photography of young girls?"

"There's nothing wrong with a beautiful woman."

"I am not saying that there is; although I didn't use the word 'woman'. I used the word 'girl'."

"I can't imagine you knowing much about either, Canon Chambers."

"That is true," Sidney acknowledged, in an irritated way, before keeping the conversation going. "But I was wondering if it was also, perhaps, something to do with the idea of time passing. I see how these animals are fixed in one moment. Perhaps photography performs a similar function. You see something at its best and you want to preserve it."

Benson gave a half-smile. "You are on the right lines there."

"You arrest decay. You believe in beauty. Do you have children, Mr Benson?"

"No, I don't."

"I've spent many hours with parents who find it difficult to accept their offspring are no longer young. They don't like the fact that they've become adults and are now beyond their control. Perhaps they want them to remain children for ever."

"I wouldn't know about that."

"Do you know Abigail Redmond?" Sidney asked.

"Who's that?"

"You may not know her by that name. She has a boyfriend with a Triumph Roadster. She was with him the first time we met; after I thought you had shot the owl."

"Oh *her*. I know *her* all right. She keeps accusing me of following her when all we are doing is travelling in the same direction. She goes to the garage; I go to my workshop. It's only natural that we're going to bump into each other."

"I suppose it is."

"I did try to talk to her but she thought I was trying to pick her up."

"And were you?"

"Of course not."

Sidney tried to appease him. "I'm sorry. I do not know about your personal circumstances."

"There is not much to know. I'm not the easiest of people."

"You must spend a lot of time on your own; watching and waiting in the woodland."

"You do need patience, yes."

"And you must have to train your eyes to look out for signs of life and movement?"

"What do you mean?"

"Since you live so close to the garage," Sidney asked, "I wondered what you were doing on the night of the fire. Did you see it at all?"

"I saw it all right; but only once it had taken hold." Benson hesitated. "You don't think I started it, do you? Morden had my best stag's head in there, and I'd already paid him to do my next catalogue. Why would I burn his place down?"

"I am not saying you did."

"You have a very odd way of going about things, Canon Chambers."

"I should not have troubled you."

"No," Jerome Benson replied. "You shouldn't."

He put on a pair of protective goggles and took up a blow-torch to cauterise the back of an alligator's head. There was little that was attractive about the man. He had no charm, he cared little for his appearance or for his effect on others, and he didn't appear interested in anything other than animals and young women.

On his way out Sidney passed a white-faced ibis surrounded by grassland in a rectangular case, and then a series of panoramas involving a selection of seabirds: a puffin, razorbill, guillemot and red-throated diver. He was depressed by this lifeless display. At least his dog still had plenty of vim in him, and his boundless enthusiasm would be sure to cheer him up. Dickens was sniffing round a low table that held an African grey parrot.

On seeing it, Sidney remembered one of his favourite stories. A friend had once told him about his uncle's funeral. His aunt had insisted that her husband's pet parrot should join the mourners but, on seeing his beloved owner's coffin being solemnly carried from the church at the end of the service, it had called out for all to hear: "Wakey! Wakey!"

The next morning Sidney was overtaken by a strange whim. He picked up a copy of *Sultry* magazine from the shelves at the newsagent's and added it to his morning purchase of *The Times*.

"Are you sure you want this?" the shopkeeper asked. It was Abigail Redmond's Aunt Rosie.

"I'm doing a little bit of research."

"Into what, may I ask?"

"Contemporary morality."

"And you need to read this to help you understand it?"

"I thought I'd see what young people were reading these days."

"It's not just young people that's the problem."

"Then it's probably more important that I take a look. I don't plan on studying it closely. I just wanted to get the general idea."

"I see. I'm sure you can imagine most of it. We only stock one or two copies. This is a decent village, after all. The taxidermist always asks for one but that's about it. I'll be glad to be rid of it, if you want my opinion."

"I'd rather you didn't tell anyone, if you don't mind."

"It'll be our secret, Canon Chambers."

Sidney knew that it would be no such thing. The news would be all round the village by lunchtime and he would have no choice but to brazen it out. Why had he done this? It was madness. He returned home and made himself a cup of tea.

As he waited for the kettle to boil Sidney skimmed through the pages of *Sultry*. It seemed harmless enough. Then he came across a girl who looked alarmingly familiar. She went by the name of Candy Sweet. Sidney recognised her to be Gary Bell's girlfriend: Abigail Redmond.

"I don't pose for no one."

Abigail was the only daughter of Harding and Agatha Redmond, a prominent farming family with plenty of land between Grantchester and Barton. Her mother was a member of the flower guild and had provided Sidney with his Labrador. Sidney presumed that Abigail had left school and wondered whether her parents would approve of her liaison with Gary Bell, or if they even knew about it. He decided to visit her mother on some canine pretext and ask a few questions.

The farmhouse stood on the east side of a large paved courtyard which contained a milking shed, a hay barn and a series of outbuildings in various stages of disrepair. Two black Labradors and a Jack Russell approached Dickens on arrival, scattering a group of chickens that had been pecking in the shadows. An outside tap dripped lazily on to the flagstones.

It was early afternoon. Agatha Redmond had been baking and she offered her guest a cup of tea and a slice of Victoria sponge cake. She explained that her husband was away at the dairy and Abigail was out seeing her Cousin Annie. Sidney was informed that it was hard to keep track of her these days and he wondered if "seeing Annie" was an excuse for something else.

"She's going to agricultural college but I can't see too much point in that. She could teach them all a thing or two. She knows how a farm works."

"I suppose there is more to it all than meets the eye."

"She could do with finding out about the financial side of things. But she's got a good head on her shoulders, I'll say that for her."

"So you imagine she will end up working on the farm?"

"I can't think of her doing anything else."

"She hasn't talked to you of anything different?"

"What are you getting at, Canon Chambers?"

Sidney took up his slice of cake. It was a Victoria sponge as he had never experienced before: light, melting and moist. He supposed it was the freshness of the eggs. "I don't know. So many girls these days are becoming secretaries or hairdressers; even models."

"I can't see our Abi doing that kind of thing. She's an outdoor type."

Sidney tried to sound as innocent as he could. "Are you having to deal with the troublesome business of boyfriends yet?"

"I know Gary Bell is sweet on her but she can do better than that. I think she fancies his car more than him. It makes a change from the tractor."

"I imagine she likes a bit of glamour."

Sidney was rather proud of the way he was directing the conversation towards photography but Agatha Redmond failed to take him up. "I don't know about that."

"Modelling is very popular these days. I understand that Daniel Morden, the unfortunate photographer . . ."

"The one whose house burned down?"

"He was very keen on the whole business of . . ."

"A lot too keen, if you ask me. There's nothing unfortunate about *him*."

"So you know the man?"

"Him and his friend Benson. They're a bit too interested in young girls, if you catch my drift. Harding had to go over and have a word with him; so did Abi's Uncle Andrew. They told him that if he ever went near our Abi he'd blow his brains out. Benson too. I'm not surprised someone burnt the photographer's place down. That taxidermist, or whatever he calls himself, will probably be next."

"You suspect it was arson then?"

"That's what people are saying."

"I don't think the police have made any announcement . . ."

"They don't need to. I think someone got wind of what those men were up to and took the law into their own hands."

"And that someone wouldn't have been your husband, by any chance?"

"We're not criminals, Canon Chambers."

"No. Although I don't think it's a good idea to go round threatening people."

"What else are we supposed to do?"

"Call the police, I would have thought."

"You think they can do anything about it? Those men can just say they're enjoying the fresh air."

"And Abigail never encouraged them or let them take her photograph?"

"Don't be daft. Of course she didn't. She would have had her father to answer for if she had."

"And she wouldn't go against her father's wishes?" Sidney asked.

"Never, Canon Chambers. She's a real daddy's girl. If there's one thing I know for certain about my daughter, it's that."

While Sidney was out on his rounds Mrs Maguire discovered the copy of *Sultry* magazine in the vicarage and took the rest of the day off to consider her future. Leonard Graham was left to do the explaining. On entering the kitchen to pour a medicinal glass of whisky, Sidney found his curate waiting. He had his hands behind his back and his facial features were in movement, unable to settle on an appropriately concerned look.

"Mrs Maguire is rather upset," he began.

Sidney added water to his whisky. "That is, if I may say, her natural condition."

"She has discovered something amongst your possessions that seems rather out of character."

"And when did she do this?"

"As she was dusting."

"It is a miracle that Mrs Maguire was doing any dusting. I presume she has put everything back in the wrong place. What did she find?"

Leonard Graham brought his hands out from behind his back and revealed the copy of *Sultry* that he had been holding.

"Oh," said Sidney. "Is that all?"

"Mrs Maguire is disappointed in you. The magazine looks well thumbed. I presume it belongs to you."

"Of course it is mine. I bought it for research purposes."

"I think Mrs Maguire would regard any descent into the pornographic, even for the purposes of research, unconvincing. Surely, in a criminal case, one can use one's imagination?"

"You might assume so, Leonard, but there are times when one needs to look for hard facts."

"And look closely, it seems."

"What do you mean?"

"You have even placed an asterisk by one of the magazine's 'naughtiest newcomers'. I assume it is your pen that has made the mark?"

"It is."

Leonard began to read with an increasing dryness of tone. "'This luscious lollipop could sugar any man's tea. Cuddly Candy Sweet loves the outdoors even when it's chilly. But don't worry, readers! She's certainly hot enough for us!'"

Sidney cut off his curate. "I agree that the prose is not up to Dostoevsky's standard. Do you not think that the girl looks familiar?"

Leonard was unimpressed. "It's not a habit of mine to look closely at seventeen-year-old girls."

"Nor of mine, but surely you can tell that Candy Sweet is a pseudonym?"

"That much is obvious."

"The girl is Abigail Redmond. Agatha Redmond's daughter."

"Agatha? From the flower guild? Labrador breeder to the clergy? I suppose you think the photographer is Daniel Morden?"

"I do indeed."

"Which might mean that anyone seeing this photograph, particularly if they were enamoured of Candy, or rather Abigail, wouldn't want her 'sweetening another man's tea'?"

"Exactly. Now perhaps you understand why I needed to buy the magazine."

Leonard paused for a moment. "But how did you know, when you were buying this particular copy of *Sultry*, that you would find a photograph of Abigail within its pages?"

"A hunch, Leonard, merely a hunch."

"And how many copies of the magazine would you have been prepared to buy in order to satisfy that hunch?"

"Who knows, Leonard? But I can assure you the study of such a bevy of beauties delights not me."

"I am glad to hear it. Will you tell Mrs Maguire or shall I?"

"You tell her, Leonard. Although . . ."

110

"You think it might be amusing to keep her suspicions up?"

Sidney hesitated. "No. I don't think so, tempting though that might be. Mrs Maguire's ideas are dangerous enough already. We can't have her spreading rumours all over the village."

"I think she's already started," his curate replied. "You have been tarred with the same brush as Morden and Benson. They assume you are all in a ring. You need to be careful. And talking of rings, Amanda telephoned. She asked if you would care to return her call?"

Amanda was asking Sidney to a concert (Isaac Stern was beginning the autumn orchestral season with concertos by Prokofiev and Mendelssohn at the Festival Hall) but the invitation was little more than a pretext to question him about an academic called Anthony Cartwright. He was a Professor of Physics in London and although she was sure that Sidney would not have heard of him, she asked him to make some enquiries amongst his colleagues at Corpus. He was, she told him, "promising".

"He's certainly got a lot more potential than that Morden chap. I was thinking about him only the other day. Are you getting anywhere on the case? I wouldn't be surprised if there was a jealous husband lurking in the background. That's where I'd start. Look to the ladies, Sidney. You'll enjoy that."

"I think Morden's more interested in younger girls."

"That doesn't mean the older women in the parish won't take a fancy to him. I'd have thought that he was

111

getting on a bit for girls and beggars can't be choosers. I should know."

"I'm interested you should be seeing an academic, Amanda. You know that they very seldom have any money?"

"That doesn't matter. Anthony has status. That's all my parents seem to care about."

"You shouldn't be marrying anyone to please your parents."

"I'm not planning on marrying anyone *yet*, Sidney. I was just saying he had *potential*. A girl has to be vigilant for she never knows the day nor the hour. Isn't that what the good book says?"

"I think that's a reference to the kingdom of heaven, Amanda."

"From the parable of the wise and foolish virgins, I seem to remember, and there's even a bridegroom in the story so I think you'll find that was rather clever of me."

"I would expect little else."

"Although I'll thank you not to make any mischievous remarks about my virginity."

"I wouldn't dream of it."

Sidney promised that he would do his best to attend the London concert and that he would make enquiries about Cartwright even if it was yet another thing to do. He made himself a cup of tea, and settled down to read a few chapters of Angus Wilson's *Anglo-Saxon Attitudes* before bedtime. After twenty minutes, he acknowledged that he could not concentrate and went into his study. There he began to make a list. He drew a dividing line down the centre of a piece of paper and wrote down his parish duties on the left, and his thoughts about the arson case on the right. When he had finished he could see that his forthcoming tasks as a detective were twice as long as those involving the priesthood. There could be no clearer example of how his priorities had changed.

He had to put the arson case to one side and make a start on Sunday's sermon. It was the eleventh Sunday after Trinity and the text was from St Mark's Gospel. He opened his Bible and pulled out a fresh piece of paper from the stand. Then, before he began to theorise on the feeding of the five thousand, he changed his mind and wrote a letter.

The Vicarage
Grantchester
4 September 1957

My dear Hildegard

It was so wonderful to see you in Germany that life in Grantchester seems very strange without you. I know it will be hard for you to think of visiting a place that does not contain too many happy memories, but I would like you to know, once more, that you will always be welcome. Having said that, I must confess that it is a strange place and that I have become involved in yet another complicated criminal investigation. I can see you smiling and shaking your head as I write. When it has all settled down, as I am sure it will, perhaps I could come and see you once more, either in the autumn, or just after Christmas? It would be good to see more of the Rhine, enjoy your company, and even improve my very faulty German. The trip would also be a welcome respite from the curious machinations of my parishioners!

Please give my best regards to your sister, who I very much enjoyed meeting, and do let me know more of your news. How many piano pupils do you have these days? Is Berlin very changed? Have you met many new friends?

I seem to live two different lives: one when I am with you, and the other when I am not. I hope that you will not be too alarmed when I say that I miss you and that I wish you were here with me now. I think of you every time I hear the music of Bach and, indeed, whenever I hear music at all.

With warmest wishes, and as ever,
Sidney

Inspector Keating was relaxed and almost amused by the gossip surrounding his friend when they met for their regular evening of backgammon. "I wouldn't take it too seriously if I were you," he smiled as he placed Sidney's drink in front of him. The froth foamed over the lip.

"But you're not me," Sidney replied indignantly.

"No, you're a one-off; and a million miles from these chaps. We've been looking into all of them, you know. Benson's had a few warnings, Gary Bell went a bit further with a girl than she wanted but then the accusation was withdrawn, and Daniel Morden has certainly had a chequered past. We even found his son."

"In France?"

Keating was rather pleased with this bit of news. "He's called Jonathan. We got him on the blower."

"Really?"

"They do have telephones across the Channel, Sidney."

"I am aware of that. What did you find out?"

"Well, for one thing, we discovered why Jonathan Morden is not speaking to his father. Turns out one of his girlfriends took rather a shine to his dad."

"You mean the father stole his son's girl?"

"I'm not sure it got as far as that. But the son said he had had enough of his dad's flirting. Couldn't stand him trying to impress her. He told her all about his time in Hollywood and I think the girl thought he could make her a film star. You hear it all the time: women taken in by predatory older men."

"It could have been the girl's fault; leading him on?"

"You can't be too friendly with teenagers, Sidney. Daniel Morden still seems a bit creepy to me. I can also see you don't like Benson. I don't care for him very much either, but I can't understand why he would burn down the summerhouse."

"No . . ."

"I understand that you don't dislike Morden, but the fact that you think he is a lovable rogue with a good heart doesn't make him innocent any more than Benson is guilty."

"I am not saying Morden is perfect."

"We need to find out more about him."

"I thought you were more suspicious of Gary Bell? After all, he has publicly stated that he didn't like Morden. He thinks everyone is eyeing up his sweetheart, and he could have set fire to the place in order to scare him off and claim on the insurance at the same time. He is the more straightforward suspect."

"But he wouldn't have been so careless as to leave a petrol can lying about. Furthermore, the fire investigator is convinced that this is not a petrol-based fire. Something else is going on here, Sidney, and I need you to help me find out."

"Are you sure you want me to remain involved?"

"Of course I do; besides, it'll help clear your name."

"Has it been so very sullied?"

"It's just tittle-tattle about mucky magazines and young girls, Sidney, but we need to put a stop to it. Buy me another pint and I'll tell you how we're going to do it. You're going to have to make a few more of your famous pastoral visits."

The following evening, Sidney and Leonard went to the cinema. The film on offer was Alfred Hitchcock's *Rear Window*. They had been expecting a tense thriller and were surprised by the slow beginning. The plot concentrated almost entirely on Jimmy Stewart's reluctance to marry Grace Kelly. He was not ready, he vouchsafed, and feared that any commitment would limit his opportunities for adventure. His maid, Stella, told him that he had "a hormone deficiency" since the bikini-clad bombshells exercising outside his window hadn't raised his temperature by a single degree.

Sidney sensed Leonard Graham's bafflement at the thought of being excited by women, but he himself was thrilled when Grace Kelly finally arrived wearing an eleven-hundred-dollar outfit and a string of pearls.

Unfortunately, the subject was still marriage. "You don't think either one of us could change?" Grace asked Jimmy with a devastatingly candid gaze. Sidney sighed.

After half an hour there was still no sign of murder, and Sidney's thoughts began to drift again to love, marriage and commitment. By the time he woke from his reverie a private detective had arrived on the scene and ridiculed Jimmy Stewart's work as an "amateur sleuth".

Leonard leant across and whispered, "This is alarmingly familiar."

"At least we have not had to deal with a case of dismemberment."

"Not yet."

"Benson confines himself to animals."

"Only as far as we know," Leonard replied before being hushed by people in the row behind.

Of course Benson may well have been nothing more than an eccentric loner, and it was wrong to suspect a man simply on the grounds of his demeanour, but there was still something troubling about him.

The next day, Sidney decided to go and see if Daniel Morden was at home and if he would be prepared to answer a few more questions. He timed his visit for midday on Saturday 7 September, after, he assumed, the photographer had got up but before his first drink. They could even go to the nearest pub, since it was unlikely that Morden would refuse an offer of hospitality.

The photographer was amused by his visitor. "It's an unexpected bonus that you keep coming to see me, Canon Chambers, I must say. You should know that I was brought up as a Roman Catholic. Once a Catholic . . ."

"Give me a child until the age of seven . . ."

"*And I will show you the man.* Ignatius Loyola. I think I have learned to subdue my fears of eternal damnation and the fiery flames."

Sidney seized the chance to raise his subject. "I suppose you will have had enough of fire in this life."

"Yes, indeed. And that is why you have come, I suppose. It can't be the joy of my company." Morden lit up a cigarillo.

"I like hearing you talk about photography. The stopping of time, the creation of a moment, the preservation of memory . . ."

"You have to be careful about that."

Sidney remembered the albums his parents had collated, filled with images of themselves and their three children: himself as a baby in his mother's arms, the siblings on the back of a toboggan, his father shying away from a snowball, his mother trying on a gas mask, his place on the extreme right of the back row of Marlborough's cricketing First XI, his sister with her friend Amanda on the way to a ball at the Lansdowne Club, and the army line-up that contained three of his dead friends.

"You mean that we treat photography too objectively?" he asked.

"It is *only* the record of a moment," Morden replied. "And only one vision, deliberately framed to exclude, without any awareness of what has happened before or after . . ."

"But that doesn't make it unreliable."

"*Memory* is unreliable, Canon Chambers. That's the problem. We remake each memory every time we recall it. It's a constructive and adaptive process."

"I am aware of its fallibility."

"You must be aware of its duplicity. Photography is something different. It has a separate, distinct reality."

"So you have to separate the image from its representation?" Sidney asked, feeling that he was getting lost.

"That is what people are teaching in the universities these days."

"So a photograph of, for example, a young girl is not so much the record of a specific time in her life but a separate work of art?"

"That's the idea; although such concepts are rather too elevated for the work I do."

"Yes, I don't imagine that someone like Abigail Redmond was aware of such a distinction. Did she know that you were going to publish semi-naked photographs of her?"

"Not exactly, no."

"So you sold them on?"

"Anyone who takes their clothes off for a photographer must know that she's not the only person who's going to see the final result. That would be naïve in the

119

extreme: and one thing about Abigail Redmond is that she is not naive."

"So you did know her name?"

"I'm sorry?"

"When we first met you said that you didn't know her name. She poses as Candy Sweet. But in fact, you knew her name all along."

"It's hard to remember everything. Sometimes you'd rather forget. Memory, again . . ."

"Did Abigail ask for any special treatment?"

"She made a few advances, I think, but then they all do. They are so desperate to escape. They don't want to be wives or secretaries. They want to go to London, but most of the time it's just a pipe dream. There are so many girls, and very few come up to the mark."

"Was Abigail one of them?" Sidney asked.

"I told her that she needed to slim down and that her nose was a bit squat but she wouldn't listen. She was convinced she was going to be a glamour model. From the way she dresses, I think she still believes that. How little she knows of life."

"So she was angry when you told her that you didn't think she had what it takes?"

"Yes. I'd say she was."

"Angry enough to burn down your studio?"

"Probably."

"You don't seem very concerned about this line of enquiry, Mr Morden. Are you sure you are telling me everything you know?"

"You want my life story?"

"No, just the facts as they pertain to this case. I am not sure you have been honest with me about your relationship with Abigail Redmond."

"There was no relationship. That's the point. I hate that girl."

"Hate?"

"Yes, hate. I bloody hate her."

"What do you mean?"

"Can I have a drink? I think I need one if I'm going to tell you all this." Morden stood up. He looked frailer than Sidney had ever seen him before; frailer, and almost frightened. "Could you take me to the pub? It should be open by now. I can't tell you all this on an empty stomach."

Once Sidney had established all that he needed to know from Morden he recognised that he had to take the initiative. He would leave Leonard Graham to hold the fort back at the vicarage and get this whole arson business out of the way.

He was bicycling towards the Redmond farm and had just passed a bus stop when he realised that the girl standing there was none other than Abigail Redmond. He turned round, propped his bike against the bus-stop pole and started to question her. Abigail was dressed in a tight white cotton blouse with the top two buttons undone, a striped pirouette skirt, short white socks and tennis shoes. She looked bored and was embarrassed to be seen in the presence of a priest. Sidney knew that he would have to make his enquiry simple and direct.

"I was coming to ask you about the fire."

Abigail looked into the distance, perhaps imagining that if she could not see him then Sidney would not be there. "Nothing to do with me."

"I am not saying you started it."

"Gary didn't do it either."

"I know that."

She turned to Sidney as briefly as she could and looked away as soon as she had finished her sentence. "Someone put the petrol can there to make people think he did it and that's no lie."

"I'm sure that's the case. I've also come to talk to you about the photographer, Daniel Morden."

"That pervert."

"I'm not sure he is a pervert."

"What would you know about it? You're a priest. Though Gary says you're as bad as the others. You've been watching me as well and all."

"I don't think everyone's looking at you, Abigail."

She took out a cigarette. "Could have fooled me."

"I'm asking because you went to have your photographs taken by Daniel Morden; and without anyone else knowing."

Abigail used the time needed to light her cigarette to think about her answer. "What's that to you then?"

"And you went more than once, didn't you?"

Abigail exhaled, the smoke only just missing Sidney's face. "So?"

"You wanted to be a model in London and you asked him to help."

"Nothing wrong with that."

"Did he tell you what he was going to do with the photographs?"

"He was going to show them to a few people. See if they were interested. That's what he said. But nothing happened so I went round again to ask what was going on."

"And what happened then?"

"None of your business."

"No. It isn't. But it might be."

"What do you mean by that?"

"You offered him something more. If he could try a bit harder."

"I don't know what you think that could be."

"We both know what it is, Abigail. But Daniel Morden resisted, didn't he? And you decided you had to do something about that."

"I didn't burn down his studio, if that's what you're thinking."

"I'm not thinking that at all, Miss Redmond. I am thinking of something very different indeed."

When he returned to the vicarage Sidney was distracted by the arrival of a letter from Germany. Hildegard had written at last and the omens were good.

Berlin
14 September 1957

My dearest friend

I hope you will come after Christmas. Perhaps this will become a routine? I hope so. I always like

123

to see you. I am most myself. I wish we had more time. I have been thinking that it is my turn to come to you and that I will soon be ready to make a return visit to Grantchester. We should not let the past ruin the present. That is a lesson from the war. It has been long enough now and as long as you are there then I can be strong. Everything is easier when you are with me . . .

Sidney wished he was with her too but instead, after allowing himself a few minutes of romantic reverie, he decided that he really had to see Morden once more.

"I thought we'd got everything out of the way the last time you came," the photographer began. He was dressed in pyjamas under an old Paisley-patterned dressing gown that might have belonged to his father. "I haven't been in bed all day, if that's what you're thinking. I got up early to take some photographs. I'm planning on doing my own project about the sunrise."

"I see."

"It would be a portrait of Britain; not so much about who's up and who's going to bed, but what the streets are like in the silence in between; when there's no one around. I love that time of day. Everything is held up, in stasis, and yet you know that stillness can be broken at any moment. It's so fragile and transient and the air's filled with that grey-blue light that can't decide whether it's day or night."

Sidney remembered just such a time during the war. The tanks had stopped in steep fields under the Caumont ridge, just east of the town. The night had been warm and quiet but at first light the shelling and mortaring began. His battalion were due to attack Lutain Wood and Sidney was convinced, despite the beauty of the dawn in a French field so far from home, that he would die that day. It was the first time the fear of death had been so specific, and even though there was nothing unusual about the sniper fire as they advanced through the woodland, he saw a man he had always admired, Captain Campbell, killed in front of him as he got out of his tank to rescue a wounded hull gunner. Sidney ran out to help but the tank was hit again through its heaviest frontal armour, the ammunition exploding and the turret leaping clean off. For a moment he had stood there, frozen in uncertainty, with the detritus of death all around him, anticipating that he was next to be killed. Yet he had survived, and ever since that terrifying stillness in the early morning light, he had determined to live each day as if it was his last; and to recognise the gift of life above the eventual certainty of death. This was the seeding of his decision to become a priest.

"It's like seeing the world when no one is looking," Morden continued. "Nothing is certain and no one is there. The ghosts have left and new people are yet to appear. I'm using the little Minox camera I told you about. I can take photographs without anyone knowing I'm doing it; as if I've dropped down from outer space. That's the effect I'm after: to see the world as if it's only just been discovered for the first time."

Sidney thought for a moment before replying. "I suppose that you and I are both trying to do the same kind of thing; you're asking people to stop and look, while I'm asking them to pause and be silent."

Having expressed his new manifesto, Daniel Morden was not keen to elaborate any further. Sidney recognised that his timing had not been ideal. "I am sorry if I am calling at an inconvenient moment."

"I was planning on a nap. I've done my work for the day. Now I can't find my cigarillos. I suppose you've come to ask me a few more questions?"

"I'm very sorry, Daniel, but I have reached the conclusion that you started the fire in your studio deliberately."

The photographer was unsurprised and kept looking for his cigarillos. "Yes, I imagined you would be thinking along those lines. It's the only plausible explanation for your visits. I'm not self-confident enough to believe that you came to hear my memoirs or enjoy my conversational virtuosity."

"Although that has been entertaining."

"I do prefer pictures," Morden replied. "Words can only do so much, *Satis verborum* being my motto. I think I told you the first time you came."

"You did. 'Enough of words.'"

"Although you seem to go in for rather a lot of them."

"That is a fault of mine, I am afraid. A priest should always begin with silence."

"Then you're not doing too well, my friend."

126

"Although, in this instance, I am not really a priest. I am hoping that you will admit to starting this fire so that the case can be closed and we can get on with our lives."

"Well I'm afraid you're in for a disappointment. Even if you were to make a case, despite my being in London at the time, I can always put it down to carelessness; or the demon drink. There is absolutely nothing to suggest it was started deliberately."

"But why did you do it?" Sidney asked. "It was because of Abigail, wasn't it?"

Morden tried to appear disinterested. "Intriguing."

"I think Abigail Redmond made some kind of threat. It might have been to tell her boyfriend about an incident that had passed between you, or she might have been tempted to make something up. Her father had already gone to see Benson, and Gary Bell was, I think, no friend of yours. So she knew that she could be in a strong position if . . ."

"Blackmail," Morden interrupted. "She was blackmailing me. She said that unless I got her a modelling job in London she would tell her boyfriend and her father that I had given her too much to drink and molested her — or worse."

"And none of this happened?"

"Of course not. I thought I had had enough experience of young girls to know what to do in these types of situation, but even I knew that it would be hard to defend myself against that kind of accusation. She wasn't asking for a great deal of money. It was just that I didn't have it."

"And you couldn't get her a modelling job?"

Morden snorted. "I don't think so. I have no influence these days, and she's too small and chubby."

"Even though you sold her photograph to *Sultry* magazine without her knowing?"

"They'll take anything . . ."

"And then she came back. How much did she ask for?"

"Fifty pounds."

"Why didn't you call her bluff?"

"I panicked, I suppose."

"And the only way you could liquidate the money quickly, apart from selling your mother's flat, would be to burn down the studio and claim on the insurance?"

"I can see how easy it is for you to think that."

"Then you would also be taking some kind of revenge on Gary Bell at the same time."

Daniel Morden poured himself a small tumbler of whisky and went through to the kitchen to add water. He called out, "Sounds rather good. I wish I'd thought of it." He came back into the room. "The only thing is that I was in London at the time of the fire."

"I know you were," Sidney replied, "but that doesn't mean that you didn't start it."

"And how would I do that? The fire investigator didn't discover any timing device as far as I am aware."

"You didn't need one."

"What do you mean?"

"You had the sun."

Morden was still standing. He took a sip of his drink. "Would you care to elaborate?"

"It was a hot day in the middle of August," Sidney explained. "The preceding days had been sweltering; the weather forecasts had predicted that it was likely to get hotter. The windows of the summerhouse faced south. I would suggest that you removed your old silent films from their cans, laying the cellulose nitrate film on the window seat and on the floor. The sun was a natural timing device. The windows became a magnifying glass. You left the summerhouse in the morning, taking the empty film cans to London where you disposed of them. Then you let the sun ignite it all while you were giving your lecture. It was a simple idea. You let nature do the work."

"It all sounds rather implausible," Morden replied, already finishing his whisky. "And I don't think there is any way of proving this."

"No. There was too much destruction."

"And Gary Bell's petrol can?"

"You placed it there afterwards."

"You think so?"

"I cannot prove anything."

"What gave you the idea to think how I might have done it?"

"Gary Bell saw you taking two films cans away with you. Then I discovered why there is no good print of *Sunrise*. The original negative was destroyed in a fire. It was a famous incident in the history of cinema and yet you never mentioned it. Pointing out that cellulose nitrate was highly flammable was too much of a risk."

"What are you going to do?"

"I will have to tell Inspector Keating what I think. He may not believe me. But I am sure the insurers will."

"I don't think they're going to pay out, in any case."

"You may be liable for prosecution."

"I suppose I might. But I don't have much to live for these days."

Sidney was surprised by his host's resignation. "But what will you do with the rest of your life, Daniel?"

"It's a question of confidence." Morden began moving about the flat, looking for whisky, cigarillos and distraction from what he was saying. "Once you've lost it, often for the smallest, pettiest reason, someone says something or a job doesn't go your way, then it can be very hard to get back. That's the great conundrum of ambition: knowing when to acknowledge one's own mediocrity. I'll probably sell this flat. It's depressing being surrounded by memories of your mother. I don't know why I've stayed so long. I thought I might try and see my son again in France. We had such a stupid misunderstanding."

"I think you should always try to make your peace with people you have loved."

"Provided the police don't take my passport away. Do you think they'll arrest me?"

"I don't know. As you point out, there is no evidence. I could be wrong."

"The rumour in Grantchester is that you are never wrong, Canon Chambers."

"That is a myth."

"Then I must congratulate whoever does your publicity. Perhaps I could hire them for my first exhibition?"

"You are planning to paint after all?"

"If I can." Morden sat down once more. "You are right, of course. I must make something of the days that I have left. I'm going to try and look at life more closely: pictures not words. That can't be so bad, can it — to study the world as hard as you can before your eyes close for the last time?"

Sidney was pleased with his ability to winkle out a story from his suspects and he was looking forward to a celebratory drink with Inspector Keating. It came, therefore, as something of a shock when he was confronted by the unexpected arrival of the Reverend Chantry Vine, archdeacon of Ely, early on the Monday morning.

The archdeacon was considerably smaller and rounder than Sidney, and in his late forties, practically bald, with short arms and broad shoulders, flattened ears and a grim-looking mouth which turned any attempt at a smile into a snarl. It was unlikely that there had ever been such a gulf between a man's name and his physique. He looked more like a rugby player than a clergyman.

Chantry Vine was concerned about the rumours and stories that had been emanating from Grantchester. He spoke with an accent Sidney had never quite been able to place (Bristol was the most likely candidate) and what he had to say combined disappointment with attack. There had been, he told Sidney, "rather too much going on".

Sidney pointed out that he could not be held responsible for other people's criminal activity.

"I also think that you should give up this detective nonsense," Vine continued. "Let the police get on with their job while you get on with yours. I hardly need to remind you of the primary duties of a priest, do I?"

Sidney confirmed that he had been called to be a messenger, watchman and steward of the Lord. He had a bounden duty to exercise care and diligence in bringing those in his charge to the faith and knowledge of God. And he had made a solemn promise at his ordination that there be no place left in him for error in religion or for viciousness in life.

The archdeacon lit up his pipe. "I think you should consider whether there is a difference between the man you are and the priest you need to become . . ."

"We all fall short, archdeacon."

Chantry Vine leant back in Sidney's armchair. Clearly the conversation was not going to end soon. "I agree, but there are times when a man can be too wilful in the pursuit of what he may think to be the common good. He may confuse it with his own interests."

"I have tried to involve myself in the concerns of my parishioners."

The archdeacon pretended to reflect on what Sidney had said but was in no mood to let up. "But should you be 'involved', as you say? Isn't there a case for detachment? By coming too close you are in danger of failing to see the whole picture. Sometimes a priest needs to step back and take a more dispassionate view.

'Watch ye and pray, lest ye enter into temptation.' You will remember: Mark 14.38."

Sidney resented being lectured in this manner (and he hardly needed to remind the archdeacon that the next line in the verse was "the spirit truly is ready but the flesh is weak"). He knew perfectly well the difference between seeing the detail and the wider picture and he didn't need Chantry Vine to keep going on about it.

"I have also heard rumours . . ."

"I can guess what they are."

"And they seem to have got rather out of hand, Sidney. I trust there is no substance to them?"

"If you are referring to the purchase of a salacious magazine . . ."

"I didn't know anything about a magazine," the archdeacon replied, taking his pipe from his mouth. Sidney had walked straight into his trap. How could he have been so stupid?

"It was nothing. My housekeeper found it. I needed to do a bit of research."

"Into salaciousness? I heard it was more to do with the closer observation of the younger members of the parish. I am all for a younger, broader Church, of course, and we need to start up as many youth clubs as we can, although they cannot, alas, consist entirely of young women. That is a job for the Girl Guides." The archdeacon put his pipe back into his mouth and smiled, as if he had only just remembered who the Girl Guides were.

"I have done nothing wrong."

"I only hope that you are right. You're a good man, Sidney, but easily distracted. We had you down as a possibility for my successor but this kind of thing doesn't help your case." The archdeacon stood up. "Surely it's time you were getting married? The bishop tells me that he is a good friend of the Kendall family in London. Haven't they got a rather attractive daughter?"

"They have."

"Can't you marry her?"

"It's not quite that simple."

"Nothing is simple in this world, Sidney, but the life of a priest is a good deal easier if he's got a decent wife, I can tell you that and no bananas. I'd be lost without my Claire."

Distracted by the phrase "and no bananas", Sidney found himself unable to concentrate on the archdeacon's advice. It was simply annoying that so few people understood what he was trying to do. He needed a holiday. As soon as he thought of the idea, another word popped into his head.

Germany.

Michaelmas term was beginning and the first autumn rains watered the parched lawns and gardens of Grantchester at last. Sidney met up with Inspector Keating to catch up on the facts of the case. There would be no arrests. Abigail was still only seventeen and it was felt that she could be discouraged from any further actions with a strong warning. There was also not enough hard evidence to present a case against Morden. His insurers had, predictably, refused to pay out, his mother's flat was on the market and he was already heading for a reunion, of sorts, with his son in France.

"So the only person whose reputation might have taken a slight dent is you, Sidney. Leonard told me that the archdeacon gave you a hard time."

"The Church is not supposed to draw attention to itself."

"If that is the case then why do you have all the tall spires?"

"I think he means 'in the wrong way'."

"You mean priests looking at girlie magazines?" Sidney gave the inspector a hard look. "I am joking. They can't take it that seriously, can they?"

"We are expected to be above reproach. Like the police."

"How did you work it all out, by the way? The arson and the blackmail?"

"I don't really know, Geordie. Perhaps you just have to spend time with people."

"The problem with our line of work is that you never know how long anything is going to take. A bricklayer can tell you when he's going to finish but I can't predict things at all; although with you around they tend to happen a lot quicker. I don't always tell you this but I am grateful to you, Sidney. Let me buy you that second pint."

Later that night, Sidney took Dickens out into the meadows for his evening constitutional. It was still just about light and he was surprised to hear footsteps behind, catching him up. He turned round to see that it was Abigail Redmond. She clearly wanted to speak to Sidney but hadn't prepared what she was going to say.

"I've broken up with Gary."

"I'm sorry to hear that."

"I'm not sure you are, Canon Chambers." There was an awkward pause before Abigail continued. "I'm following you now. Perhaps you'll get to know what it's like."

"Did the police come and see you?"

"Gave me a warning they did. My dad went mad; wondered what they were doing in the house. I had to make something up."

"And what did you say?"

"I told him that Benson was following me again and the police had caught him."

Sidney stopped. He wanted to take Abigail by the arm but knew that he could do nothing that might provoke her. "But that's not true."

"Doesn't matter, does it?"

"It does. You must stop making up stories about people."

Abigail looked at her shoes. The recent rain had muddied them. "He *was* following me, though."

"Not recently. He's been warned."

"Everyone's following me, Canon Chambers."

Sidney wasn't putting up with any nonsense. "No, they're not. This is a small village. There are only so many ways people can get in and out of it."

"You don't know what it's like."

"Of course I can't know exactly, but I cannot believe what you are saying. You should leave if it upsets you so much."

136

"That's what I've been trying to do but Dad wants me to work on the farm."

"You don't have to do that."

They had reached the end of the meadows and Sidney needed to turn back to go home. He called Dickens. He wasn't quite sure where his dog had gone. He had not expected that, at the end of a long day, he would have to counsel a teenage girl whom he could not find it in his heart to like very much.

Abigail was in no hurry to end their conversation. "I could be a secretary, I suppose."

"You could train to be anything," Sidney replied. "A woman with your determination, and . . ." here he paused ". . . imagination." He decided to be firm. "You just have to stop thinking that people are looking at you all the time. They're not. Most of them are far too preoccupied to think about you."

"You mean they're not looking at me?"

"No."

"Not even you?"

"Not even me."

"Are you sure?"

"Yes, Abigail, I'm sure. Now stop making accusations about other people and leave them to get on with their own lives." Sidney was infuriated by the way in which rumours spread and reputations were compromised. He decided that he would preach a fiery sermon about it on Sunday.

He walked back with a tired but contented Dickens by his side and within a few yards he saw Jerome Benson in the shadows. That is all I bloody need,

Sidney thought. Any proof that Abigail was not making things up and the whole thing could start all over again. He picked up a stick and threw it into the distance. Dickens ambled, rather than ran, to fetch it. Sidney knew that he would have to keep a watchful eye on the Redmond situation because he didn't want everything to simmer down only to blow up in flames once more.

Flames, he thought, as he felt the first autumn chill in the air. It wouldn't be that long until Bonfire Night. He remembered the first one he had shared with Amanda three years ago, after the murder of Hildegard's husband.

He opened the meadows gate and walked up the path that led to the main road. The past few weeks had been a strange time and it had made him think of the way in which people saw themselves in the world. How accurate is their perception of who they are and what they have become? Should people really try to see themselves as others saw them? He was not sure that they should. The important thing was to learn to like ourselves, and strive to be better. One shouldn't keep looking to see what other people thought.

When he reached home he found a rectangular box wrapped in brown paper on the kitchen table. Leonard told him that he had discovered it on the doorstep. There was a letter resting under the string. Sidney opened it and began to read:

Dear Canon Chambers
    Thank you for understanding me and for your forgiving heart. I recognise that I no longer have a

good name; and you know, I think, from recent weeks, how easy it is for a reputation to diminish. People are not kind. They may well tell you stories about me after I have gone, but all I can say is that I have tried to lead a good life even if I haven't always succeeded. I need to start again, and I need to stop drinking. I am going to France. I will see my son. And then I will make my peace with him and the world. I am grateful to you for your patience, and I apologise if I was ever rude. I have not been myself for many years. Here is a token to remember me by. Perhaps every great detective should have one. Look at the dawn. Wait for the sunrise. *Satis verborum*.

Sidney opened the box. Inside was Daniel Morden's Minox camera.

Unholy Week

Sidney was nearing the end of his annual Lenten abstinence, a time that always made him grumpy, and the Master of Corpus had asked him to take the three-hour service in the college chapel on Good Friday. There was nothing unreasonable about this request but Sidney was going to have to preach a demanding sermon slap bang in the middle of Hildegard's first visit to Grantchester since the death of her husband. There was nothing he could do to change things. The dates had been set, the travel arrangements agreed, and the accommodation booked. He was tense.

The sermon was, in effect, a series of meditations, reflecting on each of the seven sayings of Jesus on the Cross. Sidney had to begin with "Father, forgive them, for they know not what they do", and discuss the idea of eternal salvation and the nature of the relationship between Jesus and his mother. These would be interspersed with music chosen by Orlando Richards, the Professor of Music, and sung by the college choir. Sidney then had to move on to contemplate Christ's feelings of abandonment and distress ("My God, my God, why hast thou forsaken me") before ending by concentrating on the final triumph and reunion with God ("Father, into your hands, I commend my spirit").

He decided to dedicate a single day of preparation for each meditation and he took Dickens on a walk across the meadows for inspiration. It was dark and windy, with the clouds low and heavy with rain. Sidney recognised that, although the atmosphere was brooding enough to contemplate the Passion of Christ, his muse had failed to strike.

He tried to imagine himself into the scene at Golgotha. He looked at a tall elm tree that fringed the River Cam and thought of the wood of the cross, the two thieves and the agonising death. He wondered what it would be like to talk about the event as a crime scene with Jesus as the victim. Perhaps he could go through the list of suspects? Judas would be an accessary to murder, the High Priest was guilty of sentencing an innocent man to death, and Pilate was the representative of a weak government that failed to intervene. How responsible was Jesus himself, who "answered him to never a word"? How provocative was his silence in court?

Sidney could then perhaps meditate even further, to investigate the direct responsibility of the Creator himself. In sacrificing his son for the greater good was God himself the murderer?

Although this argument would be familiar to many from wartime, and Sidney would be able to expound on the theory of beneficial sacrifice, it was a risky strategy. He would have to make it clear that the story of Jesus was different from any other. Because, he concluded, this was the first death that led to resurrection, the central character changed from victim to hero. Easter represented the death of death. The resurrection was the solution to the crime; the solving of the ultimate mystery, not just of Christ's death, but the meaning of man's existence on earth.

Sidney called Dickens back from rootling around the hedgerows, and waved to a passer-by. He would need to write things down before he forgot what he wanted to say. He was prevented from doing so by the arrival of Orlando Richards.

A kindly man, with a large and thoughtful face, Orlando wore a navy suit that was on the baggy side, and a white shirt with an enlarged collar that gave him a little more neck room than normal. As a singer he could not feel constricted, and his burgundy tie was loosely knotted. His most prominent feature consisted of his large, and slightly pointed, ears. Every time they met, Sidney tried not to stare at them, but he didn't think he had ever encountered anyone who was in possession of such magnificent lugholes. It was as if a life spent listening to music had magically increased their size.

Orlando had made his visit in order to ascertain if Sidney had any musical requirements to match the thrust of his argument during the three hours. "I was also wondering if you had any plans to come to evensong this Sunday?"

"I am not sure. Why do you ask?"

"If your friend from Germany is coming then I thought that we might prepare a little surprise for her."

"That's very kind of you; although I have learned to be wary of surprises, Orlando."

"You do not need to worry about things like that. I think we all want any time she spends in college to be as pleasant as possible; even if life has been rather disrupted of late."

"I presume you are referring to the rewiring."

Orlando was not keen on the work of the college handyman and was glad of the opportunity to have a little rant. "I appreciate that the job needs to be done but Charlie Crawford is an absolute menace. The place is a death trap of frayed cables. Dr Cade has already had words with him both about his electrical ability and his overtime payments. The man is nothing but trouble. He never seems to finish one thing before he starts on the next. The whole place will have to be redecorated. And the noise is dreadful . . ."

"I can imagine."

"The man bangs about all over the place. Even his whistling is out of tune."

Sidney tried to see the positive side of the college modernisation. "I suppose redecoration might be a plus. You could have your walls painted a dark Georgian red, or a restful green."

"I don't know about that. Crawford keeps telling us how the whole college could go up in flames at any moment."

"Well, we certainly wouldn't want that."

"It's hardly likely. It's been going for hundreds of years without any mishap."

"I'd still be wary," Sidney replied. The previous year's arson had been a solemn warning about the ease with which a conflagration could take hold.

Hildegard's train was due to arrive that afternoon and Sidney was determined not to be late. The tension induced by their imminent reunion made him bicycle faster than normal, and despite his best efforts to steer with care and concentration, his thoughts kept drifting away, even back to the time when he had initiated the capture of Annabel Morrison at this very station. She had been Stephen Staunton's murderer, and Sidney had not only been responsible for her arrest but it was he who had to tell his widow, Hildegard, all that had happened. In doing so, he had withheld one critical piece of information, the very reason for the murder, her husband's infidelity with a second woman. He had decided that it was too hurtful to tell Hildegard, but he was still uncomfortable with the fact that he knew more than he should. It was the duty of a priest to keep confidences (a task Sidney found difficult when acting as an amateur detective) but he was unsure of the amount a prospective couple, if that was what they were, needed to know about each other. How much should be disclosed and how much kept secret? He had known men who had never spoken about the war, or their previous marriage, or even the children that they had had in what they might refer to as "an earlier life". They had insisted on a fresh start, without any reference to anything that had happened before. Hildegard could, perhaps, do the same. Sidney was, however, wary of burying the past. It might be a foreign country, but the temptation to revisit it remained stronger than people realised.

He tried to reduce his anxiety by wondering what Hildegard would be wearing: a loose open-fronted jacket in black serge, perhaps, with a slim straight skirt, stockings with seams, and sharply pointed pumps. He loved the little hats she often wore, tilted to one side, casting no shadow over her green eyes and her lightly quizzical eyebrows.

He imagined her stepping off the train and walking towards him. He prepared himself by anticipating that their behaviour would be quite formal at first, even guarded. It had been such a long time. What did it mean to watch a woman walking towards you and to know that anything you said could make the difference between a life spent together or apart?

He looked at all the other people standing on the platform: worried parents, expectant children, hopeful lovers. As the travellers alighted, he could see many women who might have been mistaken for Hildegard at a distance and he suffered a momentary loss of confidence. Perhaps he would not recognise her or, even worse, she had decided not to come at all? But then the smoke cleared and she was there. Sidney felt his heart lift into a place he did not think he had known before.

Hildegard was dressed in a black knee-length coat with a large cape collar that stood away from the throat, with unpadded low-set shoulders, and a silhouette tapered to give an oval effect. Her blonde hair was shorter than Sidney had remembered, and it was cut almost boyishly, sweeping back at a level with her grape-green eyes. Her eyebrows were pencil thin and she wore the subtlest lipstick. All the warmth that he felt for her came flooding back; her wry, almost judgemental smile; the surprised amusement in her eyes; the way she would open her mouth with a gasp and take a little step back at the same time when Sidney said something that she would not dare say herself.

She held out her hand and Sidney took it, and she then leant forward to let him kiss her on each cheek. This was the greeting they had settled on, and it was only after it had been achieved that she said hello.

"Good journey?" Sidney asked.

Hildegard gave him a tired smile. "I am here at last."

"I hope you feel it was worth the effort."

Sidney remembered that there was always a touch of awkwardness when they saw each other after an absence; the result of something yet to be defined.

"Of course," she replied. "Although I am nervous."

He showed her to a taxi and stowed her luggage, telling the driver that he would follow on his bicycle. It was strange to be separated from each other as soon as Hildegard had arrived, but it was the most practical solution. He would reach her lodgings only moments later.

Hildegard's landlady was Grace Wardell, the sister of the college handyman who was busy with the rewiring. She was smaller than Hildegard, with dark hair and watchful eyes. Her husband had died in a road accident and her son had been shot down over Stuttgart in 1943. "Staunton's an Irish name, isn't it?" she asked.

"It was my husband's."

"And he is no longer with us?"

"I'm afraid not."

"In the war, I suppose."

Hildegard had imagined that Sidney might have explained about her situation and worried that Mrs Wardell might guess her nationality and refuse to accommodate her. She would not have been surprised. She was used to the discomfort caused by her accident of birth and it was often the first impression she made in England. She remembered her arrival almost ten years ago; how her every interlocutor would react with disbelief, mistrust, and then mainly, but not always, with a recovered sense of decency and fairness, recognising that she could hardly be held personally responsible for the war.

Mrs Wardell was already on to the next thing. "Well you're staying for ten days. You can tell me all about it if you'd like, but if you don't then there's nothing to worry about. The room's fresh and clean and tea is at half past six when my brother Charlie gets in. I hope that'll do?"

"That will be satisfactory."

"You'll have to mind his moods. He's got a bit of a temper but he means well. If you'd like to go out after tea then I can give you a key but we retire by ten and I'd be grateful if you could do the same. We like to lock up and go to bed, knowing where we all are."

"I am sure Mrs Staunton will follow your house rules," Sidney answered.

"They aren't rules, Canon Chambers, just suggestions."

"But I am sure you would be grateful if people followed them."

"It does make life easier, I find."

Hildegard asked if Sidney could wait while she hung up her clothes and saw to her make-up. Whereas Amanda had no qualms about putting on her lipstick in front of him, Hildegard always made a tactful retreat to a nearby bathroom in order to fulfil the necessary adjustments. Her discretion gave her dignity, poise and grace.

He took her out to supper at his favourite restaurant, Le Bleu Blanc Rouge, where they enjoyed a simple meal of homemade pâté and toast, a chicken breast with the first new potatoes of the year, followed by a chocolate mousse that had been laced with a little Grand Marnier. It was the only alcohol Sidney allowed himself and although he offered Hildegard a glass of wine she refused it in order to keep him company and share his abstinence until Easter Day.

It was good to catch up on each other's news, but the conversation became more serious when Hildegard questioned Sidney about the forthcoming three-hour service.

"I think you have to go straight to the heart of the nature of suffering," he replied. "That is the message of Jesus on the Cross. You have to tackle Christ's passion head on, and then come out the other side. You cannot have the triumph of the resurrection without the devastation of the crucifixion. It is something the more evangelical amongst us tend to gloss over."

"You are more serious than people think, Sidney."

"I don't like it when they ignore the pain at the heart of the Christian message and take the clergy to be figures of fun."

"They are not regarded so in Germany."

"No. There, they are all very serious. In England, we are embarrassed by solemnity. People like to laugh at life's unpredictability because they are afraid of it."

"Are you saying the Germans have no sense of humour?"

"My dear Hildegard, I am not saying that at all."

"You are suggesting it. In English it is easier to be amusing, I think."

"The richness of the language is something of which we are proud."

"But it is difficult to learn! The same words have different meanings. One day I will try to make a pun but it is hard for foreigners. Sometimes with one letter a word can become its opposite: fast turns into feast, reign becomes resign, laughter becomes slaughter. And in Germany the verbs are at the end of the sentence, not the nouns. It is harder to surprise the people you are talking to."

Sidney ordered coffee. "I sometimes think that faith is rather like explaining the punchline of a joke. If you have to take it all apart then the joke doesn't work any more."

"You should preach about that. I am looking forward to hearing you again."

"You don't have to come to all the services."

She put her hand on his. "I do, Sidney. That is why I am here. To listen to you."

"Then I hope I will not be a disappointment."

"You never disappoint me, Sidney."

"So far, perhaps. But I wouldn't like to take anything for granted."

"Except my friendship."

The next morning, Hildegard was treated to a hearty English breakfast. Grace Wardell was a solicitous hostess but her guest was expected to leave after the meal and make herself scarce for the rest of the day. It was not a house for sitting about. Her brother Charlie would give Hildegard a lift to Grantchester.

Charlie Crawford was in his early fifties. A small man, of five foot six, who wore his regulation overalls by day, he often transformed himself into a snappy dresser by night, slapping on so much Brylcreem he looked as if he was Elvis Presley's dad. He was an impatient enthusiast with a short concentration span, a dedicated union member and a committed socialist. He was currently in dispute with the junior bursar about the overtime required for the work he was doing on the rewiring; an amount that would almost double his weekly wage. "Dr Cade owes me for four weeks and he's always late to pay. I'm going to have to sort it out."

"It's very kind of you to take me," said Hildegard as she climbed into his works van.

"It's no trouble. I should go to church myself but there's too much work to be done."

"Even on a Sunday?"

"The married fellows are at home. I can get on and do their rooms while they're out. But it's impossible for one man," he complained. "And that's typical of the college. They want everything on the cheap. Even then, they try and cheat you on the overtime. The junior bursar's the one that's the trouble."

"Is it dangerous work?" Hildegard asked.

Rain struck the misted windscreen. Charlie leaned forward to wipe away the steam. "Electricity is always dangerous, Mrs Staunton. People take it for granted but they don't know what it can do." He turned on his wipers. "I'm worried about this weather. I don't want lightning."

Hildegard thanked him for the lift and stepped into the dark simplicity of the church at Grantchester. The statuary was covered in cloth and there was little light through the windows. The last time she had been here had been at her husband's funeral.

Orlando Richards had come over from Corpus to rehearse the choir and at the service they sang "*Jesu, deine Passion ist mir lauter Freude*", the chorale from Bach's Cantata 130 for Palm Sunday "*Himmelskönig, sei willkommen*". Hildegard was so touched that she went over to thank him after the service.

"I thought it might make a nice surprise. I am a great admirer of German music; although, of course, the national character gives me pause."

"I can understand, after the war, but I hope you will make an exception in my case."

"Of course," Orlando replied. "Although it is a complicated matter, is it not? Character is music. You cannot have one without the other."

"I agree but great music is not always produced by great men."

"You mean men of morality? They may be wonderful musicians but their lives do not live up to their creations."

Hildegard smiled. "We must work hard at everything. That is why we need to practise. I was hoping that you might be able to help me."

"In what way?"

"I do not have a piano."

"Why didn't you say? You can use my room if you can stand all the banging," the Professor of Music offered gallantly. "I have taken to using a room in Peterhouse in the daytime. The noise of the rewiring has almost polished me off."

"I wouldn't want to be any trouble."

"There is a perfectly decent Bechstein if it makes you feel at home. What are you playing at the moment?"

"Bach, of course. Some Mozart. Late Beethoven."

"That's getting dangerously late for me, I am afraid."

Sidney stepped in and tried to explain. "Orlando is our Early Music specialist. Anything after 1800 is decidedly avant-garde."

"As for Sidney's jazz," the Professor of Music shuddered, "I don't know how anyone goes near it. Such a racket."

"Do you think so?" Hildegard smiled. "Sometimes I find Bach is like jazz. The Concerto in D perhaps . . ."

"Yes, I can see that: but there is a difference, is there not, between Bach or Buxtehude and the music of Bix Beiderbecke, don't you think?"

"Of course, but the similarities are often as interesting as the differences."

Sidney thought it best to stop this dangerous line of conversation. "Careful, Hildegard, or you will lose Professor Richards' goodwill."

"Then perhaps I will confine my practice to music no later than the eighteenth century. Do you have a harpsichord?"

"Of course. There is a harpsichord and a piano. You could practise as Wanda Landowska does. You know how she has started to perform the Goldberg Variations twice in one concert: once on the harpsichord, then again on the piano?"

"I found it amusing when she told people that they could play Bach in any way they chose but that she thought it better to play it in his."

"It's fascinating to hear the contrast," Orlando agreed.

"The difference in technique is critical."

"I look forward to discussing it. Where have you been hiding this magnificent woman, Sidney?"

"Ah well," said Sidney, momentarily jealous. "That is quite a story." He began to usher Hildegard away. He did not want some upstart music professor monopolising his guest. There would be little enough time for Hildegard as it was.

★   ★   ★

Sidney spent the Monday morning of Holy Week giving Hildegard a tour of the college so that she would know where everything was when she practised in Orlando's rooms.

He had chosen to enter via St Bene't's Church rather than the Porter's Lodge as he thought it best to start on the site where the college had been founded. He then ushered Hildegard into the formal nineteenth-century elegance of New Court with its prominent chapel. To its right and left there were the library and the hall. This triangular arrangement of buildings reflected the balance between academic, spiritual and social life in the college community.

Sidney's careful explanation of this fact was marred, however, by an argument in front of the library. Charlie Crawford, carrying a large roll of copper wiring, had been heading towards G staircase where Adam Cade, the junior bursar, stopped him. It was clear that Dr Cade had some form of protest, either about the nature of the rewiring or its ever-increasing cost, and Charlie was seen to drop the copper and fold his arms. He then made off, in haste, to the Porter's Lodge where, Sidney felt sure, a complaint would be issued.

"Oh dear," he observed. "I think that's best avoided."

Hildegard kept peering into the narrow openings that separated the more formal buildings. She remarked that nothing was quite what it seemed: behind the bright spacious courtyards lay dark corners, eerie passages and narrow stairs. "It's like living in a monastery," she said.

"I think that was the founders' idea. A secluded world of scholarship, without distraction."

"With women offering the greatest danger of distraction, I suppose. What happens when a fellow wants to get married?" she asked.

"They move out; although they keep their rooms for tutorials. And they still dine in college."

"It must be lonely for the wives."

Adam Cade crossed the court to say hello and Sidney made the necessary introduction, pointing out that Hildegard was staying with Charlie Crawford's sister.

"Well I hope he doesn't display the temper at home that I've just experienced here."

"I have not seen it," Hildegard assured him. "Is something the matter?"

"Something is always the matter with Crawford. That man would start a fight in an empty room. If he stopped complaining and got on with the rewiring it would have been done by now. He's left stuff all over the place, even though I have told him repeatedly about my need for tidiness and cleanliness so that I can concentrate on my work. I've had to ask him to leave it and clear it all up over the weekend. I'm late to deliver a book to my publisher and I can't lose any more time."

"He is worried about money, I think."

"So he's complained to you as well, Mrs Staunton? That's not very discreet. I've warned him that he needs to be much more meticulous about his overtime sheets. He can't make rough approximations and charge what he likes. The figures don't add up and I don't believe that he has done as much work as he says he has. But then I'm no electrician. College administration can be such a bore. You're lucky to be able to swan in and out, Canon Chambers. I think it must be fun being a clergyman."

"I do have my cares as well," Sidney replied firmly. "But I admit that there are benefits to the priesthood."

"Not least, the companionship of your charming guest, I should imagine."

Sidney thought it time to explain. "Mrs Staunton is a pianist and Professor Richards has kindly lent her his rooms in which to practise."

"I hear he keeps clearing off to Peterhouse. I wish I could do the same."

Hildegard was concerned. "I hope I will not disturb you."

"I do not think you will. Professor Richards and I have had many a discussion about the relationship between music and mathematics."

"It is close," Hildegard observed.

Dr Cade appeared grateful for her interest. "We talk about mutual codes, repeated patterns and numerological similarities. But you probably don't want me to bang on about all that. I look forward to hearing you play."

"I am sure I am not as able as Professor Richards."

"That may be the case, although I suspect that you are being modest. If it is true, then I do not doubt that you more than make up for any lesser ability with charm." Cade lifted his hat.

Sidney took Hildegard to the Porter's Lodge and explained the arrangement with Orlando Richards. Hildegard would practise for two hours every morning and afternoon for the next few days and Sidney would collect her every lunchtime. The head porter, Bill Beagrie, took a dim view of letting a woman have such a free run of the college, particularly one that was German, but once Hildegard had spoken to him his fears were allayed. Sidney assured him that he might even enjoy the sound of preludes and fugues wafting their way from an upper room in the south-easterly corner of New Court.

Sidney was happy that her piano practice left him time to perform his duties without losing out on the pleasure of lunch and dinner in her company. He felt sure that her presence could ease the penitential pattern of Lent.

Such hopes, however, were forlorn and short-lived. The following morning, Hildegard's practice session was interrupted by a scream from Doris Arnold, the bed-maker who had been cleaning the room opposite.

Inside lay the figure of Adam Cade, junior bursar and Research Fellow of Mathematics, dead in his bath.

On being informed of this untimely demise, Sidney felt not only immense sorrow for the unexpected loss of so young a life but anxiety about the effect of the news on Hildegard. He prayed that there was nothing suspicious about it. He did not want any investigations to take place while she was staying.

Dr Michael Robinson pronounced the cause of death as heart failure, which was somewhat strange as Dr Cade had only just celebrated his thirty-fifth birthday. "He's a bit young for that, don't you think?" Sidney asked.

"He was very highly strung. And I'm told he tended to work through the night. He had a set routine. Having a bath very early in the morning was his way of taking a break."

"And there is nothing unusual about his demise?"

"No, Canon Chambers, nothing at all. It is unfortunate that he had the attack and then appears subsequently to have drowned in the bath but this is not, in itself, unusual. Death comes to us all and there are times when people are unlucky. He had a weak heart. He was alone. He could not summon help."

"You mean that, had he not been in his bath, he might have survived?"

"That is possible."

"But he was looking so well . . ." Hildegard observed.

"Sometimes that makes very little difference," the doctor replied.

Hildegard was in no state to continue with her piano practice and Sidney suggested that it might be best if she went back to her lodgings for a lie-down. There, however, she was met by Charlie Crawford.

He was ranting.

Professor Todd had insinuated that Dr Cade's heart attack could have been caused by his inability to work as normal. The stress induced by the rewiring of the college, the costs involved and the difficulties in finding time to fit his academic commitments around his duties had proved fatal. Ceaseless complaint from certain college workers, and Crawford in particular, could only have added to the pressures upon him as junior bursar, and a review of the events leading up to the death was therefore in order.

"They're going to try to pin the whole thing on me, I can tell. But it was a heart attack, plain and simple. Then the man drowned. I've done nothing wrong."

"They will try and find something," his sister warned. "I'm sure they've been looking for an excuse to get rid of you."

"The head porter will back me up."

"That may not be enough."

"I can ask Sidney," Hildegard offered. "I am sure he would say something."

"I don't think they take much notice of clergymen. All I do know is that Todd's got it in for me."

"But why?"

"They're cooking the books."

Hildegard was bemused. "I do not understand that phrase."

"They've both got their hands in the college till. They stint on the workers and help themselves to whatever money they can. It's one law for them and another for the rest of us."

"Did they know that you thought like this, Mr Crawford?"

"I told them all the time."

"And what did they say?"

"That if I didn't like it I could go and work somewhere else."

"And why didn't you?"

"Because they owe me so much back pay. If I left I'd never get it unless I went to court. And then God knows what would happen. My old man spent enough time with the law to last the rest of us a lifetime."

"There's no need to go into that now," his sister counselled.

"They pretend to be fair but there's only one thing they're concerned about and that's themselves," Charlie replied.

The following morning the Master telephoned to ask if Sidney could pop over and discuss Dr Cade's funeral arrangements. He was sure that Easter would make a difference, but he hoped the event could be kept as low-key as possible. "I don't want the college acquiring a bad reputation. We've had enough trouble as it is."

"I am not sure I can hide a funeral, if that is what you are asking," Sidney replied, "although I was wondering how much of a family Dr Cade might have. I do not think he was married?"

"No, Sidney. Although he must have relations somewhere."

They were interrupted by the irascible figure of Edward Todd who had asked how soon they might be able to seek out a replacement for Dr Cade. He didn't want to take on the extra burden of teaching before the summer tripos exams. "I can farm some of the undergraduates out to other colleges but I need to be sure that they're not going to any duffers. The Professor of Mathematics at Fitzwilliam leaves a lot to be desired, I must say, and Catz isn't much better."

"Was Dr Cade a good tutor?" Sidney asked.

"One of the best, I'd say," Todd acknowledged, "although he was almost certainly bound for America. He was not without ambition."

"That must be a good thing in a mathematician, surely?"

"Better than in a priest," the Master observed.

"Of course," Sidney replied. "I try not to think about aspirations."

"Nonsense. We all know that you will be a bishop one day."

"That is unlikely."

"Provided, of course, that you detach yourself from the world of crime."

"Surely a wife will help?" Dr Todd asked.

Sidney tried to contain the conversation to matters in hand. "I don't have any marriage plans."

"That's not what it looks like, if you don't mind my saying so."

Sidney did, indeed, mind him saying so. "How things look and how things are can often be very different matters," he replied, hoping that he could escape this subject as quickly as possible.

"Your friend is staying with Crawford's sister, I believe?" Professor Todd continued before turning to the Master. "I am afraid I've had to sack him."

"Oh dear," the Master replied, "and in the middle of the rewiring. Are you sure that's wise?"

"On what grounds?" Sidney asked.

"Dr Cade was already on to him. He had started to charge whatever overtime he felt like and his attitude was surly. We can't allow trade-union mentality to take over the college when there's a perfectly good electrical company in town."

"But Crawford is a member of the staff. Shouldn't we give him a warning? Isn't it rather brutal to dismiss him out of hand?"

"We need to get on with things, Master. The college needs to steady itself and concentrate on its academic duties. Everything else is a distraction. Wouldn't you agree, Sidney?"

"Of course," his clerical companion replied, without thinking fully about his answer.

He was already wondering why Professor Todd should be keen to dismiss Charlie Crawford so soon and whether Dr Cade's heart attack was all that it seemed.

Later that day, Hildegard confirmed the news of Charlie Crawford's dismissal and asked Sidney to intercede. "An injustice has been done. He is very upset."

Any involvement in the disciplinary proceedings of the college would have to be handled with caution. "Being distressed does not necessarily qualify a man for sympathy," Sidney replied. "Perhaps he is showing remorse."

"He isn't showing any at all. In fact he is making terrible accusations."

"I suppose that is understandable."

Leonard Graham entered the room to refill his cup of tea. "You think that Charlie Crawford has been wrongfully dismissed?"

"I do. He has even suggested that Dr Cade has been, I think his words were, 'bumped off'."

Leonard Graham raised a clerical eyebrow. Sidney tried to pin down what Hildegard was saying. "Why on earth would he suggest that?"

"He speaks very wildly. I think you should talk to him, Sidney."

"We can't have him going all over town making accusations. Sooner or later we'll have Keating in the college again and who knows where that will lead?"

"Dr Cade was young."

"And with a weak heart. We have no evidence that there has been any malpractice."

"Charlie Crawford has been got out of the way."

Sidney could not believe that Hildegard was thinking along these lines. She was jumping to a conclusion that he had already begun to fear himself. "You are not suggesting that these two incidents are related? Surely they are coincidental?"

"We witnessed an argument."

"Which would lead anyone to conclude that if Dr Cade was murdered then Charlie Crawford is the most likely culprit. So why would he suggest such a thing?"

"I do not know, Sidney. But I do think that he is a man of principle."

"I tend to agree with you, but this line of enquiry will do us no good. The last thing we need is to raise the question of one man's murder and why he died."

"Oh really?" Leonard Graham began to wash up his teacup and saucer. "I thought that was the point of Easter."

Hildegard decided that she would eat with the Crawfords that evening. She knew that Sidney was expected at High Table and that he still had work to do on his sermon. Time spent at her lodgings would also give her the opportunity to ask her landlady a few questions.

Sidney was grateful for her interest, and recognised that she had a logical mind and a clear, direct way of thinking, but he was concerned that Hildegard took Charlie Crawford's suggestions so seriously. Any uncertainty would necessitate further probing and yet more distraction from his duties.

He spoke the college grace at High Table, hoping the familiar repetition would restore his religious sensibility: "*Benedic, Domine, nobis et donis tuis, quae de tua largitate sumus sumpturi, et concede ut illis salubriter nutriti, tibi debitum obsequium praestare valeamus, per Christum Dominum nostrum. Amen.*"

As he sat down to partake of his beef consommé, he was troubled by Hildegard's vehemence and by the disregard of the fellows for the working men of the college. They were, it had to be admitted, an odd group of people with which to spend his time, and although they had their eccentricities, he could not believe that any of them was capable of murder.

He observed them eating their soup in ruminative silence.

There was Clifford Watts, Professor of History and constitutional historian. He was now an elderly don, but even in his prime he had been so flummoxed by the reduction of staff during wartime that he had needed to ask how to draw the curtains to his room at night, never having done so on his own before. Neil Gardiner, the admissions tutor and Reader in Jurisprudence, kept a private aeroplane for trips to the country. This was a man who, it was rumoured, liked to dress up as an old lady and get himself helped across the road when the volume of bicyclists was at its height.

Then there was Marcus Mortimer, the English don, a charming but alcoholic womaniser who took most of his tutorials while lying on the floor. So hopeless was he that Sidney had often been called in to help out his students when they were studying the metaphysical poets, after Mr Mortimer had declared the work of Donne and Herbert to be "too Christian" for his taste.

Apart from Orlando Richards, there were few dons with whom it was possible to sustain conversation. Edward Todd, the Professor of Mathematics, was particularly bad-tempered and was continually making comments about the college catering. He had recently complained that redcurrant tart without raspberries ought not to be offered, that stewed rhubarb was a weed unfit for human consumption, and that sherry should always accompany turtle soup and that it was a trivial and exasperating economy to withdraw it.

Sidney was seated next to him at dinner that night and asked what Adam Cade had been working on at the time of his death.

"I am not sure that's relevant now."

"Perhaps not, Professor Todd, but if Dr Cade had a work that was close to publication perhaps it could be produced in his memory."

"I doubt that anyone would understand it."

"From what you said earlier, I gather that he had a growing reputation. Such a work could add lustre to the mathematical reputation of the college."

"I am not sure about that. I have a forthcoming publication myself."

"Would you care to explain what it is about?"

"Percolation theory. Do you know what that is, Canon Chambers?"

Sidney smiled ruefully. "I'd have to hazard a guess. Is it a study of the way in which water passes through or around rock?"

"Not quite. It is a mathematical examination of the behaviour of connected clusters in a random graph. It is an attempt to model the flow of liquid through a porous body."

"You look for pattern or repeated incidence so that you can predict the flow or spread of the percolation, I imagine?"

"Well, that is how I might describe it in simple terms. One predicts across two- and three-dimensional lattice structures. Two dimensions are clearly more straightforward than three but the aim is to develop a coherent theory of random spatial processes; an attempt to marry geometry with probability."

"Was Dr Cade aware of your work?"

"We worked in the same department."

"I mean to say, had he read anything of it?"

"Dr Cade was interested in the practical application; how you could use percolation theory to model the spread of a forest fire, the course of a disease or the increase of populations. I was more interested in the core mathematical material."

"And had you read any of Dr Cade's practical applications of the theory yourself?"

"You are taking an unusual interest in this, Canon Chambers."

"I believe there is always room to improve one's knowledge. And there have been suggestions that mathematics and theology are not as far removed from each other as people might think."

"I hope you are not going to start talking to me about numerology," Todd warned.

"The number twelve in the Bible is significant, I think."

"Not mathematically. It is thematic. Twelve tribes of Israel, twelve disciples, twelve foundations in the heavenly Jerusalem, twelve gates, twelve pearls and twelve angels. This is mere repetition."

"I am aware that it can be taken to extremes, but the number three, for the Trinity, is also important."

"Or six. Man was created on the sixth day, six words are used for Man and the mark of the Beast is 666, a mockery of the Trinity. You can do anything you like with the Bible. Dr Cade was more interested in musical numerology. He used to talk to Professor Richards about it all the time although, as far as I am concerned, most of the theories were too far-fetched to be given credence."

"Did you work closely with Dr Cade?"

"Mathematics requires intense solitary concentration and that is precisely why Crawford's rewiring was such a distraction. He kept coming in and out all the time. Neither of us could get any work done."

Professor Todd had finished his soup. Sidney had abandoned his. "Why did you suggest that it might have been a cause of Dr Cade's death?" he asked.

"I said no such thing."

"Crawford has stated that you did."

"I can assure you that I did not. I hope that you are not going to take his word against mine?"

The soup was removed from the table and spring chicken was served.

Sidney recognised that Edward Todd was irritated and that he would have to be careful not to press matters further. There was, however, something about the tone of this conversation that was fiercer than mere donnish superiority. Todd had been quick to dismiss the college electrician, and he appeared to Sidney both defensive and aggressive. Sidney wondered if there might be a reason why he had wanted Adam Cade dead and Charlie Crawford so conveniently removed from the scene.

He would have to make some discreet enquiries and then, if his fears were confirmed, he would have to tell Inspector Keating. It was not a prospect to which he looked forward. He could not quite believe, having often involved Amanda in his previous escapades, that

Hildegard could already be embroiled in another. He worried how it might affect the future of their relationship, but if he were still to be, in Bunyan's words, "valiant for truth", then everything else in his life would have to be secondary to the process of investigation.

Orlando had been happy to let Hildegard play Bach in his rooms and expressed the hope that the recent death of someone in such close proximity did not put her off her piano practice. He was clearly nervous about the situation and Hildegard wondered if the Professor of Music had even anticipated the death of a colleague. Perhaps he had deliberately made sure that he was conveniently out of the way and in another college at the time? It certainly seemed odd to give up such wonderful rooms for the sake of a little rewiring. But then much of Orlando's behaviour was odd, she realised, even down to his bathing of hands in warm water before taking to the keyboard. He believed that he could only play well if his fingers were warmed slightly higher than the body's natural temperature.

"I think they are at their most dexterous at ninety-nine degrees Fahrenheit," he said, "and so in summer I sometimes have to cool them down. The only concern is that you have to be careful not to play with damp hands."

Although Hildegard had already recognised the influence, and thought it precious to the point of being neurotic, Orlando went on to explain that he was following some of the techniques used by Glenn Gould.

He wore gloves indoors, kept plunging his arms into hot water, and had his two-bar electric fire on in his rooms the whole time. Hildegard decided not to comment on such behaviour, believing that it had little to do with achieving any extra sensitivity of touch, but let Orlando explain that his nervousness had been recently increased by the pressure of a new composition for Good Friday. It was a setting of Psalm 44:

If we have forgotten the name of our God, or stretched out our hands to a strange god; shall not God search this out? For he knoweth the secrets of the heart.

Yea, for thy sake are we killed all the day long; we are counted as sheep to the slaughter.

He had chosen the verses as a prefiguring of the Easter sacrifice. On being shown the score, Hildegard had noticed that the piece was in 4/4 time and also that the fourth of the fourth month would be 4 April, the date of the first performance that Good Friday.

Orlando was impressed that she had spotted his play with numerology. "I can see that nothing gets past *you*," he observed.

"I think you have been very clever; a marriage of music and mathematics."

The Professor of Music tried to brush off her appreciation with false modesty. "Of course one can get carried away with this kind of thing." He leaned forward and smiled. "They are the little touches, perhaps, that only musicians are aware of."

"And mathematicians, I would have thought." Hildegard smiled back. Her green eyes sparkled. "But only the most intelligent." Anyone watching from outside would have thought that she was almost being flirtatious. "Do you think they will know?" she asked.

"Dr Cade always used to have a good stab at understanding what I was trying to do," Orlando continued, "and Professor Todd always knows more than he lets on. But they are philistines when it comes to proper musicianship . . ."

Hildegard moved to the table where the score was laid out. "I have also noticed something else, if you don't mind my saying so?"

"Is there no limit to your perception, Mrs Staunton?"

"Your scoring of the word 'killed'. It sounds odd, I think?"

Orlando gave his companion a somewhat shifty look before he made his explanation. "That is deliberate. The word "killed" should sound odd, don't you think? Bach, for example, is onomatopoeic all the time. The bass aria from Cantata 130 has the devil singing *Der alte Drache brennt vor Neid* and the music twists like the flames of hell. I am trying to do something similar."

What he did not admit, however, was that the word "killed" was set to the notes C, A, D and E.

Hildegard wondered when Orlando Richards had started to write the piece. It seemed unlikely that he could have composed so much music in the short time that had passed since Adam Cade's death; but if he had begun it earlier, then how coincidental was the

171

reference to the murder victim? Was Orlando issuing some kind of warning, or was there something even more sinister going on: a conspiracy, even?

As soon as Sidney collected her for luncheon he could tell that Hildegard was preoccupied. She began to talk to him, carefully and quietly and without giving too much away.

"I was thinking," she began. "When am I going to meet your friend Inspector Keating?"

Sidney had instituted the new tradition of washing the feet of his parishioners on Maundy Thursday as a mark of priestly humility in commemoration of the Last Supper. He was inappropriately proud of the idea, and he brushed aside Leonard Graham's observation that there would be a sharp drop in his enthusiasm when it came to the actual performance of the task.

The curate's instincts were, of course, correct. This irritated Sidney beyond all reason as, with rising reluctance, he began to wash the feet of the thirty or so members of his congregation that evening. There was Hector Kirby, the over-hearty butcher, Mike Standing, the businessman with halitosis, Harold Streat the undertaker, Francis Tort, the dentist with a drink problem, and his new-found friend, Mark Bowen, the fire investigator. At least, Sidney felt, he now knew what an annual convention for chiropodists might be like.

He moved on to Mike's girlfriend Sandra, the East Anglian judo champion, Martha Headley the nervous organist, and even Mrs Maguire who had come with her spiritualist sister Gladys. Sidney was convinced that the latter two had decided to attend the service not for religious reasons but simply to enjoy his discomfort. He wondered if Hildegard would join the queue of bare-footed penitents.

As he knelt down and sponged away the water from Mrs Maguire's bunioned white feet, he thought not of Martha, pouring oil on the feet of Jesus and using her long hair to caress them dry, but of Adam Cade, dead in his bath. If he had not suffered a heart attack then how had he died? Had Michael Robinson, the doctor at this very service, examined the body in any detail, and had Harold Streat, the undertaker with whom the body was now lodged, noticed anything amiss? It would be unlikely that either of them had looked at Dr Cade's feet, for example, with Sidney's current level of attention. He would have to talk to them both and then, even if they expressed no concern, he would suggest that Derek Jarvis, the coroner, might take a look. He would have to ask Keating's permission, of course, and he knew that this would not go down well, particularly since their meeting that evening would also be the inspector's first encounter with Hildegard. But it was essential to do things properly, and Sidney was alarmed that no one, apart from Hildegard, was taking Cade's death as seriously as he thought they should.

She sat on the stool before him and took off a pair of simple black pumps. Sidney did not need to look up to know that she was there. He took her naked left foot and let it rest in his left hand. It was pale but warm, with a delicate, almost Romanesque arch, and her toenails were trimmed, childlike and ageless. Sidney

173

sponged each foot in turn, taking his time, feeling their weight in his hands, before using a cloth to pat them dry. When he had finished, he held her right foot for a little longer than was necessary and gave it a little squeeze before looking up and daring to catch her eye. She smiled down at him. Sidney held the moment. He imagined that everyone would surely notice that he had spent more time with Hildegard than with anyone else but he didn't care who knew it.

It was the only gentle moment in an evening that became a good deal rougher when the two of them raised the subject of Adam Cade's possible murder with Inspector Keating.

"I can't believe that you are attempting to ruin a perfectly convivial night out with anxieties about a death that the doctor has assured everyone necessary was perfectly natural," was his infuriated response to the suggestion that all was not as it seemed. "Mrs Staunton, I must apologise on behalf of my friend. There are times when he can't help himself."

It was eight-thirty in the evening and the three of them were sitting in the RAF bar of the Eagle. Hildegard recognised that it was a privilege to share in what was a traditional, masculine routine, and was apologetic. "I feel that I must take some of the blame."

"On what grounds? Please don't tell me," and here the inspector's face began to suffuse itself with dread, "that this is all your idea? It was bad enough with Miss Kendall."

"Miss Kendall has nothing to do with this, I can assure you," Sidney began.

174

"Honestly, Sidney," the inspector continued, still trying to make a joke out of it all, "where do you get these women from?"

Hildegard turned to Sidney, her tone changing more rapidly than he could have imagined. "I wasn't aware that we are many in number?"

"Two is bad enough," Keating said as he stood up, headed for the bar and ordered another pint for himself and two bitter lemons for his Lenten troublemakers.

Sidney was feeling distinctly uncomfortable in the silence that followed and could not think how to remedy the situation. In fact, for the first time in his relationships with both Hildegard and Inspector Keating, he was lost for words.

"What evidence do either of you have for any malpractice?" Keating asked on his return.

Hildegard looked to Sidney before answering. "There is too much coincidence."

"That is not sufficient."

"Dr Cade was young," Hildegard added.

"I realise that this is a delicate situation, and I do remember that sad business with your husband, Mrs Staunton. I was as reluctant to get involved then as I am now. However, what do you want me to do about all this? I can't go poking my nose into college business. I am unlikely to be the winner of its annual popularity contest as it is."

"Fortunately, we do not have one," Sidney replied, collecting himself at last. "All I am suggesting is that you have a word with Derek Jarvis and persuade him to have a look at the body."

"You want me to try and sort out an unofficial post mortem?"

"What harm is there? If nothing is amiss then no one need know."

"Honestly, Sidney . . ."

"It can be our little secret."

"And if something is amiss?"

"Then you can thank me for bringing it to your attention."

"I'll have to think about it. Haven't you two got better things to do than embroil yourselves in all this?"

"Mr Crawford has been wronged," Hildegard added quietly.

"He has been dismissed. That is, I am afraid, what happens," Keating continued. "And people react very badly to that kind of thing. But to start accusing people of murder . . ."

"He hasn't accused anyone directly."

"Well, you should tell him to keep it that way. You are quite sure that something is awry?"

"Oddly enough, Geordie, I am."

"Well, I'll see what I can do. I am not promising anything, mind?"

"I wouldn't presume to expect anything more than your consideration."

"Are you teasing me, Sidney?" Keating asked.

"No," Sidney replied. "I am merely being careful. I do not want to make you angry."

"And when have I ever been angry with you?" Keating asked, already forgetting the temper he had displayed not half an hour previously.

The evening wound to a close and Sidney escorted Hildegard back to her lodgings in Portugal Place. As they walked down Trinity Street, Hildegard slipped her arm through his and asked: "Are you really as sure as you said you were?"

"Of course I am not. But if I expressed any doubt at all then the inspector wouldn't have agreed to do anything."

"He still hasn't."

"He will. I know it will prey on his mind."

The night was cold and clear. Hildegard shivered and Sidney gave her arm a little squeeze in silent comfort. She looked down at their feet as they walked and then back up at her companion. "Do you think it is the same with faith? If you express any doubt, people won't believe what you are saying?"

They stopped outside the university bookshop. "Sometimes, Hildegard, I think criminal investigation needs a certain hardness of heart, a grim determination, whereas faith requires an open heart . . ."

"And an open mind."

"I see you are beginning to get the idea."

"I wish I didn't have to."

"It is difficult," Sidney replied, "Once you start out on these investigations, I am afraid there's no stopping them, and you can then end up in all sorts of trouble."

"Curiosity killed the cat? Isn't that an English expression?"

"Yes, but the death of the cat probably still needed investigation in order to ascertain that curiosity was the cause of its demise. It could be that someone might have placed something deliberately in the cat's way, knowing that it would arouse its curiosity. Then the cause of death becomes more complicated. Is it the cat's fault for being curious, or the person who aroused his curiosity?"

"So," Hildegard continued, "if someone knew that Dr Cade always took a bath at a certain time and in a certain way, he might have been able to arrange the murder without arousing any suspicion."

"Or even curiosity," Sidney agreed.

Corpus Christi Chapel was almost full on Good Friday, although Sidney knew that some members of the college would drift in and out during the service. Three hours was a hefty undertaking, and although many of the fellows regarded it as too much of an effort, Sidney had requested that the college kitchens be shut so that there was no chance of a luncheon alternative. If the more corpulent "corpuscles" could not fast on one day of the year then there really was no salvation for them.

The service began in silence, followed by solemn music and a first meditation: "Father, forgive them, for they know not what they do". Sidney had decided to concentrate on the concept of responsibility. Although Jesus claimed that those responsible for his death were ignorant of the consequences of their actions, those in college today could have no excuse for their sins. This was a day on which they should look into the darker recesses of their hearts, bring their sins out into the light and ask God for mercy.

178

The opening anthem was taken from the Book of Lamentations, chapter 5, and had been set to music by Professor Richards:

> The joy of our heart is ceased; our dance is turned
>   to mourning.
> The crown is fallen from our head: woe unto us,
>   that we have sinned.

Hildegard was impressed by the stark simplicity of a composition that was sung without accompaniment building up to the word "sinned" in a way that perfectly matched Sidney's preaching. Orlando had thought very hard, dwelling on the "i" of the word "sinned", using six notes to spread out the two syllables, elongating the idea of crime and guilt.

The Master then stepped forward to read from the Liturgy of the Passion:

> I gave my back to the smiters, and my cheeks to
> them that plucked off the hair: I hid not my face
> from shame and spitting.
>   For the Lord GOD will help me; therefore shall
> I not be confounded: therefore have I set my face
> like a flint, and I know that I shall not be ashamed.

Hildegard was still thinking about Orlando's composition, and took out a small notebook and pencil from her handbag. The piece was written in E flat major. She quickly marked out the lines of a score, and jotted down the music that she had just heard.

The word "sinned" was set to the notes E flat, D, E and A with the second D repeated. The notes spelt out the phrase E-D-D-E-A-D.

Sidney preached again. This time he spoke on the idea of eternal salvation from death; that human death also brings with it the death of mortality itself, the end of doubt and pain. This life is but a prelude to the fugue of eternity.

When he had finished, the choir sang Bach's "*Komm, sü□er Tod*". Hildegard knew it was, of course, a coincidence that the surname of the Professor of Mathematics, Todd, echoed the German word for death, but to place this anthem in such close proximity to the previous composition was more than happenstance.

"*Komm, sü□er Tod, komm selge Ruh!*"

Was Orlando Richards threatening Edward Todd through music, she wondered, making each piece more obvious? Was he implying that he would avenge Adam Cade's death himself, or even that he might expose Todd as a murderer and obtain justice through the death penalty?

Hildegard was further troubled after the service when Orlando sought her out. He asked if she had enjoyed the experience.

"I am not sure if 'enjoy' is the right word."

"It was a solemn meditation."

Hildegard was sure that Orlando almost wanted her to confront him. "I did notice something a little unusual in the anthem from the Book of Lamentations?"

"Did you? And what might that be?"

"The melody over the word 'sinned'?"

"I see. Of course, anything you might have read into the piece would be entirely accidental."

"And you repeated the motif of C-A-D-E that I had noticed in your earlier composition, playing with the letters of his name and the German word for death; connecting the two men through music."

"It is a bit of showing off. I thought you might appreciate it."

"I hope it was not done for my benefit."

"Not at all."

"I was only thinking if other people would notice the codes in your music; the college mathematicians, for example?"

"Music allows for several different interpretations at the same time, Mrs Staunton. I do not think mathematicians are too concerned about that. An answer is either correct or it is not. They have a clear sense of right and wrong."

"Do you think that applies to their morality as well?"

"I do not think Professor Todd and Dr Cade were friends."

"And so you like to point this out musically?"

"It is a private observation."

"Perhaps it is not so private if others can recognise it?"

"I am assuming that not everyone is as clever as you, Mrs Staunton."

Hildegard looked at him coolly. "I hope you won't score any music with my name in it."

Orlando thought for a moment, as if he was glad to talk about music rather than murder. "It would be difficult with the letter H but, as you know, I can use B natural, with B flat as the letter B."

"As Bach did."

"Indeed, as in the last contrapunctus in *The Art of Fugue*."

"Before he died." Hildegard's gaze was unflinching.

Derek Jarvis conducted his affairs with a brisk efficiency that had irritated Sidney when he had first met him a few years previously, but now he was grateful for the speed and diligence of the Coroner's Office. He paid a visit to the vicarage in the early evening of Good Friday, just as Sidney was thinking of putting his feet up.

"Inspector Keating telephoned last night," Jarvis explained, "and I thought that I might as well get it out of the way. The undertaker was a little surprised, I must say, but I thought that I would just look in to say how impressed I am with what could only be guesswork on your part."

"You mean that something is, indeed, amiss?"

"The cause of death is almost certainly drowning."

"Almost?"

"Yes, Sidney, 'almost' and not 'certainly'. There are scorch marks on the toes of Dr Cade's right foot, signs of dialectic breakdown of the skin, and a branching redness on the veins in his leg . . ."

"Perhaps from the hot-water tap?"

"Yes, one imagines he topped up the hot water with his foot while lying in the bath . . ."

"And then the hotness of the tap surprised him . . ."

"Particularly, Sidney, were it in some way connected to the live wiring to the boiler."

"You mean that there is a possibility of electrocution?"

"An electric circuit through the right-hand side of his body and across the heart leading to ventricular fibrillation."

"No?"

"It'll be hard to prove."

"I'll need to get into the room."

"That would be both dangerous and sensible."

"I could take Charlie."

"And who is he?"

"The college electrician."

"He may be culpable."

"Do you think," Sidney asked carefully, "that if your theory is correct, Adam Cade's death could, in any way, be accidental?"

"I am afraid that I do not. How you came to suspect that something was wrong is quite beyond me, Sidney. You will need to proceed very carefully."

"The college will want a discreet and straightforward solution. Whether it is the correct one, I cannot say."

"You are anticipating the possibility of some kind of cover-up?"

"My taking an interest in affairs that are not strictly my business never goes down too well."

The coroner gave Sidney a steady look. "It hasn't stopped you in the past."

"That is true."

"And I sincerely hope, Canon Chambers, that it will not stop you now."

Sidney knew that it was time for a quiet word with Charlie Crawford but he was not looking forward to stirring up trouble. However, he didn't want the college handyman making any more accusations. "I do understand how upsetting it must be for you," he began, "but I think we all have to be careful what we say in public."

"I don't care about anything like that any more. I have nothing to lose."

Sidney decided to spell things out. "Except, of course, your life."

"What are you suggesting?"

"If someone really did murder Dr Cade they won't want you telling everyone about it."

"But no one believes what I say."

"They might feel they have to make sure."

"I am not afraid of any man."

"Unfortunately, I am. And so I thought it might be helpful, Charlie, if we established a few facts."

"As long as it doesn't involve the police. My old man was always being pulled in for questions and once they start . . ."

"We don't need to involve them at the moment."

"Mrs Staunton says you have already."

"Inspector Keating is a friend of mine. As you know, he cannot get involved in college business unless he is invited to do so."

"And have you done that?"

"Not yet."

"Good."

This was harder than Sidney had been expecting. "I was wondering how you think Dr Cade met his end?"

"Someone drowned him."

"The door to the bathroom was locked from the inside. There was a bolt across it."

"I can't explain that."

"I was wondering, Charlie, if you could tell me how to electrocute someone?"

"You are not going to blame the rewiring, are you? Then they'll definitely pin the whole thing on me."

"Just tell me how it could be done."

"Most people just throw a fire in the bath. Or a radio. Something live."

"But I was wondering, Charlie, could the bath itself be made live in some way? The soap dish, for example, or the taps."

"You would need to wire it up. There would have to be switches — wiring from another room."

"Such as the one belonging to the Professor of Music?"

"You're not suggesting he had anything to do with it? You'd have to go over the ceiling and across the hall for that."

"Someone could have used his room."

"Like Mrs Staunton, you mean?"

"I am not suggesting she had anything to do with this."

"But she was playing the piano across the corridor at the time. If you start talking like that, Canon Chambers, then they will blame her as well as me."

"I was wondering if you would be able to tell, from the wiring, if such a thing were possible?"

"You would have to get the bath away from the wall."

"That should be simple enough."

"It would take some force and there would be quite a bit of noise. Then, if there were wires, you would have to follow them back to a switch; some kind of device for making the bath live and then dead."

"But it is possible?"

"Anything is possible, Canon Chambers, you just have to have the mind to do it."

"Could I persuade you to come back into the college and have a look?"

Charlie was unconvinced. "I'm not sure about that. What if we were discovered?"

"It would have to be at night and I would be with you."

"They could get me for trespassing."

"I don't think they would go as far as that. Besides, you would be with me as a guest of the college. If there has been a crime, which I think we both believe there has been, then we should return to the scene."

"I'm worried it could get me into even more trouble. They're going to fix me up for this."

"The thing is," Sidney replied, "I fear someone has already thought of that. My job is to get you out of it."

★ ★ ★

Sidney had left his clerical clobber in the college Combination Room and returned to collect it, eschewing the possibility of an alcoholic sharpener when there was still another day of Lent to survive. He also wanted to press on with his investigation into the professional rivalry between dons, the open nature of the research, and the livelihood, therefore, of plagiary. It was surely possible that one man's thinking could "percolate" into another's, almost without him knowing it, but there would have to be a difference between influence, whether acknowledged or not, and theft.

He had to understand the practical application of the theory Edward Todd and Adam Cade had been working on, and so he sought out his friend Neville Meldrum, Professor of Theoretical Physics, to discuss the matter. He needed to discover the likely financial advantages in advancing such a theory, its use in epidemiology, the spread of fire, and even in patterns of immigration. How universally could such theories be implemented and how close was Adam Cade to exploiting the work commercially? Was he, for example, likely to be richer and better known than Professor Todd, and could this have intensified the competition between them?

Professor Meldrum was amused by Sidney's earnest attempts to ask intelligent questions concerning contemporary research, but anticipated the direction of his friend's enquiries.

"You might like to think of it in another way," he suggested, leaning forward in his armchair. "Human skin, for example, is also a porous substance, taking in

187

material through the pores of the sweat glands, the hair follicles, the sebaceous glands and the keratin matrix, or even lattice, that links them."

"You mean it is subject to percolation theory."

"It absorbs water, germs, disinfectant, and also, of course, electricity. The resistance of human skin varies from person to person and fluctuates between different times of day. Under dry conditions, the resistance offered by the human body may be as high as 100,000 Ohms. Wet or broken skin may drop the body's resistance right down to 1,000 Ohms."

"I was wondering," Sidney began tentatively, "if you could therefore apply such a theory to the principles of electric conductivity . . ."

"You are beginning to catch my drift, Canon Chambers."

"You might model, for example, the pattern of the absorption of an electric current, first through water and then through skin?"

"I would not have thought that much modelling would be required."

"But you could calculate the strength of the current, the quantity of water and the likely length of time needed for full percolation?"

"I think there have already been experiments in this regard. The electric conductivity of a non-ionic water-in-oil micro-emulsion has been measured in the presence of small amounts of carrier electrolyte, yes."

"And so, having done such an experiment, it might be possible to ascertain the critical probability . . ."

"Of an infinite conducting cluster, yes."

"Which might lead to electrocution."

"Indeed it might; although there is, of course, a difference between modelling such activities and committing a murder. You would need to be able to link the experiment to the crime."

"A question of cause and effect?"

"Or, to put it in your terms, Sidney, of practising what you preach."

It was a mad idea to allow Hildegard to come with Charlie Crawford on what was, technically, an illegal mission to search Dr Cade's rooms, but Sidney decided that he wanted her to witness the exact nature of his extra-curricular activities in order to show her how seriously he took them. Furthermore, her doubts about Professor Richards had only increased since the three-hour service, and she was all for searching his rooms at the same time. She still had a key, and the rooms were on opposite sides on the same floor of the same staircase. If there had been any criminal activity it could easily have been swift, and such had been Orlando's willingness to let Hildegard play on his keyboards that he might even have employed her as a fortuitous decoy.

Sidney had not told Inspector Keating of their plans. This was a research mission with three people, one torch and a handyman's toolbox.

Dr Cade's rooms still contained his books, his research and his personal possessions, all neatly stacked, but it was not the main room of the set that

189

aroused Sidney's interest. It was the small bathroom off the bedroom.

Charlie found the boiler and pronounced that the old wiring was a death trap. There was no earth bonding, the volt trip switch to the main board was not working, and the oil-filled heater had a damaged flex and the wrong-sized fuse.

Instructed by Sidney, he dragged the bath away from the wall and crouched down behind the taps. "Amazing," he said. "It's been wired up as you suggested; the metallic soap dish and all. If it goes directly to the mains we're in business."

"How can you tell?"

"I'll have to hack at the wall a bit; that might make a bit of noise. Do you think we are safe?"

"I can't imagine there's anyone on the staircase," Sidney replied. "Professor Richards is in Peterhouse and it is Easter."

Charlie took a hammer to the wall and pulled away at the plasterboard, following the newly exposed wire against the brick. He wedged himself into the gap and shone his torch above his head. "It's going up. It may turn by the ceiling and link back to the circuit board; or it could go on up. I'll have to hack away a bit more. The bathrooms and boilers are all on top of each other."

"And who lives in the room above?" Hildegard asked.

"Professor Todd," Charlie replied. "I was just about to start on his room when I had the argument with Dr Cade."

190

"So we would need access to his room in order to find out where this wire leads?"

"That will not be necessary," came a voice from the door. It was Professor Todd himself. "May I ask what on earth it is that you are doing at this time of night and on private property?"

Charlie dropped his torch in surprise and began to pack up his toolbox as quickly as he could. Hildegard stooped to help him, as if this burst of activity could distract their accuser from his questioning.

Sidney tried to take matters in hand. "We are investigating Dr Cade's death."

"Of a heart attack?"

"I am not so sure about that."

"If you have any suspicions you should go to the police, although, as you know full well, only the Master can invite them into the college. I can't think what you are up to. Crawford has been dismissed, and this woman has no place in our midst."

"She is not 'this woman'. She is my friend Mrs Hildegard Staunton."

"I don't care who she is. Get her out of here."

Hildegard refused to be spoken to in the tone Professor Todd was employing. "I am a guest of Professor Richards, as well as Canon Chambers."

"This college has a curfew, madam. You have broken it."

Hildegard spoke with icy charm. "Professor Richards invited me here to practice. We have been discussing how musicians often borrow ideas from each other."

"And what is that to me?"

"We have been talking about the differences between being influenced by someone else or making some kind of homage to one's predecessors. We have also been talking about the outright theft of other people's musical ideas and how coded messages can be placed in pieces of music; warnings, for example. Threats."

"What are you implying?"

"I am suggesting that you think about the music that you heard in chapel today."

"I am aware that Professor Richards seems to think my surname is of interest when it comes to German music. That is tiresome in the extreme. But that is not the business that we have in hand. An official complaint, Canon Chambers, will I think be in order."

"We will leave now," Sidney said firmly. "And are sorry to have disturbed the calmness of your evening."

"I would have thought that you had better things to do on this holy night," Professor Todd replied.

"I do. But there are times when darkness needs a little light." Sidney glanced at Hildegard. She said nothing but raised a quick and quizzical eyebrow meant only for him.

After he had seen Hildegard home, Sidney sought out Inspector Keating. They were just a few minutes shy of closing time and this was the ideal opportunity to discuss the current situation and the likelihood that Dr Cade had been murdered.

"I don't know what made you so suspicious in the first place," Keating began. "Do you worry about every death you hear about?"

"I try to pray for every soul that is in my care. I didn't know Adam Cade well, but the circumstances of his death were unusual, and the college was in too much of a hurry to get Charlie Crawford out of the way."

"And you don't think he could have done it?"

"I know it is not impossible for a man to deliberately implicate himself, but I do think that, in his case, it is unlikely."

"Mrs Staunton has expressed concerns about the Professor of Music. She told me about the musical code. Do you think that's showing off, or something more sinister? I imagine both Richards and Cade preferred the company of men to women."

"I believe that may be the case but I don't think that this is a matter of *sexual* jealousy."

"A different kind then?"

"I think it is more to do with professional *envy*; with being outclassed or exposed."

"Which leads us back to Professor Todd."

"We need to get into his rooms."

"I imagine that is straightforward enough. You lot are always in and out of each other's rooms. And there's the rewiring as well."

"Todd has put himself in charge of all that. I imagine that if there is any evidence he will have got rid of it by now. But I'd like to know if the wiring to the bath continued into the rooms above."

"Professor Todd's?"

"Exactly."

"This is a very complicated case, Sidney. A man has been electrocuted in a locked bathroom. The only chance we have of proving Todd's culpability is if he tries to strike again. Do you think he knows we are on to him?"

"I think Mrs Staunton may have let something slip about the music in chapel."

"To Todd himself?"

"I think so."

"You mean that if Todd is the guilty party she has been deliberately putting Professor Richards' life in danger?"

"I don't think she has been doing it on purpose."

"Good God, man, I have warned you about this before. You can't entrap people."

"Mrs Staunton is rather new to the game, I am afraid."

"It's not a game, Sidney. Do you mean to say that Todd might try the same thing on Richards?"

"It is a possibility. That is why I have come. I'd like us to put a watch on Richards and his rooms."

"I have to be invited into the college, you will remember."

"We can act under cover of darkness."

"You want to start on all this tonight?"

"Time is of the essence. I will clear everything with the Master in the morning."

"Are you sure this is wise?"

"Trust me, inspector."

"Sidney, you know I don't like it when you ask me that. It always leads to trouble."

"And sometimes," Sidney answered firmly, "it also leads to a conviction."

He returned directly to the college. Before he could proceed any further, one of the porters told Sidney that the Master wanted to see him in the Lodge. He was agitated that a search had been conducted of another man's rooms with a former employee and a mere guest.

"You do not want to make an enemy of Professor Todd," the Master advised.

"I am aware of the dangers."

"What were you doing in Cade's rooms anyway? This whole business has caused enough trouble. I do wish that you would keep out of the way."

"I was worried about the rewiring."

"That is nonsense. I do not believe you for one minute. It is also no concern of yours. As you know perfectly well, Professor Todd is dealing with all matters electrical."

"I have every confidence in him."

"It is clear that you do not. But I do not think you understand. The cost of the rewiring is likely to be far higher than we originally anticipated."

"Although not as costly as the life of a man," Sidney said almost to himself.

The Master heard his words all too clearly. "What are you implying?"

"I would rather the task of overseeing the rewiring was given to someone else."

"That is quite absurd."

"I would feel a little easier."

"Sidney, this really is none of your business. You are surely not volunteering for the job yourself?"

"Charlie Crawford knew what he was doing. He thinks the wiring has been tampered with. I would like your permission to bring in the police to deal with matters."

"Again?"

"I am afraid so."

"You are fully aware of what you are asking?"

"It is why I have delayed this request for so long."

"Can they be relied on to act with discretion?"

"I hope so."

"That is not very reassuring."

"I am trying to be honest with you, Master. This is a very delicate situation."

Sir Giles poured himself a stiff whisky. "When is Dr Cade's funeral?"

"Wednesday."

"Very well. You can have until then to prove any theory that you might have. I am not at all convinced that Dr Cade met his end through foul means but I will allow you limited freedom to investigate. If you are proved wrong, it will be the last time I concede to such a request. Then we must let the funeral take place in peace."

Hildegard tried not to let her worry about the dangers of the situation show and felt guilty about returning to her piano practice. It was selfish, she thought, to resume normal life, as everyone else in the college seemed to be doing, so quickly after a death.

She was working her way through Beethoven's last piano sonata, No. 32, Opus 111. The first movement, *Allegro con brio ed appassionato*, was in one of Beethoven's most emotional and impassioned keys, C minor, and the underlying melody was the text of Bach's famous cantata *Ein feste Burg ist unser Gott*. It lay behind the main theme, just as her anxiety underpinned each current thought.

Was it really Sidney's duty, she worried, to involve himself in Adam Cade's death? If she were to see him more often, and even perhaps become his wife, would the business of criminal investigation become part of their marriage on a regular basis or would Sidney consider giving it up? She could tell that he enjoyed the thrill of investigation more than he was prepared to let on, and she knew that once he had started it was impossible for him to content himself with the business of being a priest. Faith alone was not enough to quell his curiosity about life.

She turned to the second movement of the sonata, the arietta, and struggled with the trill and the subsequent division of bars into eighty-one parts. She slowed her performance down, first to half tempo and then stopped completely in order to work methodically on each individual bar, going over it again and again, gradually increasing the speed as she became more aware of the technique required.

The third variation, with its dance-like character, felt like playing boogie-woogie and she smiled at the notion of telling Sidney how close she thought it was to ragtime. She even imagined the horror that would spread across the face of Orlando Richards if she expressed the idea that Beethoven was one of the founders of jazz.

As she did so, she wondered how possible it would be to return to England. She couldn't imagine Sidney going to live in Germany and assumed that if they were to spend more time together then she would have to come back to Grantchester: unless, of course, her future husband had some form of promotion. She could tell that he had the intelligence and the talent to rise through the ranks of the Church of England but she worried that his detective work was impeding his career. He had already confessed to the archdeacon's warning. But perhaps the fact that he was involved in all these investigations was an inevitable part of his character; testimony to his willingness to engage in the darker side of the human story? To take away this sphere of activity would make him a lesser man; less involved, less committed, and less like himself.

Her task, she decided, as she took the music at a run once more, was to help him become a more complete priest; and *his* task was to realise what she had to offer and how much more they could achieve if they were together. In the meantime, however, there was a mystery to solve.

Hildegard sighed as she finished the piece and closed the keyboard. She could play so much better, she knew, and there was so much more work to be done.

It was not clear how soon Keating's "watch" on G staircase would begin and Sidney asked Hildegard whether they should warn Orlando Richards that a surveillance operation was about to commence. She reminded Sidney that, despite his undoubted charms, the Professor of Music had still not been ruled out as a suspect. What exactly were his motives in planting coded messages within his compositions? Could their implementation simply be explained as some kind of donnish exhibitionism and was there anything that had been overlooked? Why, for example, had the professor so willingly vacated his rooms to Hildegard, and was there anything significant in the choice of Peterhouse as his place of refuge? Had he either suspected that some foul play was in the air or even been the perpetrator?

Sidney walked across New Court and climbed to the first floor of G staircase. Cade's rooms were closed but the Professor of Music was not only sporting his oak; the inner doorway was ajar. On pushing it open Sidney could see Edward Todd in the far corner of the room in a kneeling position behind Orlando's two-bar fire. He was fiddling with the back and rummaging around by the socket. After Sidney had expressed surprise at finding the dean of the college in another man's rooms he asked what was going on.

"This is my fire. I am collecting it. Professor Richards has failed to return it to me."

"Then why do you not simply unplug it?"

"That is what I was doing."

"I don't think you need a screwdriver to do that." Sidney had noticed the thin metal object in his hands. "What are you doing in his rooms in any case?"

"I might ask the same question of you."

199

"Professor Richards has invited me in for a drink. He will be along shortly," Sidney lied.

"I wanted to get my fire back."

"How did you know Professor Richards had it?"

"The porters asked me. It was meant as a temporary measure. It was an act of goodwill on my part, if you must know. Not that this is any of your business."

"And are you aware of Professor Richards's routine?"

"What do you mean?"

"You know that he plunges his hands into warm water before playing?"

"No."

"And you are aware of the dangerous combination between water and electricity?"

"Of course."

"Then you will not mind if I examine the plug that is affixed to his fire."

"Why would you want to do that?"

"Because I believe you have hard-wired the fire to the mains. A man touching it with damp hands would receive a severe, possibly fatal, electric shock."

"That is nonsense."

"There is a basin in the room behind you. Perhaps you would like to wash your hands and touch the fire yourself."

"Don't be absurd."

"Touch it."

"I will not."

"Touch it."

"For God's sake."

Edward Todd made a quick, and potentially fatal, decision. He advanced with the screwdriver in his hands, the metal tip raised as a weapon. Sidney took a step back and realised that he was either going to have to dodge his assailant's approach, enter into some kind of fight, or retreat through the door as quickly as he could.

Todd blocked off the exit. "None of this is any of your business."

"Everything is my business."

"You are only making matters worse, Canon Chambers."

Sidney wanted to say that the reverse was the case but knew that such a remark would only place him in further danger. "Put the screwdriver down."

"I need it. It is about to come in very useful."

Sidney played for time. "Why have you done all this, Todd?"

"I haven't done anything."

"You killed Cade."

"I did nothing of the kind. It was a heart attack."

"No," Sidney replied. "It was an electric shock."

"I don't know how you've come to that conclusion. By what logic . . ."

"You know far more about wiring and are more practical than you have been prepared to let on. I see that . . ."

"Then I'm going to make sure you don't see anything else."

Todd lunged forward. Sidney picked up a chair and threw it in his way. He was going to have to get to the

201

door as soon as he could. "This is not going to help, Todd."

"No one has ever helped me. I have to do everything myself."

"That's not strictly true, though, is it?"

Todd stopped for a moment. He was still holding the screw-driver. "What do you mean?"

"You used some of Cade's work in your thesis. He certainly helped you, not that he was aware that he was doing so."

"I'm not admitting to that kind of nonsense."

"He was about to accuse you of plagiary, wasn't he?"

"That is a lie."

"No, Todd. It's why you killed him."

"No one can prove that."

"When you explained your theory . . ."

"I don't expect a man like you to understand any of this. You are a troublesome priest and you are out of your depth."

Sidney was still far from the door and wondering how on earth he was going to attempt an escape when it opened suddenly, a whistle sounded and Inspector Keating came into the room with two police officers.

"How dare you?" Todd shouted before he was brought to the ground. "You can't interfere in college life like this."

He was disarmed and handcuffed. "You have no authority here," he complained.

Inspector Keating was having none of it. "Professor E.D.F. Todd, I am arresting you for the murder of Dr Adam Cade and for the attempted murder of Professor

Orlando Richards and Canon Sidney Chambers. You do not need to say anything now, but anything that you do say . . ."

Hildegard did not hear the news of the night's events from Sidney but during a surprise visit to her lodgings by the Master of Corpus. He had come to explain the situation in person to Charlie Crawford, to apologise for all that had happened, and to offer him his job back.

"That's a relief, I must say," Charlie began. "I have a reputation, as well you know. That man was trying to ruin me."

"I think he was trying to protect himself, Charlie."

"With no thought for the working man."

Rather than accept a swift return to full employment, Charlie now used the opportunity to negotiate a rise in salary and the full payment of all the overtime that he considered due.

"I must say," the Master had replied, "I think perhaps they could do with some of your negotiating skills in the Foreign Office."

"I just want to be paid for the work that's done."

"At least in your line of business it is easier to establish what is being done and what is not. Within academia it is so much harder to tell whether anyone is being productive or not."

"That's why they pay you more."

"I'm not sure they do, Crawford," the Master added wistfully. "If you divided a fellow's annual salary by the number of hours he works then he's probably paid less than a plumber."

"I promise that I won't charge you for this hour, Master."

"Then," Sir Giles observed tartly, "I won't charge you for my time either."

After he had left, an appalled Grace Wardell tackled her brother, as she laid the table for their Saturday tea. "That took some nerve," she said.

"You have to let them know where you stand. The fellows like a bit of banter anyway. Wouldn't you agree, Mrs Staunton?"

"I am not sure what you mean by 'banter'?"

"Quick chat, having a laugh."

Mrs Wardell poured out the tea. "It's just being cheeky, if you ask me."

Her brother offered Hildegard an explanation. "You have to be English to understand it. It's not something you'd find on the Continent, I imagine."

Grace Wardell was fussing. "I don't know how you can be so sure about that. Do sit down, Mrs Staunton."

Hildegard was thinking about Dr Cade's murder and how differently her stay had been to anything that she had been expecting. Tomorrow would be Easter Day and lunch with Sidney and they had hardly had a moment alone together.

Her landlady put the food on the table. "Sausages in batter," she announced. "You know we have a special phrase for this dish, Hildegard?"

"Yes, I think I know it. And in another house in Cambridge it would not be 'toad in the hole' but 'Todd' in the hole."

"Very good," said Charlie. "I see you have a sense of humour after all."

"Not really," Hildegard smiled. "After all that has happened, I am only just beginning to put my toe in the water."

"Now that," Charlie Crawford laughed, "is what I call banter."

Earlier that afternoon, Sidney had looked in on Keating in the police station in St Andrew's Street. He wanted to discover if Professor Todd had made a full confession and if his suspicion as to the motivation of the murderer had proved correct. Todd had at first refused to answer any questions, quoting the ancient charter of 1231 given by King Henry III that awarded the university the right to discipline its own members, *ius non trahi extra*, and expressing a haughty disdain for the workings of the police.

"But of course the fellows always think they are immune from the real world. The only way to fight back is to get them on their own terms."

"And how do you do that?"

"We referred to the statutes and ordinances of the university itself."

"I didn't know you had a copy."

"You'd be surprised what we have here, Sidney." Keating opened a large volume on his desk and began to quote from it: "'No member of the university shall intentionally or recklessly disrupt or impede or attempt to disrupt or impede the activities and functions of the university, or any part thereof, or of any college.' I think electrocution counts as disruption, don't you? However, we still haven't got to the real reason why he did it."

"Adam Cade was threatening to expose Edward Todd as a plagiarist."

"Some kind of blackmail, you mean? Is plagiarism so dangerous that a man would want to murder to prevent it being known?"

"Creative theft, which is, I think, the more polite way of explaining it, happens all the time with the flow of ideas. Musicians and writers are always stealing from each other. Hildegard has been telling me how Beethoven's last sonata contains a hidden theme from Bach; and how, in turn, Chopin's revolutionary étude takes up the theme and Prokofiev's second symphony follows its structure. Eliot's *The Waste Land* is full of quotations and borrowed ideas. But only the truly creative person can get away with this. They have to have enough originality to acknowledge their sources. Those who do not are on shakier ground, and my friend Professor Meldrum assures me that there is no more precarious territory than mathematical and scientific research. Professor Todd's forthcoming volume on percolation theory owed much to the work of his research fellow and yet this is not acknowledged, even in the publisher's proofs. Cade had got hold of a copy and threatened to expose Todd and ruin his reputation."

"Who told you this?"

"Professor Meldrum. He didn't have much time for either of them."

"Isn't that usually the case with those fellows?"

"Alas, it is so."

Keating was unimpressed. "We'd have a fine police force if none of us talked to each other. So I take it that Adam Cade kicked up a fuss and Edward Todd recognised that he needed silencing. But surely he could either have acknowledged Cade's work or talked his way out of it?"

"In this university once the accusation of plagiarism is made it is hard to brush it aside. If word had got out then Edward Todd would have been forced to resign and give up his post as dean of the college. His reputation would have been in ruins. He lived for nothing else."

"A lesson to us all. It's just as well you have more than one string to your bow, Sidney. However, I'm not sure Mrs Staunton needed such a vivid reminder of your double life. How is she, by the way? She seems a very fine woman."

"I've no doubt about that."

"Good. For a man of doubts you sound surprisingly certain. I have noted that we haven't seen very much of Miss Kendall of late."

"She is coming for Easter."

"At the same time that Mrs Staunton is here? Isn't that a bit risky?"

"I think that it's about time she met Hildegard."

"I would have thought that it was better to keep them apart."

"I'd like to see what they make of one another."

"You can't play women off against each other like that."

"That is not my intention."

"Then what *is* your intention?"

"I think I want Amanda's approval. Her blessing, as it were . . ."

"You have chosen Hildegard above her."

"Amanda has always said that I must approve of the man she marries. It seems fair that I should offer her the same right of veto."

"If I was Mrs Staunton, I wouldn't be too pleased about that. It shows a lack of confidence. You would be better off doing the deed and seeking the approval afterwards."

"It's a bit late for that. Amanda's coming for lunch."

"Are you going out somewhere? The Blue Boar, perhaps?"

"No, I think Hildegard is doing the cooking. We're having roast lamb and some kind of German pudding. There may even be simnel cake."

"So the whole thing will seem a *fait accompli*. Do you want that?"

"I'm not sure what I want."

"Well, Sidney, you had better make up your mind, or you'll end up losing both of them."

On Easter Day, Orlando Richards brought a group of musicians from the college to perform Bach's great cantata *Christ lag in Todesbanden* with the choir of Grantchester church. It was his way, he explained, of apologising for the coded compositions that had so nearly led to a disastrous misunderstanding.

Just before the service began, Leonard told Hildegard that the parishioner who had been due to give the first reading had been struck down with influenza and he asked her, as a favour, to read instead. It was only after she had begun to read the passage from the Song of Solomon that she realised that the parishioner in question may never have been asked in the first place.

"I will rise now and go about the city, in the streets and in the broad ways; I will seek him whom my soul loveth," she began. She was wearing a narrow streamlined chemise in navy blue with a matching cardigan jacket.

Hildegard looked out at the congregation and cast an anxious glance at Leonard. He really had a nerve asking her to do this: "I sought him, but I found him not. The watchmen that go about the city found me; to whom I said, 'Saw ye him whom my soul loveth?'"

Sidney was moved by the clarity of her speech, and the simple sensitivity of her interpretation. When he preached his sermon he tried not to let nerves get the better of him, but found himself being more emotional than he might normally have been. It had been an upsetting few days but now, on Easter Day itself, he had to concentrate on the core of his faith.

"Christ is risen!" he pronounced and looked down from the pulpit to see Hildegard staring straight ahead at the clean white altar with its golden Alleluia and replying: "He is risen indeed."

The congregation stood to say the Creed, and Sidney led the congregational prayers towards communion.

After Hildegard had taken both bread and wine, she returned to her seat and sat in contemplation. As she did so, she listened to the choir sing a special unaccompanied anthem. It was dedicated to the fire of the Holy Spirit, the life-force of creation, the fountain of holiness and the robe of hope.

At its end, Orlando Richards turned to Hildegard and gave her a little nod. She smiled. She had recognised the piece almost as soon as it had started: *O ignis spiritus*, by her namesake, Hildegard of Bingen.

Amanda was expected for Sunday lunch and was driving up from London in her MG.

Leonard had shopped for the groceries, receiving a special clerical discount both on the lamb from the butcher's and on the cabbage and potatoes from the grocer. He told Sidney that they should contemplate shopping more often. It was a good, quick way of meeting the parishioners and a demonstration that they were at one with their people rather than closeted in their studies. Sidney was somewhat unwilling to take lessons in pastoral care from his curate but let the matter pass. He had more important things to think about, not least the first meeting between his two greatest female friends.

"She is a very fine woman," Leonard had told Hildegard, as he accompanied her back to the vicarage, "but she can be somewhat eccentric."

"Sidney has told me about her but he is very anxious about our meeting."

"With good reason," Leonard replied as he held open the front door. "Amanda can be loud and judgemental but, of the two of you, I think she will be the more nervous. Remember, you are in the driving seat."

"But I don't know where we are going . . ." Hildegard smiled.

"I shouldn't worry too much about that. Let me make you a cup of tea. As soon as Miss Kendall gets here we will be on to the Easter champagne."

"Is that a tradition?"

"It has become one. Miss Kendall believes in extravagant gifts. She always thinks we need cheering up."

"And do you?" Hildegard asked.

"Well," Leonard replied gallantly, "the Lenten abstinence does make Sidney rather grumpy. He says so himself. Of course, now that you are here he has perked up considerably. But life does have a way of creating nasty surprises."

The door burst open and Amanda walked into the room. "I hope that I do not count as one of them, then." She had her hair swept back and she wore a bright-red tailored coat that demanded attention. "You must be Mrs Staunton . . ."

"Hildegard, please . . ."

"Of course. Leonard, will you do the honours? I'm too hot already." Amanda put down her handbag and began to shrug off her coat. "How have you found your return to Grantchester?" she asked. "Leonard, be careful. Put it on a hanger. Don't leave it over a chair like you normally do. I've brought the champagne. We must have some straight away."

"I was making some tea . . ." Leonard replied.

"Good heavens, Leonard, what is wrong with you? It is already after midday. Where is Sidney? I do hope he's delayed so that Hildegard and I can get to know each other a little. Shall we sit down?"

"Of course," said Hildegard. "Although I must also see to the lunch."

"Isn't Mrs Maguire to hand?"

"I said I would cook."

"Are the men making you slave away already? I thought you were a guest?"

"Leonard is in charge but I am helping. I have noticed that both men sometimes forget what they are doing."

"Have you spotted that already?" Amanda smiled conspiratorially. "They can't concentrate on anything at all. They like to think they have their mind on 'higher things' but most of the time they are wondering who has murdered whom. I do hope you have been spared any of that nonsense. Leonard: will you hurry up with the champagne? I am gasping." Amanda's nervousness in meeting Hildegard was shown in her refusal to maintain silence. "It must be very hard for you to come back here, I would have thought?"

"I have memories that are difficult, yes."

"Can you imagine living here again?"

Sidney entered the room and threw his cloak on to a chair. "That is a very leading question, Amanda."

"I think it's an important one. You may kiss me."

Sidney obliged. "Is there any chance of a cup of tea, do you think?"

212

"Oh, we are well past tea," Amanda continued. "The champagne is on its way. But I am keen to hear Hildegard's answer."

Hildegard put her hands on to her knees. "I am not so sure. We have not talked about this. It depends on the circumstances. I think I would be uneasy."

There was a pop from the kitchen and Leonard emerged with a tray and four glasses of champagne. "You have your work in Germany."

"I have heard you teach the piano?" Amanda checked.

"Do you play yourself?"

"I play the clarinet rather badly. I think it would be all right for jazz, but not Mozart."

"You don't like jazz?" Hildegard asked.

"I can't stand it, I am afraid."

Leonard handed round the drinks, and the four companions wished each other a Happy Easter before Sidney tried to explain. "Amanda has yet to be convinced of its wonders."

"There is nothing wondrous about it as far as I can see."

Hildegard smiled. "And there is with Mozart."

"I think the Clarinet Concerto is one of the finest pieces of music ever written," Amanda pronounced.

Hildegard turned to Sidney. "You know they say that when the angels are on duty they play Bach, but in their time off they play Mozart. Not jazz, I am sorry."

"That's the devil's music," Amanda continued, "as I believe 'jazzers' call it."

"I think you'll find that's the blues," Sidney replied before enquiring, "Have we put the roast potatoes on?"

"Oh, Sidney," Amanda answered. "You look annoyed. Are you put out that we are getting along?"

"I wasn't expecting to be teased."

Hildegard was surprised by this little streak of humourlessness. "Then you shouldn't have asked us to come at the same time."

"I wanted you to like each other."

"We do," they said in unison.

"I just want a quiet life, really," said Sidney.

Hildegard was quick to answer. "Oh I don't think you want that at all. You would be very bored."

"And in any case," Amanda continued, "we are not going to give you one. From now on you'll have to deal with both of us."

Leonard returned to the kitchen to check on the lunch. "Two for the price of one," he smiled. Sidney followed.

"Have you known him for a long time?" Hildegard asked Amanda.

"Technically, yes, but it's only recently we've become chums."

"Chums?" Hildegard asked. "I am not sure I understand that word."

"Special friends. I don't know if there is a German word for it?"

"'Vertraut' perhaps. It is something more than 'Freund' but not too much more."

"I never think it's too helpful to try and define things," Amanda replied. "There are so many different

214

terms for friendship. Do you think there are more in German than there are in English?"

Hildegard thought for a moment. "'*Vertrauter*' is a trusted friend. '*Wegbegleiter*' is someone who shares your path in life. '*Verbündeter*' is someone you feel joined to."

"That just about covers it, I would have thought."

"Then there is a meeting of minds — '*Geistesgeschwister*' — or even of souls, as in '*Seelenfreund*'. We like to be precise in Germany. We want to know how things stand. Tell me, do you have a boyfriend?"

Amanda was momentarily taken aback by Hildegard's direct tone. "I have my admirers. I don't think that any of them count as 'boyfriends'. None of them quite live up to Sidney, of course. They all fall short when I compare them to him."

Their host overheard this remark on returning to the room. He had timed it so conveniently that Hildegard imagined he might have been listening at the door. "I am sure that is true; but we must not flatter him too much."

"I rather enjoy teasing him," Amanda smiled. "And in any case, vanity is more of a problem for him than embarrassment. You know he has his admirers too?"

Sidney tried to put a stop to the conversation. "Come, come, Amanda. Wouldn't it be better if we got on with the lunch?"

Amanda would not be silenced. "I've seen those women helping out at the church fête. They've all got names like Veronica and Margaret. Then there's Agatha

Redmond. She provided Sidney with his Labrador. She gets herself into quite a tizz whenever she sees him. In fact I wouldn't be surprised if even Mrs Maguire was secretly in love with him."

"Mrs Maguire?" said Sidney. "Don't be ridiculous."

Leonard Graham returned with a tea towel over his arm. "I think that is perfectly plausible."

"Don't you start . . ."

"It's not impossible," said Hildegard.

"Mrs Maguire is not in love with me," Sidney snapped. There was a pause, and a silence which he tried to fill by standing up. He thought of walking out but realised that such an action would appear childish. Then he sat down again. "Is there any more champagne?" he asked.

"The lady does protest too much, methinks," Leonard added as he shared out the rest of the drinks.

"Honestly, will you all stop it?" Sidney asked. "It's not funny."

"Does anyone ever call you Hildy?" Leonard asked, consciously changing the subject.

"I don't think so," Hildegard replied. "But I have no objection if you'd like to call me by that name."

"There's a Hildy Johnson in the film *His Girl Friday*. Do you know it?" Leonard asked.

"Is that the one based on *The Front Page* with Rosalind Russell?" said Amanda.

"It is," Hildegard stood up. "But I should check on the lunch." She put a hand on Sidney's shoulder. "I am 'His Girl Sunday'."

216

"That would be kind," Sidney replied, rather too brusquely.

Amanda noticed Hildegard's proprietary gesture and tried not to mind. "I suppose I could always content myself by being 'His Girl Saturday'."

Leonard could not resist continuing. "Which would leave Mrs Maguire free to be 'His Girl Monday to Friday'."

"Will you all please stop going on about Mrs Maguire?" Sidney said, as quietly and as firmly as he could, only to find himself met by communal laughter and an outright refusal to obey him. He couldn't decide what he would have to do to regain his authority, or if he had lost his sense of humour altogether.

After lunch they took a walk down to the river while Dickens leapt around them. Sidney let Amanda and Hildegard talk to each other and discussed a few impending matters with his curate who was keener to return to his studies of Dostoevsky than concentrate on his parish duties. It was odd that both men had such strong outside interests, a peculiarity that was enhanced by a fortuitous meeting with Inspector Keating's family who were enjoying a similar constitutional.

The three young Keating girls were delighted to play with Dickens, throwing him sticks and chasing after him, while Cathy Keating reflected that it was her husband's first day off in months.

"He's always telling me that he never has days off," Sidney replied.

"I think you both like working too much to do anything else. You're both in love with your jobs."

"I wouldn't put it as strongly as that."

"Well, Canon Chambers, that may be true in your case, since you seem to want to do my husband's job as well as your own."

"Believe me, Mrs Keating . . ."

"Cathy . . ."

"I do not seek these things out."

"You enjoy it, though."

"As a matter of fact I do not. I wish people would lead better lives and did not resort to violence and murder in order to pursue their objectives, but if they insist on so doing then I will do everything in my power to help your husband."

Hildegard put her arm through Sidney's. Amanda noticed. "He can't help himself. He is what he is."

"And that's a good man," said Keating.

"I'm not so sure about that either," Sidney replied, immediately realising that, on this day of days, he was as reluctant to be praised as he was to be teased.

Amanda drove back to London on the Sunday evening, having kissed Hildegard goodbye and told her how much she had enjoyed meeting her. Sidney found that her manners had been impeccable, and was delighted that his two closest friends seemed to get on so well.

"She has sparkle," Hildegard told him afterwards. "And she is cleverer than people think she is. Is that deliberate?"

"I'm not sure. Amanda doesn't put on any airs and graces."

"Perhaps, because she is privileged, people think that she does not need to work."

"She takes her job very seriously, I do know that," Sidney replied.

"More seriously than she takes you?"

"She thinks I need to be teased."

"And do you?"

"I'd rather be loved."

Hildegard smiled. "I think you have to earn that, Sidney. It, too, requires hard work."

The couple spent Easter Monday and Tuesday together. They walked in the Botanical Gardens, went to a concert in one of the college chapels and visited the Fitzwilliam Museum.

Sometimes, in front of a painting, Hildegard stood almost too close to Sidney, and he liked it. She was five or six inches smaller than him and he recalled once, when she had said goodbye to him, that she had stood on a higher step so that they were almost level and she had looked him straight in the eye before kissing him on each cheek. He remembered the first time they had sat together on the sofa, when he had had to tell her that they had discovered who had killed her husband, and how natural it had felt for them to be so intimate, even in the silences. He had never experienced the freedom to say nothing at all before.

"When will I see you next?" he asked as they made their farewells at the railway station.

"You could come in the summer," Hildegard replied, "and see more of the Rhine. We have less murder in Germany. It is safer."

"I don't know what it is about Cambridge."

"It is enclosed, so the rivalry is greater."

"You would have thought that they all would have better things to think about. Wasn't it Friedrich Richter who said 'a scholar knows no boredom'? German of course."

Hildegard smiled. "Are you ever bored, Sidney? I sometimes worry that I am not enough for you. You need these distractions."

"I do not think I need them exactly, but they certainly put me on my mettle."

"As long as you do not get too many shocks."

"I'm sorry?"

"I think that was another joke. Mettle and metal. I think you would say it was feeble."

"Nothing about you is feeble, Hildegard."

"Perhaps you will start to make jokes in German."

"I think I am quite a long way from that. Herr Gruner is very concerned that I should master the basics. I am still very much a beginner."

The train pulled into the station and its noise drowned out Hildegard's quiet observation. "And perhaps not only in German."

She could not comprehend why a man who was so demonstrably adept at solving crime and understanding human character could be so dilatory with the love that was right in front of him. When, she wondered, would Sidney do anything about it?

The Hat Trick

It was a saturday in mid May, and Sidney had been prevailed upon to umpire a cricket match between Grantchester and Whittlesford at Fenners. The rain looked as if it was going to hold off, the wicket was good, and by mid morning an expectant crowd of picnickers had begun to gather at one of the most idyllic grounds in the country.

In truth, Sidney was slightly irritated that he had been invited simply to umpire. In another life he might well have been a professional cricketer. At the age of eleven he had been the first boy in his year to get his colours. Then, at public school, he had scored a momentous seventy-eight runs in a tight-fought victory over Wellington. At thirteen his parents had taken him to see Bradman bat on this very ground only to see him bowled for a duck by J.G.W. Davies, misreading a straight one from the renowned off-spinner. Sidney had even played at Cambridge himself, batting at five for Corpus, hoping that he might take part in the annual Varsity Match. But then the war had come.

He missed playing cricket. He bought his copy of Wisden each year, listened to the Test matches on the wireless, and whenever he passed a match on a village green he would always stop to watch an over. The game created a parallel world, Sidney thought. It was drama; it was excitement; it was a metaphor for the vicissitudes of life.

It was also quintessentially English: democratic (there were teams with all levels of ability), communal (the cricket "square" was often at the centre of the village green), and convivial (the game was full of eccentric characters.) It was the representation of a nation's cuisine, with its milky tea, cucumber sandwiches, Victoria sponge and lashings of beer. It was also beautiful to watch, with fifteen men, dressed in white and moving on green, creating geometrical patterns that looked as if they had been choreographed by a divine choreographer.

As Sidney approached the ground he could feel both the humidity and a touch of moisture in the air. It was definitely a day on which to bowl first. There was enough to give the seamers something to work with and, provided Grantchester won the toss and had a couple of men who knew how to move the ball about a bit, there was a good chance of early wickets.

Sidney believed that there was a science to it all. A bowler who was able to read the prevailing conditions, and work with the moisture in the air, could disguise the flight of the ball or make it swing so that even a degree in physics might prove beneficial. A batsman facing such a bowler would need an anatomical knowledge of the human hand, recognising the different ways in which the fingers could grip a ball and the wrist could spin out any number of trajectories. It was a world in which the application of the scientist met the mind of the psychologist. A batsman who inspected the wicket in front of him, anticipating how it would wear and crack over time, would be better prepared to confront the wiles of a bowler who had undertaken a similar study of that very same patch of grass. And then, at the end of every summer, no matter how brown the surface or how weathered the pitch, there was a need to understand botany and geology as each twenty-two yards of hallowed turf rested over the winter before renewing itself each spring in order to offer another season of possibility.

Sidney felt at home at Fenners. The ground was graced with a handsome pavilion, a separate wooden scoreboard and a couple of nets. Soon the air was filled with the familiar sounds of bags being thrown down, bats being knocked up and cricket studs scraping on the concrete flooring. He had a brief and poignant memory of his schooldays: the smell of freshly mown grass, the sight of the roller on the wicket, the sound of the scoreboard ticking over; a day filled with promise.

He asked the two captains to step out into the middle and tossed up his half-crown. The opposition captain called out "Heads" correctly and opted to field. This was a man who wanted to take advantage of the conditions, capture a few early wickets, and then know how many runs his team would have to chase if they were to win the game. Sidney looked across to see two fast bowlers loosening up in the nets. They looked formidable.

His mood lowered when he saw two of the Grantchester wives arriving with picnic hampers. As the home team took to the field the women smiled and waved, holding up Thermos flasks, sandwiches wrapped in greaseproof paper, and the all-important bottles of beer. How he wished Hildegard could be here, sitting on a rug by the boundary, with her legs stretched elegantly to one side and a wicker basket in front of her.

"Come on, Sidney, let's get out in the middle. You must be dreaming."

It was Roger Wilson, the second umpire and one of Inspector Keating's Special Constables, a man whom Sidney knew he should like but was unable to do so because of his relentless attempts to look busy when he was not.

Grantchester began badly, losing both openers to some frisky bowling by Horatio Walsh that provoked considerable muttering back in the pavilion. Was it fair, their captain Andrew Redmond wondered, that a West Indian should be able to turn out for Whittlesford? Should there be eligibility requirements, for example, stating that a person must have lived in a village for at least five years before being allowed to play for them? And what was a West Indian doing in Whittlesford anyway? Sidney had to point out that since Horatio had been allowed into the country, and probably on a colonial passport, he had every right to play for whatever team he chose. Furthermore, Grantchester could hardly complain when they had, in their Indian bowler Zafar Ali, one of the most devastating leg-spinners in the game.

Sidney found the process of umpiring more tiring than he had anticipated. He had to remember to count the number of balls for each over correctly, moving six pebbles from one pocket to another. He had to check the bowlers' footmarks for no-balls, judge whether the numerous leg-before-wicket appeals were correct, assess whether catches were thin edges off the bat or if they had come off the pad, and anticipate what might happen next. It was exactly like being a detective, he decided. Nothing should pass him by.

After twenty minutes, Grantchester were 8 for 2 and Sidney had already given Geoffrey Thomas, the local grocer and number four batsman, the benefit of the doubt in an extremely close LBW decision. A few runs later, and without a single boundary to trouble the scorer, Grantchester were in deep trouble at 15 for 3. They needed the incoming batsman, Derek Jarvis, to steady the ship and find his form when he joined his captain at the crease.

Sidney had not expected the coroner to be such a good judge of line and length but he could clearly pick which ball to play and which to leave alone. Extraordinary, Sidney thought, how cricket revealed character so clearly; the patient and the impatient, the methodical and the careless, the brave and the fearful.

He was also reminded of the nature of timing. Some players were almost effortless in their stroke-play, letting the ball come on to the bat and guiding their shots with a minimum amount of back-lift, while others took wild swings and hoped to God they made a connection. Once again, Sidney marvelled at the different ways in which people could strike a ball.

After six overs, two maidens and figures of 3 for 15, Horatio Walsh was given a rest. The less troublesome medium pace of the Whittlesford undertaker replaced him, and soon both Derek Jarvis and Andrew Redmond were able to pile on the runs. They formed an easy, confident partnership, and Sidney was delighted when the coroner reached his fifty after little more than an hour at the crease.

He was impressed by his application. A man couldn't arrive on a pitch and expect to play well. There had to be preparation. Of course there were events within a game that one could not necessarily anticipate, and Dame Fortune would always play her part, but Sidney believed that, over a sustained passage of time, a man could make his own luck. The cricketing averages did not lie, and although there could be magical days when all the predictions were confounded, it was important to study the statistics and take a long view. As the old adage had it: a man's form could be temporary; class was permanent.

Derek Jarvis had made a chanceless fifty but his innings was ended, as was so often the case after a milestone had been reached, by a lapse of concentration. After edging the ball down to third man, he looked behind and called for a run, only to be sent back by his captain with a shouted "NO!" It was Andrew Redmond's call, and Derek Jarvis was forced to turn round when he was already halfway down the wicket. A swift and accurate throw back to the keeper made sure that he was unable to make his ground and he was soon back in the pavilion. From a confident position of 140 for 3, Grantchester slumped. At half past three Andrew Redmond flashed at a ball that was short of a length and was caught at point. Grantchester had reached 188 for 8 and the last two wickets fell in quick succession. The innings ended when Zafar Ali, their Indian spinner, was out for a duck, his middle stump ripped clean out of the ground by a snorter from Walsh.

Tea followed, and Sidney was pleased to see that Mrs Maguire had contributed two of her lardy cakes and was on hand to dispense the meat-paste sandwiches. Rosie Thomas, the grocer's wife, doled out the tea from a large urn, while her daughter Annie offered homemade lemonade to the sweatier players after their exertions in the field.

It was an agreeable occasion, further enhanced by an impromptu visit from Leonard Graham, who had brought Dickens out for a walk and who required a quick consultation about parish matters. (One of the bellringers had fallen from a ladder and required a home visit; the churchwarden had forgotten to mow the verges at the front of the graveyard.) As the two men began their "quiet word", Mrs Maguire intervened.

"I hope you'll keep that ruddy dog away from the food. You know what he's like."

"I am sure he won't do any harm, Mrs Maguire."

"Harm?" their housekeeper replied. "That's his middle name."

As soon as her back was turned, Zafar Ali began feeding Dickens an egg sandwich.

"Don't encourage him!" she shouted but Sidney's dog was already sniffing around the lardy cakes and sidling up to any player who showed the slightest encouragement, giving them his most mournful "nobody ever feeds me" look. It was extraordinary, Sidney recognised, how successful the Labrador's patient and determined appeal could be. By the time he had finished he must have sampled everything the tea ladies had to offer.

Now it was Whittlesford's turn to bat, and the two Redmond brothers, Andrew and Harding, opened the bowling. It was quite a family affair, Sidney noticed, since their sister Rosie was in charge of the catering, and her husband Geoffrey was fielding at deep mid-wicket. During the tea interval, Sidney also spotted that Rosie's daughter Annie was on very friendly terms with Zafar Ali, a situation that appeared to create tension within the family. He only hoped that what looked like a burgeoning romance would not be cut short by prejudice.

Whittlesford made a confident start, reaching thirty without loss and, after watching their assured opening pair, Sidney fully expected them to win the game. However, nothing in cricket was ever predictable. Andrew Redmond took a few quick wickets, the game began to ebb and flow, and Whittlesford reached their hundred. Zafar Ali came on for some trademark leg-spin, licking his fingers before gripping the ball and flipping it out of the back of his hand, deceiving

Whittlesford's captain with a well-disguised googly that dislodged his leg bail, and soon the game was more evenly poised. At 160 for 6, the visitors began to take back the initiative but Grantchester were not out of it yet. A loud shout of "CATCH IT" woke Sidney from a momentary loss of concentration, as the Whittlesford batsman skied a slog-shot to deep mid-wicket. Geoffrey Thomas ran to a position underneath it, steadied his stance as it reached the top of its trajectory, cupped his hands in expectation . . . and dropped it.

Sidney was reminded how quickly the game could change. He couldn't switch off, even for a second, because, in cricket, no matter how long the game felt or how dull the passage of play, a chance could come off every ball. The fielder had to wait for the moment: expecting it, trusting that it would come eventually, and then seize it. So much depended on whether that chance was taken or dropped, and those quick, unpredictable flashes of action could influence the outcome of the whole match. It was a game that, like many a crime, balanced patience with opportunity.

The Whittlesford captain edged a streaky four through the slips off the fast bowling of Gary Bell, and then cut for two. Whittlesford required four more runs to win with three wickets in hand. They were coasting. At the end of the over, Sidney walked over from short-leg and took his position at the Gresham Road end. He then checked the six pebbles in his right pocket, ready to transfer them, a ball at a time, to its opposite side.

The sun was lower, and shadows had begun to lengthen over the boundary. This would be the last over. Andrew Redmond asked for the ball, inspected it, rubbed it against his thigh and threw it to his spin bowler.

Grantchester's only hope lay in the fact that Whittlesford's star opening batsman, who had scored seventy-three runs, was stranded at the opposite end, and Zafar was bowling to their number nine. The batsman took a swing at the first delivery and missed it completely. He was determined to win the game in style, and his partner walked down the pitch to urge patience. A quick single was all that was required and the better player would be on strike.

Andrew Redmond was fielding at mid on and the players threw him the ball between each delivery. He had a little routine going now, inspecting the ball, rubbing it on his cricket whites, and then handing it to the bowler. The Whittlesford number nine defended the second delivery of the over with a simple prod to short extra cover, but there was no run. Zafar's third ball offered plenty of temptation in the flight, and with a rush of blood to the head, the Whittlesford man skipped down the pitch to meet it, was deceived by the spin, missed the ball entirely and was well out of his crease when stumped by the wicket keeper.

The new batsman arrived and took guard. Andrew Redmond rubbed the ball on his thigh once more before throwing it to Zafar, who licked his fingers before applying them to the seam of the ball. He walked to the end of his short run, turned, and

THE HAT TRICK

delivered a quicker ball to the batsman's feet which span sharply through the gap between bat and pad and lifted the bail of the off-stump.

Jubilation! Zafar was on a hat trick, and, with only one wicket remaining, Grantchester had more than a chance of victory. Whittlesford needed four runs to win and there were two balls left. The new man at the crease was Horatio Walsh, the West Indian fast bowler. Because he was a left-handed bat, Sidney wondered whether Zafar might opt to bowl round the wicket but the canny Indian was more concerned with moving the position of his fielders.

Zafar smiled as he contemplated a delivery that might bamboozle Horatio Walsh. The two men were, perhaps, amused at the irony of the situation, complicit foreigners able to decide the fortunes of an English village cricket match between them: it was four runs on one side and a single wicket on the other.

If their roles had been reversed Zafar knew that Horatio would bowl fast and straight as he had done in the first innings, an in-swinging yorker straight to the feet. Zafar was a spinner, but that meant that he probably had a few more tricks up his sleeve. Would he bowl a straight leg-spinner and perhaps get an LBW? Or would he try a googly, anticipating Horatio's expectation of a leg-spinning ball and delivering the exact opposite, hoping for a little nick that would go through to the keeper or edge to a fielder in close? The bowler needed to guess how well his opponent could read the grip in his hand or spot the flick of his wrist. Would Horatio dance down the pitch and attempt to

231

meet the ball before it span; or would he stay in his crease and watch it carefully, defending with a straight bat? Zafar needed to decide whether Horatio was going to be adventurous or cautious. If cautious, then he would give the delivery plenty of air in the flight; if adventurous, he would give the ball more zip, expecting it to fizz off the wicket.

Andrew Redmond adjusted the field, adding a silly point and a short leg to the two slips and the wicket keeper. There were five men in close-catching positions, another at short extra cover, with the remaining fielders stationed at mid off, mid on, long leg and on the mid-wicket boundary. All the spectators were standing either directly outside the pavilion or at the edge of the ropes. This was Zafar's chance to make local history. He could, perhaps, be the first Indian bowler to take a hat trick in England.

Sidney had raised his arm out to the left to hold up the game while fielders moved into their new positions. Andrew Redmond rubbed the ball against the side of his trousers one last time before handing it to his bowler.

Horatio Walsh walked down the pitch, gave it a little prod, smiled at Zafar Ali, and took guard. Sidney dropped his arm.

Zafar turned his back to the batsman, licked his fingers, and assumed his grip on the ball, shielding his right hand with his left so that no one could see the delivery he had in mind.

He turned. He looked the batsman in the eye. Then he ran.

He took seven steps.

He placed his left foot firmly on the ground, raised his right arm, and bowled. The ball span out of the back of his hand and into the air. It hovered in the trajectory, as if buoyed up by some invisible force, and then pitched on off-stump. The ball turned in towards the batsman. Horatio rocked on to the back foot and defended his off stump with a straight bat. But the ball swept past, keeping low off the seam, and hit him firmly on the right pad. Although his foot was quite far forward, it was dead in line with leg stump. There was the slightest of pauses. Zafar turned to Sidney and enquired: "How was that?"

The outcome of the game rested on a single decision. Sidney removed his right hand from behind his back. At first it looked as if he might be moving the fifth pebble from one pocket of his coat to another, but no. Slowly, but with calm authority, Sidney raised the finger of doom. The batsman was out LBW, Grantchester had won the game, and Zafar Ali had a hat trick to his name.

The players gathered round, shook each other by the hand and patted Zafar on the back in congratulation. Geoffrey Thomas, the captain's brother-in-law who had dropped what might have been a crucial catch, was visibly relieved as his wife and daughter came to meet him.

His daughter Annie walked up to Zafar and touched his arm. "We're so proud of you."

Thomas restrained her enthusiasm. "That's enough, thank you. He was only doing his job. Let's get the beer out."

Soon the players were lost in the kind of celebration and conviviality that, Sidney thought, only cricket can foster. He downed a glass of beer, thanked the cricketers for such a warm-hearted game and made his excuses to leave. He walked over and congratulated Zafar Ali once more.

"Not a beer drinker?" he asked.

"I have a delicate stomach, I'm afraid. No alcohol. Mrs Thomas has kindly made me up a jug of lemonade."

"It looks good."

"Certainly your dog seems to think so. I put some in a bowl for him. I hope you don't mind . . ."

"Not at all."

"It's a hot day. He looked thirsty."

"I hear you run a restaurant: is business going well?"

"So far, so good. We stay open late and we are busy on Sundays. You English like your curry."

"I should pop in some time."

"You'd be very welcome. And thank you for the decision. I thought it might have been missing leg but I had to appeal."

"Not at all," Sidney replied. "I can assure you it was plumb."

"I wouldn't want any favouritism."

"No," Sidney replied. "I try to avoid that. But it's good to have you on our team. Might I see you at church one day?"

"I am a Muslim, Canon Chambers."

"We are all children of Abraham," said Sidney. "I suppose if a man has God and cricket he doesn't need much else . . ."

"Except perhaps a wife . . ." Zafar Ali finished his lemonade and poured out another glass. "Are you sure I can't tempt you?"

"No thank you. I've had a good beer and now I have my dog to walk. And we'd better not get on to the whole question of wives; unless, of course, you are thinking of getting married yourself?"

"It's a complicated situation."

Sidney looked anxious. "Does your family have someone in mind?"

"There are expectations, yes."

"But you would rather decide for yourself?"

"As I said, there are complications. And in more than one family."

"Well, if you ever need to talk about it, you know where to find me."

"Do you know the Redmond family, Canon Chambers?"

"Not well, but I often pass by the family shop. Do they supply your restaurant?"

"Annie delivers our vegetables and household supplies."

"And is she, perhaps, the complication?"

"You are perceptive, Canon Chambers."

"I saw the manner in which she greeted you and the way her father slapped her down. I am afraid you will have to make it a little less obvious if you wish to keep it a secret."

"That is the problem. We do not want it to be a secret at all."

"I could have a word with the family; if you think it might help?"

"I need to talk to Annie first. Her parents and her uncles are always polite, but I can tell they want to keep me at a distance. I am their customer, nothing more. I know they are not happy."

"And you are?"

"Not at the moment, Canon Chambers. I think none of us are very cheerful. But perhaps, with God's help, things will come good."

"I certainly hope so. I will pray for you, Zafar, if you think that would be helpful."

"I need all of God's help."

"Then that is what you shall have," Sidney replied, as kindly as he could, and looked for Dickens to take him home.

His Labrador seemed unusually sluggish. Sidney wondered whether the heat had exhausted him, or if he had eaten too much of the cricketers' tea. Cheese never agreed with him, and the egg sandwiches had possibly been left out on a warming day for too long. In fact, Dickens became lethargic all evening, sleeping more than he usually did; so much so that Sidney thought that something must be wrong. He decided to telephone Agatha Redmond, who had provided the Labrador in the first place and whose brother Andrew, Grantchester's captain, was, after all, a vet.

"It is odd that you should telephone as Dickens is not alone in feeling a little under the weather. The men in the family are ill too and I don't think it's the drink. They seem to have come down with some kind of food poisoning, Canon Chambers. We can't think what it could be. I hope it wasn't Mrs Maguire's lardy cake."

"I very much doubt that."

"Has Dickens been sick?"

"Not as far as I know."

"And what about you?"

"I am well. But I didn't really eat very much."

"Make sure Dickens has plenty of water. I can look in after church tomorrow."

"I am sure that will be fine," Sidney replied, although after looking at his exhausted dog, he was not sure that it was.

The following morning Dickens seemed to have returned to his usual self, and the Sunday was taken up with Sidney's regular activities. It did seem strange that so many of the cricketers had suffered from upset stomachs as well as sore heads but there was nothing to cause any real anxiety, and in the days that followed Sidney was more interested to hear about Colin Cowdrey's 176 not out for Kent against Lancashire, an exhilarating century for D.W. Richardson for Worcestershire against Gloucestershire at Stroud, and Miss Truman reaching the Lawn Tennis singles final in Paris. In fact he had put the weekend's cricket out of his mind until Inspector Keating raised the subject at their regular backgammon contest on the Thursday evening.

The conversation began innocently enough. "I heard about the game," Keating noted after he had thrown a double three. "I was wondering about the origin of the word hat trick. Where does it come from? Cricket doesn't have much to do with hats, does it?"

"I think it was at Sheffield's Hyde Park ground in 1858. An All-England cricket team was engaged in a cricket match against the Hallam XI. During the match, H.H. Stephenson of the All-England XI took three wickets in three balls. As was customary at the time for rewarding outstanding sporting feats, a collection was made. The proceeds were used to buy a white hat, which was duly presented to the bowler."

"And was Stephenson grateful?"

"History is, I fear, silent on this important subject, Geordie. But Mr Ali's hat trick certainly made our own little contribution to cricketing statistics."

"Although many of them drank so much afterwards I am surprised they are able to remember anything about it."

"Yes, I heard there was quite a celebration. There were plenty of sore heads and upset stomachs."

"Although that Indian chappie doesn't drink alcohol, I'm told."

"And he was the hero of the hour."

The inspector gave Sidney what was becoming one of his all-too-familiar steady looks. "You know he's not well?"

"I did not."

"Mr Ali has even had to close his restaurant. I am surprised you hadn't heard anything. Mrs Maguire must have been keeping it quiet."

"What's she got to do with it?"

"Well it could have been one of her famous lardy cakes, couldn't it?"

"I doubt very much that Mrs Maguire's cooking is to blame." Sidney was annoyed that he had to keep defending his housekeeper. "Baking is her absolute forte."

"The doctor's been but I've also sent one of Jarvis's men round to ask a few questions."

"That seems rather zealous."

"You can't be too careful. Mr Ali has said that there might have been something wrong with the lemonade."

"Surely not?"

"You would have thought not, but back in Newcastle there was a bit of an incident twenty-odd years ago. I was a small boy, mind, but there was something about the fruit crystals in the drink. They dissolved some of the coating of the pail it was in. Seventy people were poisoned."

"And that coating contained?"

"Antimony."

"Isn't that what Mozart died from?"

"I wouldn't know that, Sidney."

Although Keating was exasperated by his friend's flight of fancy his impatience did nothing to stem Sidney's impromptu peroration. "I think it may have been in a pork chop. Trichinosis, I think it's called. It's ironic because Mozart's last opera *La Clemenza di Tito* contains the poisoning of the Emperor Titus."

"I am sure it does."

"And so if you were correct then those who drank the lemonade would be the most affected: men such as Zafar Ali?"

"Indeed, that would be the case. He may have been bowled without scoring," Keating observed, "but he's certainly getting the runs now."

Sidney wondered whether his friend had brought up the entire conversation in order to deliver his joke. He was certainly pleased with it. "You know he's sweet on Annie Thomas, the grocer's daughter? That's not going down too well with the rest of the Redmond family, I am afraid."

"On the grounds of his race?"

"And his religion. We can't all be as broad-minded as you are, Sidney."

"I am not always tolerant. Poor Zafar. Such a nice man." Sidney finished his beer. "You're not too worried about all this, are you?"

"No, of course not. Although I wouldn't like to think we had a poisoner in our midst. It can sometimes take a heck of a long time to rumble them. You know the case of George Chapman?"

"The Arsenal manager?"

"No, Sidney, that is Herbert Chapman; the man who had the idea of putting numbers on the backs of players' shirts. I wish you knew as much about football as you did about everything else. George Chapman was a pub landlord, although his real name was Severin Klosowski. He polished off three of his wives by lacing their drinks over a sustained period of time and then blamed their delicate constitutions. I wouldn't want the same thing to happen here."

"I am sure the Eagle is perfectly safe," Sidney replied as he took their two empty glasses over to the bar.

There was no point looking for trouble, he thought to himself, and stomach bugs were common enough in Grantchester. He certainly wasn't going to worry about such things now.

The barmaid leaned forward, and Sidney tried not to look too obviously at her cleavage. "What's your poison?" she asked.

The following Saturday was the day of Grantchester's annual fête. Witnessing everyone going about their daily business, during a weekend when they were no longer defined by their professions, Sidney saw his parishioners with their guards down. This was when they were most themselves; more committed to their hobbies, perhaps, than their jobs. They were doing their best, as their ancestors had done before them, and he felt humbled by their quiet acts of goodness. Of course there were difficult people who were determined to make things awkward for everyone else, but they were in the minority, and as the day progressed Sidney felt a growing sense of pride for the people he served.

Amanda had been summoned from London, and she arrived with her friend Martita, an actress who was beginning to make her name in the film business and who had been prevailed upon to open proceedings by cutting the ribbon.

Sidney was cheered to show both girls off, and Amanda was looking spectacular, dressed in a silk French summer dress, based on a champagne ground and white spots, with a full knee-length skirt and a fichu top.

"Martita keeps me on my toes," she whispered to Sidney after he had complimented her on her appearance. "And I don't want to let you down."

"You are the most glamorous woman here," he replied.

"Well, that is as it should be. I like to make a bit of a splash. It's also good to give them a bit of gossip. I'm sure they were expecting Hildegard. When is she coming back?"

"I'm off to Germany next week."

"Then do send her my love."

"Your love?"

"Yes, Sidney, 'my love'. I do like the woman."

The vicar's only duty at the fête was to judge the most beautiful baby competition. This event, like so many in Sidney's life, may have seemed trivial but it was, in fact, a social minefield. It required a level of tact and diplomacy that would have tested the highest Foreign Office official, never mind a clergyman. He had learned that the best response to the presentation of a particularly ugly child was simply to say, "What a baby!"

The next most important thing was to select Mrs Maguire's offering at the bring and buy stall and prevent the humiliation of the previous year in which her Victoria sponge, of which she was so proud, had been the last cake to sell.

Sidney knew what he had to do. On scouring the stall he saw a coffee and walnut loaf that he had to purchase if he was to retain the affections of his housekeeper. It cost him one and six; a small price to pay for a clean house and regular meals. He made sure that Mrs Maguire was aware he had bought it.

"Oh, Canon Chambers, how did you guess?" she laughed nervously.

"It was the first cake to be sold. I had to fight other women off," Sidney lied.

"It's a pity you didn't make two," Amanda joined in.

"Oh but I did," Mrs Maguire replied. "There's a Victoria sponge as well. I like to think of it as my trademark recipe. You can buy it now, if you like, Miss Kendall. It's only a shilling."

"Of course," Amanda smiled. "I'll be delighted. You must be relieved the stall is so popular."

"Relieved?"

"I heard there were a few mutterings after the cricket last weekend?"

"It was nothing to do with my baking, I can assure you."

"I am not suggesting any such thing."

"I think you were, Miss Kendall." Mrs Maguire was on her dignity. "I'll have you know that everything I prepared for the cricket was made in hygienic conditions. No members of my family have ever had any food poisoning in their lives. And if you have any doubts," and here Mrs Maguire produced a moment of impromptu triumph, "look at Dickens."

Sidney turned to his dog. "What has he got to do with it?"

"He ate all the food, as well you know, Canon Chambers. He couldn't get enough of it. And he's been as right as rain ever since. So it can't have been any of my food."

"Then, perhaps for the first time, you are grateful to him."

"I wouldn't go as far as that. But he is the proof. If you ask me all those stomach upsets are caused by one thing and one thing only."

"The demon drink?" Amanda asked.

"Exactly, Miss Kendall. My father never touched a drop and he lived until he was ninety-seven."

"What a life he must have had," Amanda smiled, as sweetly as she could. "I'll take the Victoria sponge, if you don't mind."

"I don't mind at all. Just so long as you enjoy it."

"I am sure I will."

Amanda took out her purse and paid for the cake. Once they had left the stall she turned to Sidney and told him that at least her cats would like it.

"Don't be beastly," Sidney said. "She means well and she's had a tough life."

"I'm sorry, Sidney. I'm just not a cake person."

"And what kind of a person are you, Amanda?"

"Oh, you know, more cocktails and canapés."

Once the tug of war had ended and Martita had driven off to stay with friends in the country, Sidney found himself alone with Amanda. They walked down to the river to see the light fade on the water and amongst the willows. It was a glorious evening and Sidney was looking forward to dinner at the Red Lion before Amanda caught the last train back to London. It would be the culmination of a long and happy day, he felt; a day on which she had seen him at his best, as a generous host, loved by his parishioners and in control of the fluctuating organisation of the fête.

The shadows lengthened across the meadows as the river flowed lazily away from them. The church tower glowed in the evening light.

"It's idyllic in the summer, isn't it?" Amanda said, taking Sidney's arm. "I wish I could spend more time here."

"You can spend as long as you like. You know that, Amanda."

"I'm not sure Hildegard would approve."

"You'd be surprised. She's not a jealous woman."

"Is there anything about her that is not good?"

"Nothing, I think, Amanda. But, like you, she may be too good for me."

"What rot. You do talk nonsense sometimes, Sidney . . ."

Their conversation was interrupted by the sight of Inspector Keating walking briskly towards them. "I am glad I've caught up with you. I'm afraid there's some bad news."

"Oh no," Amanda replied.

"Mr Ali is dead. He failed to recover from the food poisoning and we've called in Jarvis. The only problem is that the family are Muslims and they want a quick burial. You've got to talk to them, Sidney, and hold it off for as long as possible."

"I am sure they have their own imam."

"Not here. You'll have to talk to the cemetery too. You'll need to make up something appropriate probably. Get Leonard to help. Don't worry if you take your time as long as it is all explained. They are upset and confused. Annie Thomas is with them. You'll have your work cut out but we have to get to the bottom of this."

"And you suspect foul play?"

"I'll need you to think over everything that happened last Saturday, Sidney. Did you notice anything? Who else had the lemonade? And was Zafar singled out or was his constitution more delicate than everyone else's? If he was singled out then who on earth would want to kill him?"

The Ali family lived in a small flat above the Curry Garden in Mill Road, a restaurant that offered delicacies including a classic Bengali Sea Bream Paturi, Murgh Nizami, Nihari Lamb and Kashmiri Rogan Josh. Looking at the menu, it occurred to Sidney that it would be extremely unlikely for someone so familiar with these dishes to have their insides troubled by an innocent lemonade or a slice of Mrs Maguire's lardy cake.

Sidney took off his shoes and expressed his condolences to Zafar's parents, Wasim and Shaksi, as their three surviving children, Aaqil, Munir and Nuha, watched uncertainly. They did not speak but followed their parents as they showed Sidney into a small dark room that contained a low sofa and a few wooden chairs. The curtains were drawn and a candle had been lit. A framed passage from the Koran was the only decoration on the anaglypta-covered wall. Life had come to a stop and was now as empty and forlorn as a swimming pool drained at the end of summer.

Wasim asked Sidney to sit down but the family remained standing, uncertain why he had come and how long he might stay. The children hovered in the doorway. There was nothing else for them to do.

Shaksi offered refreshments, but her heart wasn't in it. Sidney asked for a glass of water. He did not want to put the family to any trouble, he said. He assumed that most of their time was spent remembering Zafar. If they hadn't come to Britain, he imagined them thinking, then their son would still be alive. The thought remained unspoken in the air.

Sidney asked if there had been anything unusual in the days leading up to the death, recognising, as soon as he had uttered the words, that Zafar's illness must have sent everything out of kilter. Wasim said that his son had complained of a metallic taste in his mouth. There had been a swelling in his hands and feet, and he had suffered from nausea, vomiting, stomach cramps and fainting. The only thing he had found to alleviate these symptoms was the Earl Grey tea that Rosie Thomas had provided from the grocer's shop. The rest of the family all took Darjeeling, but Zafar preferred the more delicately scented China tea and had joked that he hoped such a preference could not be seen as a betrayal of his country.

"It is such a terrible turn of events," Sidney said as he prepared to take his leave. "And after such a triumph. I have never seen a hat trick before. It's very unusual, and he did it with such agility and style. His final appeal was admirably, enquiringly civilised and bore no sign of any excitement even though he must have felt triumphant inside. Did he bring the match ball home with him?"

"I don't think so. Why do you ask?"

"Normally, in a game of cricket, if a bowler takes a hat trick he gets to keep the ball."

"I don't think he brought a ball home. But he was in bad shape. He could hardly walk."

"It's very odd if the ball had disappeared entirely. It doesn't make sense."

"Nothing about what has happened makes any sense, Canon Chambers. All we can do is pray."

"We could pray now. In silence."

"Yes. Let us do that, Canon Chambers. I would be grateful. Peace be on you and the mercy of Allah."

Sidney decided that he had to see Annie Thomas to talk about the funeral and, at the same time, ask a few discreet questions in order to discover if there was anything unusual about Zafar's last days.

Her mother said that she was not yet ready to speak to anyone. In fact she preferred not to talk at all, and had hardly uttered a word since the death, shutting herself in her room, rejecting her food, drinking only water. She would not even get dressed, moving only to the bathroom and kitchen, wearing a pair of pyjamas, her face pale and swollen. Dr Robinson had come and said that it was too dangerous to give her anything that might help her sleep for fear of an overdose. She needed the time and rest for grief.

Sidney insisted that he at least try to see her, and although Annie's mother was doubtful, he was shown up to the bedroom door. He knocked carefully and explained who he was and why he had come. There was nothing he could do to change what had happened but he wanted to help her be a recognised part of the funeral and for her love for Zafar to be publicly acknowledged. People should know, he told her, and he would help them know.

It took some time for the door to open and when it did he saw a young girl whose eyes had had the light taken out of them. She looked down at the floor, at Sidney's shoes, and stepped back. She held a crumpled handkerchief in her hand, said nothing, and returned to her bed, pulling the sheets and blankets over her, turning her face away from her visitor and back towards the wall.

Sidney sat at the foot of the bed. He acknowledged that it was hard, almost impossible, for her to speak and that it was quite all right if she said nothing. He could not imagine what it was like for her. He would pray if she liked or not.

She did not.

It was only that he wanted her wishes, whatever they were, to come first.

"I wish that he was alive again. That's all. And you can't give me that."

"I can't."

"If I close my eyes, if no one comes, if I am alone, then perhaps I can wake up and find it hasn't happened."

"You've had a terrible loss." Sidney did not know what to say. It was too soon to touch her or take her hand. All he could do was wait until she was ready to speak.

It took a long time.

"He was such a gentle man," Annie continued at last. "And he would never harm anyone. He was going to be a doctor."

"What did he think it was?"

Annie still had her back to Sidney but now turned and sat up in her bed, looking not at him but at her own knees. "He didn't like to blame anyone, but he thought it was the lemonade. Only he can't understand why he didn't get any better. I know the jug will have been washed out by now, so there isn't any evidence and we can't prove anything."

"It's a very unfortunate turn of events. How much did your parents know about your relationship?"

"They knew we were friendly."

"But they didn't know that you were planning to marry?"

"How did you know that?"

"Zafar told me as much himself."

"I don't know why he would have done that."

"You would need your parents' approval. I offered to help."

"You would have been prepared to do that? I am only nineteen."

"I would have needed to talk to you both properly first. I would have wanted to see that the relationship was genuine, and that it was founded on mutual respect. Then I would have spoken with your parents."

"I don't think they would ever have agreed."

"I suppose parents think that their children are too young to know what to do with their lives."

Annie's face livened with anger. "Do you know that I am a year older than my mother when she had me? They like to cover it up and say that I was a bit premature, but I know that she only got married because she was pregnant. And now they want to take control of my life."

"Perhaps she doesn't want you to make the same mistake."

"Zafar's family is very hardworking. They are all ambitious; far more than other families round here. Unlike us, they don't expect an easy life just because they have had the privilege to be English."

"Ah yes," Sidney replied. "The idea that you have won first prize in the lottery of life simply by being born here. I have always thought that to be a very dangerous assumption."

"We don't have to do what is expected of us all the time, do we? Sometimes the unexpected can be better. You have to take a few risks, and trust that the person you love is right for you, don't you think?"

"I do. Although I haven't always acted on that idea. Perhaps you have more courage when you are younger."

Annie smiled. "You're not old, Canon Chambers."

"I am thirty-eight."

"You'd better get a move-on."

"People do keep telling me."

"But you won't act on their advice," Annie replied. "A bit like me. I'm always doing the opposite of what people tell me. But now look where it's got me."

She turned abruptly away, her face to the wall once more as if, like a child, she imagined that if she could not see Sidney he would no longer be there. She had strayed too far from her grief and now wanted only to return to it, filling her heart with its exclusive sorrow.

On Monday morning, Sidney tried to cheer himself up by reading the latest cricketing news. *The Times* reported that England were going to be represented at Lord's by the same eleven that had beaten India by an innings at Trent Bridge and that there were predictions of a good batting surface. The correspondent thought that the home side needed to think about the options for their spin bowlers and hoped that Taylor and Barrington would be able to improve their leg-breaks.

The concentration on spin made Sidney return once again to the fact of Zafar Ali's death and reminded him that he needed to see the coroner. When he arrived he found that Derek Jarvis was already expecting him and the post-mortem report had been typed up.

" 'The mucous membrane over the fore border of the epiglottis and adjacent part of the pharynx has been destroyed by sloughing,' " Jarvis began. " 'The ulceration extends into the upper part of the oesophagus. About an inch below its commencement, the mucous membrane has been entirely removed by sloughing and ulceration, the circular muscular fibres being exposed.

Above the upper limit of this ulcer, the mucous membrane presents several oval, elongated and ulcerated areas, occupied by slips of mucous membrane which have sloughed. There is redness, swelling and general inflammation in the stomach, there are ulcers and pustules in the lining membrane of the mouth, and the lungs of the deceased are hepatised and gorged with blood.

"'There are traces of thallium in both the kidneys and intestines, but insufficient to be the cause of death. More significant is the presence of antimony potassium nitrate in the stomach (0.000282 oz), kidneys (0.000705 oz), liver (0.01464 oz) and intestines (0.017636 oz).'"

Jarvis was in no doubt. "There's rather too much antimony for this to be an accident."

"So you are suggesting . . ."

"Indeed I am . . ."

"What does antimony look like?" Sidney asked.

"They are faint yellow crystals."

"Lemon yellow? As in lemonade?"

"They can also be mistaken for Epsom salts. And so if a patient is given that for an upset stomach, for example . . ."

"He could be given antimony instead."

"It would be interesting if the grocer's sold both lemonade crystals and Epsom salts. And who was administering any medicine the patient was taking?"

"I think we can rule out Annie Thomas."

"Do you, Sidney?"

"We can't suspect everyone, can we?"

"We need to know who made up the lemonade on the day of the cricket match, exactly who drank it, and who washed up the jug afterwards. My suspicion is that there wouldn't have been enough antimony in the drink to kill a man outright . . ."

"Which leads you to conclude?"

"Nothing at this point. Only it may not just be the lemonade. There could be other possibilities."

"You mean that the poison could have been applied to a number of different foodstuffs? I think Zafar had an egg sandwich and that was about it."

"We must find out everything he ate and drank and touched. I'm worried where the trace of thallium has come from. He could have been taking different poisons at different times."

"Are you also implying that there could be more than one murderer on the loose?"

"We can't rule anything out, Sidney. You could start by talking to the suppliers. But you will need to be careful not to reveal your role in all this. I don't want you falling victim to anything untoward. If you feel at all unwell, then you must see your doctor immediately and inform me. In fact, it would be a good idea to keep a diary of everything you eat and drink, where it has come from and who has provided it."

"Do you really think that's necessary?"

"I do. You are building quite a reputation in these parts. If you let anyone know that you are suspicious of them then you will be putting yourself at risk."

"That seems a bit fearful."

"You can't be too careful, Sidney."

"What on earth is the matter with these people?"

"Perhaps they do not spend enough time in church?"

"I know I certainly don't," Sidney replied.

He had not joined the priesthood to investigate murders and antagonise grocers, and yet here he was, planning to do just that.

Annie's mother, Rosie Thomas, was a forthright blonde woman with a reddish face, a thin mouth and an upturned nose. Cruel observers would remark that her salad days were over and that she had let herself go, but Sidney could tell that with a proper hairdresser and some instruction from Amanda, she could easily be transformed into a stylish and handsome figure about town should she so wish. However, it was the desire to do this, the need for time, patience and, above all, confidence, that was clearly lacking. She had made a niche for herself as the efficient manageress of the grocery stores and this, she had clearly decided, was her lot in life. Sidney had never seen her without an apron.

Rosie revealed that she did indeed supply the Indian restaurant, and that her daughter Annie made her deliveries every Thursday, although she was unlikely to be resuming her duties soon as she was still confined to her bedroom.

"They don't like them on a Friday because they go to prayers all day. Still, it suits us. We can get them out of the way. Although Annie takes long enough about it."

"She and Mr Ali were friends, I hear."

"I am not sure how much you have heard, Canon Chambers, but it won't do to listen to gossip. You

255

wouldn't catch my girl going off with a foreigner, I can tell you that for nothing."

"I wasn't making that suggestion. I was only asking if they were friends."

"We are friends with all our customers."

"You treat them all equally, I am sure."

"We try to. Once you start having favourites they ask for discounts. It never works."

"And did Mr Ali pay the full whack?"

"Of course."

"And what did he buy?"

"Vegetables when we had the right type for him, a few gherkins and pickled onions. He used to order the less perishable stuff on a monthly basis; you know the kind of thing: tinned salmon, peach slices, Carnation milk. I think he went to London for the more exotic ingredients. We don't sell spices."

"But you provided him with the basics? Milk, sugar and tea, and lemonade, of course — as you did on the day of the match."

"You can't blame my lemonade for what happened. It was more likely to be your housekeeper's cake."

"I very much doubt it. Her baking has never caused any trouble in the past."

"There's always a first time."

"I am sure there is. But about the lemonade . . ."

"I can show you the powder we sell — it's like crystals — they dissolve in water."

"And do you also supply Epsom salts?"

"We are not a chemist."

"Baking powder?"

"Why are you asking? Are you unwell?"

"No, it's not that." Sidney panicked. "Mrs Maguire asked me to get some baking powder."

"Mrs Maguire normally does her own shopping."

"I thought I would help out."

"You need a wife, Canon Chambers."

"People keep telling me."

"Is your German friend coming again?"

"Not imminently."

"Nothing wrong with an English girl. Have you thought about my niece?"

"Abigail Redmond? She is far too young for me. And anyway, isn't she spoken for?"

"Not any more. We put a stop to all that Gary Bell nonsense as soon as we found out. She's a good-looking girl."

"Really, Mrs Thomas, this is not what I came to discuss."

"What did you come to talk about?"

"I came for baking powder, I remember that now, and to ask about Mr Ali."

"Well that's all over now, God rest his soul; not that he believes in God."

"His is a Muslim God. Allah."

"That doesn't really count, though, does it?"

"We are all children of Abraham, Mrs Thomas."

"You mean we are all Jews? I don't think so."

"It is a figure of speech."

A queue was forming in the shop behind him, and now was not the time to talk to Mrs Thomas about the similarities between the great religions. "Could I also have some lemonade crystals?" he asked.

"What do you want them for?"

"For lemonade, of course," Sidney answered, knowing that he had every intention of proceeding directly from the grocer's shop to the Coroner's Office.

"You are a funny one," Mrs Thomas replied. "There are times when I just can't make you out, Canon Chambers."

"You are not the first person to tell me that."

"You should spend more time in church rather than poking your nose into other people's business. It doesn't do any good, you know."

After long conversations with the Ali family, Harold Streat, the undertaker, and the staff at the Mill Road cemetery, Sidney organised a simplified Christian funeral ceremony followed by Muslim prayers in which the imam spoke out the Takbirs. Members of both cricket teams were in attendance, and there was a large turnout from both the Muslim community and patrons of the Curry Garden. It was clear that Zafar was much loved and that his future would have been bright. It made his loss hard to understand and the thought of the crime horrifying.

Annie Thomas had chosen to read a Christina Rossetti poem for the service. She wore a black dress and had a pale, determined look that commanded attention and refused interruption. She wanted it to be publicly acknowledged that she was unembarrassed by her affiliation with the deceased, and was determined to let everyone know she had loved him:

> He was born in the spring,
> And died before harvesting:
> On the last warm summer day
> He left us; he would not stay
> For autumn twilight cold and grey.
> Sit we by his grave, and sing
> He is gone away.

After the service, Sidney took pains to tell her how brave she had been and that she should come and see him if she ever felt vulnerable or afraid. He hoped that she would not return to the confines of her bedroom. "I know it is hard," he began. "Eventually, I hope, this grief will lessen. Time will pass."

"What if I don't want it to pass? If I forget this pain then I will forget him, and I don't want to do that."

"I don't think he would want to see you like this."

"Anything less would be a betrayal." She looked at Sidney for as long as she had ever done. "I want my parents to know it wasn't just some teenage thing."

"I am sure they don't think that. It's why they were so concerned."

"Mum said you came round asking weird questions."

"I just needed to put my mind at rest."

"You think it was the lemonade?"

"I am not sure." Sidney did not want to arouse any suspicion or provoke any blame, and Annie's conversation forced him to be far more careful than he might normally be. "Will you be going home?" he asked.

"No, Canon Chambers, I am going to stay with Zafar's family for a few days."

"Do your parents mind?"

"Yes. That's why I am going."

"And do they have a room for you?"

"It's the room Zafar slept in. That's why I want to go there."

"Are you sure that's good for you?"

"I don't want it to be good for me, Canon Chambers. I want to do what is right."

Sidney could tell that it was going to take years for any grief to lessen or for the tensions in the Redmond family to die down, and he needed some guidance from the coroner if he was going to pursue his suspicions.

"There is nothing untoward about the lemonade crystals that you brought me," Derek Jarvis told him. "We would have anticipated that. You can't expect the family to have handed over the poison."

"You think they are responsible?"

"I think they could be as guilty as hell. It's often the closest family members. But proving that is a job for you and Keating."

"The supply could have been adulterated without their knowledge, I suppose. At the cricket ground, for example."

"It could," Derek Jarvis agreed.

"Which would mean anyone?" Sidney asked.

"Anyone and everyone. The whole bloody village, if you like."

★ ★ ★

The next morning Amanda telephoned to ask how the funeral had gone. She also wanted to tell Sidney that she had been to hear Claudio Arrau continue his cycle of Beethoven sonatas at the Festival Hall and wished Hildegard could have heard it with her.

"I am still so glad you like her."

"Of course I like her," Amanda replied. "And you must be careful not to lose her. If you don't watch out someone else will snap her up."

"I don't think she intends to marry again . . ."

"I wouldn't be too sure of that, Sidney."

"I can't think about all this."

"Honestly, Sidney, I know a man may have been killed and that you have your duties to attend to, but your future happiness is equally important. You can't spend your whole life in pursuit of murderers. Are you still involving yourself in the inquiry into the death of that poor Indian boy?"

"I was there, Amanda, just before he became unwell."

"And is there evidence of foul play?"

"I am afraid there is."

"What kind?"

"Antimony poisoning."

"I have heard of that. It's the same as tartar emetic, isn't it?"

"I believe so. How on earth do you know?"

"They give it to horses to bring down their temperature."

"Horses?"

261

"It's called 'Hind's Sweating Ball'. It can be quite dangerous if taken in large quantities . . ."

"And is it difficult to get hold of?"

"Not if you are a vet. I could put you in touch with one if you wanted to pursue that particular line of enquiry."

"The captain of our cricket team is a vet."

"Oh, good gracious, Sidney."

"I will have to go and see him."

"You will be careful, won't you? I am always fearful when you embark on your investigative escapades."

"I'll be perfectly safe, Amanda."

"That's what I thought in the past but now I worry about you all the time. I only wish Hildegard was there to look after you . . ."

Andrew Redmond lived in an end-of-terrace house on the edge of Grantchester which opened out into farmland. The third Redmond child, and something of an afterthought, he was twenty-nine years old and unmarried. This was surprising given his relative good looks, his sporting abilities and his professional assurance. A few cards from a recent birthday stood on the mantelpiece but this was clearly the home of a man who lived on his own, with horse brasses and fire tongs, and framed photographs of cricket teams from both school and university. Andrew was always in the centre of the front row: A.P.D. Redmond (Capt.).

The house smelled faintly of antiseptic. On being asked if he would like a cup of tea, Sidney noticed that, unlike in many a bachelor's house, everything had been tidied from the kitchen, the surfaces had been newly wiped and the floor had been mopped so recently that it still carried a faint, wet gleam.

Sidney had used Dickens as the excuse for his visit. It was time for a regular check-up and he wanted his Labrador to get the once-over just to ensure that all was well. "He has had the odd poorly moment after the cricket, and I just thought that I should make sure there is nothing more sinister," he explained.

"That is wise," Redmond replied, as he settled Dickens on his examination table and ran a firm professional hand over the dog's head and ears. "These have been strange times."

"I gather," Sidney began as tentatively as he could, "that since the match you have not been well yourself."

"I think it was the beer. There was a new barrel in and I suppose it must have been more potent."

"You don't strike me as being much of a drinker," Sidney pressed.

"I'm not. It's only after the cricket. And when I'm thirsty."

"Did you have any of the lemonade?"

"No, I didn't touch any of that. I hear that you think that's what might have done it for poor old Zafar."

"You hear?"

"From my sister. Rosie said you'd been in at the shop. I thought your housekeeper did that kind of thing."

"No, I like to do the odd bit of shopping myself. Mrs Maguire's cooking has, alas, come under a bit of suspicion, but you can see that I, for one, am still standing."

"I'm glad to see it. I suppose some of us react differently to others."

"Presumably, as a vet, you know how to deal with an upset stomach."

"Animals and humans are very different, Canon Chambers."

"And you cater for every animal?"

"I do my best. Of course it's mainly cattle round here." He finished his examination of the Labrador. "Dickens seems in good shape."

"I am glad that he managed to restore himself so quickly."

"I could have given him something to settle him down."

"It's an emetic that's normally required, is it not?"

"That's right."

"And do you have different emetics for different animals? I imagine that a treatment for a dog would be very different to that for a horse, for example?"

"Of course, Canon Chambers. Horses require a particular treatment of their own."

"Hind's Sweating Ball, I believe."

"You are well informed."

"With antimony as the core ingredient."

"Why are you asking about this, Canon Chambers? You are a dog man. And your Labrador is perfectly fine. There's plenty of life left in him yet."

On Friday 19 June Sidney joined his father and twenty-two thousand other spectators to watch the second Test match between England and India at

Lord's. India had batted first and were all out for 168, five of them falling victim to Tommy Greenhough's leg-break googlies. Clearly this was a wicket that would take spin; the kind of bowling that Sidney was sure Zafar Ali would have loved.

England resumed the second day on 50 for 3 with Colin Cowdrey and Ken Barrington at the crease. Sidney's father had been very keen to get to the ground early in order to see the two men bat: Barrington for his powerful drives, pulls and square cuts; Cowdrey for his elegance and timing. Sidney had first seen him when he scored a century for Oxford in the 1953 game against Cambridge. His father, Ernest, had been a tea planter in Bangalore and it was remarked, even then, that he had clearly foretold his son's destiny by giving him the initials MCC.

Before the teams emerged from the pavilion, Sidney's father asked for news of the parish and said he assumed it would be something of a relief for his son to absent himself from felicity awhile.

"I am, although I am sure Felicity will be missing me."

It was a joke they shared together almost every time they met, and they never tired of it. Sidney loved the easy companionship with his father; a friendship that had probably begun at the age of six when he had been given his first bat and been shown how to prepare it with linseed oil and knock it in, how to hold it (the left hand above the right), what guard to take at the crease ("middle and leg, please, umpire"), and how to survey the imaginary field that was set before him, searching for gaps that would yield the most runs. Their shared interest in the game had developed over thirty years and deepened their friendship, allowing ruminative conversation that could be adjourned and resumed at leisure whether at Lord's, the Oval, Fenners or the Parks. Sidney sometimes felt that while they were watching the cricket he could tell his father anything, although he liked to keep matters of the heart close to his chest.

"Are you planning any more of your German sorties this summer?" Alec Chambers asked, with an intentionally light curiosity, as if his son was only going to the shops.

"No, I think that may have to wait. I've rather a lot on."

"And have you seen much of Amanda recently?" Alec Chambers probed as Cowdrey cut through the covers. "Shot!"

"She came to the church fête."

"And did that prove a success?"

"I think so. Unfortunately I was called away."

"A pressing parish matter, no doubt. I suppose Amanda must be used to it."

Foolishly, but in order to avoid further questions about the women in his life, Sidney confessed that there had, in all likelihood, been another murder in the village.

"Good God, man, it's like the Battle of the Somme out there."

"I wouldn't quite put it like that."

"At least the cricket takes your mind off things."

"Although I have been thinking," Sidney replied at the end of the over, "how some of the greatest criminologists have been cricketers. Do you know, for example, that Arthur Conan Doyle once bowled out W.G. Grace? Extraordinary to think that the creator of Sherlock Holmes was a dab hand at bat and ball. In his first game at Lord's he scored a hundred . . ."

"I don't know how much that would have helped to solve a crime . . ."

"Lord Peter Wimsey once made centuries in two consecutive innings. A.J. Raffles was considered a dangerous bat, a brilliant field and the finest slow bowler of his decade . . ."

"These are fictional characters, Sidney. You are getting carried away. Let's concentrate on the game . . ."

Colin Cowdrey continued with a snick for four but was then caught behind off the fast medium-paced bowling of "Tiny" Desai for 34. England were now in a spot of trouble at 69 for 4. The Indian fast bowlers were able to move the ball off the seam at a lively pace, with short balls lifting unexpectedly, making conditions difficult for the England batsmen.

Although Barrington proved steady in defence, Desai bowled Horton for two, and Godfrey Evans followed with a duck. England had slumped to 80 for 6. Alec Chambers was worried that Barrington would soon run out of partners.

"Those players look a bit timid. You can't play if you're scared of the ball. It's hardly going to kill you."

"Didn't the English experiment with cricket-ball grenades in the Great War?" Sidney asked.

"The number fifteen?" his father remembered. "You could throw it by hand or catapult. It was used at the Battle of Loos, and also, I think, in the Gallipoli campaign. But it didn't like wet conditions . . ."

"Rather like a real cricket ball."

"The match-head fuses failed to light and so it was withdrawn the following year. A pity. It would have been rather good to beat the Germans with a symbol of our national game."

Barrington reached his fifty and the Indians opted for a change of tactics. The sky had begun to cloud over and Subash Gupte, known as "Fergie" to his friends, came on to twirl a few leg-break googlies, changing the pace and flight, offering up a good, kicking top-spinner, as well as the standard leg-break with dip and bounce. He kept varying his trajectory so that the batsmen had considerable difficulty reading his wrist. Within minutes he had Fred Trueman LBW and England were 100 for 7.

"Done him up like a Christmas turkey," Alec Chambers mused. "Although I don't know why he keeps licking the ball."

"I think it gives him extra grip."

"I would have thought that might make it more slippery."

"Not if you apply it to the seam."

"It doesn't seem very healthy to me. Think of the germs he could pick up . . ."

Sidney hesitated and a memory came to him with sudden dread. It was of Andrew Redmond rubbing the ball into his cricket whites between each delivery, and of Zafar Ali applying his fingers first to the ball and then to his tongue.

Had Grantchester's captain poisoned the ball?

"Did you like Zafar Ali?" he asked, the next time he saw him.

"He was the best player in our team."

"I didn't ask about his cricketing ability. I asked if you liked him."

"We got on well enough."

"Are you aware that he was fond of your niece?"

"I think it was more of a case that she was fond of him. It was a form of rebellion."

"So your family knew about it?"

"We all knew about it. We didn't think it was serious until we saw how upset she was when he died. She's still hardly speaking, you know."

"I think it was serious enough for them to be secretly engaged."

"I think you must be mistaken, Canon Chambers. If there had been any possibility of that kind of nonsense her parents would have put a stop to it."

"She is nineteen years old and I am sure she could find her way to Gretna Green. She does not necessarily need their permission."

"She does if she wants their financial support."

"I think she was going to help manage the restaurant."

"I can't imagine that. It's full of Indians. It's not her culture. His parents would never accept it, let alone Annie's."

"I think they were preparing to welcome her into the family."

"The Muslims? I don't think so."

"I admit it might seem unusual."

"Unusual, Canon Chambers? It's not right. If there's anything being a vet teaches you, it's about keeping the bloodstock pure. You can no more mix a Christian with a Muslim than you can a Lipizzan Maestoso with a Shetland pony."

Sidney was fairly sure that Lipizzan horses were originally crossbreeds but didn't pick him up on his observation. "And you are a Christian family, of course."

"My sister-in-law does your flower rota week in, week out. You can hardly get more Christian than that."

"It's certainly evidence of fidelity to a cause."

"I do have further appointments, Canon Chambers."

"I understand. And I must let you get on, Mr Redmond. However, I did want to ask you what happened to the cricket ball after the game. I don't seem to have been given it."

"I don't know. You were the umpire. It's your job to pocket it."

"Indeed, but I think we all got caught up in the excitement. Did you pick it up, Mr Redmond? The last batsman was LBW."

"I think he kicked the ball away. I don't know what happened to it after that. Why are you asking about that now?"

★ ★ ★

Although Sidney was convinced that he had never been given the cricket ball he had to accept that there was a slight possibility that he could have forgotten all about it. He was prone to absent-mindedness. There were times when he blamed Mrs Maguire for tidying the vicarage in a manner that defied logic, but even she could not be blamed for the disappearance of so many of his possessions. Although he was proud of being able to think hard when it mattered, his ability to focus on one specific problem frequently meant that everything else was pushed to the periphery of his consciousness. Everyday concerns and responsibilities were then sacrificed on the altar of concentration.

As a result, umbrellas were left on trains, scarves were abandoned on hot days, his favourite pen had been left God knows where because it had begun to leak, and his watch, the strap of which was too tight, had been removed in a library, a school or a bookshop (he couldn't remember which). The only way he could retain his more valuable possessions was to keep them at home and in close proximity to his desk, but even there, as papers, books, notes and unfinished thoughts mounted alongside plates of biscuits, cups of tea, and even an abandoned whisky glass or two, Sidney was forced to acknowledge that he did, indeed, have a tendency to lose things. It was the price he had to pay for conjecture. How was he expected to remember the minutiae of daily existence when he had so much else to think about?

He prayed to St Anthony of Padua, the patron saint of lost possessions, for solace and guidance but most of the time he simply had to wait for things to turn up; in a less-favoured jacket or a little-used drawer, for example. It was therefore not a complete surprise when, a few days later, he noticed the very cricket ball he had been worrying about lying in Dickens's basket.

"How did that get there?"

Leonard Graham was sitting at the kitchen table, reading the appointments section in the *Church Times*. "What do you mean?"

"The ball."

"It's always been there," Leonard replied off-handedly, taking a sip of his tea before turning the page to study a report on Anglican-Orthodox relations.

"Are you sure?" Sidney pressed.

"He was playing with it after the game."

"'Playing with it'?" Sidney could not understand how they had failed to notice that a key piece of evidence had been left lying around. He acknowledged that he must have been thinking about other things, but he could not quite believe that those "other things" included a meditation on this very ball. How could he have been so stupid?

"I threw it once and he ran off and collected it. Then he wanted me to do it again and again. I kept it up for a bit but it became so very tiresome. Dickens lives in an eternal present. You wonder how he keeps his enthusiasm. It's certainly more than I can manage."

"When was this?"

"The day of the match."

"And how did you get it?"

"What?"

"The BALL."

Leonard folded up the *Church Times*, acknowledging that there was little chance that he was going to be left in peace until the enquiry was over. "I don't know, Sidney. I can't really remember. I think Dickens had it in his mouth."

"How?"

"Andrew Redmond gave it to him to stop him polishing off the sandwiches. His sister made them."

"Andrew Redmond!"

"It's been in his basket ever since. Haven't you noticed?"

"It must have been under his blanket. Perhaps Mrs Maguire . . ."

"Don't be absurd, Sidney. She doesn't go anywhere near that basket."

"But how could anyone not have told me? This could be a vital clue!"

"How was I to know?"

"A curate obsessed by murder in the prose of Dostoevsky could surely jump to the conclusion that this could be used as a murder weapon."

Leonard sighed. "A cricket ball covered in Dickens's slobber? Honestly, Sidney, that's hardly likely, is it?"

"He doesn't slobber."

"This is ridiculous. I suppose one day you'll start accusing Dickens of murder."

"Of course I won't. But this is not ridiculous. Don't you see? Nothing can be discounted. The evidence is all around us."

Leonard picked up his *Church Times* and his mug of tea and prepared to leave the room. "Am I to assume," he asked, "that every single piece of information that comes into this vicarage, every statement that is made, whether uttered seriously or lightly, and now every little thing that Dickens happens to pick up, is to be treated as evidence in whatever mystery happens to be preoccupying your very existence? Please don't tell me that the answer is yes?"

Sidney took the cricket ball to Derek Jarvis for analysis and was depressed to discover that although there was, indeed, a faint trace of thallium on the seam, it was not enough to kill a man and his theory that it had been impregnated was likely to be far too fanciful.

"It's an ingenious idea, I will admit," Jarvis acknowledged. "But you would need to keep reapplying the poison. So unless the perpetrator carried thallium in his cricket whites . . ."

"I was thinking he could have tampered with his own trousers and then, by rubbing the ball in an ostensible attempt to shine it, he would, in fact, have been secretly applying the poison."

"You've got the wrong end of the stick here, I'm afraid, Sidney, and you're going to have to let it go. A man would have to put so much thallium on his trousers they would disintegrate. I agree you could soak the ball overnight in thallium, and even reapply it before your team goes out to bowl, but I can't see how you could sustain the amount of poison you need to kill a man. It must be something else, equally slow,

274

perhaps, and given over a longer period of time. Do you think it could be a member of Ali's own family?"

"They seem so close."

"Who nursed him in his final days?"

"His girlfriend, Annie."

"Then you need to find out exactly what she gave him."

"I think she just made him cups of tea and sat by his side."

"Then you need to get me that tea. I need samples of everything that he took."

"Do you think Annie could have poisoned him unwittingly?"

"Or deliberately."

"Surely not? I can't believe that at all."

"Everything is possible. Find out what actually poisoned Mr Ali, then let's worry about how it got into his body. After that we can start to work out who might have been responsible. It's not going to be easy, I can tell you."

"I can't think Annie has anything to do with it."

"You have to believe every possibility, Sidney."

"Well, I won't believe *that*."

"Then you need to prove otherwise."

"I will, Derek. If it's the last thing I do."

"Don't say that, Sidney. Don't even joke about it."

"I am not joking. I have never been more serious in my life."

It was so depressing to think that Annie might have been poisoning her beloved unwittingly. If this was the case, then it made Sidney despair at the capacity for human sickness; that a brother and sister could collude not only in the murder of a young man, but also disguise their responsibility by implicating their niece and daughter.

It would have been such an extreme thing to do; to interfere so ruthlessly in the future of a child in their care, justifying their intervention by claiming that they were acting in her own best interests. If challenged, Sidney could already anticipate how they might explain their behaviour. They would probably defend themselves by saying that they were responsible family members who had been forced to take extreme measures to protect Annie's long-term reputation and her future social and economic wellbeing. They had even been forced into it, under provocation and as a last resort, in response to her wilful adolescent rebellion.

This was a vile lie.

Sidney could imagine their protestations already, when all the time Andrew Redmond and Rosie Thomas had been behaving with extreme prejudice, self-interest, ignorance and hatred.

The selfishness was almost beyond comprehension, and Sidney's mood alternated between despair and fury. He could find no redeeming feature in the case, and his fears were confirmed on another visit to the Curry Garden. In the final week of his life Zafar Ali had drunk nothing except tea.

"Annie brought it herself," Wasim confirmed.

Sidney was only delaying the inevitable revelation. "I wondered if I could have a look at the packet she brought?"

"It is almost finished."

"Have any other members of the family been ill?"

"No, but we normally have Darjeeling. I think we've already told you this. Zafar preferred Earl Grey."

"Did he have his own pot?"

Husband and wife looked at each other as if they were worried about giving something away. "Yes," Shaksi replied. "It was a little confusing at times, but that is what we did. Zafar was very particular about his tea."

"I will need to have a look at it. Do you think I could take it to the coroner?"

"You don't think it was the tea, do you?"

"I'm not sure." Sidney already knew that his attempt to buy time was futile. The truth would soon be out.

"Mrs Thomas ordered it especially for us. It was a special blend."

"And when did she start to provide this for you?"

"A few weeks before the cricket match. We thought it was kind of her to take such trouble. She didn't even charge us any money. It was a present; the least she could do, she said."

Keating told Sidney that there had been plenty of similar cases that year. A man in South London had put rat poison in his wife's chocolate; a woman in Durham, Mrs Mary Elizabeth Wilson, had been accused of despatching two husbands with elemental phosphorus; and only that week, twelve ounces of potassium cyanide had gone missing from the chemistry labs at Sidney's old school, Marlborough College.

The following day Rosie Thomas was arrested for the murder of Zafar Ali. She had added antimony both to the lemonade, and then to the tea.

A modest amount, drunk by the family, would cause them some upset but to a man who was already vulnerable from the lemonade, such a topping-up of the poison that was already in his body would eventually prove fatal.

"So the cricket ball wasn't to blame," Keating told Sidney. "Although it wasn't for want of trying. We've brought in Andrew Redmond for questioning. Attempted murder."

"Will the charges stick?"

"Probably more than the poison did to the ball. As Jarvis suspected, the slow release can be activated by contact and saliva but it wasn't enough to kill a man. Instead the Redmond family decided to build up the amount gradually."

"And both brother and sister were in on it?"

"I think most of the family knew something about it."

"Except Annie."

"Yes. It was, in a way, an honour killing. You suspected them from the very beginning, though, didn't you, Sidney?"

"It's perfectly natural for a captain to field at mid on, and even to receive the ball and have a little look at it between deliveries, but it's unusual to give it a shine when the spinners are on. That would help a seam bowler but not a spinner. It seemed an unusual tactic."

"He was trying to rub more poison on to the ball?"

"It seems so."

"But he hadn't perfected the technique. Hence their need to go for the lemonade and then the tea. A triple dose, as it were."

"The fact that the ball disappeared after the game is also important. Normally a player always keeps the hat-trick ball, but in this case . . ."

"He let your dog slobber all over it."

"He doesn't slobber . . ."

"It was one way of removing all trace of the poison." Keating looked up into the night sky as if, for a moment, the mysteries of the universe could be explained within it. "It is amazing when you think about it. Three different types of poison; an unholy Trinity, if you like . . ."

"Or, indeed, a hat trick," Sidney replied.

Annie Thomas was devastated by the news. Sidney sat with her at a restaurant table in a darkened room on a summer afternoon of shimmering heat. She had only just begun to dress and leave Zafar's room. She had not been outside since the day of the funeral. Instead she had helped in the restaurant, working in the kitchen, keeping away from the public and her family, far from anyone who might remind her that her future husband was not likely to return to the restaurant and live above it as if nothing had happened and he had merely been away.

"My mother must have known that I was killing him. It's too cruel."

"It's the product of a sick mind."

"We should have run away."

"Did they warn or threaten you beforehand?"

"All the time. My family is racist, Canon Chambers, I can't pretend otherwise, but I didn't think they would take the law into their own hands. We are supposed to be a responsible family. This is meant to be a decent place. How could they hate me so much?"

"I don't think they hated you."

"It would have been easier if I had killed myself. Then Zafar wouldn't have died."

"You mustn't think like this."

"How else can I think, Canon Chambers? It's all my fault."

"No. It's not."

"Zafar died because of me. If he hadn't met me he'd still be alive. That's what I can't stop thinking about. You knew right away that something was up, didn't you? There's something very wrong about this place, Canon Chambers, very wrong indeed. Why do people do such things?" she asked.

"So many reasons," Sidney replied. "Desperation, loneliness, revenge."

"Revenge?"

"For one's own lost chances; revenge against life, against fate."

"So what should we do?"

"I think we should still try to make things better; to leave a better world than the one we found. You have already made a difference."

"I don't think I have."

280

"People will remember what has happened. By loving Zafar you have shown that things can change. People will think harder about what love means."

"It's too late, though, isn't it?"

"But not for the rest of us, and not for you. That love will live on, Annie."

She stood up and looked at him directly. "Do you think so?"

"It cannot be undone. It will be remembered."

Sidney placed his hand on hers. She looked down and let it rest. There was nothing more to be said.

A few weeks later, after the trial, when both Rosie Thomas and Andrew Redmond had escaped the death penalty but been sentenced to life imprisonment, Sidney met Inspector Keating as he was coming back from the station. They had seen enough of each other recently, and would meet again for their regular Thursday-night drink at the Eagle, but the simple act of bumping into one another with nothing urgent to discuss cheered them both up.

"Canon Chambers," Keating smiled. "Are you going back into town?"

"Indeed I am."

"Perhaps, then, I can persuade you to accompany me, and delay your journey for a short while, at a local hostelry?"

"There is a pub near my old college," Sidney replied. "I believe it is on the way. If I remember rightly, it is called the Eagle. Have you heard tell of such a place?"

"I am not sure that I have. Perhaps you could point me in the right direction?"

"It would be a pleasure."

It was a beautiful summer evening and once they had ordered the drinks and sat down, Inspector Keating used the opportunity to reflect on recent events. "What a bloody terrible business."

"Awful."

"That poor girl. Have you seen her?"

"I don't think I've done much good. She never wants to see her mother again."

"I can understand that."

Sidney replied without hesitation. "Although I, of course, have to believe that it's never too late for redemption. I only wish I could have worked out what was going on a little earlier."

"I don't know if you would have saved Mr Ali's life, Sidney. It was a slow process."

"I should have looked more carefully and thought about what was going on: the lemonade, the tea, the cricket ball — all that sleight of hand."

"The disguised delivery . . ."

"I sometimes think, Geordie, that we can learn a lot from cricket. There are so many ways in which it echoes the slings and arrows of outrageous fortune."

"It takes too long though. Football: ninety minutes, perfect. Rugby: eighty minutes, even better. You wouldn't catch me going to a Test match. Five days! It seems an eternity."

"I think for some cricketers that's the point. They think they are in heaven."

"Well it's not my idea of paradise, that's for sure."

The two men enjoyed a companionable silence, resting from the rigours of detection. A group of graduate students were laughing at the next table, enjoying all the romantic promise of youth. He noticed that one of them had a cricketing jumper draped over his shoulders. "You know, I once met an old soldier who claimed that he taught Hitler to play cricket."

"Really?" Sidney asked.

"It was during the First War. My acquaintance, I won't call him a friend as he was a bit of a fascist, had been a prisoner of war. Hitler was recovering from his wounds in a nearby hospital. One day he saw them playing and he asked for the rules of the game."

"I suppose he found it hard to follow?"

"He thought he could use it to train up his men, give them a bit of discipline."

Sidney took another sip of beer. "I wonder if the war might have been different if the Germans had played cricket. It doesn't seem likely, does it?"

"No, it never caught on. Apparently Hitler found the game 'insufficiently violent'. Although he might have thought differently if he'd come to Cambridge."

"Indeed," Sidney concurred grimly.

The Uncertainty Principle

In April 1961, two weeks after an Easter weekend when he had been out walking Dickens under a moon so full and bright that you could almost read *The Times* at midnight, Sidney was sitting at home, listening to reports on the radio of Yuri Gagarin's voyage into outer space. One account mentioned that the Russian cosmonaut had complained about his inability to find God. He had looked and looked, he had apparently said, but could see no sign of his creator. Sidney expressed irritation at this glib propaganda but Leonard Graham was not worried. He replied that there was a greater chance of finding aliens floating around in spaceships than there was of encountering a physical manifestation of God in the galaxy. "I don't know if you have heard of the Fermi Paradox?" he asked.

"I most certainly have not."

"Enrico Fermi . . ."

"An Italian?"

"A naturalised American, I believe. Fermi has suggested that, given the age of the universe and its vast number of stars, extra-terrestrial life should be quite common."

284

"And does he have any evidence for this assertion?"

"Scientists are looking at various equations to assess the mathematical probability, things like the rate of star formation in the galaxy; the fraction of stars with planets and the number per star that are habitable; the fraction of those planets which develop life, the fraction of intelligent life, and the further fraction of detectable technological intelligent life; and finally the length of time such civilisations are detectable."

"How do you know all this?"

"I heard Amanda's friend Tony talking about it the last time I was in London."

"Ah," Sidney replied. "Him."

"Amanda's friend Tony" had been on the periphery of Sidney's radar but they had never met even though Leonard had been to one of his public lectures. A professor at the University of London, Dr Anthony Cartwright had written several books on the nature of time and was in his forties. He had met Amanda at a London dinner party a few years ago (she had even asked Sidney to make a few enquiries amongst his Corpus colleagues but things had soon "gone off the boil" and she hadn't followed it up). Recently, however, Cartwright had re-emerged on the London scene and he had already taken Amanda to both the opera and the Cheltenham Gold Cup.

Sidney was used to his friend's array of suitors and had assumed that none of them would ever come up to the mark. Amanda's usual line in polite society was that if she promised herself to one man now then she might run the risk of missing out on "someone better" in a few years' time, although most of the available men these days were, she vouchsafed, "the wrong side of hopeless". Privately, she often told Sidney that it was simpler to concentrate on the reliability of her profession rather than the vagaries of the masculine whim. He was therefore under the impression that, despite her public protestations, Amanda actually preferred the freedom of the single life.

Now, however, there was news. Sidney's telephone rang at eleven o'clock at night. Dickens looked up, sensing that this might delay his nocturnal constitutional and Leonard raised an eyebrow. Sidney picked up the receiver to hear Amanda start on a story that contained no introduction. "Tony has asked me to marry him and I have accepted."

Sidney was so nonplussed that it took him a moment to realise that "Tony" must be Dr Anthony Cartwright and could only offer a hesitant answer while he bought more time. "Congratulations. That's marvellous, isn't it?"

"It is." Amanda paused, expecting more. Sidney said nothing.

"Obviously we want you to take the ceremony."

"You mean you'd like it in Grantchester?"

"No, of course not. That's too far for all my friends and we don't know anyone there. We're having it at Holy Trinity, Sloane Street."

"Where they already have a vicar. I think it's Lionel Tulis . . ." Sidney wondered why Amanda had decided to do this. It was too sudden.

"He won't mind. We've even booked a date. It's July the eighth."

"I am sure the vicar will mind, Amanda. That is quite a church."

"I'll sort him out."

"I'd rather you didn't."

"What's wrong, Sidney? I hope you're happy for me."

"Of course I'm pleased," Sidney replied without conviction. He hoped he could somehow persuade Hildegard to come to the ceremony. If not, he would have to ask Keating. "Perhaps I could just preach the sermon?" he offered.

"No, Sidney, I want you to marry us. That's the whole point. We agreed, you remember?"

"I can't remember agreeing to anything."

"Well, agree with me now. I don't care what you do as long as you approve."

"I thought I had power of veto?"

"Not in this case. I'll be glad to get it out of the way. People have been nagging me to marry for years and I don't mind telling you that it's rather a relief to get it over and done with."

Sidney was unsettled by her practical tone. "You do love him, don't you?"

"Of course."

"It's just that you don't sound . . ."

"I'm trying not to be *nervous* about it, Sidney. Can't you tell? Of course I love him. He's got the most amazing mind."

"Well then . . ."

"I think I need something a bit more than 'Well then . . .'"

"I haven't met him, Amanda. It feels a bit sudden."

"One of us has to get on with it. You've been hanging about for years."

"This isn't about me."

"No, it most definitely is not. When would you like to come and meet him? I expect you'll want to give us all that marriage preparation, won't you?"

Sidney noticed that Leonard was still in the room and that he had been listening. That was almost as irritating as the telephone call. He needed to get out and walk Dickens. "Pastoral advice is customary when people are preparing for matrimony."

"Obviously you don't need to tell us anything about sex. I think we can manage perfectly well judging by the way Tony kisses me and I don't want it to be embarrassing, either for you or for us."

Sidney blanched at the revelation of information he did not require. "I will have to talk to you about the solemnity of the occasion and what you plan to do about children."

"Tony says he doesn't want any."

"That doesn't mean we don't have to discuss it. What about you, Amanda?"

"I don't mind. It's whatever Tony wants. He's besotted. Are you coming to dinner with Nigel and Juliette a week on Saturday? We could meet there."

The last time he had been to dinner with his friends Amanda's previous engagement ring had been stolen. Sidney presumed she now had another one to match

288

the new man in her life. "It's a bit difficult, coming down from Cambridge."

"What's difficult about it? Honestly, Sidney, people do it all the time."

"I've got a lot on."

"But nothing crucial, surely? There must be some respite from all your murders. In any case, what could be more important than meeting the man with whom I'm going to spend the rest of my life?"

Nigel Thompson and his wife Juliette lived in St John's Wood. Sidney's sister Jennifer had also been invited to the dinner party with her boyfriend Johnny Johnson. Juliette asked Sidney if he wanted to "bring anyone special" since she had heard news of Hildegard. When her guest informed her that Hildegard was in Germany, she offered to invite a different eighth person to make up the numbers but Sidney was insistent that he wanted to speak to Amanda and her new fiancé without distraction.

The food was quietly stylish and unpretentious (mackerel pâté with melba toast, a chicken casserole with green beans and toasted almonds, a lemon tart) because the guests had not come to assess the cuisine but Anthony Cartwright. He obliged them by talking about himself throughout the meal.

Despite the fact that he had managed to ensnare an attractive fiancée, Cartwright was not a man who set much store by appearances. He wore a three-piece tweed suit that was probably worn every day; he had a thin, long face with small, pale-blue eyes, a tight little mouth and a chin that compensated for his reduced features by jutting forward. Sidney thought that he could have done with a beard to soften the impact of the jawline, but conversation was clearly more important than his looks and he spoke with a lifetime of assuming that he was the cleverest man in the room. He didn't offer any questions but waited to be asked himself, regarding the time in which others were speaking as an opportunity to prepare for his next salvo.

Amanda was girlish in his presence and anxious to please. "We are such opposites we should complement each other perfectly," she laughed.

Cartwright was eager to point out that he was a key member of a research team in America, and that he would be spending most of his vacations across the Atlantic, engaging in vital enquiries into the nature of movement, velocity, time and space.

"Which suits me very well," Amanda smiled, reaching out to hold her fiancé's hand. "I can continue my independent life in London while Tony masters the secrets of the universe. You will hardly notice the difference."

"And what is the nature of your research?" Sidney asked.

"I wouldn't expect a priest to understand, Canon Chambers," Tony Cartwright replied.

"Try me," Sidney bristled.

The professor took a patronising sigh before telling the assembled party that he was working on an extrapolation of Heisenberg's Uncertainty Principle, a theory which stated that the position and the velocity of an object cannot both be measured exactly and at the same time.

"And why is that?" Juliette asked.

Cartwright was irritated to be interrupted but continued. The act of measuring precisely the velocity of a subatomic particle, such as an electron, he explained, will always knock it about in an unpredictable way, so that the simultaneous measurement of its position has no validity. He was therefore seeking funding to build a sophisticated (and expensive) resonator circuit that could not only measure position and velocity more exactly and more sensitively, but also quantify the size of what he called a "superposition principle", in which a particle could simultaneously exist in two places.

"A resonator circuit?" Sidney suggested.

"The technical term is a dielectric resonator oscillator or DRO."

"But how can anything be in two places at once?" Jennifer asked.

"I'm glad you asked that," Cartwright smiled lightly. "Consider, for a moment, the idea of a half-silvered mirror. As you know, this is a piece of glass that has just enough reflective material so that exactly half the light striking it at forty-five degrees goes straight through it and the other half bounces from the reflective surface at a right-angle. So, if a single photon of light encounters this half-silvered mirror, there is a 50 per cent chance that it will be transmitted (and pass through the surface) and a 50 per cent chance that it will be reflected back. Are you with me?"

"Of course," Jennifer replied. "The light has two choices. It either goes through the mirror or it is reflected."

"That is what anyone might think."

"But surely that is the case?"

"Not exactly. One would assume that the photon must do one thing or the other, but in actual fact, quantum mechanics tells us that it can do both. We are discovering that it may even be possible to be in two locations at the same time — at least for an atom or a subatomic particle, such as an electron. At that size range, every bit of matter and energy exists in a state of blurry flux, allowing it to occupy not just two locations but an infinite number of them simultaneously."

"Blimey, Tony," Johnny Johnson answered. "That's amazing. But does it only apply to tiny objects like electrons? I can't imagine human beings will ever be able to be in a series of different places at once."

"That would certainly help our criminal friends," Sidney observed. "You could have an alibi and commit a crime at the same time."

"But this has to be nonsense," Nigel cut in. Such a conversation was becoming an affront to the ordered expectations of a politician in government.

"It's not nonsense," Cartwright continued. "In fact, it is one of the most exciting developments in the history of science. Unfortunately we don't yet understand its implications."

"What does it mean for human beings?" Jennifer asked.

"Clearly we are not the same as electrons," the professor went on. "The world we see, and which we are a part of, follows a totally different set of rules. As far as I am aware, there's just one dinner party at this particular table in North London, there is only one decanter of wine on the table, and I'm glad to say that there is also only one, inimitable, Amanda Kendall."

"I'm glad to hear that," his fiancée added quickly.

"However, what nobody can explain is why the universe seems split into these two separate and irreconcilable realities. If everything in the universe is made of quantum things, why don't we see quantum effects in everyday life? Why can't Canon Chambers, for example, who is made of quantum particles, materialise here, there, and everywhere he chooses?"

"Sidney does that all the time!" Jennifer laughed.

Anthony Cartwright kept going. "I think it's to do with gravity. Gravity roots us in the one place at the one time."

"So we need to keep our feet on the ground?"

"Exactly. But if you experimented by removing gravity . . ."

"As in space . . ."

"Then perhaps we could exist in different times simultaneously."

"You mean we could travel through time?" Amanda asked.

"It's not necessarily impossible. How far back would you like to go?"

"To the Garden of Eden, my darling: the very beginning. Just you and me."

Anthony Cartwright took out his pipe and lit it. "I don't think there was a Garden of Eden. But I'm sure Canon Chambers will take a different view."

"Indeed I do."

Sidney was determined not to be as impressed as everyone else by these scientific discursions and kept a low profile in a following conversation in which the guests decided which period of history they would most like to have lived in. Amanda saw herself as Queen Elizabeth I, Juliette as the Greek poet Sappho and Jennifer as a character in Jane Austen. When pressed, Sidney imagined that he could perhaps have been a Victorian clergyman in a country parish, like Gilbert White, whereas Tony Cartwright said he would most like to live so far into the future that he could control his time travel and know how to get back to wherever he wanted to be.

"But what if you lived in an age that didn't have time travel?" his host asked.

"I would make sure that I could be in the past and the future at the same time. That is the idea."

"Ingenious," said Juliette.

"Doesn't leave much room for God, does it?" Johnny Johnson observed.

Sidney wanted to go home. It was ten o'clock and he had an early start the next morning. He finished his glass of wine. "I don't think God is interested in the games humanity plays with its ideas."

There was silence. Sidney had spoken more critically than anyone was used to. "I'm sorry," he continued abruptly. "I must be getting back."

"Is something the matter?" Juliette asked.

"No, it's nothing. I'm quite all right."

"I hope it wasn't the food."

"Or the company," Anthony Cartwright laughed.

Sidney realised that he was making a scene. "No. It's all right. I'm sorry. I don't want to make a fuss. Slight headache." It was the kind that no amount of Aspro could clear.

"I'll give you a lift to the station," said Jennifer.

Sidney was apologetic. "I don't want to break up the party."

"It's all right," his sister replied before turning to her hostess. "I can come back. It's not far."

"I'll come with you," said Johnny.

"No, it's all right."

"I insist."

Amanda stood up and kissed Sidney goodbye. She wanted to make sure that he was still going to take her through the wedding preparations with Tony in a few days' time. Sidney tried to smile. "I look forward to it." He shook Anthony Cartwright's hand and said that it had been good to meet him at last.

Outside, and once they had settled in the car, Jennifer drove without turning to her brother at all. "Don't tell me you're jealous, Sidney."

"I really don't think I am."

"You were in such a mood. What's wrong with him?"

"You don't think he's too good to be true?"

"There are men like that, Sidney. You should be happy for Amanda. She's found someone who loves her at last."

"I know, I know. But there's something about him that doesn't feel right."

"Oh, Sidney, don't be ridiculous."

Jennifer's boyfriend was curiously silent. "What do you think, Johnny?" she asked.

"Well, I hate to disagree with you, and I know this will get me into a lot of trouble once we have dropped Sidney off, but I think your brother might have a point."

Amanda drove Anthony Cartwright to Grantchester the following week. She had suggested that they could get through the whole "marriage-preparation malarkey" over lunch in a single session at Le Bleu Blanc Rouge but Sidney was having none of it. They would need to come for two full sessions over morning coffee in the vicarage and they would be treated in the same way as any other couple.

Sidney wondered if part of their hurry was because his friend was pregnant. Although he felt sure that his sister would have told him if that was the case, Amanda was in full organisational mode. Indeed, she had already booked a honeymoon in the south of France (revealing that she was going to pay for the whole thing since, as an academic, her fiancé had so little money, and she wanted to stay at the Palais de la Méditerranée in Nice).

Sidney was surprised by Anthony Cartwright's keenness to get the ceremony out of the way before he went on his next research trip to America. It was certainly unusual for a man to leave his wife straight after the honeymoon for six weeks but his research was, apparently, at a critical stage. Science was the new frontier and he told Sidney that all of the interesting work was being done across the Atlantic.

"Richard Feynman at Caltech is working on a pictorial representation scheme for the mathematical expressions governing the behaviour of subatomic particles. I have to be there or I'll be out of the game. I don't want to end up like poor old Meldrum."

Neville Meldrum, the Professor of Theoretical Physics at Corpus, was one of Sidney's closest friends and there was nothing "poor" or "old" about him.

"I've always said that Cambridge is a bit of a backwater," Amanda joined in. "I don't know why Sidney has put up with the provinces for so long. That's why I'm so glad that we're getting married in London. We can put on a proper 'do'."

Sidney poured out the coffee and offered round a small plate of Mrs Maguire's shortbread. "And what about your family, Dr Cartwright?"

"I'm an only child, I'm afraid. My father's long gone and my mother's on the Isle of Skye. It's very much Amanda's show, as you can imagine."

Sidney tried to smile but he could already tell that this encounter was going to be tough. He reminded the couple of the introduction of the ceremony itself: that marriage was not to be enterprised lightly, but reverently, discreetly, advisedly, soberly and in the fear of God.

"We know all that," Amanda replied impatiently. "We've both been to plenty of weddings."

"But you haven't, as far as I am aware, taken vows before God yourselves."

"Certainly not."

Sidney looked at Anthony Cartwright and waited for his answer. "No," he replied. "Of course I haven't. Amanda is the love of my life."

"I suppose, then, we should start by thinking about that phrase: 'the love of my life'. I have views on the matter but it might be helpful to hear yours first. What do you think it means when someone says, 'You are the love of my life'?"

Amanda crossed her legs at her ankles. "I thought you were doing the marriage guidance."

"This is preparation," Sidney replied. "Guidance comes when things are falling apart." Again he tried to smile but his heart just wasn't in it. "And I don't think you've got to that stage yet."

"I don't intend to get to it either."

"Good." Sidney turned to Cartwright. "You understand, both of you, that marriage is for life? It has to exist after the thrill of early love has gone."

"I don't think ours will go, Amanda, do you?"

"I should jolly well hope not. I'm expecting years of unadulterated passion."

"Some people are, of course, fortunate," Sidney replied. "But my task is to make you think of all eventualities: not only the joys of children . . ."

"I don't think we'll be having any children . . ." Cartwright interrupted.

Amanda backed him up. "I think we are agreed on that."

"But also sickness, ill fortune, even death."

"Oh, Sidney, this is very gloomy," Amanda cut in.

"I don't mean to be."

"Shouldn't this be a cheerful occasion?"

"Of course, the service itself is a great moment of celebration both of God's love for mankind and of your love for each other. But we can only enjoy ourselves once the solemnities have been observed. The use of the word 'solemn' is deliberate."

"And the church in Sloane Street is quite dark," Cartwright mused.

"Mummy's going to fill it with flowers. And it's going to be a wonderful sunny day. I just know it."

"I am sure it will be," Sidney conceded. "And I know we are all looking forward to it. But before we get to that happy day I am also charged to ask you whether you are true Christian believers?"

"Oh for goodness sake, of course we are. You know that. We go to church."

"That is not always the same thing." Sidney was not going to make it easy for them. He turned to Amanda's fiancé once more. "Dr Cartwright, we have only met on one occasion and so I must ask you to answer. Have you been baptised and confirmed?"

"I have."

"And do you believe in God the Father Almighty, Maker of Heaven and Earth? And in Jesus Christ, His only-begotten Son our Lord?"

"I wouldn't quite put it as strongly as that."

"Then how would you put it?"

Amanda was exasperated. "This is awfully serious, Sidney. If you carry on like this we'll have to consider finding someone else to take the service. The vicar's already put out that you're doing it. He's insisted on saying a few words even though he's got one of those annoying clergy voices that goes up and down all the time."

"I think you will find all priests very much the same if you want to be married in a church. If the religious commitment is all too much for you then may I remind you that there is always the registry office." Sidney did not intend to sound pompous but he was not going to allow Amanda to use their friendship to get an easy ride.

"Registry office?" she almost spat. "Isn't that for runaways and adulterers?"

"I am only reminding you that you have that choice. In the meantime, I must repeat my question to you, Anthony." Sidney used Cartwright's formal Christian name deliberately. "Dost thou believe in the Holy Ghost; the holy Catholic Church; the communion of saints; the remission of sins; the resurrection of the flesh; and everlasting life after death?"

"I do, I suppose."

"Supposing isn't good enough."

"Very well, I do."

Amanda cut in again. "You are being very fierce, Sidney. Are you going to ask me all these questions?"

"Of course. In fact, Amanda, you might find me even tougher when it's your turn."

300

"I think you're punishing me for marrying Tony rather than you."

"Not at all," said Sidney, angry that she should refer directly to their friendship. "I am simply making sure that you know what you are doing. Believe me, you'll thank me for it in the end."

"I think we'll be the judge of that."

"No," Sidney replied. "God will be." He couldn't quite work out what had got into him and why he was so intensely irritated but he wasn't going to have his faith passed over for the sake of social nicety.

The following Tuesday was a university teaching morning, and Sidney bicycled over to Corpus in good time to put some first-year undergraduates through their theological paces. As he approached the college, he realised that he was unusually early, and thought he would take a detour to see if he could find his colleague Neville Meldrum, the eminent astrophysicist. There were a few questions he wanted to ask.

Professor Meldrum was a man of fastidious precision in his late forties, and he was probably the best-dressed fellow in the college. He wore elegant three-piece suits from Savile Row (his father had been an Edwardian dandy), crisp white shirts with starched collars, and his handmade shoes were beautifully polished.

He was preparing for the morning's academic work, wiping clean a blackboard in the lecture hall that was filled with calculations Sidney could not hope to understand, setting out monochromatic absorption coefficients and opacities in stellar interiors. Sidney could just about remember the chemical symbols. "You should come to a few lectures," Meldrum encouraged. "It would help you keep abreast of the space race."

"It looks very complicated."

"No more so than theology and ancient Greek. We could exchange tutorials."

"I think I stopped at the periodic table."

"You should start again. We're moving on to discuss dark matter. Although," Meldrum paused for effect, "I imagine you have dark matters of your own."

Sidney had forgotten the limitations of Neville Meldrum's humour but he liked the man for his extreme precision. He spent his life in search of clarity and Sidney knew that he should get to the point as quickly as possible. His colleague acknowledged that he did not know Anthony Cartwright personally but had, indeed, heard of him as they had both applied for the same post in 1954: a research fellowship at the Royal Observatory, Greenwich.

Sidney began by asking how much their fields of scientific enquiry overlapped and if his friend could throw any light on Anthony Cartwright's desire to build a resonator circuit and his work in the United States.

"The Americans are ahead of us here, constructing microwave amplifiers, quantum oscillators and infrared lasers, so he's on to something. But who is funding his trips across the Atlantic and all his lab work? I wonder if it's Bell Labs, or an American university like Columbia? A few physicists even have their research specifically funded by private donation."

"That would be Amanda."

"Miss Kendall? Forgive me, Sidney, I know she is a formidable woman but surely she is no expert in quantum mechanics?"

"Indeed not."

Neville Meldrum was sufficiently surprised to distract himself with a course of action over which he had immediate control. He began to sort through his lecture notes in preparation for the next set of undergraduates. "I'm sure Cartwright's intentions are honourable," he said to himself.

"Are you?"

Neville looked up. "No, of course I'm not, Sidney. I'm just saying so to be polite, although I can't quite imagine a man marrying a woman simply to fund his research."

"People do marry for money, Neville."

"Yes, I suppose they do."

Sidney guessed that his colleague was holding something back. "What is it, Neville?"

"The odd thing is that I thought Cartwright was married already." He checked his notes once more. "Perhaps the wife died."

"They certainly haven't said anything about that to me."

"You would think they might mention it. It is peculiar if he hasn't, don't you think? I'm pretty sure they lived in Cornwall for a while. I think she breeds dogs. She was definitely Cornish. I remember hearing people say that she was quite fierce about it; wanted independence for the county and said she'd never wanted to leave — which is a bit of a handicap if you are an astrophysicist. There aren't too many opportunities for them in Cornwall."

"There's Exeter, I suppose, but that's in Devon."

"The curious thing is that when he went to London I think they bought a place in King's Lynn. I've no idea why. Perhaps she couldn't face living in the capital. Although if you're going to live in King's Lynn you might as well be in Cornwall. You'd probably get more visitors."

"This is very alarming," Sidney replied. "How easy do you think it would be to find out if he's still married to her? I don't want Amanda to enter into a bigamous marriage."

"Indeed not," said Professor Meldrum, before adding a thought that had, as yet, remained unspoken. "Then Cartwright really would have to be in two places at the same time."

On the Saturday Amanda was singing in a late-afternoon concert given by the Bach Choir at the Festival Hall and she persuaded Sidney to join both her and Tony Cartwright for drinks afterwards. There were, she informed him, quite a few matters to discuss, not least the amount of time he thought it necessary to give to religious preparation before the wedding.

"I don't know why we're having to go through all this so thoroughly. It's lovely that you want to see us but we can't all be as religious as you, Sidney."

"Sometimes I feel I'm not religious enough — but we're not here to talk about me."

Cartwright went to the bar to order the drinks. Alone together for the first time since the engagement, Amanda was keen to seek Sidney's approval. "Isn't Tony marvellous?" she asked him.

"He's certainly very intelligent," Sidney replied. "An original choice."

"You were expecting one of my posh friends whom you automatically assume to be dim?"

"I had no expectations in that matter, I promise. But you've surprised us all. I hope you'll be very happy together."

"I'm glad you approve."

"It does seem quite a hasty decision, Amanda."

"I'm not pregnant, if that's what you're implying."

"No. It's not that."

"Then what is the matter? I can tell that you are holding back."

"No, I'm not," Sidney lied.

"I'm not getting any younger . . ."

"Do you think you know each other well enough?" Sidney asked. "Have you met his family and friends? Do you know what he really believes? Has he been involved with anyone else? What do you think he is looking for in a relationship?"

"Goodness, Sidney, those are far too many questions to answer all in one go. We love each other. Isn't that enough?"

"It's only that I've always thought that love needs strong foundations. You have to make sure they are secure before you build a marriage."

Amanda could see that Tony was paying for the drinks and was about to return. "Yes, of course, Sidney, I understand all that. It's very odd, isn't it, you doling out all this marital advice without being married yourself?"

"I am aware of my limitations."

"Perhaps you'll know soon enough. Tony and I are expecting to come to Germany in the next year or two," she said, impishly.

"You've told him about Hildegard?"

"I had to assure Tony you were a man with your heart in the right place." Cartwright was smiling as he returned with the drinks. "He thought you were a pansy." Amanda looked dotingly towards her fiancé. "Didn't you, darling?"

Sidney was badly in need of Geordie Keating's advice but when they next met for their regular night of backgammon in the Eagle his friend was out of sorts. His eldest daughter, Maggie, was walking out with her first boyfriend and the inspector was struggling to come to terms with it.

"It's the end of childhood," he complained. "Maggie's not my little girl any more. I wish she was still seven."

"We cannot halt the advance of time, Geordie. In a year or two, I'm sure you'll both still love each other. And you'll always be her dad."

"But I have no influence on her any more. It's all Davie, Davie, Davie . . ."

"And what does Davie do?"

"Nothing that's going to make any money. He wants to be some kind of pop singer. They asked me for the cash to get a coach to Liverpool. Apparently it's all happening up there. She's only sixteen so I said no. What do they think they're playing at?"

"You don't want her running away. She might do that, you know."

"Are you suggesting I should just approve of the whole thing and go along with it?"

"I am suggesting that you do not fall out with her. That is a very different thing. She is still more dependent on you than she will admit, either in public or to you. Try not to lose your temper, Geordie, and be patient. They come back to you in the end."

"I don't know how you know all this."

"I do have a sister."

"The one that shares a flat with Miss Kendall? How's she getting on, by the way?"

"That is what I wanted to talk to you about."

Sidney explained the situation and Keating listened attentively. After finishing one pint and starting a second he was ready to pass judgement. "It might be worth having a word with Miss Kendall's parents: find out what they think of Cartwright. No father is going to give his entire approval to his daughter's choice and if he's got any sense he'll hold some money back. Do you know his lawyer?"

"I don't think I can investigate the family finances."

"You can get an idea. What will happen when Amanda's father dies? Or rather, both parents? What if they had a car accident or something like that?"

"You don't think that this is a deliberate plot that eventually involves the murder of Amanda's parents, do you?"

"No, of course not. Although . . ."

"You are already becoming even more suspicious than I am."

"That's the ABC of crime investigation, Sidney. Assume nothing. Believe nobody. Check everything. And there's also D — for dosh. It always finds its way in there somehow. You could then find out how much the old man is going to shell out once his daughter marries (there's often a clause in the trust fund) and how much he is holding back. You could ask him about his will, if he's made one and if his children have seen it. Miss Kendall has a brother, I believe."

"He married a divorcee and is in disgrace with his parents."

"So much so that he's been cut off? It would be helpful to find out if Miss Kendall is the sole beneficiary. How much do you think Sir Cecil is worth?"

Sidney thought for a moment. "He must be a millionaire. There's the large house in Chelsea and they've also got somewhere in Monte Carlo."

"If you ask me it could be interesting to find out how much it costs to build a new science laboratory and, indeed, to support an existing wife."

"It's a delicate matter."

"You must let me know if there is anything the police can do."

"That's very kind but I don't want you getting involved. It's a London matter and you have plenty to do here."

"I know that, Sidney, but I like Miss Kendall very much. I don't want to see her life ruined."

"Ruined? You would put it as strongly as that?"

"If Cartwright's after her money, if he's married already, or if he's simply an out and out bastard, then we need to conduct some enquiries."

Sidney was touched by his friend's vehemence but was worried about tactics. Could he manage to make Amanda see the error of her ways, or was he being unreasonable in suspecting Cartwright of such base motives? The next stage was surely to submit them to closer questioning when they came to the vicarage. He would talk to them about their future life together, and try to use the idea of a shared existence to ask how they planned to run their financial affairs.

"The important word," he began, "is 'sharing'. Through marriage the two of you become one; no longer single, but a newly created joint identity that combines the best that you both have to offer."

Amanda was still defensive and brittle, batting away searching questions with jokes. "My looks and his brains, you mean."

"No, I don't mean that."

"Rather than my looks and her brains?" Cartwright added. He seemed bored.

Sidney tried again. "It's more a case of mutual understanding. You have the same common values, the same ethical ambition, a shared outlook on life."

"Are you suggesting my values are 'common'?" Amanda laughed nervously.

"This is no time to be frivolous. Marriage is a serious and sacred step in which you acknowledge both God's love and your love for each other. It requires you to be less selfish. You have to put the other person first."

"I understand," Cartwright replied. "We work as a unit. We share the same house, the same ideas, and have a common outlook. We put everything into one pot and stir it up into some kind of marital soup."

"Yes, ideally there should be no secrets and complete transparency." Sidney had been careful not to use the word "money", and had waited to see if either of them brought up the subject. Now Amanda did so.

"I'm not worried about money or anything like that," she answered, turning to her fiancé. "All that I have is yours."

"Ditto," Cartwright replied.

Sidney thought that Amanda's future husband should have made an effort to be more romantic (he could do better than "ditto" for a start). He looked directly at them both. "You are aware that Amanda is wealthy."

"I am."

"Money can influence a marriage in many ways."

"I imagine it's better to have it than not."

"And you won't resent sharing it, Amanda?"

Anthony Cartwright cut in before his fiancée could answer. "I do earn money of my own. I am not a sponger."

"I wasn't implying that you were. Sometimes, however, a man can feel diminished if a wife has more money than he does."

"I think I have enough self-confidence to protect me from those kind of feelings, Canon Chambers."

"I'm going to fund Tony's research," Amanda explained. "I can't think of anything more important than doing that. You can hardly accuse me of being frivolous if I do, can you, Sidney? What could be more wifely and supportive? And that's what I'm going to be."

She rose, reached for Cartwright's hand, and leant across to kiss Sidney on the cheek. "Happy now?" she asked.

A week later, Sidney was dining in Corpus and took the opportunity to talk to Professor Meldrum once more. It was, however, difficult to get a word in over the braised lamb and Neville's conversation was full of his recent experiments into the gas content of interstellar space and the strong dependence of opacity on wavelength.

"You'd be better off discussing the gas content at High Table," the Professor of English joked. "There's plenty of opaque conversation here."

While Professor Meldrum thought he had as good a sense of humour as the next man, his equilibrium was easily tested. "I think it's important," he pronounced, "that we monitor solar influences, the behaviour of high-energy particles, and examples of gravitational collapse. It is a pity that those of you working in the humanities expect scientists to familiarise themselves with early medieval poetry but know nothing of the current developments in cosmic-ray research."

"It's far too difficult."

"Nonsense. Even Canon Chambers understands it when he tries."

Sidney had drifted off and was thinking about Hildegard. He worried, on waking, to think that he would have to remember Meldrum's previous conversation about the study of elementary particles and their behaviour at high energies. He changed the subject as quickly as he could and asked his friend whether he had discovered anything more about Anthony Cartwright's marital status.

"I'm glad you've brought that up," his companion replied, "since I have had rather more success in these investigations than I have had in my laboratory. I am beginning to see the attraction of having a sideline, Sidney. The results are more immediately rewarding."

"They can be a distraction, of course."

"Although, in this case, I think the diversion is definitely worth pursuing. There is still a Mrs Cartwright living and she has a house in King's Lynn."

"It couldn't be a different woman?"

"It could, but this one has the same line of business as the Mrs Cartwright I remember hearing about. Perhaps you could go and see her on the quiet?"

"Perhaps I should . . ."

"You'll need an excuse, I imagine. You won't be able to find out what you need to know from a telephone call and you obviously can't just turn up and ask impertinent questions; however, I have already thought of something that should be able to yield the necessary results." Meldrum took a sip of Beaujolais. He was expecting Sidney to be pleased with his idea. "You remember that I told you she bred dogs?"

"And how is that relevant?"

"You're being unusually slow, Sidney. Don't you see? You could take Dickens. He could be your cover."

Sidney worried how, with his severely limited expertise, he could get away with talking to a Labrador breeder with any authority. He could ask Agatha Redmond for advice, he supposed, but he was keen to give that particular family a wide berth.

Neville suggested that Sidney could have a niece or nephew who wanted a puppy. Sidney could offer Dickens's "services" to one of Mrs Cartwright's bitches in exchange.

"And what if I don't actually need a puppy?"

"You don't have to go through with it all. You can just discuss the matter and change your mind afterwards."

"I don't like to lead people on."

Neville was tempted to pick Sidney up on this but let the remark pass. "It was only an idea," his colleague continued. "After all, you're the detective."

Sidney had already arranged to meet Amanda on her own in the American Bar of the Savoy to discuss matters and he decided to stick with their plan before even thinking of making any sortie to Norfolk. He wondered if a bit of close questioning might make his friend aware of his reservations, but Amanda had already anticipated his doubts, immediately joking that she hoped Sidney wasn't planning to persuade her to call the whole thing off.

She insisted on champagne and regaled her friend with stories surrounding her preparation for the great day. Her dress had been ordered from John Cavanagh's Mayfair salon, there were going to be three bridesmaids and two pages, and Jennifer was to be the maid of honour. She had paid Henry Poole on Savile Row for Tony's morning suit and her mother was going to wear peach. Sidney was inwardly appalled by the implications of all this expenditure. He replied that he was greatly looking forward to the whole thing, it was sure to go well (the church was marvellous and the vicar was a good man), and he was convinced that the happy couple were going to have a wonderful honeymoon. He only wanted to ask Amanda, and he knew it was none of his business, whether she was happy with the idea that she and her husband planned to spend so much time apart so soon after marrying.

"But that's the beauty of it," Amanda insisted. "We have all the benefits of wedlock without giving up any independence. Tony says our marriage will be like a fulcrum; we are either side of it and connected to it. It doesn't matter whether it goes up or down, we will always be joined."

Sidney could see that he was going to have to be blunt. "Are you sure you want to go through with this, Amanda?"

"Of course I'm sure."

"What will you do about money?"

"What do you mean? We've already discussed this. I've got loads and Daddy likes Anthony very much. He says it's time we had some brains in the family. He thinks Tony's going to win the Nobel Prize!"

"But how will you manage? Who will be in charge?"

"Of the money? Why, Tony, of course."

"You'll have a joint account? How much have you given him already?"

"Really, Sidney, that's none of your business. I don't know why you're worrying about it. There's plenty of money to go round."

"I'm sure there is, but I think you should retain some control."

"Are you saying that I shouldn't trust my husband?"

Sidney had to backtrack. "I think it would be good if you had some kind of independence."

"Do you mean a running-away fund? Mummy has one of them. That's the only piece of advice she has given me. 'Make sure you have enough to do a moonlight flit if it all goes wrong. Every woman should have a year's supply and time to find someone else.' She's still got hers. Why don't you like Tony?"

"I do," Sidney began. "I admire his intelligence and I'm glad that he's so keen on you." Sidney stopped himself from using the word "love".

"He dotes on my every word. Isn't that wonderful?"

Sidney was not going to be distracted. "Do you know much about his past, I wonder? He hasn't been married before or anything like that?"

"You asked about that at our very first session. I can't imagine the situation has changed."

"No, I can't imagine it either. But I suppose people should know something about their partner's previous history?"

"I'm not so sure, Sidney. I think I'd rather keep everything in the dark. I don't want to have to talk about dreadful people like Guy Hopkins. The only person Tony knows about is you."

"I am not a former boyfriend, Amanda."

"You know what I mean."

"This is not about us. Tony is a good deal older than you. I'd be surprised if there wasn't somebody."

"But why do I need to know? Tony doesn't believe in the past anyway. He says we have to think of time in a completely different way these days: past, present and future are all one."

"I seem to remember T.S. Eliot thinking something similar . . ."

"I am 'all women' apparently: 'all women for all time'. Isn't that romantic?"

"Yes, I suppose it is."

"Don't be such a killjoy. What on earth is wrong with you, Sidney? Do you resent my happiness? I wish you'd cheer up. You're not very good company."

"I'm sorry, Amanda, I am trying to help you."

"Are you thinking I should call the whole thing off? Is that really why you wanted to see me?"

"Well . . ."

"Honestly, Sidney, I thought better of you. You can't have me all to yourself. Besides, you've got Hildegard. I haven't been at all jealous about her, have I? And if

316

you're going to keep banging on about 'the past' then she's certainly had one."

"There's no need to bring her into this."

"There is, actually, Sidney. You are being a hypocrite. It's all right for you to toddle off to Germany whenever you feel like it and see your merry widow, but it's not all right for me to find the one chance of happiness I've ever had in my life. Can't you see that what I am doing is almost exactly the same as you? I will be married to someone who is abroad, just as Hildegard is abroad. I am copying you. You should be flattered. Instead you seem to want exclusive access to both me and Hildegard at the same time . . ."

"That's not true."

"In fact, you should talk to Tony about it. That's what he's always going on about; how things can exist simultaneously . . ."

"I know. That's partly what I came to . . ."

"You're just jealous because we're actually getting on with it while you persist in shilly-shallying around."

"That's not the case at all, and well you know it."

"I don't even know why you've come here. I'm sure we've gone through all my marital arrangements a hundred times."

"Twice. It's only that I think you should consider . . ."

"What should I consider, Sidney? Come on. Spit it out."

"I'm not sure if Dr Cartwright is all that he says he is."

"You think he's some kind of impostor? For God's sake, Sidney! I've been to his offices. I've even seen him give a lecture. I KNOW WHO HE IS."

"But how much do you know about his past?"

"As much as I need to know, thank you very much. Honestly, Sidney, I've had enough of your conniving little questions. They are mean-spirited and petty and cheap and I don't think I can put up with them a minute longer. Why do you have to go on and on and on?"

Amanda stood up.

Sidney tried again. "I'm sorry if you are upset. I only want your happiness."

"That's very good of you, but I can't accept what you say when you accompany it with such perfidious and insinuating doubt. Tony loves me. And I love Tony. You can take someone else's wedding on July the eighth but you can't take mine. Consider yourself uninvited . . ."

"But Amanda . . ."

"DON'T 'BUT AMANDA' ME! Leave me alone. Don't speak to me ever again. I've absolutely had enough of this. Everyone, even Jennifer, has cast aspersions about Tony and asked me if I am serious. Well, I am. I don't care about any of you. I've got Tony and I've got money and we'll find a new set of friends and we won't ever have to see any of you again."

Amanda picked up her wrap and stormed out into the foyer. Sidney was now aware that the cocktail bar was silent and that everyone was looking at him.

He felt sick.

A waiter approached. "Is everything all right, sir?"

"I think I'd better have the bill."

Sidney had never paid at the Savoy before and he imagined the price of the champagne they had just consumed would be close to his weekly wage. He was shaking. No one had ever spoken to him in such a way. Now he would have to collect his thoughts and try to talk calmly to someone about what to do next: Jennifer, Keating, Meldrum; even Mrs Kendall.

As the waiter brought the bill, Amanda rushed back into the bar and leant down by the chair she had recently vacated.

"I left my handbag."

She looked at Sidney for as briefly as it could be construed polite before leaving once more.

"Don't speak."

Cartwright's Kennels was situated on the outskirts of King's Lynn, next to a farm on the road to Hunstanton. Mrs Cartwright was a small thin woman with tired skin and short, unwashed blonde hair that was probably cut by a friend rather than a hairdresser. She wore jeans tucked into Wellington boots and a loose olive-green jumper that seemed too hot for summer. Sidney explained that he was thinking of offering Dickens as a stud dog. This could perhaps be for free, in exchange for one of the resultant puppies.

Mrs Cartwright was wary. How old was Dickens and was he of breeding quality? Did he have pedigree and did his owner have the necessary paperwork leading back to his great-great-grandparents? Had he been checked for brucellosis, entropion, ectoprion, inherited eye disease and dysplasia? What was his hip score?

Sidney was out of his depth, and although Mrs Cartwright said that she would need far more information, she was, at least, happy to show him round. He could meet the bitches and see the scale of her operation. Her aim was to produce good-looking, healthy and well-socialised pups from carefully planned litters. It was an emotional and risky business, she told him, vet's fees were increasing all the time, and she hated saying goodbye to eight-week-old puppies after she had cared for them so lovingly and when their personalities were already shining through.

Sidney was surprised to see a set of concrete out-houses that looked too inhospitable for dogs. "Do you own those buildings too?" he asked.

"Oh, they're just storage. They're full of my husband's stuff."

Sidney could hardly believe his luck. "Does he help with the dogs?"

"He's in London most of the time. He just comes back in the holidays."

"Is he a teacher?"

The owner pushed back a strand of hair that had blown over her face in the wind. "University."

"I see. That must be difficult."

"What makes it difficult?"

"Him being away." Sidney could tell that she was only entertaining this kind of conversation because he was a priest rather than a dog breeder.

She knelt down and began a quick inspection of Sidney's Labrador. "I like it. It leaves me free for the dogs while he gets on with his work. He telephones most days."

"Don't you miss him?"

"He's my best friend."

"And you don't need to see him to know that he loves you, I'm sure." Sidney smiled encouragingly.

She did not reply and Sidney knew that he could not pursue this conversation without arousing suspicion. He needed to switch back to the subject of dogs. "I have Dickens as my best friend."

Mrs Cartwright visibly cheered. "He is?"

"What I like about him is his reliability and his optimism. If only people were the same."

"It's why we breed dogs; so we can pass on their qualities to the next generation. We're always seeking to improve the breed."

Mrs Cartwright returned to discuss the possibility of Dickens becoming a stud dog. Did Sidney know his dog's conformation well enough to be able to tell just how his qualities could improve on those of the bitch? Did Dickens have a strong rear or front that would compensate for one weaker in those areas? Did he have a good layback of shoulder, a nice "double thigh" and the proper tail set?

Sidney struggled to answer these questions but assured Mrs Cartwright that he would be happy to leave Dickens for a full assessment. There were other things he needed to do in King's Lynn.

"Would you be here for the engagement?" she asked.

Sidney was inwardly startled by the question. "How long are dogs normally engaged for?"

"At least twenty minutes."

"Is that all?"

"Canon Chambers, you do know what 'engagement' means? It's not like having a fiancé. It's mating. Is he fertile?"

"I'm not sure."

"So he hasn't been a stud before?"

"Not as far as I know. I am not always sure what he gets up to."

"I need to know if he's got the libido to do the job effectively."

"I think he's got that all right. He's very keen on lady Labradors on the meadows."

Mrs Cartwright was unimpressed. "The fact that he has a tendency to chase every bitch in sight, whether she's in season or not, doesn't necessarily mean that he will have a clue what to do when it comes to the point. Dogs can behave very differently at the crucial moment. A bit like human beings. You're not married yourself?"

Now they were back on course. Sidney laid aside his embarrassment at being asked such questions. "I am hoping to find a wife, but it's not easy for a clergyman. How did you meet your husband?"

"It was after my mother had to sell our farm in Cornwall. We've never been lucky with money. My dad dropped down dead, the debtors came and we had to do a flit. Mum came to stay with her sister up here and brought me with her. Tony was just about to leave for university . . ."

"And so . . ."

"We were childhood sweethearts. He was the first boy at his school to go to Oxford. He studied so hard, and I used to help him in the holidays until his work got too difficult to understand. His dad had passed over too and we went on these great big walks along the beach with the dogs. Have you been to Holkham? I think it's the best in the world. If we had the weather people would think it was the Caribbean."

"And you got married here?"

"In the registry office. We're not churchgoers, I am afraid, Canon Chambers."

"I suppose it's not as popular as it once was . . ."

"Never have been. That was a long time ago, though; over twenty years. Be silver soon and we're not that old."

"How often do you see each other?"

"He is always busy in London but he gets here every other weekend. We always have the summer together, and a bit of Christmas and Easter. It's easier when you don't have children."

"You didn't . . ."

"We couldn't. Don't know why. Doesn't matter too much now, I suppose. The dogs are my children."

"And is business good?"

"It's terrible really; we're always needing money. Tony sends me some whenever he can, but London's expensive and that's where he is."

"You did say what he does, but I've forgotten," Sidney remarked as casually as he could. He only needed one final confirmation and then he would leave immediately for the registry office.

"He teaches at the university."

"I do a bit of teaching myself. I wonder what subject . . ."

"Physics. It all goes over my head, but he tells me that I don't need to worry. I'm his time off. When he's here he doesn't want to be anywhere else. He says it is always such a wrench to leave but he has to earn money otherwise we won't have anything to live on. I know it sounds a bit weird, living apart, but I can rely on him and if I'm anxious about anything he will come."

"I'm sorry about the money worries." Sidney realised he was pushing it but couldn't help himself.

"There's not much we can do about that. But Tony told me last week he's got a big job coming up and that should bring in quite a bit extra. It'll mean working away from home a little bit more than usual but it'll be worth it. We can convert the outbuildings, have a bit more space, and maybe even go on holiday together. He was talking about America."

"You've never been?"

"Neither of us have. Tony's scared of flying but says he's going to treat me to a trip to California. It'd be quite something, don't you think?"

It took some nerve for a man to describe his forthcoming nuptials as "working away from home a little bit more than usual" and Sidney began to wonder about the psychology of bigamy.

"Do you want to go ahead with this?" Mrs Cartwright asked. "It's quite a procedure."

"I think I'll wait. Although I could perhaps put my name down for a puppy, couldn't I?" He thought he could give one to Leonard, if only to see the look on his face.

"I'll take your address then. We should have some in September."

"That would be most kind. It's been a pleasure meeting you. I'm sorry, I didn't quite catch your first name?"

"You can call me Mandy. Mandy Cartwright."

Sidney marvelled at the nerve of a man who was planning on having two wives with exactly the same name.

He visited the registry office and established the facts. Then he walked back through the streets of King's Lynn. People were braving the wind, hoping the rain would hold off. He telephoned his sister to find out where Amanda was and discovered that she was already preparing for a wedding rehearsal that was due to take place that night. "It was the only time the vicar could manage", she said. "I don't think gatecrashers will be welcome," she warned, "if that's what you're thinking of doing."

Sidney kept his own counsel. It was going to be quite a business telling Mandy Cartwright why she needed to join him on the next train down to London.

Holy Trinity, Sloane Street was a suitably decorative venue and the apotheosis of the Arts and Crafts movement, with an imposing Italianate marble exterior and stained-glass windows by Morris and Burne-Jones. Sidney had always found it gaudy, imposing, and a little to close to Roman Catholicism for his taste.

As he entered the darkness from the brightness of an early summer evening, he stumbled across a group of flower ladies who were preparing a series of freestyle floral displays of carnations, chrysanthemums, lilies, gladioli and roses. There was going to be a scene, Sidney knew, and for one moment he began to doubt whether he was doing the right thing. But Cartwright was on the verge of breaking the law — his wife needed to see for herself what was going on — and Amanda had spurned every attempt at a warning.

The rehearsal was already under way by the time they arrived. Jennifer stood by Amanda, and a best man Sidney had never seen before was next to Cartwright. The priest was telling the couple when to come forward, where to stand and when to kneel, and he asked the best man whether he had the ring. Everything was straightforward, he told the prospective bride and groom. It was *their* day, and the beginning of *their* happiness, and he would do everything possible to make it unforgettable.

He then proceeded to go through the order of service, casually remarking that no one had ever, in his experience, piped up to say that they knew of any just cause or impediment.

"There's always a first time," came a voice from the south transept.

It was Mandy Cartwright.

"What is going on?" the priest asked. "I can't understand that there is a problem. I have published the banns for the last three Sundays."

"That man is my husband."

"I don't think so," Amanda Kendall scoffed. "He is about to be mine."

"Amanda . . ." Sidney began.

"What are you doing here?"

"My God," said Cartwright.

"How could you do this?" his wife asked.

"For us," Anthony Cartwright replied. "For money."

Amanda realised the horror of the situation. She turned and slapped her fiancé's face.

Sidney walked up to the prospective groom. "Dr Cartwright, when I asked you at our first marriage preparation if either of you had made your vows before, you denied that you had done so."

"That is correct."

"You lied."

"You asked me if I had made them 'before God'. I made them in a registry office. That is not the same thing."

Sidney was thrown by the lack of apology or embarrassment. "The laws of the Church and the laws of man are equally binding in matters of marriage," he continued. "Dr Cartwright, you are already married. You've never been to America. You've lied about your career and cruelly deceived my greatest friend. I am too angry to explain further. You have defrauded Miss Kendall."

"I think you'll find she gave her money willingly."

"How could you?" Amanda asked at last. "How could you do this to me?"

"I tried to love you," Dr Cartwright replied. "And I almost succeeded."

"Don't make it worse," his wife said.

"You beasts," spat Amanda. "Are you in it together? Has this happened before? Were you plotting the whole thing? How could you? What am I going to do? How am I going to tell anyone? It's unbearable. You're vile. All of you. Vile."

Jennifer took her by the arm and led her away.

"Come on," Mandy Cartwright told her husband. "You have some explaining to do. Don't think you're going to get off lightly."

They walked off in the opposite direction, followed by a silent best man, leaving Sidney alone with the priest.

"I thought I had learned not to be surprised by anything," the Reverend Lionel Tulis began. "But this really does take the biscuit."

"I wonder about the origins of that phrase . . ." Sidney mused. "It doesn't seem enough to explain what we have just witnessed. Mrs Cartwright remained so practical throughout. It almost makes you wonder if it has happened before."

"I suppose we could both do with a cup of tea. Unless you'd prefer something stronger?"

"I don't suppose you have any whisky?" Sidney asked.

"I do indeed," said Tulis. "I can't stand sherry."

"Then we have much in common."

★ ★ ★

Although it wasn't one of their usual Thursday nights, Sidney asked Keating if they could meet the following evening so that they could talk through everything that had happened. The inspector described it as a "post-mortem without the dead body".

"What I'm wondering," he began, "is if the wife knew as little as she says she did and how she managed to stay so calm? Perhaps they were planning to bump Amanda off. Fortunately it didn't get that far. You did well, Sidney. How did you guess?"

"I don't know," he answered sadly, still guilty about the public nature of Amanda's humiliation. "Instinct is a funny thing."

"I'm not sure the sixth sense exists."

"Neither am I, but we have to hope."

"Do you think it's the same as knowing God?" Keating asked. "Some people have it and some don't?"

"That would put believers at an unfair advantage."

"But they have that. The opportunity of an afterlife, for a start."

"That is open to everyone, Geordie. The Church of England does not blackball potential members."

"Not even Cartwright?"

"If he is penitent, then no. Do you suppose he'll get away with it?"

"There's not much he can be charged with," Keating replied. "Intention is not the same as action. Despite the rehearsal we can't prove he was actually going to do it; and besides, what good would it do his marriage? They need to sort a few things out. But it's Amanda I'm worried about. Have you spoken to her?"

"Jennifer will tell me when she's ready."

"I imagine she'd want to give men the go-by for a few years. There's little chance of her rushing into anything else."

"I very much doubt it."

"Which leaves us with you, Sidney. When are you going to Germany again?"

"Next month."

"I wish you'd get on with it, man. It's been going on for far too long."

"I know, Geordie."

Sidney looked up and noticed Neville Meldrum at the bar offering replenishments through gesture alone. "I don't know why I feel so uncertain about these things. But I see we are to be joined by our friend, the eminent physicist. He doesn't enjoy these kinds of discussion. He is a great believer in privacy."

"But he must wonder what has happened?"

"'Wonder' is a strange word, isn't it, Geordie?" Sidney asked, moving the conversation sharply away from the subject of Hildegard. "We mainly use the idea of 'wondering' to mean 'thinking' when, in fact, it is supposed to be so much more than that. The 'wonder' felt by the shepherds at the Nativity, or the disciples at Pentecost; that sense of amazement when we experience something that is so far beyond our comprehension and yet it is still revealed to us in all its glory as a gift from the infinite. I think we've lost our awareness of what 'wonder' really means: the more we content ourselves with the narrow confines of our existence, the less we wonder. It's like the word 'awful'.

Now it's something bad, but previously it was close to wonder. People were filled with awe."

"I was only wondering where my next pint was coming from, Sidney. I wasn't expecting a free sermon."

"It's on the house, Geordie," his friend smiled. "Unlike, unfortunately, our drinks."

Sidney was tired by the time he returned home and was glad to have the vicarage to himself. Leonard was preaching in London, Mrs Maguire had left a little shepherd's pie to heat up, and Dickens was waiting expectantly. Sidney was looking forward to putting his feet up, listening to a little jazz, and rereading the letter from Hildegard that had arrived that morning.

My Sidney

I hope you are keeping out of trouble. We are all looking forward to your visit and to discover how your German has improved! I will have all your favourite food and I will arrange trips into the country. You will discover that Berlin has changed very quickly. There are builders on every corner.

I imagine your life every day. How is Amanda? I sometimes worry if she will be happy. You are so good to her, as you are to all your friends, but remember there is one who likes to think that she is special, as you are to her, and she longs for your visit. She is

Your Hildegard.

★　★　★

It had begun to rain but Dickens needed his late night constitutional. As he took him out for the briefest of jaunts across the meadows, Sidney thought of all that Hildegard meant to him. He really must not let the opportunity pass, he decided. August could not come soon enough.

When he returned he was surprised to see a car parked outside the front door to the vicarage with the engine still running. As he approached, a figure emerged to speak to him.

It was Amanda.

"I won't stay long," she began. "I'm going to see some friends in Norfolk. I need some time away from London. I came to apologise. I should not have been angry with you."

"I am sorry for what I did."

"How soon did you know?" Amanda asked.

"I had to do a bit of investigation."

"When we had those drinks at the Savoy you knew that something was wrong?"

"I didn't. But I suspected."

She put her hand to her cheek, trying to stop the tears. "Why didn't you come out with it then?"

"I had no evidence."

"But you are *always* right."

"No, I'm not. I thought it was my own foolish jealousy. Please, won't you come in?"

"I'd rather not," Amanda replied. She could not look her friend in the eye. "I'm embarrassed and I'm not at my best. I should drive on."

"Did you want anything in particular?"

"No, I just wanted to say sorry. That was all. My mother said I should, and I knew it too. I've been very stubborn."

"Well, I'm very sorry too. Are you sure you won't have a nightcap?"

"No. I can't." Amanda hesitated. She did not appear to want to leave. "I was just wondering, though . . ."

"What is it?"

"No. It's nothing. I can't say it."

"We are friends. There is nothing we cannot say to each other."

"I'm not sure. I think there is. The things unspoken."

"Ah," Sidney replied. "Those things."

Amanda looked up and spoke quickly, hoping the words would disappear as soon as she said them; or perhaps hoping that if the outcome was not to her liking she had never said the words she was going to say at all. "I've been thinking," she began, "and I know this is mad, and you probably think I am crazy, but would it be a disaster if you married me? Not in the religious sense, you understand, but in the romantic sense. As husband and wife . . ."

If she had suggested this ten years ago it would have been the most thrilling moment in Sidney's life. But now, after so much had happened, it was too late.

"Amanda, this isn't really the time," he answered, as kindly as he could. "You've had a terrible shock."

"Perhaps I needed it. It's made me come to my senses. You are the only person who understands me."

"I'm not so sure about that."

"I've been so hopeless at choosing. I always knew you were a good man, but I foolishly thought that you weren't enough for me. It was all about silly things like money and status and I've been undone by both of them. Now I've missed my chance. You're in love with Hildegard, aren't you?"

"Yes," Sidney replied. "I am."

It was the first time he had admitted it, either to himself or to anyone else. Now he had said it aloud, there was no going back.

Amanda looked straight back at him. "But you will always love me too, won't you?"

"Of course I will."

"Until death us do part?"

"Yes, of course, Amanda, always, until death us do part."

She gave him a little nervous wave. She was still wearing her driving gloves and her hand was a black silhouette against the night sky. "Goodbye then, Sidney." She opened the car door.

"Goodbye, Amanda. God bless you."

The door slammed. Sidney waited, and then watched the car drive away into the darkness. He looked up at the moon. It took him a long time to realise that he was crying.

Appointment in Berlin

Sidney had not been back to Berlin for three years and the restoration of the buildings in the British sector, particularly on the Ku'damm and around the Bahnhof Berlin Zoologischer Garten, had proceeded with such speed that parts of the city had taken on a futuristic air. He remembered talking to Hildegard's brother Matthias, a journalist who had gathered the testimonies of Berliners in the aftermath of war, walking barefoot as they cleared rubble, gathered wood and searched basements for food, stealing buttons from the clothing of the dead. It had been a different, defeated world, but now the city was razing recent history and concrete, glass and steel rose from the wreckage.

He was staying with Humphrey Turnbull, the vicar of St George's in the British sector of West Berlin, and he was very much looking forward to two weeks in Hildegard's company. The vicarage was located in Warnen Weg, in Charlottenburg, ten minutes' walk from the British Officers' Club and the NAAFI shop. Sidney knew that Humphrey would use his friend's visit to take a few days off and delegate services in exchange for the free accommodation. There would also be the usual mix of tea parties, cocktails and social dinners. Rohan Delacombe, Commandant of the British Sector, and Tristram Havers, his aide-de-camp, would whizz him round the city in their Mercedes-Benz. As a result, Sidney was worried that he was not going to be able to spend as much time with Hildegard as he wanted.

The plan was that, after unpacking and settling in on his first night, Sidney would pick up Hildegard from her apartment block the following morning. They would have a look at the shops on the Ku'damm, have lunch at the KaDeWe and take a walk in the Tiergarten. Hildegard would then cook him one of her simple suppers with *Erbsensuppe* or *Brathering mit Bratkartoffeln*.

Sidney was therefore somewhat perplexed when he rang her doorbell and discovered that there was no one at home. He wondered if he had got the day wrong, but he was sure that they had agreed on 29 July. He remembered it easily because it was his mother's birthday. He knocked on the door in case the bell was not working. An elderly lady passed on her way to the shops and an Alsatian ambled across his path. A young girl was playing tennis against the side of the building. Sidney interrupted her backhand practice to ask in rudimentary German if she knew either Hildegard or the Baumanns, her sister and brother-in law; she did not.

It was eleven in the morning and he had little choice but to wait. He crossed the street and found a table in a nearby café. It was, perhaps, the place Hildegard had intended to take him. He hoped for a moment that he had made a mistake and the arrangement was that they should meet there instead of at her flat. He could see her apartment from the café and kept watch as he stretched out the amount of time it took to drink a cup of coffee.

He allowed himself a brief moment of irritation. He felt foolish, coming all this way only to find himself facing a locked building and no one at home. What could Hildegard be doing that was more important than seeing him? Perhaps he was not the priority that he thought he was.

It was, however, out of character for her to have forgotten their meeting or to attend to more urgent business. He began to worry. Perhaps she had been taken ill? Sidney had never asked about her health and considered that a woman in her thirties should be perfectly fit but now he was anxious. Perhaps she had a heart condition that she had never told him about? Perhaps she had been hit by a car or been attacked? The streets of Berlin were so well policed that they seemed safe enough but that did not mean that either accident or murder was unknown.

As he sat in the café he began to worry what a life without her would be like. He couldn't imagine it. He wanted to spend more time with her, not less, and for her to disappear like this only brought home how much he needed her. Perhaps there was a man she had not told him about? Perhaps she was already married to someone else, and was, like Anthony Cartwright, leading a double life?

How well did Sidney really know Hildegard? It was important, he knew, that a woman retained an air of mystery, and that a couple, if that is what they were, should still have things to discover about each other. He recognised that relationships needed time to change and deepen, but he continued to doubt. Perhaps what they had was still only friendship, and although that could be strong in its own way, they did not have the passion for love. Perhaps, Sidney thought to himself, he should have declared himself sooner and more openly.

He watched people through the café windows: businessmen in tight suits with thin lapels carrying American-style attaché cases; women with headscarves holding on to recalcitrant children on the way to the Tiergarten; a gang of road-workers dressed in identical boiler suits stopping for a cigarette and a morning break. A passing tank wiped out his view. He missed Hildegard and worried whether he had done anything wrong. He remembered the last time he had come to this very café. Her sister had sat with a sketchbook, drawing customers at the bar and in the distance. She wanted to be like Heinrich Zille, she told Sidney, the German Dickens, the artist who had tried to represent the soul of the city and its citizens, *Herz und Schnauze*, heart and gob.

He paid up, left the café, and returned to the apartment. The girl had finished her tennis, the Alsatian was asleep in the shadows, and the doorbell remained unanswered. It was noon. Sidney realised that he would have to take a tram back to the vicarage and ask if Humphrey Turnbull needed anything doing. He needed to decide whether to confess to what had happened. He hoped that the vicar would not laugh at him.

He was just about to arrive at the tram stop when he heard a voice calling his name. He turned to see the sweaty figure of Matthias Baumann running towards him. He wore a dishevelled suit, his tie was loosened, and he carried a beaten-up trilby and a crumpled copy of *Der Tagesspiegel* under his arm.

"You have been to the apartment?" he asked. "I am sorry. Hildegard was worried and now I am late to tell you. Please excuse me."

"Has something happened?" Sidney replied. "Is Hildegard all right?"

"She is well. But her mother is not."

"Where is she?"

"In Leipzig. Frau Leber fell in the street. Too hot. She was wearing a coat in the heat. She always wears coat. Then she collapse. I am not sure of the word you have — *Schlaganfall*. Is it stroke? Both sisters go to see her. I stay. Give message."

"Shall I follow them?"

"Hildegard asks if you can. Is difficult. But not impossible. You need permits, visas. She told me to help arrange. We must go to Reisebüro Office."

"Now?"

"This afternoon. You have papers?"

"I think so."

"You must bring everything. They like papers. And stamps."

"I haven't brought any stamps."

"No, they have stamps. For passport. You understand?"

"I think so."

"You have been in DDR before?"

"I don't think I have had the pleasure."

"It is no pleasure. East Berlin is good. It has theatres, very good, and beer and is full of rebels. Hildegard will take you. But the rest of the country is like Russia."

"How long will Hildegard and Trudi be there?"

"It depends on mother."

"How bad is she?"

"You know what they say? In DDR you have to be very healthy to go to hospital." Hildegard's brother-in-law put his hat back on his head. "If you are not strong, you die."

The Reisebüro Office was situated near the Brandenburg Gate, and Matthias introduced Sidney to his friend Karlheinz Renke who was in charge of issuing permits. Renke warned that it would be a time-consuming process and that he couldn't guarantee success. Money would have to change hands. It would be ten Deutschmarks just for the visa and there was an enforced currency exchange of twenty-five Deutschmarks per day. Sidney worried that he did not have enough.

First he had to get an entry visa from the Soviet Military Administration in Germany. There were four kinds, Renke told him, and Sidney had to nominate how long he was going to stay and the exact dates and times of his travel. Once he had acquired both a standard entry and exit visa (*Visum zur Ein- und Ausreise*), he needed a transit visa (*Transitvisum*), which restricted him to a predefined travel route within the shortest possible time. He would also need to register with the Volkspolizei. An *Aufenthaltsberechtigung* (residence entitlement) stamp would be placed in his passport. The names of each city or region where he registered, as well as the expiration date of that registration, would be entered in appropriate spaces.

Sidney wondered how the bureaucracy had become so tortuous and who could have invented it. The authorities would have to know exactly where he was each day, and there could be no deviation in his plans, and no allowance for any unpredictable event.

As Renke processed the paperwork Sidney looked out of the doorway to see the Volkspolizei carrying out technical checks on Berlin-bound vehicles. These were the people fleeing the republic for the West. This was *Republikfluchten*, Matthias told him, and anyone coming into the city was regarded with distrust. Men were taken off to be questioned, parcels were confiscated, cars were sent back. Sidney found it ironic that in the eighteenth century, under the Elector of Saxony, the appeal of Berlin lay in its tolerance to outsiders. It was a home for freedom. Now the border guards did everything possible to discourage any love for the place. The East Germans were clearly so desperate to leave their country that Sidney wondered why on earth he was going in.

Three days later he found himself at the Bahnhof Berlin Zoologischer Garten. He was to take the stopping train to Leipzig Hauptbahnhof. It was late afternoon. There were only four platforms at the station and they were already crowded, so that Sidney had to push and jostle with the best of them to try and make his way on to the train. There was a party of East

German soldiers who were already drunk; young families with tired mothers in floral tops, sullen fathers and bored children. A group of female athletes in tracksuits were on their way to a competition in Munich; a party of young pioneers in their white shirts and blue neckties were singing in unison, while thin, hungry-looking businessmen in cheap, functional suits pushed past in search of their seats.

Sidney boarded the train and passed along the corridors. He hoped he would not have to share a noisy carriage. He had brought a book to calm his nerves before seeing Hildegard. It was the latest Kinglsey Amis.

As he made his way past families and groups of men who were standing at the junctions between carriages, Sidney worried what he might say or do if someone had already occupied his seat. His German was already at its limit. A beggar asked him for money and he felt guilty refusing, hauling his suitcase in one hand and his briefcase in the other. He stopped to check the number of one of the carriages. Inside sat a man whom he recognised as a Cambridge student: Rory Montague. He was with some kind of business associate. Sidney tapped on the window but the two men responded with bemusement as he slid the carriage door open.

"Mr Montague," he began. "What an extraordinary thing! To see you here."

The man looked up and said in German, "I'm sorry I do not speak English. I do not know what you are saying."

Sidney was convinced. He even had the same mole on his left cheek. "But I know that you do speak English. You are Rory Montague."

"I am Dieter Hirsch," the man replied in German. "And this is my colleague Hans Färber."

Sidney now spoke in halting German. "But I know you from Cambridge. You were a pupil of Valentine Lyall, the man who fell from the roof of King's College."

The man told Sidney he was mistaken. "Is this your carriage?" he asked.

"No, it is not my carriage," Sidney replied.

"Then you must excuse us. I suggest you find your seat. The train is very crowded today."

Sidney was thrown. Perhaps his suspicions a few years ago had been right all along. Montague must be a spy, but on which side?

He found his carriage crowded with a family of five. A young girl with blonde pigtails was sitting in Sidney's seat by the window and he politely allowed her to keep it, taking the one next to her in the middle of a row of three, squeezing in beside a large woman who was holding a brown paper bag full of apples. The woman shifted minimally to her left and the young girl responded to Sidney's kindness by saying that she did not want to sit next to a stranger.

"Don't argue," her mother snapped, before apologising to Sidney.

"That's quite all right."

"You are American?"

"No," Sidney replied. "I am English."

The ample woman offered Sidney one of her apples. "As long as you are not Russian," she whispered. A student sitting opposite looked up from his book.

"Be careful, Grandma," he said.

The train was heading out of the city of Berlin and the sun was still high in the sky. The two boys in the family were playing with Sandman toys, pretending they were in a spaceship exploring a world where there was no money.

From the window Sidney could see a party of soldiers marching past the propaganda posters of Soviet workers holding up their tools, expressing their solidarity with their East German comrades.

Auf DICH kommt es an!

The posters hung from bombstruck buildings above watchful crowds who seemed frightened of drawing attention to themselves.

Marsch der deutschen Jugend für den Frieden!

The train eased its way south past Wilmersdorf and Zehlendorf and out towards Potsdam. Wrecked rolling stock lay abandoned by the sidings, rusted and with bullet holes. Farmers tended the fields and, in the distance, Sidney was reassured to see a few church towers standing in compact villages. As they approached Wittenberg, Sidney thought of Luther, apocryphally nailing his ninety-five theses on to the door of All Saints' Church in an act of rebellion. Now they had undergone a different, enforced revolution, one that promised a proletarian heaven on earth. Looking out over the scarred landscape it didn't look much like paradise.

They were approaching the industrial heartland of the D/D/R and Sidney could smell the pollution from distant factories. The air had turned grey in the cool of the evening. The train ground through a series of points and chuntered on past the industrial complex of Bitterfeld before dividing at Holzweissig. The woman with the apples was sleeping with her mouth open. Sidney could not understand why she wore a coat. He couldn't imagine Hildegard's mother being similar. The girl with pigtails told her mother she was going to be sick.

The train stopped. Outside a party of soldiers were banging on the windows and waving to their friends. The train guard walked quickly past Sidney's carriage. He looked agitated. Outside Sidney could see a sign: *Alle Fahrzeuge Halt!*

The sun was hard and low. Parched leaves hung from the branches of the trees. An open truck took labourers home from the fields. The driver sounded his horn, and the soldiers jeered. The compartment was unbearably hot, even with the window open.

Sidney tried to read but could not concentrate. The little girl told her mother she needed the toilet. As he stood up to help her the carriage door slid open. It was Montague. He handed Sidney a sealed document. "Take this," he said, in English. "If anything happens, give it to the Master."

"Why?"

"Don't ask questions. There's no time."

"What is it?"

"You do not need to know. If you are questioned, make sure they see your dog collar. They trust the clergy here."

"I thought religion was banned."

"They've tried that. It doesn't work."

"I suppose it gives me an air of impartiality."

"No, it's not that," Montague replied quickly. "It's because they think the clergy are too stupid to do anything that might get them into trouble."

The mother and daughter indicated that they wanted to get past. Montague slipped away leaving Sidney with an unknown document resting on the pages of his book. It was clearly something secret and of importance but why would Montague entrust it to him? Perhaps it was a trap? But who could want to incriminate him? The best thing, he decided, would be to hide the document as quickly as possible and forget all about it. He closed the book and put it away in his briefcase. Inside he saw the little Minox camera that Daniel Morden had given him. He took it out. Now the mother and daughter had left he could get to the window and take a picture with ease. There was a lovely image before him of wheat fields and crows. It was like a van Gogh painting. He could even see the silhouette of a church in the distance. He raised the camera, framed the image, and pressed the shutter.

As he did so, the door to the carriage opened once more. Sidney had been expecting the mother and daughter but it was the train guard. A soldier accompanied him. The large lady awoke and showed her identity card. Sidney put the camera back in his briefcase and reached in for his papers. He knew they were all in order but he had been flustered by the heat of the afternoon and by Montague's interruption. He felt himself sweat.

The guard asked him for his name and his date of birth and the purpose of his visit. How long was he staying in Leipzig, where was he staying and whom was he visiting? The answers could be found on the papers in front of him, but the guard insisted on a slow, methodical questioning, looking at Sidney's face, then at his passport, and lastly at the visas and permits.

Sidney tried to be helpful and spoke in German. "I think you will find they are all in order."

The guard grunted but said nothing. He did not seem at all interested that Sidney was English and a clergyman. The army officer clicked the fingers of his right hand and pointed at the briefcase.

"Those are just my working papers and a book. I am a clergyman."

The army officer looked in the briefcase, picked out the book and flicked through the pages. Sidney was relieved that he had moved whatever the secret document was into the zipped compartment at the side. It looked like a letter. Surely it could not be too compromising; especially if it was in English.

The officer reached down into the bag and pulled out Sidney's camera. "This is not a book," he said. "Nor is it papers."

"It is just a camera," Sidney replied.

"I have never seen a tourist with a camera like this."

"I agree it might seem unusual. I had not seen one before."

"How did you get it?"

"A friend gave it to me."

Sidney was not sure that Daniel Morden was a friend; nor did he want to disclose the context in which the camera had been given to him.

"And did your friend ask you to take photographs on his behalf?"

"Not at all."

"How many photographs have you taken since you have been in the DDR?"

"One. I took some in West Berlin."

"You know that it is illegal to photograph government buildings, industrial complexes, trains, transport facilities and army barracks?"

"I think so."

"And you have not photographed any of these things?"

"Not as far as I am aware." Sidney did not think a distant water tower could possibly count.

"You could have been unaware? Perhaps you need to be more aware." The officer stressed the word in German. *Gewahr.*

"I don't think I have done anything wrong."

"You know that this camera is famous for photographing documents."

"I have not photographed any documents."

"It is used by spies."

"I am not a spy."

"We will have to look at the film. If there is nothing wrong then we will return it. We know where you are staying in Leipzig."

Sidney realised that these men were going to confiscate his camera and that there was nothing he could do. There was a shout from a nearby carriage and the sound of banging. He heard a man call out the name "Emmerich". The officer interviewing Sidney turned away, taking the camera with him, and signalled that the guard should follow. There were more shouts and Sidney could hear gunfire followed by a man telling someone else to stop. He looked to see where the sound was coming from and then, out of the carriage window, he saw Rory Montague running across the fields and into the distance.

Montague ran in a zigzag as further shots were fired and then, just before he reached a distant ditch, he was hit. Two soldiers ran out across the fields, waving at their contemporaries to join them. Rory Montague's companion Hans Färber was amongst them. They gathered round the fallen body.

Färber turned and looked back at the train. He was trying to pick out a particular carriage. He put his left hand above his eyes, shielding his vision against the low sun. Then he seemed to find what he was looking for. He stretched out his arm.

He was pointing directly at Sidney.

Two hours later he was in a police van heading towards the outskirts of Leipzig. It stopped on a hot urban street as an elderly drunk was being taken down to the cells.

"You will stay here overnight," he was told. "In the morning we will question you. We will confiscate your possessions."

Sidney was stripped, put into prison fatigues and led through a maze of corridors with internal traffic lights at the corners. When the light turned red, Sidney was pushed into a recessed niche facing in towards the brickwork. Tired and bemused, he tried to think of distracting, comforting thoughts, but they did not come. The door to his isolation cell was unlocked. Inside there was a bed and a latrine that stank. A high frosted-glass window showed a little of the lamplight from outside but Sidney could tell that he would be unable to reach it.

Sidney was in Runde Ecke, the Stasi headquarters in Leipzig. He lay down on the thin hard bed and wondered whether Hildegard would ever know that he was there.

After a hot, disturbed night, in which he had little sleep, he was taken out of his cell and allowed a cold shower. Unshaved, and with only a rinse of the mouth rather than a clean of the teeth, he was taken up to the second floor to see one of the Stasi's chief officials, Lothar Fechner, a man with a thin neat suit, oiled hair and fingernails that were so clean and precise that Sidney suspected him of depravity.

Fechner sat at an angle to the corner window. His desk was conspicuously ordered with an ashtray and telephone to the left, a blotter, paper and envelopes in front of him, and a lamp to the right. He smelt of cheap cologne, so much so that Sidney wondered if it was used to screen out the smell of alcohol. He guessed that there would be a vodka bottle and possibly a revolver in the desk drawers. From the positioning of the pen Sidney could tell that his interrogator was left-handed. He could hear music from a band playing outside: "*Auferstanden aus Ruinen*".

"Cigarette?" Lothar Fechner began. He pronounced the word in such a way that Sidney was not sure if the questioning was going to be conducted in English or German.

He replied in German. He hoped it would help. "I don't smoke."

"Neither do I."

There was a long pause. It was clear that Fechner was in no hurry and he looked at the papers on his desk as if he were a doctor about to reveal a fatal diagnosis. "Did you want to see if my hands were trembling?" Sidney asked.

Lothar Fechner did not appear to be listening. "How did you know Dieter Hirsch?" he asked.

"I didn't."

"Not a good start, Canon Chambers." The interrogator's diction was quick and precise. "You were seen talking to the man. He gave you an envelope. The little girl with the pigtails saw you." Fechner picked up a pencil and tapped it on the desk as if waiting for an answer.

"I do not know that man as Dieter Hirsch."

"You thought he was someone else?"

"I did."

"Someone English?"

Sidney had to decide how much truth to tell. "I thought he was a colleague of mine."

"A priest?"

"No, from my college at Cambridge. I am a member of the university. You have heard of it?"

Fechner paused before answering. Sidney wondered if he was deciding to sound insulted or not. "Surely you do not think that mentioning your university is going to help?"

"I thought it might be of interest."

"Cambridge is where the children of the privileged make their contacts and then find jobs in companies run by the fathers of their friends."

"The idea is one of merit; it is only elitist in terms of its standards."

"That is not how I would define elitism."

"The opportunity is open to everyone."

"Everyone who has been given all the advantages of their upbringing."

"It is true that some people are given a head start."

"Like Dieter Hirsch?"

"I imagine so."

Fechner turned and looked out of the window. There seemed no reason for doing this. A clock struck ten. After a couple of minutes had passed he asked his next question. "Why did he give you the envelope?"

"I don't know. I imagine he wanted to be rid of it."

"Then why didn't he throw it away?"

"I don't know."

Now Fechner changed tactic and asked his questions incredibly quickly, one on top of the other. "What do you think he expected you to do with it?"

"Take it back to Cambridge, I suppose."

"Did you know what was inside?"

"I don't know anything about that."

"And why were you on the train?"

"As I explained, I was going to see a friend in Leipzig."

"Which friend?"

"Mrs Hildegard Staunton."

"She is English?"

"Her maiden name is Leber. Hildegard Leber. Her father fought in Leipzig for the Resistance against fascism."

"He was a communist?"

"Hans Leber. He was shot outside the Rathaus."

"She is his daughter?"

Sidney was becoming weary. "I think so."

"You know he is a hero in Leipzig?"

"I did not know."

"We will summon his daughter and see if she is the friend you say she is."

"She may find it difficult to come. Her mother has been very ill."

Lothar Fechner smiled. "Canon Chambers, you must not worry. If we ask her to come to see us then she will come. And while we wait you can talk to us."

"I am not sure if I have anything to talk about."

"Oh, I think we will take an interest in anything you have to say. Tell me, for example, about your knowledge of chemistry."

"I don't have any."

"Have you ever been to Pieseritz?"

"I have never heard of the place."

"You are sure?"

"Quite sure."

"Then perhaps you could explain why there was a photograph of the chemical factory at Pieseritz in your briefcase."

"Was there?"

"In an envelope. Were you told about the plot to destroy this factory?"

"I don't know anything about that."

"Dieter Hirsch did."

Lothar Fechner paused once more. He looked bored and let the silence hold. At last Sidney continued, "What has happened to him?"

"For someone who is not your friend, you seem unduly worried."

"Is he dead?"

"Of course." Fechner stood up, looked out of the window, walked around his desk and sat down. Then he smiled.

Sidney could not think what the man wanted. "What was he doing in East Germany?"

"You are asking me, Canon Chambers? I thought that you would have the answer yourself."

"I do not know anything about him."

"Then let me help you." Fechner laid out a map on his desk. "We have intercepted some intelligence, some traffic, a simple matter. It is coded but it was easy to read. Perhaps too easy. It indicated a date and a time for a controlled explosion. Do you know when that could be?"

"Of course not."

"You say 'of course not' and 'of course'. I do not believe you. It was for tonight. At 11 p.m. That is why Mr Hirsch was travelling on the same train."

"You think he was planning to blow something up?"

"I do not think. I know."

"And what would that be?"

"Can't you guess?"

Sidney had become even more irritated. "Of course I can't."

"It is the chemical factory in Pieseritz. You had a photograph of it in your briefcase."

"I didn't know that at the time."

"You do now."

"So what will happen?"

"The army are there. They are searching. We are waiting. If they find nothing then perhaps, if you are fortunate, and Frau Staunton comes to your rescue, then we might be able to send you back to Britain. It will take a long time, of course. I assume you are comfortable here?"

"Not exactly."

"If you do not like it then we can find somewhere else. Although that, of course, may be less congenial."

"How will we know?"

"We will wait to see what the army discover at Pieseritz. If they do find something then it will be difficult for you."

"What do you mean?"

"I don't think you would like me to explain. In the meantime, you must wait. Do not worry. I have planned a little entertainment. A few mental exercises. You are from Cambridge so I think you might appreciate the challenge."

"What challenge?"

"I would like to research the intelligence of people from Cambridge."

"And how will you do that?"

"An examination, of course," Fechner replied. "For a man of your ability I am sure you will not find it difficult. And it will pass the time wonderfully. In fact I am sure that you will have a wonderful time. Everything," Sidney's interrogator smiled, "will be wonderful."

He was escorted back to his cell and given a pencil and a pad of paper. A guard remained with him at all times, even when he tried to rest and sleep. A bare lightbulb was constantly illuminated.

"We have two exams for you," Lothar Fechner announced later that afternoon. "You must answer as best you can. If you are awarded full marks then you will be given food that you can eat. But if you fail, and if you fail badly, then I am afraid we will only give you the minimum we can to ensure your physical survival. We do not worry too much about your mental fitness. After all, if you cannot pass an exam then what is the point of us looking after you?"

"Human decency?" Sidney asked.

"I am afraid we do not concern ourselves too much with English manners. But we will allow you to complete your tasks in your own language. The first test is a chemistry exam."

"But I know nothing about the subject."

"That is unfortunate; and unfortunately," Fechner gave a little laugh at his repetition, "we do not believe you."

"You do not believe I am a priest?"

"That will be your second test. Since what we found on your person was a cross, a prayer book and some chemical plans then the only way we can find out if you are who you say you are is to see if you can answer a few questions."

"But I never said I was a chemist."

"You will have to do your best. Perhaps you can pray. I am sure that the God that you believe in will help you."

"That is not how it works."

"I have decided that it doesn't work at all. There is no God. But perhaps there will be a miracle. Alternatively you could start to tell the truth."

"I am telling the truth."

Lothar Fechner closed the door to the cell. "I will leave you to your tests."

Sidney opened the chemistry paper and read.

Which of the following electronic transitions in a hydrogen atom would result in the emission of a photon with the longest wavelength?

(a) n=4 to n=1 (b) n=4 to n=2 (c) n=5 to n=1 (d) n=4 to n=3

Sidney remembered the blackboard in the lecture theatre where he had asked Neville Meldrum about Anthony Cartwright. He guessed that the answer was (d) and moved on. Only two years previously he had been at the Rede Lecture given by C.P. Snow in which the old man had argued that the British lived in two different cultures, one of art and the other of science, and that there was very little overlap between them. Well, he was certainly going to prove that now. Sidney was hopeless at science and the memory of chemistry at school filled him with dread. He did know his periodic table but he had never been that impressed by chemistry teachers showing off with random explosions in the lab. Then it dawned on him. All these questions might be related to the plot to blow up a chemical plant. If he was too good at his answers he would be even more of a suspect than he was already; too bad, and the authorities would not believe that he was so incompetent. He had to display a distinctly average ability. In short, he had to be English.

There were thirty more questions and he answered with blind guesswork, making up numbers and formulae as he did so, dimly remembering his chemistry O level. After an hour the game was up. The test went nuclear.

What percentage of a radioactive substance remains after 6 half-lives have elapsed? (a) 0.78% *(b) 1.56% (c) 3.31% (d) 6.25%*

Sidney plumped for (b) and then abandoned the exam. He was not going to be drawn on anything that might concern the atomic bomb. Then he turned to the other exam in front of him. This was a theology paper. Looking at the questions he was filled with confidence and could already imagine his reward: a shoulder of lamb, a nice stew or even a bit of fresh fish perhaps.

1. Explain Luther's doctrine of the Cross. What is the difference between a "theologian of glory" and a "theologian of the Cross?"

2. What does Kant mean by the statement: "A hundred real thalers would not be worth more than a hundred possible thalers."

3. "Believers have a perpetual struggle with their own lack of faith." Explain what Calvin meant by this sentence.

This was all first-year undergraduate stuff and Sidney was pleased. He wrote at length about how Calvin stressed that the reliability of the divine promises could co-exist with a human failure to trust in those promises; and that the person of Christ is seen as a confirmation of the promises of God.

It was straightforward, and Sidney used the time to think less of the circumstances he was in and more about the nature of theology and the origins of doubt. He had none about his biblical scholarship and was therefore surprised when Fechner questioned him the following morning.

"You are quite proficient in chemistry, I see."

"If I did well it must have been a fluke. I guessed most of the answers."

"Then you guessed very well. Interesting that you should do better in a subject where you have doubts than in a study where you appear to have none."

"I trust in the promises of Christ."

"So our pastor tells us. Of course we will give you food. But there are a number of questions which still need answers."

"I think I've had enough questions for one day."

"That is most amusing. Please excuse me while I allow myself a small chuckle."

Fechner stood up, looked out of the window and walked around his desk once more. Then he sat down. He said nothing. Sidney realised this was a technique to make him speak, his interrogator was forcing him to break the silence between them. He decided to say nothing and counted the seconds. After five minutes, Fechner asked him another question. "There are very many things we need to discuss, Canon Chambers; not least your knowledge of Dieter Hirsch — or perhaps I should say, Rory Montague?"

"You think that is his name?"

"You were heard to address him so."

"I may have been mistaken."

"Then why did he pass you confidential information?"

"I was not aware of what he was giving me."

"And what were you supposed to do with it?"

"I was asked to take it back to Cambridge and give it to the Master of my college. I imagined it was a letter; an explanation of some sort. Rory Montague had gone missing a few years ago."

"Missing?"

"He had been climbing on the roof of King's College with a friend."

"Is that what students normally do?"

"Not exactly."

"Surely they should be studying?"

"They should."

"Although sometimes they may not be studying the subjects they tell people they are studying, isn't that right, Canon Chambers? They could, for example, be studying the industrial infrastructure of a foreign country. They could be planning to sabotage its scientific progress. They could be working against our ideological freedom to preserve the tyranny of capitalist exploitation."

"Of course they could be doing that," Sidney replied. "But I don't think that's likely."

"I am sure you don't, Canon Chambers, but I still have not received a convincing explanation of why you are in the DDR, what you were doing on that train with a camera normally used by spies, and carrying a negative exposure of one of our most secret chemical plants. It is unusual for a priest to be in such a position, is it not? Particularly one who appears to be so adept in chemistry."

"I am hopeless at chemistry," Sidney answered. "I am far better at being a priest."

"That is not what my examiners think. Pastor Krause thought your arguments reflected the thinking of a decadent intellectual rather than the mind of a man who spends his time either in prayer or with his people."

"That is, I acknowledge, a weakness."

"Then I am sure you will not mind spending a little longer in our company. The circumstances here are not unpleasant; a man might even consider them monastic. Perhaps you could use the time to become a better man of God?"

"I am not sure I need the excuse of being here to concentrate on my duties as a Christian."

"But I am afraid you have no choice, Canon Chambers. I have taken the liberty of ordering *The Rule of St Benedict* from the library. It is surprising we still have it. Many works have, of course, been taken away, but this remains. However, it is not in German."

"I presume, then, that it is in Latin."

"It is. You speak Latin?"

"I do. I am good at Latin."

Fechner smiled. "Vanity again, Canon Chambers. You do disappoint me."

Sidney was led back to his cell, passing through the dark corridors with their exposed pipework and niches to prevent him seeing any other prisoner. He had met only guards and interrogators since his arrival. The place smelled of sewers and the warmth made it worse. He was given a few thin pork knuckles and some sauerkraut. The guard told him that it would make him healthy.

Kristian Krause came to visit. This was the man who had marked down his theology exam and accused him of decadent intellectualism. Sidney took an immediate dislike to him and felt no guilt. Some men, he thought, even if they were priests, were inherently unpleasant.

Pastor Krause gave him a copy of *The Rule of St Benedict*. "You may find it helpful in your cell."

"You think I should pretend I am a monk."

"There are worse ways of surviving."

"Have you ever been a monk yourself?"

"My duties are in the world."

"I think a monk considers himself to be in the world."

"I mean with the people."

"Are you a communist?" Sidney asked.

"It is not irreconcilable with our faith. Perhaps it is even an opportunity."

"You mean that?"

"Of course. We fight for the poor and the oppressed."

"While supporting the oppressor."

"Canon Chambers, I think your views of the DDR are naive. Perhaps you need some time alone to think. Your stay here might even be considered a blessing."

"I find it hard to see it in those terms."

After Pastor Krause had left, Sidney picked up his copy of *The Rule of St Benedict*. He chose a passage at random. "We believe that the divine presence is everywhere and that in every place the eyes of the Lord are watching the good and the wicked."

"Well," Sidney prayed, "I hope you are watching over all the people gathered in this place." It was becoming increasingly hard to make the best of things or even to think the best of people.

"You must not be proud nor be given too much wine," Sidney continued to read. There was fat chance of that.

"Refrain from too much eating or sleeping and from laziness."

Sidney hesitated. This was only making the situation worse. He tried to think positively. He could pretend, he supposed, that he was in some beautiful Renaissance cell decorated by Fra Angelico, but this only worked when he closed his eyes. When he opened them, he was confronted with grim reality. If this was God's way of making him a better Christian then it was going to be a hard graft.

"Do not grumble or speak ill of others," St Benedict admonished. "Place your hope in God alone."

The next day Sidney was taken to see Fechner again. "I thought you might have escaped by now."

"I presume that you are joking," Sidney replied.

"I like a little amusement," Fechner continued. "Don't you?"

"What happened at Pieseritz?" Sidney asked.

"I am pleased that you are concerned."

"Was there an explosion?"

"I am not sure that I am at liberty to tell you. Even if I were, I think that the information might prove too useful."

Sidney knew that an interrogator must have been trained to give nothing away but thought that a matter of fact might be allowable. Clearly it was not.

"Mr Chambers, I am sure you will not mind. I have ordered the polygraph. It is time to test whether you are lying or not."

"I try not to lie."

"You try? That means sometimes you do. You could be lying about your lying."

"I sometimes try to protect people from the truth. That is different, I think."

"It is still a lie. In this country the truth must come before everything else."

"But I have found," Sidney replied tentatively, "that there are often different kinds of truth."

He thought of explaining further but realised, by the look on Lothar Fechner's face, that any Anglican meditation on the constitution of truth could only lead to trouble.

Once he had been rigged up with galvanometers on his fingers, a blood-pressure cuff and tubes around his chest and abdomen, Sidney was asked a series of questions to test that the machine was working. What was his name? Who was the Prime Minister of Britain? When the real test actually began, he found the questions even weirder. They were nothing to do with espionage or his knowledge of chemistry but almost entirely about Hildegard. It was clear, perhaps, that Fechner was trying to destabilise him by concentrating on the personal.

"How well do you know Mrs Staunton?" he asked.

"She is a very good friend of mine."

"Is the relationship physical?"

"That's a very personal question."

"Please answer it."

"I don't see why I should."

"I would remind you that you are a prisoner."

"On what charge?"

"We haven't decided. There could be so many. In the meantime I would remind you of my original question."

"The answer is no."

"Would you like it to be physical?"

"I don't know. I haven't thought about it."

"Do you love her?"

"Again, I don't know. I don't see why I should answer these questions. This is a private matter. It has nothing to do with any case you may bring against me."

"In this country there is no privacy." Fechner lit a cigarette and let the smoke furl over his face. Sidney remembered him saying that he did not smoke. "Secrecy is the enemy of freedom, don't you find? A man with a clear conscience has nothing to hide."

"That does not mean that his conscience is a possession of the state."

"Everything is the business of the state. That is how we build socialism. Everything belongs to everybody. There is freedom and equality for all."

"I have not seen this yet."

"Because we are still building. It needs time."

"And when will you achieve this dream?"

"As soon as people like you start telling the truth."

The interrogation lasted an hour and Sidney had no idea whether he had done well or badly. He had hesitated before answering the question, "Is the Master of your Cambridge college a spy?" and did not know whether he had been caught out or not. He felt that he was in the middle of a novel by Kafka; not that he had read any Kafka.

He was taken back to his cell and given a small bowl of *Sol-janka*, a traditional Russian working-man's stew. Then, without any warning, the door slid open and his briefcase and suitcase were placed on the floor.

"Change," the guard said.

"What is happening?"

"You are free to go."

Sidney could not believe his luck. "Why?" he asked.

"You want to stay? Don't ask questions. Change and go."

The guard led him out back through the traffic-lit corridors. Every signal was at green. Sidney finally found himself in the entrance hallway that he had entered he did not know how many days previously. Fechner was waiting to greet him.

"Here are your papers. I am sorry to have inconvenienced you."

"I am free?"

"It was never in doubt."

"Then what was I doing here?"

"Oh, Canon Chambers, you ask so many questions when it would be better to remain silent. You have a powerful friend. That is all you need. I only wish you had told us earlier."

"I did."

"You should have been more believable. I found it so hard to have faith in you."

"But I told you the truth."

"I see that now. But sometimes it is hard to believe in the truth, don't you think? I find it particularly difficult, for example, with the clergy. They are so keen to tell me their version of the truth and it often has no relation to reality. I am sure they mean well but you cannot expect me to believe what they say. Perhaps you should teach me."

"I think you may be making one of your famous jokes."

"I think not."

"Perhaps in England, then."

"I do not think the English can tell me very much about morality. A pity. I enjoyed our conversations. I hope that you did too."

Sidney knew that he had to be careful. He reminded himself that this could still all be a trap. He had to remain on his guard no matter how tempting it was to be rude. "I found them stimulating."

"Then I hope you will remember them."

"Believe me, Herr Fechner, I will find it very hard to forget."

They shook hands, and Sidney was shown to the front door of the Runde Ecke. Outside, he could see Hildegard standing by a light-blue Trabant. As he made to greet her, she looked at him sternly and spoke in English. "Wait. Don't touch me. They are watching. Get in the car."

Sidney obeyed.

"Don't look at me," Hildegard continued. "Concentrate on the road ahead."

She turned the key in the ignition but put her other hand on his thigh. "Keep looking forward," she said.

Sidney obeyed. "Was it you who secured my release?"

Hildegard smiled briefly, then checked her mirrors and pulled away. "I imagine we will be followed."

"I thought they would have had enough of us."

"It's normal."

They drove into the outskirts of Leipzig. There were few people out on the streets and the trams were almost empty. No amount of sunlight could warm up the brutalist architecture. A farmer's wife was selling watermelons from a rough wooden cart attached to a motorbike. A string quartet, their members already dressed in dinner suits, stopped at a street corner to discuss directions. The female cellist was shouting, annoyed at having to carry around such a large instrument in the heat when they were lost. After braking suddenly to allow a group of young Pioneers to cross the road, Hildegard reminded Sidney that this was the first time she had driven him.

"Are you a good driver?" he asked.

"Terrifying," she replied.

They were heading for the Hotel Merkur: a rectangular building that looked like a giant wireless, dominating the old city centre with its incongruous modernity. They passed the Hauptbahnhof, the station at which Sidney should have alighted. He asked whether he should look out for Bach's church.

Hildegard had other things on her mind. "Did they torture you?" she asked.

"No. I had a lie-detector test."

"Fechner told me."

"Do you know him?"

"My father taught him when he was a student."

"He didn't tell me that."

"He has been trained not to tell you anything."

"And did your father train him as well?"

"It is best that you do not ask too many questions, Sidney. The answer is no, but you cannot be as curious here as you are in England."

"I have noticed. I presume it is all right to ask about your mother?"

"Of course. And that is kind of you."

"It is the reason I am here."

Hildegard drove through a red light. "I am sorry. There was nothing I could do. I am grateful to you for coming. I should have started by thanking you."

"There's no need."

"I think there is."

"How is your mother?"

"You will see her tonight. It is not as serious as people thought. She collapsed but it was not a stroke. Now she is frightened. I am sorry to have been away when you arrived. If I had still been in Berlin then none of this would have happened."

"It's been quite an adventure."

"Is that what you call it?"

"Now the ordeal is over I can look on the bright side."

"The ordeal is never over, Sidney. Not in this country."

"Shouldn't you be careful what you are saying?"

"I see you are learning. But I do not think you are a member of the Stasi unless, of course, they have recruited you already?"

"I don't think they would want someone like me."

"You'd be surprised."

"I think I've learned not to be surprised by anything."

"Then you haven't spent long enough in the DDR."

They were now in a residential area. Hildegard's childhood home, she told Sidney, had been on the eastern side of town, in Gustav-Mahler Strasse (even though, she said, neither of her parents had much time for Mahler). A few last-minute shoppers were bringing home jars of Spreewald gherkins, Filinchen and bottles of Vita Cola. Posters hung from government and municipal buildings displaying images of Walter Ulbricht, Secretary of the Communist Party, Wilhelm Pieck, President of the DDR, and Otto Grotewohl, the Prime Minister.

Sidney was still adjusting to the visible signs of communism. "The shops are still open, I see."

"We do have them here. Although sometimes they close early. You know we have a joke?"

"In the DDR?"

"We say that Yuri Gagarin could find more milk in the Milky Way than he could in the DDR."

"That is a joke?"

"It is the best we can do."

Hildegard parked the car outside the hotel and helped Sidney to check in. She told him to wash, shave and shower before the hot water ran out. She had prepared supper at her mother's and would wait in the lobby. Her sister Trudi was out with friends and so it would just be the three of them.

Sibilla Leber lived on the second floor of a modernist building off Konradstrasse. It had one bedroom, a small living room where she ate, and a little kitchenette. The communal bathroom was outside and down the corridor. "At least it's cheap to heat," she explained. "Not that I need to get any warmer."

Sidney remembered his father giving him a piece of advice. "If you're thinking of marrying a woman you need to take a good look at her mother because that's what you're going to get in the end."

Sibilla Leber had the same short blonde hair as her daughter but it had begun to grey as it curled down to the level of her dark-green eyes. Her nose was slightly more upturned, her face thinner and gaunter, and her mouth, while still appealing, had gathered lines around it; the result of smoking, Sidney thought. She was smaller than her daughter and wore a blue cotton suit that looked like a uniform that had seen better days. Nevertheless, she had a definite presence. Now in her late fifties, she had had both her daughters when she was very young, and been widowed at the age of twenty-seven.

The evidence of her husband's life was all around them. Hans Leber had been a prominent member of the KPD, refused to give the Nazi salute and wrote for *Red Flag*, the communist newspaper. Then, after the Reichstag fire and the Leipzig Trial, the persecutions began. The Blackshirts raided newspaper offices, smashing typewriters and duplicating machines, confiscating propaganda. Although communist activities were declared illegal Hans Leber continued to resist. "He used to say, 'It's easy to call yourself a communist if you don't have to shed any blood for it. You only know what you really believe when the hour comes and you have to stand up for it,'" Sibilla Leber explained.

A propaganda poster showing the martyred Hans Leber hung from the wall. He was a pioneer of freedom, marching at the head of an endless queue of new recruits stretching back across a long road that led from the storm clouds of fascism and capitalism to the new dawn of communism. "It was April 1933. My husband died as he lived; as a fighter in the class war."

"You must have been very proud of him."

"It is different today, but I will never abandon what he fought for. Even if the movement has changed. There will always be bad communists, just as there are incompetent priests. But the solution is to purge the undesirables and stay true to the ideals."

Sidney was not sure he agreed but tried to keep the conversation going. "You need to replace bad faith with good people."

"Exactly."

"Even if we all fall short."

Hildegard asked a question. "Do you think it is easier to be a good communist than a good Christian?"

Her mother leaned back in what was clearly her favourite armchair. "Communism is for this world. Christianity is for the next. I have two loyalties."

Sidney could see that Sibilla Leber had been, and could still be, a formidable woman. Then he remembered something his mother had told him in response to Alec Chambers' perceived *bon mots*. "I wouldn't take your father's advice too seriously, if I were you, son. If there's one thing that's guaranteed to infuriate a woman it's to tell her that she's turning into her mother."

Supper was served and Sibilla Leber explained that it was part of communist ideology to eat well and eat lots; especially fatty food. She had no real interest in who Sidney was or why he had come. Instead he was merely the audience for the recounting of her life story and her political beliefs. She hadn't even asked about his recent ordeal, presumably because she considered there had been nothing wrong with arresting a perfectly innocent priest on a suspicion of espionage.

When they had finished their main course, Hildegard cleared the plates and served up *Rote Grütze*: a fruit compote made from red berries, topped with vanilla custard. "This is a special treat," she said, "because it is the summer. Normally we have just the one course."

"I am honoured," Sidney replied.

Hildegard rested a hand on his shoulder. "Of course you are."

Sibilla Leber reminded Sidney that Karl Marx was German. "This has been Germany's dangerous century," she warned as she spooned *Rote Grütze* into her mouth. "But we still have time to redeem ourselves. Out of the evils of National Socialism will come the refining fire of revolutionary equality."

After supper Hildegard began to play the piano. Her mother carried on talking. Leipzig was the home of pianos, she told Sidney. The town had one of the first ever to be made, by Bartolomeo Cristofori in 1726, and, at the beginning of the century, the Zimmerman company in Leipzig was the largest piano factory in

Europe, producing some twelve thousand instruments a year.

"This has always been my favourite piano," Hildegard called out as she played. "It has the perfect action for Bach."

"I thought your piano was in Berlin?" Sidney asked.

"That is borrowed."

She was playing the Partita No. 1 in B major. She knew it was one of Sidney's favourites and had played it for him one of the first times they had met. He listened for a while before asking, "And what is the perfect action for Bach?"

"It must be sensitive and responsive, but still have some tension." Hildegard continued to play with a lightness of touch that concealed the strength of her forearms. "A bit like you, Sidney."

"I don't know about that."

Hildegard stopped. "There is no need to blush. I paid you a compliment. What is wrong with that?"

"I am not used to it."

"Perhaps you should get used to it. I might say it again one day," and she gave a little laugh.

Sibilla Leber interrupted. "*Warum lachen Sie?*"

"*Es ist nichts,*" her daughter replied. It may well have seemed as if it was nothing, but at that moment Sidney knew, also, that it was everything. He watched her play. He admired her concentration. It was a kind of prayer.

They left for Berlin early on Sunday morning. Sidney had hoped to attend the 11a.m. communion at St George's but their train to the West stopped earlier than its expected destination. Instead of a loudspeaker warning the passengers *Achtung! You are now leaving the Democratic Sector of Berlin* a panicky voice told them: *End of the line! End of the line! The train ends here.*

They were at Treptower Park. Once inside the station they saw a row of Trapos, blackclad transport police with semiautomatic weapons slung over their shoulders. "Something's going on," Hildegard told Sidney. "We shouldn't have stopped. There are more police than usual."

A group of soldiers was closing the ticket halls and turning people away from the platforms that led to the West.

"Come on," said Hildegard. "We can't stay."

She led Sidney out into the streets and they headed towards the Brandenburg Gate. As they did so, they could see members of the Factory Fighting Group gathering in military formation with a line of water cannon. A group of trucks arrived, piled high with barbed wire.

Hildegard asked a policeman what was happening. He told her that the border was closed. No one was going in, and no one was coming out. He pointed to a man drawing a white line on the street. "That is where the Wall will be."

Security forces were grouped all over the city: Vopos, Bereitschaft Polizei, Kampfgruppen and East German People's Army units. They were searching buildings on the sector lines, inspecting stairwells, windows and upper floors. Sidney looked up to see armed men on the rooftops.

Vopos took up assigned beats of streets, assisted by customs police. Armoured cars and machine-gun carriers assembled near the industrial site at the Rummelsburg S-Bahn station. Sentries were placed at two-metre intervals along the entire Berlin-sector border to prevent escapes, while border troops, factory paramilitaries and construction units barricaded the streets with barbed wire, tank traps and improvised concrete bolsters.

Hildegard took control. "I think we should go somewhere less dangerous."

"But we have our papers."

"You have been arrested, Sidney. They will find something wrong."

"I am willing to risk it."

"You are too reckless. Come with me."

They carried their luggage through the streets and stopped at a small café. Hildegard suggested they have a coffee and make a plan. Crowds of families, holding children to their chests and on their shoulders, pulled prams that were filled with their possessions. One man even had a mattress on his head, as if he was planning somewhere to jump.

A passer-by stopped at the window and looked straight at them.

"My God," said Sidney.

"What is it?"

The man continued to stare at them. It was Rory Montague. He held his look for a few seconds, nodded, and then walked on.

"It can't be him, but it was."

"Who?"

"The man from the train. They shot him while he was trying to escape."

"He must have survived. Did you see the body?"

"They told me he was dead."

"Perhaps they only wanted you to believe that he was dead. But, if he was not, then they must have let him escape. Do you think you are in danger?"

"I may be. Why would they shoot him and then let him get away?"

"They wouldn't do that."

"I thought he was working for the SIS. He gave me the negative to give to the Master. That's why I was stopped. I told you."

"So perhaps he was not working for the SIS but the KGB? He framed you."

Sidney tried to think it through. "He wanted me to be arrested. They arranged for me to think he was dead."

"But why would they need to do that?"

"So that I would tell people when I got back to England. I would inform the Master."

"And whose side is the Master on?"

"I don't know."

"But what you do know is that Rory Montague is alive. If he wants you to think that he is dead then that puts you into danger. We must leave East Germany today. It is too dangerous to stay longer."

Sidney hesitated. "I don't understand why he went to all that trouble. Why do the British need to know that he is dead?"

"Perhaps he was working undercover and has defected."

"But why would he have me arrested?"

"To warn you."

"Wouldn't it have been simpler to kill me?"

"Not on a crowded train."

"They could have done it when I was arrested. They could have staged a road accident or gone in for a bit of food poisoning. I am sure a doctor could have attributed my demise to natural causes. What did you say to Fechner?" Sidney asked.

"I reminded him of history. I told him I still knew people: important men who could influence his future. I assured him that you were not a threat."

"You vouched for me?"

"I also gave him money."

"You bought my freedom?"

"It is more complicated than that."

Sidney wondered where she had found the money and how much his freedom was likely to have cost when she asked him another question. "You told him that you loved me, didn't you?"

"Fechner told you that?"

"He mentioned the lie detector. So it is true?"

"Yes, Hildegard, it is true."

"Why have you not told me this before?"

"I wasn't sure if you were ready."

"We have known each other a long time now. What you really mean, Sidney, is that you were not sure that you were ready."

"I suppose so."

"Are you ready now?"

"I think I am."

"Then we had better leave, while we still have lives to live. Already it is harder to cross. Don't kiss me yet. That man has seen us, and I think your permit has expired. We must find a place and wait until night. We do not want another arrest."

Crowds were gathering on the Potsdamer Platz and in front of the Brandenburg Gate. There were tanks in the back streets, and barriers across the rail tracks in the north of the city. Warning billboards had been erected. *Soldat auch Du bist eingesperrt!*

Tanks of the East German People's Army were parked on either side of the border approaches, their turret guns pointing westwards. Armed men in steel helmets guarded the crossing as construction workers began to insert concrete posts into the cobbled streets.

Cars were being diverted to Checkpoint Staaken. A few westerners were showing their identity cards, and after lengthy conversations and interrogations they were allowed through to be greeted by students protesting at this violent division of their city. Already, it reminded them of the communist repression of the Hungarian uprising.

Ulbricht, murderer! Budapest! Budapest! Budapest!

In the Bernauer Strasse people were jumping from the windows of their Eastern apartment blocks down into Western streets, pursued by Vopos and Grepos. They were waving, calling, holding up children and pets, making their last attempts to be reunited with their loved ones. The soldiers ignored them.

An old man made his way to the checkpoint. As he did so, he threw a grocery bag into the garden of an apartment block. "I don't want those bastards accusing me of smuggling sausages."

"I can't believe that they can cut us off so quickly," Hildegard said. "There must be gaps in the barbed wire or places where we can cross."

They made their way north, following the contours of the River Spree, and could see the ruins of the Reichstag in the distance. There was no barbed wire. Hildegard turned to Sidney. "Can you swim?"

"Would you like me to carry your suitcase, Hildegard?"

"I could lighten it by wearing some more clothes."

"That might help."

In the distance they could hear gunfire. "You don't think . . .?" Sidney began.

"That they are shooting people who are trying to escape? Yes, I do."

"Wouldn't it be easier just to present our papers?"

Hildegard had opened her suitcase and was taking out a second blouse and a raincoat. "That man has seen you, Sidney. The Stasi will have already warned Border Control to check you."

"Despite your intervention?"

"One man helped us. We were lucky. And I don't trust anyone. I will take your briefcase. Do you think we can do this in one trip?"

Sidney thought about the story of the fox, the chicken and the sack of corn. Now was not the time to tell it. "I don't see why not."

"Are you a strong swimmer?"

"I was almost a Cambridge Blue."

"You are joking, Sidney."

"I thought it might reassure you. Give me your suitcase."

"How can you manage the two of them on one hand?"

"Backstroke," said Sidney, slipping into the water. "It's very warm, you know."

"Keep your voice down," said Hildegard before jumping into the dark water. "It's not so far. We need to be fast."

The cases were heavy and Sidney's progress was slower than he had anticipated. He kept checking the depth to see if he could stand up but every time he did so he feared that he would sink. "Don't drown on me!" Hildegard whispered. "Let the suitcases go if you need to. I don't care about them. All we need are our papers."

"And you've got them?"

"Of course."

"Are you a strong swimmer?" Sidney asked.

"I was champion at school."

"Are you telling me the truth?"

"No," Hildegard repeated Sidney's words. "I thought it might reassure you."

They were halfway across the river when Hildegard asked suddenly, "You do love me, don't you?"

"Of course."

"Only I have to know if there's something worth living for."

At last Sidney was within his depth. He stood up and began to wade slowly towards the edge. Hildegard knelt down and held out an arm to take each case in turn. She led Sidney through a series of alleys and side streets. "We must keep going west and avoid the main roads."

Their clothes clung to them and the night was now cold. "How long will this take?" Sidney asked.

"Less than an hour. When we find ourselves in the Tiergarten we know we are safe. People say it is very romantic at night."

"Life doesn't feel so romantic at the moment."

"You have to have faith."

They approached the Tiergarten through the ruins of the Reichstag and made their way diagonally south-west. It was dawn by the time they reached the university and a further stretch of the Spree.

"You don't want me to swim across this as well?" Sidney asked. "My clothes are almost dry."

"There is a bridge. I used to swim in the Neuer See when I was a student."

"I wish I had known you then."

"No, you don't. I was too serious."

"And you're not now?"

They left the Tiergarten and passed the Zoological Gardens. The first of the Monday-morning workers were entering the railway station and a newspaper vendor was selling copies of *Der Tagesspiegel* and the *Berliner Morgenpost* with the headline *Wir rufen die Welt!*

They made their way towards Hildegard's apartment off Schillerstrasse and climbed the stairs. Matthias had left for work, and Trudi was still in Leipzig. They opened their suitcases and discovered that everything they contained was either damp or water-damaged. Hildegard found some towels and fished out a shirt and a pair of trousers from the wardrobe of her brother-in-law. "I know these won't fit but we can wait until everything is dry. I will make coffee."

Sidney took off his jacket. "My passport has not been stamped. What about your papers? Will it be hard now for you to go back?"

"I think so."

Sidney headed for the bathroom to change. "I think I should get back to the vicarage. They will be expecting me."

"You can stay here."

Sidney stopped in the doorway. "Really?"

"Of course."

"I suppose Matthias won't mind. In the daytime."

"No, Sidney, you can stay with me. In my room." Hildegard helped Sidney off with his shirt. "I think you may have forgotten to ask me something. Perhaps it slipped your mind."

"Yes, I suppose it did. In all the fuss."

"You said that you thought that you were ready. I don't remember you asking if I was too?"

Sidney put his hand to her cheek and then let it fall. "Hildegard," he began, slowly and firmly. "I am so sorry. I do not know what to say. I have been distracted. But the truth is that I have always been terrified. I have

384

APPOINTMENT IN BERLIN

been afraid that you might say no to me. I love our friendship. I do not want to do anything to endanger it. And I love you."

"That is good."

"Then are you ready?"

Hildegard looked directly at him. "I have been ready for seven years."

That evening they returned to the vicarage and told the Reverend Humphrey Turnbull of their adventures. They did not yet tell him about their marital plans. "You've obviously been having a thrilling time. Perhaps you should write a book about your shenanigans?"

Sidney coughed. "They were a little more than that, Humphrey."

"Well you are here now. Do you have plans?"

Hildegard looked at Sidney but he refused to give the game away. "I think I'll be leaving in the next few days. Tonight, however, I thought we could have a treat. The Eric Dolphy Quintet is playing at the Club Jazz Salon. I wondered if you'd like to join us?"

"Jazz isn't really my thing, Sidney. Thank you all the same."

"I suppose you are more of a Wagner man."

"Not at all. I prefer operetta." He looked mischievously at Hildegard. "*The Merry Widow.* That sort of thing."

"I do not trust widows who are merry," Hildegard replied.

"Well, I hope you won't be a widow much longer. I'm sure that Sidney could find you an agreeable companion back in England if he put his mind to it."

385

Hildegard smiled. "I am sure he could."

They walked back out through the streets and as soon as they were clear of the vicarage Hildegard put her arm through Sidney's. "I suppose I should buy you a ring," he said.

"I suppose you should."

"What kind would you like?"

"Surprise me."

"I thought that nothing surprised you."

"Then let this be a first time."

The club was already crowded when they arrived and they were given a table at the side. All around them, people were talking about the Wall and their relatives in the East. Sidney picked up the menu and saw that everything was more expensive than he had anticipated. Hildegard could tell he was worried but told him not to be. She had enough money, not for champagne, but for a nice white wine and a little Wiener schnitzel.

Eric Dolphy's tonal bebop reminded Hildegard of Bartók and Stravinsky. Sidney was surprised how quickly she took to jazz and how much she liked it.

"It's all music," she said. "I think Pepsi Auer is very good on the piano. I wish I could play like that."

"I'm sure you could."

"I haven't got the style."

Sidney put his hand on hers. "You've got all the style I need."

Dolphy improvised on his alto saxophone and then the bass clarinet, and his set included an unaccompanied rendition of Billie Holiday's "God Bless the Child". He stretched out the central melody and experimented with wide intervals, looping scales and blistering arpeggios, pulling the main theme away into something completely different, as if the original melody was a half-remembered dream. The drinks arrived as Dolphy took to the flute for "Hi-Fly", before he began an energetic rendition of "I'll Remember April" with Buster Smith's unfortunately lengthy drum solo. Hildegard told Sidney that she was irritated that the Anglican vicar had referred to their night-time canal crossing, which had taken place under the threat of gunfire, as mere "shenanigans".

"He thinks, because we are German, that the Wall and any suffering that results from it, is our own fault. He is almost amused by it all."

"I think it must be because he is frightened to take everything too seriously. He has seen hell. He thinks our gaze should be averted."

"So he makes jokes."

"For a priest, humour is important, Hildegard. You remember that Dante called his poem *The Divine Comedy*?"

"Because it has a happy ending? What about the suffering beforehand? What about, in your words, 'the Cross': the suffering that earns joy? I think a clergyman should carry suffering with him."

"And you think that is what I should do?"

"I do not think you should be trivial. I do not want a husband who is, I think the word is, 'lightweight'."

"And I hope you have not got one. In turn, I do not want a lightweight wife."

"Then we should be well suited, Sidney. Only I would not want you to take me for granted."

"I would never do that."

"I am not so sure. Be careful, Canon Chambers. You are about to become my husband. At times you may expect me to be your little clergy wife but you will often get more than you anticipated. I will always be watching you."

"I see. You will be like the Stasi in our marriage."

"Not at all," Hildegard leant forward and kissed him on the lips. "I will be far worse than that."

The wedding was to take place in early October. Sidney returned to make all the necessary preparations, asking Leonard to conduct the service with Hildegard's sister. Trudi giving the bride away. Inspector Keating had agreed to read the lesson, but not before reading Sidney his own version of the riot act. What had his friend been doing, hunting down members of the British secret service and jeopardising missions in a foreign country? He had discovered, from his contacts in the Foreign Office, that the shooting of Rory Montague had been specially staged by a series of agents as a distraction. The last thing they had expected to find was a clergyman right in the middle of it.

"How was I supposed to know that?" Sidney complained.

"As soon as you saw Montague on the train you should have kept quiet."

"But no one warned me."

"You would have thought that the business on the roof of King's Chapel would have been enough. You must have guessed that our men were involved even if no one fully explained it at the time."

"I wish someone had."

"No one expected you to go wandering round East Germany."

"I was not 'wandering round', Geordie. I was in pursuit of the woman I love."

"I thought you were keeping to West Berlin. That seemed fair enough. People couldn't imagine you doing much damage there. A few weeks later there was even a wall to keep you in your place."

"I don't think that it was meant for me."

"It might as well have been. Honestly, Sidney, what on earth did you think you were doing?"

"I would like to remind you, Geordie, that I nearly went to prison. It's not my fault that I was on the same train as a member of the SIS who, I would also like to point out, handed me secret documents about a chemical plant. For goodness sake . . ."

"He must have panicked."

"What was he doing?"

"I am not entirely sure. They only tell me what they think is necessary. Sometimes, Sidney, it's probably quite important that you don't know everything."

"And you do?"

"I have just told you I do not."

Sidney did not think that this was the time to posit a completely different theory: that Rory Montague was still working for the Russians and had stage-managed everything. He wondered whether there was such a thing as a "quadruple agent". "Do you think I can't be trusted?" he asked.

"No one doubts your loyalty, Sidney. Only there are times . . ."

"When I am considered naive or indiscreet? That is most unfair, you know . . ."

Keating placed a hand on his friend's arm. "Let's not argue. You are back safely, and these are happy times. I imagine the future Mrs Chambers will be living with us?"

Sidney was thrown by this change of tack and had never heard Hildegard described in that way out loud. He forgot his grievances and his uncertainty and began to think, once more, how extraordinary it was that he was getting married and how fortunate he had been to find this late-flowering love.

The day itself turned into a golden afternoon. The sun was out, the leaves on the elms were just on the turn, and there was that first autumn crispness in the air. The church of St Andrew and St James was packed with friends and family for the wedding. Sidney's father, mother, brother Matt and sister Jennifer lined up in the front row alongside Inspector Keating.

Amanda gave him a little wink before the ceremony began. Sidney had expected that she might have expressed some doubt about these forthcoming nuptials, but she had been gracious and generous and had given Hildegard her full blessing. The only naysayer was, predictably, Mrs Maguire, who was unable to refrain from commenting on the bride's refusal to wear white. As it was her second wedding, Hildegard had chosen a full-length dress with flared sleeves in darkest red, providing Mrs Maguire with the simple opportunity to remark that she had always been able to spot a scarlet woman.

"It's not scarlet, it's burgundy," Amanda had informed her. "Like a fine wine."

"To be appreciated, and savoured again and again," Leonard Graham added.

"That's quite enough," Mrs Maguire replied, before moving on to pursue grievances elsewhere.

Orlando Richards began the service by playing Pachelbel's Canon on the organ. He had laid on a special choir, filled with choral scholars and third-year students, and they had prepared some of Hildegard's favourite music: "*Also heilig ist der Tag*", "*Bist du bei Mir*", and Mozart's "*Exsultate Jubilate*".

Leonard gave the address and managed to refrain from quoting Dostoevsky (something he had previously threatened). Instead he spoke of marriage as a gift and a blessing that could be shared both privately and publicly. It was like a garden, he argued. It needed to be nurtured. It had to be cared for with tenderness, for in that garden was the rose that was the bride.

The service ended with the hymn "Now thank we all our God", using the melody from Bach's cantata "*Nun danket alle Gott*". As the bride and groom turned to face the congregation, they could see the world of their friends before them, asking for a bounteous God to be ever near them, guiding the perplexed and freeing his people from all ills, in this world and the next.

Hildegard slipped her arm through her new husband's and they walked down the aisle together at last. Yes, Sidney thought, he had much to be thankful for: his home, his health, his vocation, his friends, his family, and now his wife. Life had certainly bowled him the odd googly, and doubtless there would be further tests, trials and tribulations, but just for now, and on this day, it was to be enjoyed in all its fullness and with all its wonders, the most wondrous gift of all being nothing less than the love of such a fine woman: his very own, his beloved, Hildegard.